AMBERVILLE

AMBERVILLE

TIM DAVYS

HARPER

An Imprint of HarperCollins*Publishers*
www.harpercollins.com

First published in Swedish in 2007 by Albert Bonniers Förlag.

FIRST U.S. EDITION

Translated by Paul Norlen

Designed by Renato Stanisic

Library of Congress Cataloging-in-Publication Data is available upon request.

ISBN: 978-0-06-162512-1

09 10 11 12 13   OV/RRD   10 9 8 7 6 5 4 3 2 1

AMBERVILLE

CHAPTER 1

Early one morning at the end of April there was pounding on the door to Eric Bear and Emma Rabbit's apartment on brick-red Uxbridge Street. The morning rain had let up, the wind had died down, and the sun was shining anew over Mollisan Town.

"Shut up and stop pounding," mumbled Eric Bear to himself, pulling the blanket over his head.

But the blanket was too thin; the pounding on the door echoed painfully inside the bear's head.

It was impossible to fall back asleep.

Yesterday had turned into a late and wet one. It had been the kind of evening when each and every stuffed animal seemed to have decided to go out. The restaurants up in Lanceheim were packed; along bright-violet Pfaffendorfer Tor the animals were thronging all the way from the Concert Hall, and the crowding at the bars along mustard-yellow Krünkenhagen was worse than on North Avenue during rush hour. Mammals and reptiles, fish and fowl, imaginary animals and even the occasional insect: all kinds of stuffed animals crowded into Lanceheim.

"Follow me!" Eric cried out when the animals on the sidewalk threatened to divide the group.

There had been five of them. Wolle Toad, Nicholas Cat, and a project leader from the advertising agency Wolle & Wolle whose name Eric didn't know.

But it was Philip Baboon who walked at Eric's side. This evening Baboon was the object of everyone's attention. He represented the shoe company Dot. They had been searching for a new advertising agency for several months, and Wolle & Wolle were on their way to winning the pitch. Now only that last little push was required.

Eric Bear was ready to push.

Eric set his sights on a restaurant which was not too far away. From a distance he saw the neon sign's bold yellow letters which read: "Parrot's Bar & Grill."

"Parrot's," said Eric to Philip Baboon. "Never had a boring moment there."

In fact, Eric Bear had never even heard of the place, and he would most likely never be able to find it again. But the cursive neon letters reminded him of the Art Deco of his childhood, and anyway, up here one restaurant was pretty much like any other.

"Just so there aren't any decadent females at Parrot's," Baboon said, giggling nervously. "I haven't been out in almost twenty years, I don't want to run into any . . . voluptuaries . . . the first thing I do."

Philip Baboon was wearing a gray suit, a white shirt, and a dark-blue tie.

Over dinner he had related that his greatest interests were balance sheets, rates of turnover, and the snails he collected on the beach in Hillevie. Baboon still had his briefcase in hand as he walked beside Eric Bear. He would carry it the entire evening, as if it were a life buoy.

It was obvious to everyone that Philip Baboon wanted nothing more than to meet decadent females.

"Voluptuaries?" laughed Eric Bear. "I'm sure there might well be that sort at Parrot's, unfortunately."

Philip Baboon shivered with expectation.

A new series of brutal poundings was heard from the outside door.

Why don't they ring the doorbell, like normal stuffed animals?

Eric Bear turned over in bed. Under the blanket he could smell his own breath. Gin martinis and vodka. Stale gin martinis and vodka. Had he been smoking yesterday? It felt like it on his tongue.

When they'd left Parrot's Bar & Grill—because there hadn't been any females who were sufficiently decadent for Baboon's taste there—they were all thoroughly intoxicated. They ended up at a jazz club. A dark, cellar space which couldn't possibly be in Lanceheim, but rather up in Tourquai.

"I know that we shouldn't talk shop," said Eric Bear.

He had a hard time talking without slurring. He and Baboon were sitting across from each other at a small, round table in a corner of the place. Eric sat on a chair, Baboon was reclining on a hard bench next to the wall. A saxophone was screeching from the stage and maybe someone was sitting on Baboon's lap? It was so dark, it was hard to be sure.

"I know that we shouldn't talk shop, but we're the only ones left, aren't we? You've decided on Wolle and Wolle?"

"On Tuesday," said Baboon.

At least Eric thought that's how he replied.

"Tuesday?"

"But we demand a ceiling," said Baboon.

Or else he said something else. On the stage the saxophone had been joined by a trumpet, and it was impossible to hear what anyone said.

"Is that a panda sitting on your lap, Baboon?" asked Wolle Toad.

Bear didn't know where the toad had appeared from. But Baboon had been found out, and he rose from the bench. The following moment he fell down backwards again. With the panda on top of him.

"I have never touched any panda!" he shouted.

Then Eric knew that Wolle & Wolle would have Dot as a new account.

"I'M COMING!"

Eric threw off the blanket and sat up in bed. The bedroom was swaying. The noise from the door was getting louder.

He had a vague recollection that Emma had left the house almost an hour earlier. She rented a studio in the south end of Amberville, down toward Swarwick Park. There she worked as long as the sun was standing in the east, and she liked to get going early in the morning. Eric was slower. More precise, he said.

More vain, she said.

The bear stood up and pulled on the underwear and shirt that were lying on the floor beside the bed. Those were the clothes he'd had on yesterday. They stank of sweat, smoke, and stale booze. With a sigh he went slowly out through the dining room.

The blinds had been drawn in the bedroom, but the sun was sparkling happily from a blue sky through the windows in the living room. The nostrils of Eric's cloth nose expanded and unconsciously his small, round ears moved forward. He dared not even guess who might be at the door; they seldom had uninvited guests. He furrowed his cross-stitched eyebrows and reached for his aching head. At the same time there was an amused curiosity in his small, black-button eyes.

Life often treated Eric Bear to pleasant surprises.

He came out into the hall just as the pounding resumed, and this time the animal on the other side had lost patience. The hinges rattled uneasily; the force behind the pounding could not be mistaken.

Eric hesitated.

He remained standing next to a small sofa upholstered in pink velvet which Emma Rabbit had purchased at auction at a high price a little more than a year earlier.

Perhaps it was best not to open. Eric suddenly had a feeling that he didn't want to know who was on the other side of the door. With an inaudible sigh he sat down on the pink sofa.

It became silent outside.

After that the door came flying into the hall.

The blow was loud and distinct. It was followed by an unpleasant crunching sound, and from a cloud of wood chips and wall plaster Eric discerned the outline of a small bird, who carefully stepped over the debris on the floor.

Behind the bird two broad figures loomed on either side.

Nicholas Dove and his gorillas had come for a visit.

"Eric, my friend," said Dove in his squeaky monotone as the dust settled. "I see I'm arriving at a very inconvenient time."

And the dove made a gesture toward Eric's bare legs. The bird himself wore an impeccable double-breasted jacket, with a pink silk scarf around his neck.

Eric had leaped up from the sofa as though standing to attention when the door was battered into the hallway, and now he looked down at his underwear. His heart was pounding hard in his chest, and he was much too shocked to be either afraid or angry.

"I . . ." he began.

"No problem," Dove assured him, going past Eric without need of an invitation and on into the living room.

The two gorillas remained standing in the hall, in the space that had recently been a doorway. There was nowhere to escape. Eric vaguely recalled one of the gorillas, the one who was bright red, from the distant past. It was a very unusual color for an ape.

In the living room, the dove had already made himself comfortable in one of the armchairs. Eric sat down warily on the sofa next to it. Despite the fact that practically all the stuffed animals in Mollisan Town were the same size, some seemed daintier and others coarser. Dove fell into the first category, the gorillas in the latter.

"It's been a long time . . ." said Eric. "Really . . ."

"Much too long," replied Dove, "much too long, my friend. But that's not on my account. You've always known where to find me."

That was true.

Nicholas Dove's nest had always been at Casino Monokowski. It was said that Dove seldom or never left his comfortable office, where through tinted windows he could survey the casino from above. Eric knew, however, that the painting to the left of the desk—a horse in battle gear—was actually the door to Dove's private apartment. From there he made his visits to the outside world, a necessity in order to maintain the balance of power. The bird was one of the most dangerous animals in Amberville, and directly or indirectly he controlled most of the organized crime in the district.

"Undeniably," replied Eric, trying to keep a light tone of voice, "you know where to find me, too."

"You look after your friends," said Dove. "And I must of course congratulate you on all your successes."

Eric nodded and smiled but felt a chill along his spine. He didn't know what Dove was getting at. Eric Bear was in the prime of life and felt that he had much to be proud of. Presumably Dove had read something having to do with Wolle

& Wolle. Since Eric had become boss above Wolle Toad and Wolle Hare, a fair amount had been written about him in the press.

"Thanks," said Eric.

"You've got a lovely place here," continued Nicholas Dove.

Again a din was heard from out in the hallway. Not quite as ear-shattering as when the door was knocked down, but sounds of the same type. Eric turned around and saw how the apes were smashing the lovely pink sofa to bits.

Emma, he thought in a panic that crept up from his belly toward his throat. Emma. She's going to be crushed.

"Why . . . ?"

Eric tried to sound relaxed, and nodded out toward the hall where the gorillas continued to kick and strike what was left of the piece of furniture.

"They're taking a break," said the dove. "Surplus energy. It's just as well that I get to the point before your entire lovely apartment is destroyed."

Eric swallowed and nodded. Sweat was pouring down his back, but it might just as well have been the hangover. He didn't want to appear materialistic, but the pink sofa hadn't been free. And Emma would never understand. She knew nothing about Eric's youthful years; he'd never dared tell her that he had once worked for Nicholas Dove. To others he hinted at this and that about his past because he thought that made him more exciting. But Emma wasn't as easily impressed.

The gorillas had finished in the hallway. With decisive steps they went through the living room into the dining room, where they let themselves go on the dining room furniture: the table and chairs.

Just so they don't see the crystal chandelier, thought Eric. It was a copy of an eighteenth-century piece signed de Clos, of which only four existed.

The very next moment hundreds of crystal prisms crashed against the parquet floor.

"Eric, you know me," said Dove, adjusting his scarf. "I'm not one to beat around the bush, I intend to get right to the point. I'm on the Death List."

"The Death List?" Eric repeated foolishly.

"That's right," nodded the dove without a hint of hesitation.

"But," said Eric, feeling uncertain as to whether the dove was joking, "are you really sure that . . . there is something like . . . I mean, I know that it . . ."

Eric fell silent.

"Does that have any significance?" asked Dove without interest.

Eric had heard the rumor of a Death List since preschool. As an adult it was hard for him to believe that a list actually existed. The Chauffeurs worked according to principles known only to them, and that of course gave rise to speculations. The Chauffeurs in their red pickup picked up old stuffed animals, "the worn and the weary," as the saying went. No one knew to where the old animals were conveyed, but they disappeared and were never seen again. It wasn't strange that the Chauffeurs were feared, not strange that you wished there were some sort of list; anything at all that made the Chauffeurs' nighttime runs seem less random. The Environmental Ministry was mentioned in this regard, because the Environmental Ministry was responsible for the city's transports and for the so-called Cub List. But it was improbable that anyone at the ministry had the task of giving stuffed animals a death sentence.

"Perhaps it has a certain significance," Eric said carefully.

He didn't want to glance in the other direction, toward the dining room; the sounds were sufficient to understand what was going on.

"If there isn't any Death List, then you can't very well be on it."

"That," dismissed the dove, "is a hypothetical line of reasoning that doesn't interest me. I came here for a single reason. I want you to track down the list and remove my name from it."

The silence that ensued only lasted a moment. The gorillas in the dining room were fully occupied with the chairs, which were more solidly constructed than it might seem.

"Why me in particular?"

"You owe me a few services," Dove reminded him. "At least a few."

"But that was a hundred years ago!"

"Compound the interest and you're in a bad position," sneered Dove, but quickly became stern again; these abrupt changes were one of his specialties. "Honorably stated, Eric, you in particular are a good fit. Considering your mother . . ."

The fact that Rhino Edda had been appointed head of the Environmental Ministry—the most important of the three ministries in Mollisan Town—was behind several commissions of trust Eric Bear had received over the years. At this moment he would return them all for this conversation never having taken place.

"Mr. Dove," said Eric. "I can guarantee that neither the Environmental Ministry, nor Mother, sits around drawing up any Death Lists that—"

"That's fine, that's fine," Dove brushed aside the excuses while taking the opportunity to smooth out the sleeve of his jacket. "I don't care how you go about it. The less I know, the better. I would gladly put you on the trail if I could, but it . . . the cat . . . who maintained that he knew my name was on the list . . . has unfortunately . . . disappeared. So I suppose you can begin exactly as you wish."

"But I—"

Nicholas Dove interrupted him by getting up from the armchair. A terrible crash was heard. Eric guessed that it was the glass case with the crystal glasses that had fallen to the floor.

"Now we're leaving!" shouted the dove.

It immediately became silent in the dining room, and both apes came trotting out to the living room.

Dove took a few steps toward the hall, but remembered what he'd forgotten and turned around.

"It's actually rather simple," he said, looking coldly at Eric Bear who remained seated on the sofa. "If the Chauffeurs fetch me, then my gorillas will fetch your beloved Emma Rabbit. And tear her to pieces."

The dove didn't stay behind to see how his threat affected the bear. He preceded the gorillas out to the hall. Eric was incapable of moving from the spot.

"Good luck!" the squeaky voice was heard to say from the stairway.

CHAPTER 2

Eric devoted the day to putting things in order on Uxbridge Street. He and Emma lived in a true showcase apartment three flights up in one of Amberville's older, blue, historically registered buildings. Actually it was indefensible that Eric had settled down in his childhood Amberville. He ought to have done as his creative friends had and bought something less ostentatious—but equally expensive—in one of the multicultural neighborhoods in north Tourquai. Or, even better, remodeled a loft in Yok. That would have been in accord with his image: a rebel in the business world with a mysterious past.

From his fifteenth to his nineteenth year Eric Bear lived at Casino Monokowski, one of the illegal establishments in Amberville which had its counterparts in the other districts. He slept where there was room, in a bed or under a table, on a couch or on a toilet; he wasn't sensitive in that respect. Most often the drugs made him pleasantly closed off; he could have fallen asleep on top of one of the roulette tables as well. He kept his possessions in a plastic bag in a cupboard in the employee dressing room. His best friend, Sam

Gazelle, carried the key to the cupboard in his vest pocket. Eric used the cupboard so seldom that betweentimes he forgot what was in it.

During that period Eric was living on Nicholas Dove's terms. Of this he was constantly reminded. The jobs he got were of varying degrees of difficulty. The assignments never came from Dove personally, but nonetheless there was no mistaking who was making the decisions. It might be a matter of running errands—carrying sealed envelopes that contained bundles of currency, or small packages with drugs (wrapped in so much thick, beige tape that sharp scissors or knives were required to get them open) from one corner of the casino to the other. But it might just as well be a matter of helping Sam lure money from johns in the corridor or breaking his back for an entire day as a busboy, if there were many who called in sick. Sometimes he did the more unpleasant things, such as working in the john-rooms or acting as a lookout while the gorillas did their job.

In exchange he got almost unlimited credit at the gaming tables.

In exchange he got food and shelter.

The young Eric Bear didn't complain.

But with each new marker he bought at the casino's bank and for every white pill he rinsed down with alcohol in one of the bars, he took yet another step toward the woeful end for which he seemed predestined. If it hadn't been for Emma Rabbit, the red pickup would have picked up Eric Bear before his twentieth birthday.

The first time he saw her she was standing in front of a window that looked out over the sea. In her smile was a challenge he couldn't resist. She was dressed in white. It was as though the image of Emma Rabbit was composed by an advertising designer. It was as though he'd discovered her.

It is said that love conquers all.

It does.

Starting that day, and every day since, Eric Bear had loved Emma with pain, trust, passion, and self-annihilating restlessness that he couldn't control. When she was successful, his happiness felt no limits. When things went against her, his helplessness was painful.

She didn't like that.

She quarreled with him and accused him of taking over her feelings. She said that he was smothering her, that he was erasing the boundaries between their lives. She said that wasn't the way you showed love.

If he'd had an opportunity, he would gladly have loved her in some other way. But where Emma was concerned, reason was out of the running. He reacted like a little cub, instinctively and without reflection. It had always been that way, and so it would remain.

While Eric Bear was cleaning away the traces of what had happened and thinking up reasonable explanations for why the hallway and dining room furniture were missing (to gain time he thought about saying that he had loaned out the hall furniture for a photography shoot and that the dining room furniture had been sent off for refinishing), he realized he had no alternative.

He was compelled to try to find out if there was a Death List, and if such was the case, to remove Dove's name.

He didn't know how much time he had, but he suspected that time was short. He would not succeed on his own.

Once again on this April day in the life of the middle-aged bear his thoughts returned to the bohemian existence of his youth. None of the comfortable project managers, TV commercial directors, or spoiled marketing executives with whom he hobnobbed nowadays would be able to help him with the mission Nicholas Dove had given him. He would be forced to call together the old gang.

CHAPTER 3

Grand Divino was a paradise for anyone who thought they could afford to throw away money. Fashion, food, home decor, or culture, most everything was to be found at Grand Divino. An overabundance was offered for sale in a magnificent setting of marble, velvet, oak, and glass; a department store had been created which was at the same time welcoming and spacious. The building was salmon pink; the massive entryway stood open from the Forenoon Weather to the Evening Weather. When Eric Bear stepped into the perfume counters' sea of glass and mirrors, he was one of the day's first customers.

As usual, the aromas made him dizzy. Intoxicated by lavender and mint, musk and lily of the valley, he remained standing for a few extended moments of daydreams about Emma Rabbit. They were lying in the tall, green grass under a summer sky, embracing each other and saying the sort of things you only say to your beloved. It was as if he'd let himself be taken in by his own slogans. "Giselle—a scent of spring." Or "Number 3 from Max Loya—dreams of love." He liked perfumes and had worked with many of the major brands. He had even worked with products he didn't like, but actually that didn't make any great difference. What he liked most of all was success. He realized that this was not a charming feature of his character, and tried to gloss over it as much as possible.

But he wasn't a good liar, and Emma had always been able to unmask him. She hadn't believed what he'd said about the furniture yesterday evening. She had accepted all his inventions for the sake of household peace, but this morning she had gone on the attack: even a cub would realize that he'd been lying!

Eric responded to the best of his ability. Hard-pressed, he nonetheless decided not to tell the truth. The truth would not make anything better.

Eric Bear started breathing through his mouth. In that way he avoided the aromas of the seductive perfumes and regained his power to act. With decisive steps he walked over toward the escalators and went up to the fifth floor. There were elevators at Grand Divino as well, but he could never remember where they were. It was the escalators, constructed of glass, plastic, and Plexiglas, that were the backbone of the department store. Their complicated mechanisms were exposed in what looked like glass drawers on the underside, and like perpetual-motion machines they kept the urge to buy going from morning to evening. Being slowly lifted up toward Grand Divino's sky roof, where small lamp-stars sparkled against a dark-blue background, gave a sense of divinity. After that it appeared small-minded to get cold feet if a pair of boots cost a few thousand.

On the fifth floor, to the right of the beds and linens, was the sewing notions department. And farthest in, alongside the knitting needles and yarn, the massive Tom-Tom Crow sat on a stool. He was a peculiar sight. He was sitting behind a long, white table, sorting sewing needles according to eye size. The crow's black form was hunched over the table, and he used the long feathers farthest out on the fingerbones for this detail work. It was not least thanks to the red spot on the underside of his beak—apparently a manufacturing defect—that Eric recognized his old friend. The crow was so large that the table in front of him appeared to belong in a preschool.

There were two more clerks in the sewing notions department, a pair of sows getting on in years whom Eric didn't notice at first. One of them was standing, unobtrusively folding flowery pieces of cloth not far from Tom-Tom; the other was over at the register, ironing aprons marked down twenty percent.

Complete calm prevailed in the department. Eric Bear placed himself at a safe distance, in the shelter of a bunk bed, and gathered courage. It seemed almost impossible that the slow needle-sorter was the same bird Eric had once known. Twenty years earlier the crow had been able to break two bricks between his wings. Back then Eric had laughed many times at the poor things who disturbed Tom-Tom by mistake when he sat absorbed in his thoughts; you couldn't imagine a more meaningless way to have an arm torn off. Most often Tom-Tom Crow was nicer than most, but sometimes he exploded in a madness that he couldn't control.

And now? Could the crow's loyalty still be counted on?

Eric took a few cautious steps into the sewing notions department and carefully avoided landing in the ironing sow's way. As Eric passed the embroideries, the crow looked up from his needles. For a fraction of a second a surprised worry was seen in his small, black eyes. Slowly he pushed the needles aside and got up from the stool.

"I'll be damned!" he burst out.

The crow ran over, taking the bear in his arms and lifting him up from the floor in a mighty embrace that caused Eric to laugh. Above all in relief, but also because he realized how ridiculous this had to appear.

After the friends exchanged the phrases that two old friends exchange when they haven't seen each other for a long time, Tom-Tom sat down on his stool and resumed his sorting. Eric leaned toward the table and watched for a while.

"And how the hell did you end up here?" he finally asked.

The swearword was a clumsy attempt to ingratiate himself. Nowadays Eric Bear swore so seldom that it rang falsely when he tried.

"What do you mean?" asked the crow.

"Yes . . . well," said Eric, less cocksure, "how did you end up here . . . knitting and crocheting and . . . sows?"

"Josephine and Nadine," said Tom-Tom, smiling, "are the flipping best. They help me with the embroideries. At home I'm working on a big frigging wall hanging. It's for the bedroom. It's going to be a fantasy landscape. Stay for lunch, then I can show you. I have the sketches here somewhere . . ."

Tom-Tom looked around with uncertainty. His sketches were somewhere.

"To be honest," said Eric, "I was thinking about freeing you from lunch. For good."

"There's nothing wrong with lunch," said Tom-Tom. "They have an employee lunchroom in the basement. Today there's vegetable soup. Maybe it doesn't sound so frigging cool, but it's better than you might think."

"I thought we could do a thing together," said Eric. "You and me and Sam and Snake."

"A thing?" repeated Tom-Tom.

Eric had a hard time reading the crow's tone of voice. He nodded.

"All four of us?" asked Tom-Tom.

Eric nodded again.

"Snake is never going to join in," objected the crow. "I

ran into him a few years ago, here at the department store. He pretended not to recognize me. I thought it was a frigging joke, I thought . . . I called him a few times, but he never answered."

"Snake will join in," Eric assured him.

"You guarantee?"

"I guarantee."

"I'll be damned," said Tom-Tom.

The crow became absorbed in thought.

"Economically you'll be set for the rest of your life," Eric interjected without having any idea of how he could fulfill that promise.

"You say so?"

"I say so."

"And if it goes to hell?" asked Tom-Tom, wise from experience.

"Then it goes to hell," confirmed Eric.

The crow nodded as though something profound had been said, and sank into reflection. When Eric started to doubt whether Tom-Tom even recalled what he was thinking about, the crow got up from the stool. It was a slow movement, not hesitant but not aggressive either.

"What the hell," he said. "Let's go, then."

"Good," answered Eric without sounding surprised.

Tom-Tom undid the apron which everyone in the sewing notions department was forced to wear. He folded it up neatly and placed it next to the needles.

"Nadine," he called to the nearest sow. "Nadine, you'll have to sort the needles. I'm quitting."

Nadine looked confused. She must have quickly found herself, however, for as Eric and Tom-Tom reached the escalators on the fifth floor their way was obstructed by a stern walrus. It was the department head. He riveted his gray eyes on the crow and asked what was going on.

"I'm quitting now," Tom-Tom answered amiably.

"I don't think so," the walrus hissed authoritatively. "You can't just leave your job like that. There is something called notice. There is something called responsibility."

This self-importance caused both Eric and Tom-Tom to break into a smile. The memories of youthful adventures returned to them both, of days that would never come back and that the Vaseline-coated lens of time had made infinitely lovely.

"Toss him," said Eric.

"You think so?" asked Tom-Tom.

"I think so," Eric nodded.

Whereupon Tom-Tom took a step forward, pressed his claws down into the parquet floor to get a solid stance, and then lifted the walrus from the floor and heaved him off into the bed department, where he landed on a pile of mattresses that fell over with a leisurely crash.

"Just like before, eh?" laughed Tom-Tom, proceeding calmly to the escalators.

Eric Bear didn't dare admit even to himself how bubblingly, inappropriately happy he felt.

"Do we have time to swing by the employee lunchroom before we take off?" asked Tom-Tom. "It would be a shame to miss out on that frigging vegetable soup."

TWILIGHT, 1

He stood in his tower, looking out over Mollisan Town in the twilight. Deep within his small, cold eyes there burned a fire, a white fire of unshakable will. He revealed this will to no one; he understood that it would frighten any stuffed animal who saw it. And he could keep it concealed, because he never lost control. If you couldn't control yourself, it was impossible to control others. And from his perspective, control was equivalent to power. That was how he lived his life. He seized power, and he administered it. In the shimmering orb of his eye a smile glistened fleetingly, but this smile was impossible to see. It was the smile of power, self-satisfied and terrified at the same time.

He was standing in the darkness. Down below his lookout point the two rectilinear avenues divided the city into four districts. His city, a world of objects and desire. He stood completely still, observing how the cars skidded around like fox fire on ingeniously labyrinthine streets. Every street in the city had its own characteristic color. Every important building was painted, from foundation to roof—including doors and windowsills, roof tiles, and chimneys—one of the rainbow's many shades. From his tower, Mollisan Town was an explosion of colors during the daytime, but after darkness set in, it was the neon lights instead that gave life and personality to asphalt, brick, and cement. He loved this city.

Mollisan Town was a few kilometers from the coast. To the west was the great sea and Hillevie, the resort town for the well-to-do. Otherwise they were surrounded by deep forests to the north as well as to the south and east. And the city was growing: at its edges trees and brush were being shoved aside to establish heavy industries. With each century the stuffed animals had conquered a few kilometers of the forest in every direction. Yet the forests were endless; no one had ever succeeded in exploring or mapping them in their insurveyable immensity, despite attempts being made.

The stuffed animals were curious by nature, he thought. That was their joy, and their misfortune.

The four districts of the city, distinct in their differences, competed at being the largest. In the past they had been independent villages, but they had grown together inexorably and been forced to share resources. Amberville's bourgeois prosperity; Tourquai's hectic urban life; Lanceheim, which remained a city within the city; and, finally, Yok, which with each year in the present century had grown to be a greater and greater problem for the city's administration. Today in each of the city's districts there lived more than a million stuffed animals, of all types and colors, dispositions and mentalities. Sometimes he saw himself as their puppet master; it was a matter of power and control. If he closed his eyes he could envision four million thin threads running from his brain, binding each and every animal in his city.

Pride, he thought. A mortal sin.

The cat who spilled the beans, the cat who had tattled to Nicholas Dove . . . the thought made him furious. Unconsciously his muscles tensed and he grabbed hold of the arm of the chair. The thought that such an insignificant animal, such a fool, had been able to upset a circle . . . that the almost perfect world he'd built—not for himself but for everyone—might crack apart so easily . . . that over the years he'd become so spoiled and lazy that he no longer worried . . . let himself be taken by surprise . . . surprised by something as obvious as . . . the spinelessness of stuffed animals.

He shook his head.

He breathed slowly.

He was forced to turn the argument around so as not to explode. Without insignificant errors like this thing with the cat, he thought, life would be all too easy. If chance didn't remain his opponent, who would be able to challenge him? Standing here, cursing the cat, led nowhere. The time for action had come.

CHAPTER 4

Along sky-blue South Avenue and mint-green East Avenue, the district of Yok reminded a careless observer of the well-cared-for townhouses in Amberville. After a few moments of scrutiny the differences became apparent. In expectation of good times that never came, the landlords had evicted their impoverished renters. The hope was for new, wealthier animals, but no one like that appeared. The years passed, the unoccupied buildings fell into disrepair, and finally they were so decrepit that the owners no longer had the means to keep them up. Especially now, because they had evicted the renters who up till then had provided them with their sole source of income.

In time the buildings along South and East Avenues came to be regarded as the boundary line between a functioning and a nonfunctioning society. Many had business in Yok, because both the Ministries of Finance and Culture had chosen to relocate certain aspects of their operations there for social reasons. Visitors took the bus along the deep-blue Avinguda de Pedrables, the street that flows from north to south like a broad river through that part of the city.

Those who lived in the chaos of streets running in all directions without name or number, the stuffed animals who made decrepit or improvised buildings their miserable homes, would all have moved to Tourquai, Amberville, or Lanceheim if they'd had the opportunity. No one chose of their own free will to live with the stench from the overloaded sewer system and the garbage fermenting in the streets. No one enjoyed the insecurity, the unpredictable aggressiveness of the homeless, or the fistfights and gunfire that were part of everyday life there. It was easy to hide in Yok, to lie low year after year without the risk of being discovered. In the food stores, on the streets, or in the bars, it was wisest to look only at the person you were talking to, or even better: at nothing at all. The inhabitants of this part of the city knew how to take care of themselves, ignore others, and secretly hope to get a chance one day to leave Yok for good.

Eric Bear and Tom-Tom Crow left Grand Divino, crossed the mint-green avenue, and took the way into Yok via Rue d'Uzès. Eric had written down the address on a slip of paper that was in his pants pocket: 152 Yiala's Arch. They walked rather quickly. The crow had always felt uncomfortable in Yok's decrepit poverty; he had grown up in Tourquai. He was the cub as well as grandcub of a long line of successful shopkeepers. He was slurping on a bag of salty pretzel sticks he'd brought with him from the department store, which meant that he didn't complain about having missed out on the vegetable soup.

In silence they continued due south, and after a half hour or so they could no longer distinguish one block from the next. Gray concrete buildings, four or five stories high, whose lowest floors were covered with sun-bleached graffiti over rain-tattered advertisements. Here and there were shops that lacked names and that often sold unexpected combinations of wares: vegetables and handbags, liquor and plastic furniture. Eric and Tom-

Tom were alone on the streets, and yet they felt they were being watched.

"Damn, how I hate this," said Tom-Tom.

"Don't forget that you're the one who's big and dangerous," Eric reminded him.

Tom-Tom nodded to himself. He appreciated being addressed in a sort of familiar understanding, like two grown-up stuffed animals making conversation. Eric Bear was the only one who used that tone of voice with him.

Just when Tom-Tom was thinking for the third time about asking whether Eric really knew where he was going, the bear nodded toward a narrow, grass-green alley some ten meters farther along on the left side. The alley seemed to disappear down a steep slope between the buildings, and it was so narrow that Tom-Tom was unsure whether there would be room for him with his wings.

"There," said Eric.

"Are you sure? I mean, it's frigging hard to find your way around here," Tom-Tom pointed out, taking the last pretzels from the bag. "But I'm guessing you must have been here before."

Eric nodded. True, it was a long time ago, so long that it almost didn't count, but yesterday afternoon he had hastily checked. Sam Gazelle was still living at 152 Yiala's Arch, which, by the way, was one of the few green streets in this neighborhood.

"Hope the poor devil is home," said Tom-Tom.

"Worst case, we'll just have to wait," said Eric.

"Hope he's alive," said Tom-Tom.

"He's the type who never dies," said Eric.

Tom-Tom nodded and smiled. There was something to that.

The alley was not quite as narrow as the crow had thought, but the stench of urine was so overpowering that he almost turned around because of it. In some remarkable way, he had the idea that the buildings were closing behind him. When he looked over his shoulder he realized that there was nowhere to flee, if that should be required. In these neighborhoods you never knew. The crow was filled with fear. The reason he'd abandoned his previous life and started working in the notions department at Grand Divino was that he never wanted to feel like this again. Others related what happened when he fell into his black holes of panic; he himself recalled nothing. Sometimes it went well, other times not so well. It was after one of these memory losses—after he'd long since left the Casino—that he'd returned to consciousness in a small sewing notions boutique in Lanceheim. The event had awakened an interest in handwork that surprised him, and when he started at Grand Divino, life took a positive turn. His needs were not great, either. To be able to one day finish his embroidered wall hanging was a dream sufficient to give the crow happiness for many years to come.

It hadn't taken more than an hour with Eric Bear before Tom-Tom again found himself in the situation that he thought he'd left behind for all time. His pulse pounded so that it hurt. He looked around yet again, and he thought he glimpsed something or someone there, far away. Fear seized him with a firm grasp, and the world began to spin.

"Here it is," said Eric.

"What?"

"It's here."

Eric nodded toward an entryway, the first and only door in the entire long, narrow slope.

"Sam lives here?"

Eric nodded.

"What the hell!" said Tom-Tom with emphasis.

. . . .

The entryway to 152 Yiala's Arch was broken. The bear and the crow went into the building without encountering anyone, and when they reached the first stairway landing the screams were heard.

"He's home," declared the crow.

Eric nodded. The scream they heard was one of pain, but there had also been a concealed note of pleasure. They continued purposefully up the stairs, and right before they reached the fourth floor it became silent.

On three floors there were two closed, unmarked doors, and Eric was on his way over to the one on the right when he became hesitant. He stopped, taking a step to the left, but then made a decision.

"No, it's the one to the right, I'm sure," he said.

"We could always knock and ask," suggested the crow.

He took a step past the bear and knocked firmly on the door to the right. If it were possible, the stillness in the building seemed to intensify during the seconds that followed. They stood, waiting, but nothing happened.

The crow knocked again, harder this time, calling out at the same time.

"Sam! It's us! It's Tom-Tom!"

Another minute passed without anything happening, and Eric lost patience.

"It's no coincidence," he said, "that the screams we heard have gone silent. Knock down the door."

"Should I?" asked Tom-Tom.

"Knock down the door," repeated Eric.

Tom-Tom moved away a little, took a deep breath, and ran up against the closed door, heaving himself against it with his whole body and feeling how it gave way. In order not to give Sam a chance to take the back way out, both

Tom-Tom and Eric stormed in. The gazelle was sitting on a little stool next to a bed on the farther wall.

The gazelle looked up in terror. His torso was bare, his naked, white belly turned toward the door, and it seemed as though the black rings around his eyes had become even larger. His sand-brown fur glistened beautifully thanks to expensive shampoo, but the freshness of the fur stood in stark contrast to the horizontally ringed horns. The right horn had broken off in the middle even before he'd started at Casino Monokowski more than twenty years earlier, and he'd never managed to get it fixed.

In the bed next to Sam an old duck was lying, tied up. He looked unusual, mint-green with a blue beak. Alongside him, both on the mattress and on the floor, newly plucked feathers were whirling in the draft from the broken-in door. Certain feathers were scorched on the edges, and there was a faint odor of burnt animal.

The old duck stared at Eric and Tom-Tom with a look of panic.

"Help," he said unexpectedly.

There was no strength in his voice, the word was more like a statement.

Sam twisted toward the duck and looked at him with surprise. The old bird took a few breaths, filled his chest with air, and cleared his throat.

"You must help me," he said in a somewhat steadier voice. "The gazelle has hurt me. He has really hurt me."

And tears ran from the duck's eyes.

"Sam, let him loose," said Eric.

Sam gave a start. He'd thought there was something familiar about the figures who had broken down his door, but in his clouded brain he had a hard time placing them. Now that there was a voice to go along with the bear's face, the lights came on.

"Eric?"

"Send the duck away, Sam," Eric repeated. "We have to talk."

"Eric, darling!" exclaimed Sam, and now there was an exaggerated delight in his voice. "And Tom-Tom! You look really old!"

And with a laugh like the ringing of small bells, Sam got up from the stool. In a particular way that couldn't be accused of being exactly feminine, but definitely wasn't masculine, he minced over to his uninvited guests and embraced them both. Eric froze. He'd always had a hard time with touching. Tom-Tom, on the other hand, squeezed back, hiding the gazelle under his wings, feeling that he'd missed this fragile being.

"Damn, it's been a long time," said the crow. "And I didn't even know I missed you."

"You're sweet, darling," Sam smiled. "Thank the good Magnus for dumb crows!"

And he giggled happily. Eric nodded toward the duck. Sam shrugged his shoulders, but went over to the bed and loosened the ropes that bound the duck from head to foot.

"That you come here to visit," said the gazelle elatedly while he struggled with his own buttons, "in the middle of the night . . ."

"Sam," said Tom-Tom gently, "for heaven's sake, it's the middle of the day."

"As if that should be important, sweetheart?" said Sam. "When you come here to visit . . . at last . . . finally . . . and together. It almost makes me want to cry. I guess it's just Snake that's missing."

"Soon it'll be his turn," informed Eric.

The duck got out of the bed, recoiling from the gazelle and making a large detour around him in order to make his way to the door.

"I'm thinking of calling the police on you," he said, pointing at Sam.

Eric Bear and Tom-Tom weren't fooled. They both knew that the duck had paid Sam Gazelle for . . . special services. The duck disappeared out to the stairway and they heard his rapid, flat footsteps echo on the way down to the entry.

Sam went over to the kitchenette and poured himself a glass of water. He looked at Eric and raised his eyebrows, but Eric shook his head.

"I'm fine, thanks."

"Okay, talk," said Sam.

"Hell, Sam," said Tom-Tom, looking after the duck, "are you still carrying on with . . . you are after all . . . that bird must have been over sixty?"

"Sweet crow, as long as they pay they can be over a hundred," Sam replied. "And that goes for you, too, Eric. And if you ask really nicely you might not have to pay at all."

The bear ignored the invitation and got right to business.

"This is how things stand," said Eric, who knew that Sam wouldn't be satisfied with anything other than the truth. "I've gotten an assignment from an old acquaintance. We're going to find the Death List. And we're going to be sure to remove his name from it."

For once—this happened very seldom—Sam Gazelle had nothing to say. He was taken by surprise, astonished, and he stared suspiciously at Eric, who realized that the moment was perfect for proposing the first part of his plan.

"Sam," he said, "I was thinking I might rent your apartment. Starting now, and for a week or so going forward. As long as needed. This will be our headquarters."

"Darling, I haven't even said if I want to be involved or not," the gazelle protested.

"I'll pay more than the rent, of course. And whether we

end up succeeding or not, I guarantee that you will be liberally paid for your efforts."

"Exactly what do you mean by 'liberally'?" asked the gazelle.

And Eric Bear concocted a story about how much Nicholas Dove would pay, and half in advance if they failed, and it was no more difficult than that to entice Sam Gazelle to join up as well.

Sam filled two more glasses with water, and the three animals made a toast.

"An advance in case we don't succeed sounds good," said Sam, "especially since there isn't any Death List, is there?"

His light, whinnying laughter rang again like a small bell.

CHAPTER 5

Back then the four of them had never been inseparable musketeers. Sam Gazelle was most often so drugged up he had a hard time telling one musketeer from another, and Snake Marek was only loyal to a single animal: himself. Eric Bear never counted; everyone knew he was only passing through the underworld.

On those occasions when Nicholas Dove commissioned them to work together it had always been a matter of chance, but each time they were surprised by how well they functioned together. No one encroached on the other's territory. Eric was the energy; he was the ignition key while Tom-Tom was the motor, the force. Sam was the one who supplied courage and irreverence and found paths that no one else dared to tread. Snake Marek was the uncrowned king of intrigue who anticipated their opponents' responses and removed obstacles before anyone even had time to set them up.

Snake was the first in the foursome to make himself independent from Nicholas Dove and move out of Casino Monokowski. That was a great, difficult decision, and no one criticized him for not keeping in touch. It was all or nothing, and that's how it had to be.

Snake found a small apartment up in north Lanceheim and, after a few lost years in the finance business, landed in the environment for which he was intended. He applied for, and got, a job as administrative assistant at the Environmental Ministry. He understood very quickly that his particular talent for persuasion suited public administration. He was not a social snake, seldom evoked sympathy among his closest associates, and didn't have a favorable appearance. He was a pale-green reptile with yellowish eyes, and despite the fact that he slinked upright through life, he needed something to stand on—a bench or a table or a box—so as not to feel inferior. Nevertheless, he made a career. When Eric Bear found him—roughly the same time as Tom-Tom and Sam came to life on Friday morning in the newly established headquarters at Yiala's Arch—Snake Marek had held the position as head of the Office of Grants within the Ministry of Culture for many years.

Marek's office was at the end of a long corridor of linoleum floors and dark-blue walls where posters advertising obscure cultural events were taped up. The office was a narrow cubicle with a rectangular window which the sun never reached. There was no smell whatsoever, neither in the office nor out in the corridor, and no other animals were to be seen.

"I only have ten minutes" was the first thing Snake Marek said to Eric Bear after a little less than twenty years.

Eric was invited to sit on a narrow Windsor-style chair at the short end of the desk, the only piece of furniture in the office for visitors. There was an antipathy in Snake's voice that was not even concealed. (On the phone with the receptionist Snake had maintained that he wasn't in, but when he realized that Eric was calling from down in the lobby he changed his mind and unwillingly gave his old friend permission to come up.)

After neutral, friendly exchanges about health, Eric got to the point. Could Snake help out? Take a leave of absence for a week or two. It wouldn't need to be longer than that, and then he was back to his routines again. At this point the bear made a vague gesture toward the small cubicle that was already feeling claustrophobic to him.

Snake replied at length. He didn't say either yes or no, and Eric realized that what he was listening to was a prelude to refusal. Snake talked and talked, and finally the bear lost patience.

"Do you think," said Eric sharply, "that I'm sitting here for the fun of it? If you think I'd be looking you up for the first time in twenty years if it wasn't a matter of life or death, literally, then you're not in your right mind."

Snake Marek changed tactics. He ignored Eric's questions, and spoke instead of the past. Precisely and at great length he pulled out old injustices and long-forgotten conflicts. It was no secret that Snake had always harbored an envy, to a certain degree justified, of Eric.

Eric tried to interrupt, tried to correct him, but to no avail.

After ten minutes Eric rose from the chair, held his paws over his head, and admitted defeat. This didn't get Snake to quit talking. Eric backed slowly out of the small office cubicle. Harried by complicated sentence constructions filled with ironic poison arrows, the bear hurried along the dark-blue corridor back out into reality.

He needed a new strategy.

Snake Marek was an animal with a calling.

Even at a very young age Snake's brain could be compared to a generator working dangerously near the limits of its operating capacity. Apart from a few hours of quiet at night, it glowed, sparked, and hummed from early dawn until long after sundown. When Marek reached his teens, his need to communicate all of these thoughts, ideas, feelings, melodies, and visions was as physically tangible as his need for food and sleep. The surrounding world must find out. The surrounding world must hear, observe, and confirm.

So thought the young Snake.

He wrote poems that he hid in his desk drawer, because he knew that posterity would one day discover them there. He wrote editorials for the school newspaper under a pseudonym, but signed his arts columns with his own name. He started a pop band as a twelve-year-old, and compelled some schoolmates who were several years older to accompany him when he performed his profound lyrics. His first exhibition as an artist took place two days after his sixteenth birthday. What he exhibited were predominantly charcoal drawings; the forests around the city were his still life.

Snake Marek's artistic production knew no limits. From his thirteenth to his eighteenth year he poured forth no less than seventeen collections of poetry and five novels. In addition he made daily contributions to the newspaper. To begin with, he wrote in Amberville's school newspaper, but later he did double duty as a reporter for *The Daily News* as well. During the same period he wrote more than a hundred songs, none with fewer than four verses, and produced twice that number of paintings, if you only counted oils and watercolors. Thanks to his manic disposition, Snake Marek managed to suffer, ponder, and produce in a feverish, unceasing cycle. He, however, didn't have time to notice the surrounding world's complete lack of interest in him.

The summer he turned eighteen everything fell apart. Burning yourself out was of course a kind of merit badge for a hard-pressed artist, and therefore he felt rather satisfied with the entire course of the illness.

The triggering factor was his fourth art exhibition, which, exactly like the earlier ones, was met with haughty silence.

This was the final drop that caused the goblet to overflow. Two days after the exhibition Snake Marek made a large pyre on the street outside his entryway. All the handwritten poems and manuscripts of novels, all the demo tapes and paintings, framed or not, soon formed a neat pile on the sidewalk, albeit considerably smaller than Snake had wished for and imagined. Before anyone was able to stop him he lit it, and when the flames were leaping high the neighbors called the police. Sirens were soon heard at a distance, and Snake—who hadn't foreseen this—went into a panic. He fled from the scene, and ended up—after a cold night in a foul-smelling trash room—at Casino Monokowski.

The years he then spent along with Eric, Tom-Tom, and the others, Snake chose to conceal deep down in the archives of his memory when he took over the position as administrative assistant at the Environmental Ministry.

For Snake Marek had a Plan.

During his time at Casino Monokowski his artistic endeavors weren't given up, but the surrounding world was no longer allowed to share in the development that Snake Marek underwent as a poet, prose writer, musician, and artist. The insight had smoldered the whole time in his subconscious. His talent was depicting Reality. Cut the symbolism, skip the subtexts, and weed severely in the poetry. He would become a Realist.

And the time at Casino Monokowski gave him, if nothing else, stories enough to tell for the rest of his life.

So with great and somewhat unexpected patience he set to work. Day after day, well-formulated and then corrected and edited manuscript pages were added to the others; notes were joined with care to notes; colors blended with a careful, sensitive brush, without anyone on the job knowing of it. It didn't go quickly, it was an artist's life as far from the romantic myths of impassioned creation as you could go. Nonetheless, Snake Marek found a deep satisfaction in his methodical mission. By day he lived like a normal office rat at the ministry, evenings and nights and dawns he returned to being an all-around artist in the small apartment he'd purchased on Knaackstrasse in northwest Lanceheim.

Even if Snake Marek began his career in the public sector in the Environmental Ministry, from the first he already had his sights set on the Ministry of Culture. And when the possibility of changing departments arose, he seized the opportunity. So many signs, he felt, indicated that the grandiose—not to say fantastic—Plan he had put together in orgasmic haze was completely plausible.

For three long years he was forced to carry out idiotic office tasks at Culture before the next move became possible. But only a few days after he had taken the position at the Office of Grants, the years of waiting proved to have been worth the trouble.

He became one of five processing assistants to the department's then boss. Snake was responsible for poetry and related cultural manifestations, that is to say sung, improvised, and dramatic poetry, and no one questioned the proposals for nominations that he sifted out from the applications. As long as there were candidates to give grants to, everyone seemed to be in a good mood.

But in the energy that he showed, Snake was alone in the Office of Grants. The other administrative assistants were older culture workers who capped unsuccessful careers with jobs in the department, and in that respect Snake stood out as an obvious candidate when, a few years later, a successor to the boss's position was discussed. No one put as much effort into preparatory work as he did, no one showed as much interest in the individuals behind the applications as he.

One fine spring day a little less than five years after Snake Marek had changed departments, he was named head of the Office of Grants in the Ministry of Culture, and the distinction was celebrated at a run-down tavern right next to the office in east Lanceheim. Snake was a happy, contented, newly named boss; it was striking with what ease he took on his new role. In his imagination he'd had it for a long time.

His first decision was to refrain from replacing himself with a new administrative assistant. When another one of the assistants took retirement six months later, this position as well remained unfilled. Snake himself took on these duties. In the ministry this unwillingness to recruit personnel was seen as positive. Reality beset the Ministry of Culture's finances, and having a manager who was not too refined to do some of the heavy work was unusual.

Four years after Snake Marek had become head of the Office of Grants, only he and a secretary were still working in the department. During the same period the combined appropriations for grants had been reduced by a six-figure amount. Snake had made himself known as a reflective authority, cautious with the taxpayers' money.

All, of course, in accord with The Plan.

Only extremely deserving poets, prose writers, musicians, and artists were awarded grants nowadays. The ones whom the reviewers in the daily papers scarcely dared judge. The ones who were introverted and self-referential and impossible to have in a furnished room. Snake knew their secrets. They were all drug-abusers, psychopaths, and obsessive-compulsives.

And this, all while Snake Marek's own artistic production of easily accessible books, songs, and paintings simply grew and grew at home in his dark apartment.

It had been a long time since a young, promising novelist had the economic opportunity to grow into a great body of work. No popular poetry was being created, because the poets were forced to work as dishwashers and language teachers and were completely spent in the evenings when they came home. The authorities seemed only to encourage navel-gazing and experimentation, and soon there was nothing else.

But all this would be transformed.

Soon the city's yearning cultural consumers would have their fill of Snake Marek's collected works. In one stroke he would then become the leader in every art form.

It was therefore not strange that Snake Marek reacted coldly to Eric Bear's proposal of a leave of absence; Marek had things to do.

In the afternoon after Eric Bear had met Snake at the Office of Grants, the bear went straight to his childhood home on Hillville Road. As always in the middle of the day the house on the peaceful light-flame-yellow street was empty. Father was at school, Mother was at the ministry.

In the secretaire in his parents' joint office on the second floor, Rhinoceros Edda kept everything she needed to carry on her correspondence. Among other things, official Environmental Ministry stationery, watermarked with her own monogram. Eric Bear used this paper to write—in Rhinoceros Edda's name—a brief message, addressed to Snake Marek.

At the Environmental Ministry, wrote Eric, a document was circulating at the present time that dealt with gambling and alcohol abuse. In one of the addenda, which discussed the problem from a historical perspective, Snake Marek was mentioned. It would be unfortunate, wrote Eric, if Snake's past were to make his political future impossible. If Snake took an immediate leave of absence, then Rhinoceros Edda would see to it that the document in its present form would not be distributed.

Edda was doing this for the sake of her cub, wrote Eric, because she knew that Eric needed Snake's immediate assistance.

After that, Eric signed with his mother's signature, which he'd learned to copy in his early teens, and sent the letter by courier to the Office of Grants. It would reach Snake Marek before the end of the business day.

TEDDY BEAR, 1

In a way my twin brother Eric and I are married to the same she.

But she doesn't know it.

It's a complicated situation.

But love is a world unto itself.

The crooked path that led me to love: How did it happen? Emma Rabbit was an angel, I an ordinary bear. She both was and is worthy of someone better. And yet she chose me. The ways of love are unfathomable.

Love is lethal for a bear who has consecrated his life to goodness. Love is the victory of feeling over reason. Is that why my thoughts become cloudy when I think about Emma and what led up to our wedding?

Is Emma good? Could I be married to someone who isn't good? Could I be married to someone who doesn't strive for the same goodness as I myself do?

I'm no missionary. I'm no hypocrite, either. But I was in love with Emma even before I met her. Paradoxically enough, the fact that Eric had my job at the advertising agency Wolle & Wolle made the decision easier.

Emma Rabbit was the most beautiful bride I'd ever seen.

Around her head, where the fur was combed so it looked like the softest lamb's wool, rested a garland of fresh dandelion leaves and pink roses. I had braided the garland for her that same morning, according to tradition. A sheer bridal veil of silk brocade fell across her slender back and drew attention to her sweet face where her nose glistened moistly and her cheeks were glowing with expectation, anxiety, and happiness. But it was her gaze that bewitched me. The solitude in her large peppercorn eyes that had enticed me to tenderness and affection was temporarily gone, replaced by conviction.

She was strong and beautiful.

Emma was standing in one of the narthexes of the church along with her mother. Her mother was nervous. I had never met her. Or perhaps I had met her. She was not angry, only worried about all the hundreds of details that might go wrong. She was worried about whether her cub had chosen the right mate or not. I'm not criticizing her. I was not an unequivocal match. Despite my successful parents, I probably made an unstable impression at times.

Outside the narthex Emma's girlfriends stood waiting. They spoke loudly and shrilly with one another. They were nervous, too.

Neither the nervousness of her mother or her girlfriends could, however, compare to Emma Rabbit's own. She had awakened with a lurch when the half-moon was still high in the sky. She sat up in bed and called out, "The ring!" with such panic that I threw off the blanket and leapt up.

"The ring? Is it gone?"

The ring was in secure keeping in the blue case that I had set on the nightstand. Yet Emma did not go back to sleep. Her anxiety kept us awake until dawn. Then we fell asleep for a few hours until it was time for me to go gather flowers for the garland.

They grew in the flowerbeds outside Lakestead House.

"You're completely sure now, aren't you?" asked Emma.

She was waiting for me in the corridor. She was driving her wagon.

I went up and looked her deep in the eyes. I nodded.

"I'm sure," I answered without the least hint of doubt.

"Why?"

There was anxiety in her eyes and her nostrils flared involuntarily. A moment later they narrowed again.

"Because I love you," I replied.

"But you were so hesitant," she said, exactly as I knew she would, "you were occupied with your evil and good. You said that making promises you know you can't keep is lying. And the more you cared about someone, the bigger the lie. You said that marriage was the worst kind of lie. Because even if you wanted to be faithful . . . even if you wanted to love for your whole life . . . even if you wanted . . ."

"Darling," I interrupted, "I know what I said."

"Even if you wanted all that . . ." Emma continued without paying attention to my objection. "You said that the rest of your life was too long a time to foresee. You said that things always happen that you can't control. You said that, knowing all that with certainty, an animal with good intentions, an animal with a thoroughly good heart, ought never to get married."

"Dear," I interrupted a second time, "I know that I . . ."

"But everything you said," said Emma, looking at me at the same time as her nose carried out the same sort of unregulated expansions and contractions as before, "doesn't that mean anything anymore?"

I sighed and tried to calm her.

I didn't want to take back what I'd said.

I couldn't take it back; I stood by every word.

But to profess my love to her, to describe her as I saw her, with her secure self-confidence, her creative talent, and last but not least her remarkable beauty, wouldn't be telling lies.

"Many struggle their whole lives to find the empathy which is completely natural for you," I said. "It makes you sensitive and strong. If you find yourself in a difficult situation some day, your empathy will help you through the sorrow."

"What difficult situation?" asked Emma.

"I mean," I replied, reining in my irritation so that it was impossible to hear, "that you can rely on yourself, darling. You don't need me, or anyone else, either. You are your own happiness. If you can't see that yourself, which in a way is part of your charm, you're going to find out what I mean the day you need to."

I don't know if she understood what I was saying.

She leaned forward and hugged me hard. When at last she released her hold, I went down the stairs and gathered my flowers.

I hadn't lied.

I hadn't held back the truth.

Yet it was with a heavy heart that I cut pink roses from the bushes growing in the backyard.

A good bear.

That's what I want to be.

That's not a humble desire.

In the afternoons, after reading and before I go down to dinner, I sit in the armchair and think about everything that separates good from evil. Some days I sit for a quarter of an hour. Other days I don't get out of there for two or three hours. They are punctual at Lakestead House, and it's unfortunate when this drags on.

Evil is a serious subject. Many have immersed themselves in it. Yet one of the greatest problems is the definition itself.

Being a good bear demands that you know what evil looks like.

I know what evil looks like.

My forty-eighth summer of life is approaching. It is not without experience that I look back on my life. I don't want to call it a happy life. It was never a question of making a happy life for myself. But I feel satisfied; there is a certain calm. It occurred to me yesterday. Few grains of sand from the past chafed in my soul as I walked along the shore in the pouring rain of the Afternoon Weather.

Involuntarily my mood darkened.

And in my armchair before dinner, my childhood was waiting for me.

The day my twin brother and I were delivered to our parents I already knew everything about a mother's and a father's love for their cubs. I knew that my brother would come to experience that kind of love. And I knew that I wouldn't. It was not an insight expressed in words; I was two days old. And yet the certainty of it was in my heart. It marked my upbringing. I loved Mother and Father. They loved me back. But never like they loved Eric.

Never.

We came direct from the factory, a troupe of parentless cubs being driven out to their future homes by the Deliverymen in their green Volga pickup. Stuffed animals out taking a walk that morning stopped to look at the truck. The males clasped their females closer to them. The females tipped their heads to one side and smiled tenderly.

I can imagine how it was.

I myself have been walking on a sidewalk like that and seen the green pickup driving by. A truckbed full of cubs who will long for love their whole lives. A longing that is going to lead them astray, and destroy them.

Almost nothing is more difficult than keeping the longing for love free from demands.

It is a struggle.

I struggle every day.

Mother liked to say that the Saturday when Eric and I came to flame-yellow Hillville Road, nature appeared in sparkling garb. The sky was light blue and the pleasantly warm sun put the cascades of red, yellow, and green foliage in light and shadow by turns.

The Deliverymen drove across the Star—the golden square that was the absolute midpoint of the city—and continued along mint-green East Avenue. The carillon in the highest of Sagrada Bastante's thirteen towers struck its cheerful melody.

There's no symbolism to be found in those thirteen towers.

The four rectilinear avenues toward east, west, south, and north were the skeleton of our city. During the week these were heavily traversed thoroughfares. On the weekends, the east and west avenues were transformed into walking streets. In the middle, between three lanes to one side and three lanes to the other, grew massive oaks and maples. They formed a long avenue on either side of a wide gravel walkway.

The trees provided shelter from the rain that passed over the city twice a day, in the morning and in the afternoon.

In the fall thousands and thousands more lamps were set up in the foliage. The first of November every year the lamps were lit just before the Evening Weather, and the two avenues pierced the city like sabers of light.

You shouldn't look for any symbolism in that either.

The Deliverymen drove Eric and me to Amberville, the district whose boundaries are formed by East Avenue and the beautifully sky-blue South Avenue. Here the two-story buildings stand wall to wall in seemingly endless rows. Up the street and down the street, most in shades of green or blue, with more or less identical buildings. White wood-work against dark-red or dark-brown plaster. Sloping roofs shingled with black mosaic tile. Two garrets with transom windows on each attic. Narrow ribbons of smoke rise from the chimneys in the twilight. Red and pink geraniums spiral from the flowerboxes.

Details set the houses apart. Growing up in Amberville, we often knocked on the wrong door.

"We've got two units to number 14," said one of the De-liverymen to the other.

With the point of a pencil he checked off Eric's and my names on his list.

"Two units?" the Deliveryman commented behind the steering wheel.

"Twin bears. Don't see that often."

We were a sensation even when we were made. Two iden-tical stuffed animals. Indistinguishable.

The green pickup swung onto the sidewalk outside 14 Hillville Road. The Deliveryman who was sitting on the passenger side jumped out and went around and opened the back door.

There we sat. We were neither shorter nor taller than we are today. We were less worn around the knees and elbows. That was the main difference.

But we couldn't do anything. Couldn't talk, couldn't think, couldn't walk. The Deliveryman took us, one under each arm, and carried us up to the house which was to be our parental home.

Mother and Father stood waiting at the door. Our father, Boxer Bloom, was wearing his best white shirt, and a bow tie besides. Our mother, Rhinoceros Edda, had on a dress that was as big as a tent.

"Finally!" said Mother.

"Now it begins," said Father.

I have few memories of my own of early childhood. But Mother told us stories when we got older. Funny stories about how Eric or I said something silly before we understood what the words meant. Dramatic stories of illnesses and escapes. Mother liked to tell stories as she was preparing food. She stood at the old, wood-fired stove in our narrow kitchen. Eric and I sat at the kitchen table and listened.

She told about when we drove the car out to the lake in the summer and when we ate our picnics in Swarwick Park in autumn. In Mother's stories Eric was the initiator and I was the follower. Eric was the star and I was the audience.

I was a cub, and needed no explanations for why things were that way. It was natural that Eric was promoted at my expense.

We loved him.

I have never felt, and never will feel, envy in relation to my brother. Bitterness, it is said, is an inborn talent. Roughly in the same way as music. I've never been able to hold a tune. My anxiety is of a different type.

The memory of Mother's tale changed in time to a memory of the event itself. There have been times in my life when I believed that these implanted memories might replace the real ones. That's not the case. What Mother told and retold were situations that were especially meaningful to her. Not especially meaningful to me or to Eric. If you think about it, you might more than suspect that Mother's stories were keys to her inner life.

The keys to my life were kept in a different drawer.

There was a time when I tried to force it open.

Then I understood that that was meaningless. Being a good bear is a constantly ongoing project in the present tense.

Eric and I shared a room. It was the highest up, on the fourth floor with the sloping roof over our beds. That early time was dizzying for our new parents. They had lived for each other, now Eric and I made our demands. There was a lot we needed to learn. Simple things like walking down the stairs to the kitchen. Or expressing the simple feelings that filled us. We were cold. We got hungry. And sleepy. One time we ate too many cookies and got a stomachache.

At this time our mother had not made a name for herself at the ministry. Like hundreds of other paper-pushers she plodded along, and her coworkers hardly sensed that she would become one of our time's most talked-about politicians. It was both obvious and easy for Mother to go to half-time, and she continued to work half-time until Eric and I had learned the most necessary skills.

It was different with Father.

Our father, Boxer Bloom, was rector of Amberville's Secondary Grammar School. The school building was a chalk-white fairy-tale castle, adorned with towers and pinnacles. The building was designed by Toad Hendersen, who had also renovated the city's massive cathedral. The school's main entry faced toward moss-green All Saints Road, but from the hill in the schoolyard at the back the forest could be glimpsed beyond the city limits.

For Father the job was a calling. Between the present day and the future there were some animals who made a difference, and he counted himself among them. He was bringing up the coming generations. If he succeeded, the city we'd known until now would be a pale prototype of that which was to come. Father was careful about describing his visions concretely, but I sensed that what he especially disliked about his own time was its lack of order.

He wanted to sort things out.

The barbarous by themselves, and the civilized by themselves.

The reliable here, and the unreliable there.

The heart knew which was which, even if the brain confused the issue with doubts.

Whatever happened, we could rely on Father keeping his promises. The ministry responsible for the Cub List had inquired as to whether our parents were really ready for a set of twins; wouldn't it be difficult to treat the cubs alike?

Father guaranteed that on that point there was no danger. We cubs could always rely on a promise from Boxer Bloom. And by cubs, Boxer Bloom meant all the cubs that went to his school. Eric and I would start there eventually. In that respect we were no exception.

Eric's and my room on the fourth floor was a perfect boys' room. Our beds with their tall, white headboards, our nightstands with cute soccer lamps, and our little desks with their wheeled stools, were just about identical, exactly like us.

At first glance.

If you looked, there were differences. Small, hardly noticeable, but nonetheless undeniable differences.

I'm describing outward appearances.

Inside, an abyss was growing between us.

It happened late one evening when we were six months old; it became one of Mother's most important memories. Mother and Father had invited some friends to dinner. It was later asserted that their many dinner parties were one of the reasons for Mother's career. Thanks to her cooking skills, the dinner guests became eternally loyal to her. The network she created was wide-branching. Two or three evenings a week we had animals in our home. While others in the neighborhood were pottering in the garden, reading books, or being consumed by their careers, Mother prepared food for her dinner guests.

Eric and I grew up in the kitchen. In the heat from the oven that never cooled, in a throng of bubbling kettles, unwashed saucepans and bowls, recently used cutting boards and graters that smelled of garlic, parmesan, and horserad-

ish left standing on benches and tables where we often discovered a lamb filet or a sliced eggplant when we picked up
a plate or decided to rinse out a cup in order to fill it with
hot chocolate. In the midst of this chaos stood our mother,
Rhinoceros Edda, like a commander on her captain's bridge,
careful not to stir the béarnaise sauce with the wooden spoon
she'd just fished out of the cauliflower pan.

Mother made no mistakes.

That evening baked cod was being served with puréed
almond potatoes. The gravy was served in the gravy boat
that we'd inherited from Grandmother. A silver gravy boat
that was very valuable.

At the table, besides Mother and Father, sat their best
friends, Mouse Weiss and her husband, Cat Jones. Penguin
Odenrick was there—at that time still a deacon in the church
on Hillville Road, unaware that he would soon be made
a prodeacon—along with Jack Pig, whom Mother would
later succeed as head of the Environmental Ministry.

It was Odenrick who heard it first.

"Excuse me," he said in a loud voice, "but did I just hear
a scream?"

Conversation ceased. Odenrick had been right. In the silence a screaming cub was heard. From up on the fourth
floor a howl forced its way down to the dining room. Boxer
Bloom got up. There was still explosive force in his legs
after many years of soccer-playing in his younger days.

"It's the cubs," he said, his face pale.

He ran out of the room and up the stairs.

All of the guests, with Mother in the lead, followed.

When they came into the nursery, Father was already
standing by my crib. I was the one who was screaming. I
continued screaming, despite the fact that Father lifted me
up and held me to him. It was silent from Eric's bed. Nonetheless Mother took the few steps across the room in order
to see to her other twin.

It was her instinct, to see to Eric first. But the suspicion that that's the way it was—that she set one twin before the other—was, and is, the most shameful thing in Mother's life.

Not even now will she admit it.

Nonetheless, all her friends from that time bear witness to that.

That time she relied on her intuition. Subconsciously she understood that her twins' symbiosis was such that what one of them saw could be perceived by the other, and vice versa.

I was screaming because Eric was in danger.

Mother saw it.

"A moth!" she screamed.

Father more or less threw me down on the bed again, where I immediately fell silent. It's unclear whether I fell silent due to Father's brusque treatment or if I stopped screaming because I had done my duty.

With a tremendous leap Father threw himself across the room and killed the moth before anyone had time to react. With that the drama was over. It was only when the guests returned to the dining room and the cooling food that they realized what had happened.

I had saved Eric's life.

Deacon Odenrick taught me to distinguish good from evil. The penguin was one of many deacons who worked in Amberville, but the only one with whom I came in contact.

The structure of our church is simple.

In every district of the city there are several parishes. In Amberville there are four. Working in the parishes are all-deacons, a kind of apprentice, who are paid by the church. Each parish has its own deacon who leads the organization and does most of the preaching. Among the deacons in the district, a prodeacon is chosen. In turn, the four prodeacons of Mollisan Town have a leader, the church's high-est representative: the archdeacon in the cathedral Sagrada Bastante. No one in my surroundings would have guessed that the hard-tested Odenrick would, in time, come to be the new archdeacon in Mollisan Town.

At that time, Odenrick was completely lacking in such ambitions.

Perhaps that was why he was chosen?

The pious penguin with his worn deacon's vestment came to visit us on our light-flame-yellow street a few times each week. Every time he came by he took time to sit a while on the edge of my or Eric's bed and say a bedtime prayer with us. This started when we were six years old. We lay on our backs with our heads on the pillow and paws on our stomachs and closed our eyes while Father Odenrick spoke with Magnus, the creator of all things, on our behalf.

"Deliver them from evil," the penguin prayed tenderly.

"What is evil?" I asked.

"Things that make you feel bad," said Eric precociously, without being asked.

"So the stone I fell down on yesterday is evil?" I asked, just as impudent and precocious as my twin.

Odenrick wrinkled his gray plastic beak and became absorbed in reflection. He was sitting on the edge of my bed, and in the glow from the lamp on the nightstand I could see how his large eyes became cloudy.

"Things that make you feel bad in your heart, Teddy," he said at last, looking down at me. "The kind of things that cause pain in your heart, inside you, are evil. The one who wants these bad things makes you sad and unhappy, and the sadder you get, the more evil the one who wishes you to feel bad is."

As soon as he finished the sentence Odenrick heard how frightening this must have sounded to a six-year-old's ear, and he tried at once to cheer us up.

"But thank goodness," he said, "there are also those of us who want what is good. The church wants what is good, all believers want what is good, and with good it's exactly the opposite. You know that someone wants what is good for you when you feel satisfied inside. When you feel well."

"But why doesn't everyone want to feel good?" I asked. "Why does anyone want to do something bad?"

"Because otherwise you wouldn't know when someone was good," said my brother Eric slyly, but his voice was trembling.

"There you're wrong," Odenrick smiled tenderly in Eric's direction. "There is evil in the world, cubs. Hopefully you'll never have to encounter it, but you should know about it. For it is going to entice you when you get older, and then you must recognize it and resist it."

Eric had turned toward the wall. Sniffling was heard coming from his bed. Deacon Odenrick sat silently and listened. I was so surprised I didn't know what I should say.

"Eric?" said Odenrick at last. "Is there something you want to tell?"

I felt confused. Up until that evening I'd believed that Eric and I shared everything. Feelings as well as experiences. There and then I was forced to realize that that wasn't the case. This was at the same time a relief and a disappointment.

Penguin Odenrick and I listened together to Eric.

"It's Samuel Pig," Eric sobbed. "He calls me a thief. He says that I'm bad. He's says that I've stolen the Ruby."

"The Ruby?" asked Odenrick.

"That's his red marble," Eric explained, sniffling. "He says that he's going to whip me. With his friends. That they're going to give me such a whipping that I'll never be able to walk again."

All the cubs at preschool played marbles. For most of them it was no game, but rather completely serious. We were cubs, but we were particularly superstitious where it concerned our marbles.

"Samuel Pig?" Odenrick repeated.

Eric nodded and tried to wipe away the tears from his cheeks.

"I know Samuel Pig's parents," said Odenrick. "I'll talk with them."

"No, no!" howled Eric, terrified. "You mustn't say anything."

"But Samuel can't threaten you unpunished," said Odenrick, and his voice was quivering with indignation. "I'll speak with your principal."

"No!" howled Eric again.

"But what—" Odenrick began.

"Nothing," interrupted Eric. "It's just that I'm scared. He's mean, Samuel. He lies. And he fights. Promise not to say anything."

"But I . . ."

"Promise?" nagged Eric.

"I promise," said Odenrick. "We deacons have a duty to remain silent. You can count on me. I'm not going to say anything. But if Samuel so much as . . ."

The penguin didn't finish his sentence. When we saw Odenrick's threadbare appearance on the edge of my bed, we thought it was wise that he didn't express any sort of threat.

He didn't look as though he could live up to it.

The preschool was five blocks north. The pride of the school was the playground behind it. There we spent at least a few hours every day, most often during the Forenoon Weather.

Eric and I went to preschool because Mother wanted us to. We could have been at home, but Mother thought that the most important thing in life was to correctly understand how to manage your social environment. We went to preschool to learn to play with others, not just ourselves.

It happened less than a week after Eric's confession. It was a Thursday. That I know. We sang on Thursday mornings, and I liked to sing. After singing we ate the fruit we'd brought with us from home, and then it was time to go outside. There were thirty of us cubs, and it quickly became chaotic in the hall when everyone was putting on their outdoor clothes at the same time.

Eric vanished out of sight. It was not unusual; we often kept a little distance from each other. Twins have different strategies at various periods of life. At the age of six Eric and I were careful about not choosing similar clothes and keeping ourselves a little apart from each other. I used to go down to the lawn by the great oak tree where there were always a few playing soccer. I was no star. I could just as happily play defense as be goalie. This made me popular. This particular Thursday, however, I was too late. I don't know how it happened, but when I came over to the lawn a match between two teams was already in progress. I watched for a while, but soon lost interest.

That was why I walked over toward the storage sheds.

They were a short distance away. They were simple structures where the preschool stored nets and rackets, balls and bicycles and other things that could be used for outdoor games. I knew that there were cubs who hung around behind the sheds. They could play there without the preschool staff seeing them. There were corners there where you could be in peace. But I didn't know more than that; it was seldom that I had anything to do with cubs who had secrets.

I heard the muffled screams long before I arrived at the sheds, and I heard who was screaming.

Eric.

I started to run. When I rounded the nearest storage

building, I was out of breath. I will never forget the sight that met me.

Eric was standing upright with his back against one of the sheds. In front of Eric stood Samuel Pig, and on either side of Samuel a polar bear and an elephant whose names I didn't know. Samuel pressed Eric against the wall of the shed with a fat fist around my twin's neck.

"And one for Mama!" screamed the elephant who stood alongside, at the same time as he took out a marble, a little glass marble with all the colors of the rainbow, and pressed it against Eric's lips.

Eric already had something in his mouth. When the elephant continued to press the marble against Eric's lips, it finally had the opposite effect. Eric opened his mouth and out sprayed all the marbles the cubs had already forced in.

Samuel Pig let go of Eric so as not to get spit on his hand; Eric fell down on his knees and gasped for air like a fish. The pig showed no mercy. He kicked Eric in the stomach and screamed, "Take out the Ruby!"

Eric whimpered and sniffled. He didn't have the Ruby, he said. This led to more kicks.

The entire course of events took no more than a few seconds. Eric was lying on the ground, crying, when I shouted, "Three against one! That's brave."

The elephant and the polar bear gave a start.

I'd scared them, and they took a step away from my brother. As if to deny that they'd had anything to do with him. The pig gave me a superior look.

"Go away," he said, turning toward Eric again. "You've got nothing to do with this."

"Help," whimpered Eric.

"Two against three is at least a little better," I continued and took a few steps forward.

I was not a champion fighter.

Actually I'd never been in a fight. I would never ever fight again. But my twin was lying on the ground and I couldn't do anything other than try to help him.

"Go to hell," hissed Samuel.

His companions were excited by his courage. They turned toward me with a kind of impatient energy that scared me.

"He's going to give us the Ruby," the polar bear explained.

"Otherwise he's toast," the elephant chimed in.

"But . . . I don't have—" said Eric, and got yet another pig-kick in the stomach.

That was enough for me.

I rushed up toward the three perpetrators with my sights on the pig, and managed to push against him so hard that he stumbled over Eric and fell down to the ground. Eric took the opportunity to pull himself up on his knees at the same time as Samuel got back up on his hooves faster than I'd thought possible. With a howl he threw himself over me.

After that my memory of the fight is more diffuse.

I knew for sure that Eric got away.

I'm unsure whether that happened immediately after the pig tackled me or somewhat later, but I have the feeling that Eric got moving as soon as he had the chance.

The polar bear, the elephant, and the pig belted me green and blue. They didn't stop before we heard the bells ringing us in. I was a threadbare teddy bear who with great effort dragged myself up the slope from the storage sheds back to the school.

As was her habit, Mother came and picked us up right after lunch. She greeted the preschool staff. She asked if we'd been good. She asked if we'd had a good day.

Then we left.

Without looking at us she directed her steps toward the market hall in Amberville. It was a few blocks from the school, and we followed in her wake. The market hall was a magical oasis of scents and colors, a temple of food filled with loud-voiced hawkers and choosy customers. For several hours we wandered around in there, until we had almost forgotten the drama at the schoolyard.

It wasn't until that evening that we had a chance to talk about what had happened. When Father turned off the lamp in our room and we heard him go down the stairs toward the living room, Eric whispered his thanks for the help.

"If Samuel played marbles a little better he wouldn't be so angry all the time," said Eric.

"He was angry," I said in confirmation and felt how my body ached.

"It serves him right," said Eric.

"What?"

Then Eric turned on the lamp above his bed, and in the light he held out the glittering marble: the Ruby.

"I nabbed it from that fat pig a long time ago. It serves him right."

I looked at Eric and saw the expression on his face for a fraction of a second. Then he turned out the light.

It was that evening the abyss between us opened.

That evening defined us as each other's opposite.

The cubs at the school had almost beaten me to death, for good reason. My twin brother was a thief.

My twin was the opposite of a good bear.

CHAPTER 6

They usually met at Zum Franziskaner on North Avenue, a lunch restaurant on the lemon-yellow avenue for those who would rather see than be seen. For many years Rhinoceros Edda had had the goal of seeing Eric at least once a week. They had an uncomplicated relationship, mother and cub, in contrast to Eric's more contentious connection to his father. His mother dismissed his destructive teenage years at Casino Monokowski as a healthy and necessary rebellion; his father had been less understanding. And even if at first Eric loved his mother for her broad-mindedness and despised his father for his narrow-mindedness, over the years he'd acquired a more nuanced picture of the situation.

"You look tired," remarked Edda. "Are you sleeping properly?"

Eric Bear said that he was sleeping properly. In addition he promised that he would stay inside during the Afternoon Rain, and if he did somehow get wet he would change into dry socks. He was forty-eight years old. His wife was living under a death threat. But in his mama's eyes a good night's sleep and clean underwear were the most important things. Perhaps that was the way you should live your life?

Sure, he said, he'd gone to see Teddy since they last met.

There was something liberating in sometimes being treated like a child.

As lunch progressed, Eric asked about the Cub List. He'd heard the story so many times that he practically knew it by heart; it was one of the few truly exciting routines there was to tell about in the otherwise ordinary, bureaucratic ministry. And Mother told it exactly as he remembered.

The Cub List was drawn up based on the applications that were submitted and registered. All incoming letters to the department were entered into a journal, and the order of priority followed the same chronology. A test of the applicants' suitability was always carried out; this was a necessary routine which sometimes meant that the process was delayed. Only in exceptional cases was it necessary to dig deeply into the animals' past. Most of those who applied for cubs had sense enough to see for themselves what the authorities demanded. A final Cub List was drawn up each month, where the names of the fortunate, but not yet notified, future parents were noted.

None of this was particularly startling, but then came the part of the story that, to the young Eric, was exciting.

When the list was ready, it was to be sent to the Deliverymen, the uniformed heroes who drove the green pickups. Now, the physical transport operation was not run from the Environmental Ministry's head office on Avenue Gabriel, either. Therefore it was a question of how the list should be sent to the shipping agent. The list was considered a sensitive document, and there was risk of manipulation. Despite everything, every year the ministry rejected applicants, and it was understandable if this led to frustration. The risk could not be taken that one of those rejected might get hold of the Cub List and write their own name there, and therefore it seemed dangerous to simply put it in the mailbox.

Finally someone came up with the idea of the Order Room. The Cub List left the office on Rue de Cadix with an internal courier, who went through an underground tunnel to the headquarters on Avenue Gabriel. The courier took the elevator up to the ninth floor and left the list in a sealed envelope on the table in a room to which there were only two keys.

The Order Room.

After office hours that same evening—always the sixteenth of the month—the Deliverymen came. They unlocked the door with the other key, picked up the list and thereby all risks had been minimized.

"But are there only two keys?"

"Well," answered his mother, "perhaps there's one more."

And the very young Eric understood that it was his mother who had the third and final key, which of course caused him to look through her key rings and finally find it. He made an impression in modeling clay and, along with Teddy, made a plaster key that they played with for a week or two. A not entirely scrupulous locksmith helped Eric make a real key a few years later—Eric had an idea about how he might use it in order to pay a gambling debt, which thank heavens he never put into effect.

Eric and Teddy had asked thousands of questions about the Cub List and the Order Room when they were smaller, questions which to a large extent had to do with the question all animals asked themselves at some point in their lives. Why was it just me who grew up with my parents? Was it by chance, or was there some intention? And the same questions appeared in the mind of the adult bear while he listened to his mother as she told the story again.

Was it really no more than that? An official who placed a list in a locked room, someone else who picked it up?

When they'd each had a cup of coffee and were getting up to leave, Eric finally asked the question that had been his whole reason for this lunch:

"And a corresponding Death List?" he said. "Does it exist?"

"There has never been a Death List," sighed Edda. "But I understand that animals want to believe in it. That death should only be by chance feels somehow . . . unworthy."

After Eric Bear said goodbye to his mother, he went straight home to Emma. She never stayed in the studio very long on Fridays; she was concerned about making her way home before the lines bottled up the avenues before the weekend. Eric found her in the living room, where she was absorbed in one of the many novels she read, the titles of which he didn't even know.

"I've got to go to Teddy's," he said without sitting down. "I have to stay a few days, perhaps a whole week."

The words just came; the lie wasn't something he'd planned.

"A week?"

He felt false and treacherous, but nonetheless continued without a quiver in his voice. "I don't know if it's some kind of breakthrough or if it's just routine. They phoned this afternoon and said that it was important that I be there."

"Then it must be important," Emma confirmed amiably.

"I'll pack a suitcase with a change of clothes and toiletries. I'll be in touch as soon as I know anything more."

"Are you leaving right now?"

He cast a shy glance toward her and shrugged his shoulders.

"I suppose it can wait until tomorrow," he said.

"No, no. If they've said it's important that you should come, then of course you should take off."

Eric phoned the office before he left the house. It was right after the wind stopped blowing during the Afternoon Weather, but Wolle and Wolle almost never left the office before midnight. Eric told them the same story, that he had to spend the coming week with his twin brother, Teddy, and that therefore he couldn't come in other than for exceptional reasons. There was a meeting on Wednesday afternoon he was thinking of, and one on Thursday morning, but more than that he couldn't promise. Wolle and Wolle promised to cover for him. And thus Eric had freed himself from his marital as well as his professional duties. He departed toward Yok and Yiala's Arch; it was time to find the Death List, even if it didn't exist.

CHAPTER 7

Snake Marek knocked on the door to Sam's apartment at grass-green Yiala's Arch just as the breeze started blowing and the Evening Weather began. The friends didn't make an event of the fact that he came. Tom-Tom Crow was standing in the kitchen, shaking an enormous cocktail shaker; Sam and Eric were out on the balcony, talking. The crow let the snake in, and after a guarded nod, Snake wriggled out through the balcony door. He made his way up onto a rusty table that had presumably been on the balcony when Sam moved in and wheedled his way into the conversation. When Tom-Tom joined the friends after a little while, Sam cleared his throat solemnly.

"It's time to make a toast," he said as the crow poured cocktails, "to a reunion. And to success, of course. And to time, which hasn't made us uglier or older, simply wiser and"—Sam winked at Snake—"more cunning."

And with his tinkling-bell giggle Sam raised his glass. The others did the same, and the cool alcohol warmed their frozen souls. As always, the evening was lovelier than it was warm.

"I'm extremely grateful," said Eric, "that you're willing to help. And I was thinking that we might devote the evening to trying to figure out how we should go about our task. You know what it's about. The dove believes he's on the Death List, and he wants us to remove his name. An impossible task, it might seem. But we've done the impossible before. So just let it flow. No suggestion is wrong, no associations too far-fetched . . ."

Sam giggled again.

". . . except the indecent," added Eric.

Everyone laughed, Snake with a contemptuous sneer.

"But, what the hell," said Tom-Tom, stealing a glance at Sam as the laughter subsided, "is there really a Death List?"

"Darling, you're so clever," said Sam shrewdly. "Or what, Marek? The crow is sharp!"

Snake's head swayed back and forth, indicating his ambivalence. He was much too gloomy to let himself be provoked. He had been forced to leave the ministry, but no one could force him to be happy about being at Yiala's Arch.

But before anyone had time to comment on the Death List's existence or lack thereof, the sound of a broken bottle was heard in the Dumpster down in the courtyard. Up on the balcony all four of them felt ashamed. Here they stood like rank amateurs, discussing secrets so that everyone could hear. Quietly they finished their glasses, went inside, and sat down around the deplorably moldy kitchen table.

"What do you say?" said Eric to Snake as Tom-Tom set vodka, juice, and ice out on the table. "Is there a Death List?"

"Rumors about the Death List have always flourished," replied Snake. "You can find references to a Death List in poetic refrains written hundreds of years ago. It has been maintained that the list is depicted on each of the three frescoes of the Preachers on the ceiling of Sagrada Bastante, but in actual size so that it is impossible to see it from the floor. It is said that the Twenty-Years War was really about control of the list. It is maintained that during the entire Prohibition period at the beginning of the century not a single animal was picked up. And it is maintained that during the sixties, the lists were made in the form of concealed messages on vinyl records by well-known artists. If you played the records backwards, the names on the current list were heard."

"But how the hell can that be true?" said Tom-Tom.

"That doesn't matter," Snake hissed with irritation. "The essential point is, it's not by chance. A myth can only survive for so long for two reasons. Either because those who are in control for some reason want the myth to survive. Or because . . ."

"Why, why?" repeated Sam with ominous exaggeration.

"Because it's true," said Eric.

"Yes, damn it. I've always thought it existed," said Tom-Tom, looking defiantly at Sam, who shrugged his shoulders and turned his attention toward the bottle of vodka. "There's nothing strange about a Death List, is there? Would the Chauffeurs drive around at night and pick us up at random? But of course it's not random. You can almost always tell who's on their way. It's not the case that the Chauffeurs pick up some wretch who's young or healthy or . . . you know . . . someone who's good . . ."

"That's happened, too," Sam interjected.

"You know what I mean," said Tom-Tom. "It's less damn strange that the Chauffeurs have a list to go by than that they should drive around at random."

"And who do you think makes that list, my friend?" asked Sam amiably. "The creator of all things, Magnus?"

"No, I don't think so. I don't believe in Magnus. Do you think I'm completely frigging stupid, or what?"

Wise animals had done Sam more ill than stupid ones. He felt at ease with Tom-Tom Crow.

"It is sometimes said," said Sam. He looked at Snake Marek. "What do you say, old animal, that because the Cub List is drawn up by the Environmental Ministry, it's not impossible that there is some shady section of the Environmental Ministry that makes the Death List, too?"

"Ask Eric," hissed Marek. "Perhaps it's his mother who personally draws up the Death List. At least she's dictatorial enough. The Environmental Ministry deals with so many strange things that I can't even count them all. No one can. But one thing I can say, and that is that we at Culture would never use government appropriations to purchase artworks for our conference rooms in the way that—"

"No Death List is made at the Environmental Ministry, that I can guarantee," interrupted Eric.

He'd forgotten how much Snake talked, and how hard it was to get him to stop.

"I know you're thinking that the Environmental Ministry takes care of transports, and thereby has ultimate responsibility for the Chauffeurs," he continued. "But that takes place through a type of contract. Certain logistical matters are controlled from the ministry, but beyond that . . . nothing."

Conversation ceased and a few fresh bottles of vodka were taken out while everyone thought about the Chauffeurs. It was almost impossible to mention these messengers of death without darkening everyone's mood. No animals were so feared as the Chauffeurs. Even if few had seen them, all were aware that they drove the red pickup through the town at night, in pursuit of their victims. They did what they had to do, and picked up those animals whose lives were over. But where were the animals taken, and what happened to them? Was there a heaven, a life after this one? Every time you saw a red pickup or thought about the Chauffeurs, your faith was tested. Was it strong enough to chase away your fears?

The stuffed animals sipped the vodka in silence. The alcohol had its effect, and the conversation became less structured. For another half hour or so they succeeded in keeping on the subject. Snake talked, the others listened. He attacked the problem from a series of different points of view and after considerable anguish came to the conclusion that it was more probable that the Death List existed, in some form, than that it did not.

The weather was approaching midnight. Sam left his guests in the kitchen and went into the bathroom where, in one of the hollow feet of the bathtub, he stored the green tablets he usually took along with alcohol, and which provided a dreamless sleep. When he returned, Eric and Tom-Tom were no longer responsible for what they were saying.

"Death takes us all," exclaimed Eric gloomily.

"Lanceheim LOSERS," Tom-Tom cried out. "They ought to be called Lanceheim LOSERS and not Lasers."

He was talking about the district cricket team. No one paid him any attention.

"You were always a sports nut, sweetheart," said Sam sentimentally. "You always liked sports. I remember one time . . . one time . . . no . . . no . . . I don't remember."

Tom-Tom broke out in violent laughter.

"There's no way out," Eric continued on his introverted track. "Sooner or later it ends. That's all we know."

"And can you turn sooner into later, that is the question," Snake interjected.

"A question many of my customers would gladly have an answer to," Sam smiled hazily.

"You fucking creep," snapped Snake.

"Listen up now," said Tom-Tom threateningly. "You can be damn creepy yourself."

Sam looked gratefully at the crow.

"Death," said Eric, "is perhaps the start of the next life?"

"There's a story," said Snake, "of how a name was once removed from the Death List. That must be the one Dove's heard."

"I don't know what story you're thinking of," said the bear, who if he'd been more sober would have noticed that Snake Marek—in contrast to the others—didn't seem especially drunk.

"The one about Prodeacon ... what was his name ... Prodeacon Poodle?"

"I seem to think that I've heard it," said Sam.

"I've never heard it," said Eric firmly.

"If it's something frigging dirty, I don't want to hear it," said Tom-Tom, who feared it was time to tell dirty stories. The crow had always felt uncomfortable where dirty stories were concerned.

"Prodeacon Trew Poodle lived just under one hundred years ago—he was prodeacon down here in Yok, and the story is about his goodness," said Snake. "The three prodeacons in Amberville, Tourquai, and Lanceheim saw Trew as their spiritual leader, despite the fact that he was considerably younger and not at all as experienced as they. One night Trew called the other prodeacons to him and told them the unbelievable: all four of them were on the Death List. In just a week they would be picked up by the red wagons that were used at that time."

"I've heard this story," mumbled Sam.

"Prodeacon Trew could not let this happen," Snake continued relentlessly.

This was Snake's best routine, a long, morally instructive story; he'd used the story about Prodeacon Trew Poodle as a starting point in several novels over the years; it could symbolize just about anything.

"With a frenzy that astonished his three colleagues," said Snake, "the prodeacon fell on his knees before the altar and started to pray. He prayed for their lives, he prayed to

Magnus to spare them, he implored Him to remove them from the list."

"Now I know," said Sam. "Now I remember this."

"Well, I'll be damned," said Tom-Tom hesitantly. "So it's Magnus who writes the list?"

"Prodeacon Poodle prays and prays," Snake continued without letting himself be distracted, "while the prodeacons from Tourquai, Lanceheim, and Amberville hurry back to their respective parishes and devote themselves to more practical details. Who should succeed them, who should inherit their possessions, who should write their obituaries."

"Vanity," interjected Eric, and added, mostly to himself: "Not the least bit important."

"However that might be," snorted Snake, "Prodeacon Poodle prays for a week at a time while the others are busy with worldly things, and the following Sunday they meet again in Sagrada Bastante. And while they are standing there, discussing practicalities, the doors of the church open and in come the Coachmen."

"The Coachmen?" wondered Tom-Tom.

"The Chauffeurs of that time, sweetheart," explained Sam.

"The Coachmen pick up the prodeacon from Amberville, the prodeacon from Lanceheim and the prodeacon from Tourquai," continued Snake.

"And the point of the story is that Magnus doesn't hear prayers?" said Eric with surprise.

"Prodeacon Trew Poodle was also on the list," said Snake. "That was why he was praying for the others' lives, so that all the city's four prodeacons wouldn't disappear at the same time. But thanks to his unselfish prayer, he was the one whose name was removed."

"What the hell, couldn't he save the others?" asked Tom-Tom.

"It is told," said Snake, "that at that time only one animal could be removed from the list every fifth year."

"At that time?"

Snake Marek would have shrugged his shoulders if he'd had any.

"It's a morally instructive story, not historical truth."

Snake fell silent and sipped his vodka without drinking it.

"Let's hope that this is the fifth year, darling," whispered Sam to Eric.

Sam finally went and lay down. Tom-Tom moved over to the couch, taking with him a giant bag of cheese doodles.

Eric remained at the kitchen table, gloomily collapsed with a mug of vodka in his paws and with his thoughts far back in time. The memory of the years at Casino Monokowski were usually pleasant, but now the usual feeling refused to make an appearance. Instead of being happy at seeing his old companions again, he felt downhearted.

"I think the crow is right," hissed Snake in his ear.

Eric winced. Snake was standing on the kitchen counter, right behind him.

"The Chauffeurs don't drive around at random," Snake continued. "It's completely obvious, of course, but it takes a stupid crow to put it into words. Our best possibility to get on the trail of the list is through the Chauffeurs."

Eric got up from the kitchen table, realized that he could hardly stand straight, and infinitely slowly and carefully he went over to the balcony door. Cold air, he thought, was what he needed in order to think clearly. Snake followed behind. Out on the balcony Eric noted that the breeze had not yet died down. He had thought that dawn was quite near. The chill worked its way into his fur and there was a faint odor of bacon in the air.

"There's something to that," said Eric after taking a few deep breaths. "We have to find the Chauffeurs. If there's a list, someone must deliver it to them."

"That's exactly what I was thinking," said Snake.

"That's why I asked you to come along," said Eric. "To think. How do we go about this?"

"There are not an infinite number of ways to go about this."

"I have a tougher nut to crack," Eric added. "A problem worthy of you, I believe."

They stood a while in the moonlight, looking into the lighted but deplorable apartments on the opposite side of the courtyard. Neither of them had mentioned a word about the letter Eric had written in his mother's name and which had forced Snake to Yiala's Arch.

"Let's hear it," said Snake without enthusiasm.

"Let us say," said Eric, "that there was not only a reward offered if we succeed. Let us say that there is a punishment as well if we don't succeed."

Eric fell silent. Snake said nothing; the hypothesis spoke for itself.

"Let us say," continued Eric along this rhetorical path, "that the threat looks like this: if Dove is carried off by the Chauffeurs, an animal close to me is going to be carried off in a comparable way by the dove's gorillas."

"I understand," said Snake.

"Just as important," said Eric, speaking more slowly than he had during the evening up till now, "as you helping us find the Death List, is that you give me an answer to the question of how I'm going to be able to save that animal close to me if we don't succeed. And, Snake, I believe we don't have very much time."

TWILIGHT, 2

He turned slowly toward the skyline of Tourquai, a pin-cushion of the vanity and ambition of the builders. It was not by building monuments to himself that his greatness was manifested; that was not his way of defining power.

He himself was not interested in material things. He pretended to be materialistic because that gave him a kind of alibi; he owned a car he never drove and a house he seldom visited. His eyeglass frames were of the latest model, he wrote with an expensive pen and his shoes were purchased five floors up at Grand Divino. But these were disguises.

Power was not in owning, power was in directing.

He had the necessary means at his disposal, and he made use of them. He was a master of manipulation; with his words he could entice and seduce, poison and crush. It was a matter of logic. To have the ability to conceal it and then let it appear again in a manner which suited the overarching context. Nothing gave him the same satisfaction as when he succeeded in converting a resistant stuffed animal for his own purposes. Then he experienced moments of the dizzying intoxication of power, more powerful than anything else. Then life was a matter of pursuing this intoxication over and over again.

The secret of the Chauffeurs was well hidden.

Eric Bear perhaps realizes that that is where he should begin, he thought, but it's not going to come to anything. The Chauffeurs aren't communicative, they're completely inaccessible; it was for their lack of animal qualities that they were chosen for their filthy occupation once upon a time.

He laughed drily at the thought. A hollow laugh, which hurt at the top of his throat. He had never been good at laughing.

If for some reason the bear should get on the trail of something—he reminded himself that humility is a virtue—if the bear were to get on his trail, well, there were occasions when the patience-testing methods of manipulation didn't suffice. There were animals who lacked sufficient comprehension to allow themselves to be guided by razor-sharp logic. There was a quicker, more direct language of power at hand when such was required. Physical violence didn't fascinate him in the same way as lies and treachery did, but the effects of violence produced the same results. This applied to threats, bribery, and empty promises as well. The palette of techniques he used varied in beauty, but the end was, despite everything, more important than the means.

The bear could be stopped the moment he understood anything about the secret of the Chauffeurs. The next step, the step over that boundary, the bear would never have the opportunity to take. There were animals who could easily detach a head from its body and bury the two parts in the forests on either side of the city.

He tried to laugh again.

It didn't go any better this time.

CHAPTER 8

Sam Gazelle hated being alone.

Nonetheless he was sitting by himself in an old Volga Combi, staring out toward the night that had just settled over East Avenue. In the glow from the streetlights the broad street's mint-green pavement was no more than a variation of black. A sparkling cross was hanging from the rearview mirror and there was a faint odor of damp fur from the car's backseat. The avenue was empty. Cars were parked densely along the sidewalks on both sides. Sam could make out the Star in the rearview mirror. He was parked a few hundred meters onto East Avenue, five or six cross-streets from the roundabout, but he hardly knew how he'd managed to get himself there. He despised cars. There was hardly room in the compartment for his left horn. He had a crack in his right hoof that risked being caught in the gas pedal. The reason that he hadn't refused was spelled l-o-v-e.

He couldn't help it. Despite all the years that had passed. There was something quite special about Eric Bear.

Sam sighed heavily.

In honor of the evening, he had put on his light-blue velvet jacket, and from the inside pocket he pulled out a small plastic container. Originally filled with throat lozenges, the container had been Sam's mobile lifesaver for a long time; whenever he left home, he brought enough pills to gobble them all day. Now, as he was shaking out a portion of the contents of the container onto the passenger seat, it meant nothing to him. Two capsules and the rest compact, little round tablets. White, red, green, and one blue. He didn't know what the pills were called, he hardly knew what they cost, and had no idea what effect they had in combination with each other.

He picked up a couple of them, assured himself that he'd gotten one of the blue ones, and collected saliva in order to swallow them all down in one gulp. The remainder could go back in the container. Hopefully he would feel less lonesome in a little while. Otherwise he would have to take a few more, perhaps more of the red ones?

On the street outside nothing was going on. You might think there ought to be more life and movement; the evening was young, and a few kilometers farther east on the avenue the first night animals were venturing out onto the sidewalks. Sam had forgotten the years when he'd been forced to search for company on the street, despite the fact that they weren't so long ago. But sometimes the pain from a certain moment in the past might come racing through the years and torment him in the exact same way now as it did then. Therefore it was better to concentrate on what was going on around him.

But no red pickup drove past.

Snake Marek sat tensely coiled around the steering wheel of a Volga Sport GTI, wondering how he would even be able to drive the car. He'd gotten a vehicle with reptile-adapted instrumentation, with automatic transmission, and with the gas and brake pedals within a tail's-length distance, but he hated twisting around the steering wheel and crawling back and forth in order to turn. He'd always thought that snakes that drove cars made themselves ridiculous. And in addition, he was still bitter about finding himself in this situation, together with his companions from before, and commanded by Eric Bear. His life was so lamentably unstable, he thought, and so impossible to calculate, since chance could never be determined, anyway.

The fortress he had constructed for himself at the Office of Grants had been demolished in a mere moment by a letter from a stupid rhinoceros. And Snake was not even sure Rhinoceros Edda had written the letter; it might just as well have been Eric Bear. This was a lesson, Snake thought with suppressed fury. When this little excursion was over and he returned to the ministry, he must take a look at his situation. He'd gotten too comfortable, he'd forgotten the rules of the game. In order to sit securely as boss, you had to conquer the next position in the hierarchy as well. And the next, and then the next.

Snake had gotten the bear to set out one car and one driver per avenue, and even if they didn't get a bite this evening, there would be a bite during one of the coming nights. The city's four great thoroughfares were used by everyone sooner or later, because these were quite simply the fastest alternatives. Mollisan Town was a massive city, and professional drivers soon tired of all the traffic lights and one-way streets, roadwork, and unreliable nighttime wanderers on the smaller streets. The Chauffeurs used the avenues; anything else was unthinkable.

North Avenue divided Tourquai to the west from Lanceheim to the east. In the middle of the lemon-yellow street a magnificent lane of willow trees had been laid out. It ran the entire way from the Star out to the end of the developed part of the city, after which the lane was absorbed into the surrounding forest. Seen from the other direction, it was as though the forest had sent a scout right into the heart of the city via North Avenue.

Snake's car was parked facing south, in toward the city. Due to the dense foliage of the willow trees, he had a hard time seeing very far, but nonetheless he'd managed to get a parking space which made it possible for him to discern a red pickup on its way north at a reasonably long distance. On the other hand, having time to turn around and follow after didn't feel equally obvious. A U-turn of that type demanded that he writhe all the way from the right side of the steering wheel to its left, hop down onto the seat, and make the maneuver again. That took time.

He swore to himself, shaking his head.

In addition, it irked Snake Marek's vanity that the assignment itself wasn't more complicated. That self-righteous bear hadn't needed to sabotage his life for this. Any fool whatsoever would have been able to figure out you have to find the Chauffeurs.

"Thus," Snake Marek had said to his suddenly very anxious companions, "we follow a red pickup until dawn. The Chauffeurs are where the pickup is parked. And where the Chauffeurs are, we're going to find the list."

Snake's need of sleep was minimal, and he had no problem keeping himself alert. A car or two drove past, mostly taxis, the typical, black cabs. He rolled down the window a few centimeters and listened to the restful, verging-on-poetic sound of the willow trees' hiss as the night breeze passed through their foliage. There was a rhythm in the movement that inspired Marek. Perhaps the night would not yet be wasted?

Snake jumped down from the steering wheel. From the glove compartment he took out a pale-yellow notebook; he'd bought the surplus stock down at the stationery store.

The cover was tattered and worn, but there was nothing wrong with the paper inside. He grasped the pencil with his tail and quickly wrote:

a horseshoe, a sickle
a metaphoric tickle
the clever, the obtuse
continue to seduce

He lifted the point from the page and looked down at what he'd written. As usual he was seized by a kind of dizziness. It was so ingenious, so amazingly beautiful, that he scarcely dared believe that he himself had thought of it.

Perhaps he hadn't?

And deep inside in his cold-blooded heart a faint hope was awakened to life. It was a feeling he hadn't felt in almost twenty years. He knew that the surrounding world was still not ready for Snake Marek's life's work. That they wouldn't understand, that no one could grasp it. No one.

Except possibly Eric Bear.

If each and every one of the buildings which lined blood-red Western Avenue between Tourquai and Amberville had been a block in a box of toys, Eric Bear would probably have been able to take them out one by one and place them in the right order all the way from the Star out to the city limits. This was his childhood neighborhood; on the gravel path that ran parallel to Western Avenue on the Amberville side he had jogged every morning during all of secondary school. Unfortunately the familiar environment lulled him into a secure feeling of well-being that made it more and more difficult for him to keep his eyes open when the weather passed midnight. Ever since Nicholas Dove's gorillas had broken down the door at Uxbridge Street, the adrenaline had been supplied to the bear's system in the same way as the injection engine on a Volga GTI. Now the direct infusion was cut off and Eric felt how exhausted he was. At this pause in the flood of events and demands, his eyes shut and he felt how his head began to whirl with fatigue. There was a faint aroma of vanilla in the car, and he wondered how that had happened.

He'd borrowed the cars at work. From his employees. For his own use he had humbly chosen a gray Volga Combi. It was owned by a mouse in the accounting department whose name he still didn't know, despite the fact that she'd worked at Wolle & Wolle at least as long as he had.

He leaned his head against the neck rest and at the same time fingered the walkie-talkie lying on the seat beside him. In the shop he had been assured that the frequency which had been installed was unique. There were few walkie-talkies on the market with a comparable range, and thereby you avoided worrying about eavesdropping and interference. It could of course have been sales talk, if it hadn't been for the price. Eric paid with a strained smile, and realized that there were few—if there was anyone—prepared to lay out a small fortune for a couple of phones.

He lifted the walkie-talkie, pressed the button on the side, and called the others. "Bear here. Everyone awake? Over."

"Snake. Over," said Snake.

"Gazelle. Over," said Gazelle.

Then it was silent.

"Crow?" asked Eric at last, but he received no answer. "Crow, press the black button on the side. Over."

There was a crackling sound. "Sure thing—damn—Crow here. Over."

"We'll check in again in an hour. Over and out."

Eric put down the walkie-talkie on the seat, felt a violent

dizziness, a feeling like sitting in the first car on a roller coaster on its way down the first slope, and before he'd reached the bottom he was sleeping soundly.

Tom-Tom Crow had brought four bags of peanuts and some knitting with him in the car. It was not a coincidence that they'd let him have the only Volga Mini that Eric had borrowed; it was so enjoyable watching the massive crow fold himself into the little car. But there was nothing wrong with the size of the interior, and Tom-Tom was sitting in the front seat, deeply absorbed in his knitting, when the red pickup came driving along South Avenue.

Tom-Tom saw it from the corner of his eye, but didn't make note of it. He had just reparked the car to be able to keep better track of the stitches with the help of the streetlights. The knitting project Tom-Tom had embarked on was going to be a navy-blue sweater with a skull pattern in white on the back. The pattern demanded that he concentrate on the purls, and the red pickup drove past just as he was brooding over whether he'd made thirty-two or thirty-three stitches with the white yarn. On the thirty-fifth stitch he would change color.

There was a delay of a few seconds before the information which nevertheless had passed through his eye and moved on farther into the mysterious windings of the brain registered in his awareness.

He looked up.

"But . . . what the hell . . ." muttered the crow in surprise.

CHAPTER 9

Tom-Tom Crow threw down the knitting on the passenger seat and turned the key in the ignition. The little car coughed and the motor came to life with a kind of low buzzing. Without a glance over his shoulders or any warning signals, Tom-Tom swung out from the parking place, took a proper grip on the gas pedal with the claws of his feet, and pressed it to the floor. The various Volga models all went roughly the same speed—even if the GTI reached its top velocity more quickly than the others—and soon the crow had the situation under control. In contrast to most of the others, the red pickup kept to the speed limit on South Avenue.

Tom-Tom was a good driver. For several years, before he started working in the sewing notions department at Grand Divino, he had driven one of the city's massive buses, route 3 from Rosdahl in Lanceheim to Parc Clemeaux in Tourquai. He was used to city traffic, comfortable behind the wheel.

Without letting the red pickup out of his sight, he found the walkie-talkie under the knitting on the passenger seat.

He picked up the apparatus, conveyed it to his beak, and pressed the black button.

"Contact," he said, as they'd agreed upon.

He released the button and waited for a reply, but nothing was heard. Then he pressed the button again.

"Driving southward," he said.

This time when he let go of the black button, there was a tremendous commotion in the walkie-talkie's speaker. Three animals who were screaming, each one in his own way, congratulations and admonitions, advice and warnings.

The red pickup turned off the main highway and drove into Amberville. Tom-Tom turned off the walkie-talkie, set it on the seat next to him and devoted all his concentration to driving. On the side streets it would not be as easy to follow without being noticed.

Amberville was not a part of the city that Tom-Tom Crow knew especially well. Raised in Lanceheim, it was true he had worked at Casino Monokowski for many years, but during that time he had hardly left the casino. On the few occasions when the personnel had gone out and partied, they had chosen clubs up in Tourquai, where there wasn't the risk of running into their own guests.

Immediately after the exit from South Avenue, the pickup turned left, onto a street whose creamy-white luster even the night couldn't conceal. Uncertain as to exactly where he was, Tom-Tom didn't intend to take a chance. At the risk of being discovered, he followed, as fast as he could, only to find an empty, sleepy cross-street with apartment houses lying desolately before him.

The red pickup was gone.

Eric drove as fast as he could.

"Tom-Tom," he called. "Position?"

The walkie-talkie was mute. Eric reduced his speed

somewhat. He was on his way down toward the golden Star, the roundabout where the four avenues ran together.

"You have to help out," he asked the snake and the gazelle in the walkie-talkie. "We'll meet in ten minutes at the starting point. Come."

The "starting point" was the massive stairway up to Sagrada Bastante at the east corner of the Star, and exactly ten minutes later Sam and Snake came walking and winding, respectively, to meet Eric. The Star was illuminated at night; the golden roundabout and the small park in the middle glistened and glowed even stronger than during the day.

"There's only one button to push in," hissed Snake, creeping a few steps up in order to be at the same level as the others, "and that stupid crow doesn't even get that."

"Old man, perhaps it's not a good idea to get surly and pout just now," said the gazelle, immediately coming to Tom-Tom's defense.

Eric brushed aside their squabbling.

"We have to do this more methodically," he said. "I can't manage this by myself. If I drive east to west, and you north to south along different streets, we ought to be able to catch sight of him at last."

"Darling, there's nothing that says he's still in Amberville," Sam said.

"There's nothing that says he's driven away from there," said Eric.

"That's the problem with fools," hissed Snake. "They're hard to understand."

"The crow saw the pickup," reminded the bear. "We have to try to find him. What's the alternative? Stand here and chat?"

It was three skeptical companions who departed from the Star in their respective Volgas to try to crisscross Amberville like moles in pursuit of the red pickup.

. . . .

Tom-Tom Crow was certain that the Chauffeurs must have noticed him by this time.

For every kilometer he continued, he marveled at the fact that they didn't stop and wave him over to the side. He could not recall if he had ever been so afraid.

If the Chauffeurs waved you to the side, then your life was over.

After having lost the pickup down in Amberville, he'd driven around the nearby neighborhoods without a plan. All the buildings looked alike, with their black tile roofs and small stairways up to the outside doors. He turned left and right and left again; in the darkness, all the subtleties of blue and green looked alike.

And then, suddenly, after yet another right turn, there it stood: the red pickup. And for the first time Tom-Tom saw a living Chauffeur. The Chauffeur was wearing a gray mantle which completely covered his body. His face was concealed by a large hood. He was carefully leading an older parrot out of one of the buildings. As they came down the steps, the glow of the streetlight fell such that Tom-Tom was able to see that the Chauffeur was nonetheless a stuffed animal.

It was a wolf.

Perhaps the wolf didn't appear particularly fear-inducing, but the circumstances caused a cold shiver of terror to pass down the crow's back. The Chauffeur and the old parrot got into the pickup, which immediately drove away, and Tom-Tom—who had still not put the brakes on during these ominous seconds—continued straight ahead, after them.

As though in a trance, the crow followed the red pickup onto South Avenue and farther out of the city. Tom-Tom had never been outside the city limits. He turned off the headlights and continued in the darkness. The red rear lights on the pickup in front of him were soon the only thing he saw.

They drove deeper and deeper into the dense forest. Hundreds, perhaps thousands of trees were dimly seen in the darkness to the sides of the narrow road. After half an hour they arrived at an enormous, hangar-like structure standing dark and deserted in the middle of nowhere. The red pickup stopped there.

Tom-Tom pressed the brake pedal to the floor, and without turning off the engine saw the door on the passenger side of the pickup open and the old parrot got out.

Quickly and simply the Chauffeurs then turned around in order to drive back.

The road was so narrow there was scarcely room for two cars to meet, and the crow didn't know what he should do. He couldn't reveal himself. In pure panic he threw the car into reverse. He stepped on the gas and turned right into the forest. That the little car inserted itself between two tree trunks instead of crashing against them was pure chance. Only ten seconds later the red pickup passed, and Tom-Tom waited half a minute before he returned up onto the road and followed the distant rear lights back toward the city.

He was not interested in what the Chauffeurs did with worn-out animals like the old parrot. Tom-Tom's mission was to find out where the Chauffeurs themselves hung out. And it was obviously not in the forest.

Sam and Snake drove around Amberville for almost an hour before they gave up.

"The crow went the wrong way, and he's struggling to find his way back," said Snake into the walkie-talkie. "Or else he's still wondering how the walkie-talkie works."

"Whatever," replied Sam. "I'm going home and sleep now, old man."

Snake kept him company, and they turned both of their cars and drove back toward Yok. But Eric could not give up.

The bear continued untiringly, driving from east to west and from west to east through the dark streets. However deeply this part of the city was sleeping, it was pure chance that no one called the police; seeing the same car drive back and forth during the darkest hours of the night ought to have aroused suspicion.

Finally the walkie-talkie crackled to life.

Eric slammed on the brakes in pure terror.

"Hello? Come."

"It's me," Tom-Tom's voice was heard. "I have contact. Come."

Holy Magnus, thought Eric to himself. It had been more than two hours since the crow had been in touch. "Where? Come."

"In Yok. Come."

"I'm on my way."

Eric turned east at the next intersection and drove quickly through the empty streets. Driving was something he'd devoted all too little time to in his life. He was an unaccustomed driver, but each time he sat behind the wheel he was filled with a kind of childish joy. The adrenaline again streamed out into his body and there was no trace of the tired resignation he'd felt previously.

"Passing South Avenue. Come," he let Tom-Tom know.

Only a few blocks into south Yok, however, Eric's frustration increased anew. The rectilinear streets in Amberville, where the cars stood neatly parked along the sidewalks and made the streets easily navigable, were replaced by a labyrinthine muddle where a steady stream of obstacles forced him to take detours. The walkie-talkie lay silent on the seat beside him; he didn't want to use it unnecessarily and was quite certain besides that the crow would not be able to help. Tom-Tom didn't know these neighborhoods either.

Eric swore and sweated. He backed up and turned. Accelerated and jammed on the brakes. And after ten minutes he no longer had any idea where he was.

. . . .

The Chauffeurs were about to fool Tom-Tom in the end.

After a great deal of back-and-forth on their way through Yok, the crow lost sight of them now and then in his fear of coming too close. He hesitated before he turned around the street corners, and at the last corner he hesitated longer than usual. Then he screwed up his courage, put the car in first and arrived just in time to see the pickup driving toward a building with a speckled-gray brick wall.

But the pickup didn't slow down. Instead the wall opened, closing itself around the pickup again so quickly that Tom-Tom felt uncertain for a moment about what he'd actually seen.

He slammed on the brakes.

The building whose wall was a disguised garage door was not particularly large: three stories high, ten meters across, with no windows on the ground floor. Which, on the other hand, was not unusual in Yok. There was no door, either, but Tom-Tom suspected that there was one on the other side. On the façade was an unlit neon sign: "Hotel Esplanade."

"They've driven down into some infernal garage," Tom-Tom reported on the walkie-talkie. "I believe we're here."

"Where? Come," asked Eric.

"Don't really know," said Tom-Tom, "but I'm checking."

Eric turned onto the sidewalk and waited impatiently while the walkie-talkie crackled. Then the crow was heard again: "I'll be damned," said Tom-Tom. He sounded surprised. "They're hanging out a few blocks from where we're staying."

"Where we're staying? Come," Eric repeated stupidly.

"I flipping believe you can see the Chauffeurs from Sam's apartment," said the crow.

TEDDY BEAR, 2

One evening I awakened with a jolt.

I was in the eighth grade and stood with one paw in childhood and the other in early maturity. I slept soundly at night and had good reason to do so.

My heart was pure.

Eric and I were still living in our boys' room highest up in the house on flame-yellow Hillville Road. The staircase leading down to the hall passed by Mother and Father's bedroom. It was old, creaking and squeaking when you walked on the steps. I thought it was the sound of footsteps on the staircase that caused me to awaken. In a fog I got up on my elbows. Then I saw.

Someone was on his way out through the window.

A figure crawling out of the room was outlined against the dark night sky outside, palely illuminated by the stars. I let out a sigh of despair. It was so loud that the figure in the window opening stopped dead in his tracks.

"It's only me," hissed Eric.

A few seconds passed before I realized that it was my twin brother who was in the window, and not in his bed.

"Go back to sleep," he hissed.

He's running away, I recall thinking.

The phrase "running away" came to me so immediately that I didn't even make note of it. Eric and I had reached puberty's subversive jumble of emotions. We were living in the midst of our childhood, among well-worn children's books, model airplanes, and soccer balls. Opening the window and fleeing seemed equally cowardly and enticing to me.

The evening breeze caressed my brow, our thin curtain danced before the open window and from somewhere outside a faint aroma of grilled meat reached me.

This abyss that had opened between me and my twin brother.

I carried the heavy knowledge with me constantly that Eric was in some kind of trouble. I had even spoken with Archdeacon Odenrick, in a roundabout way, about lost souls. We had spoken about lost animals. Odenrick was a penguin of the church and refused to give up hope on anyone.

There is always salvation, said Odenrick. For one who feels remorse, there is always forgiveness.

I myself had nothing to regret, and my twin brother never asked for forgiveness.

What kept me awake at night was not so much the question of where Eric had gone as the fact that something—presumably a great many things—had been going on prior to this night. Without my having a clue about it. How many encounters and conversations had he withheld from me? Had it been difficult or easy, and was his other life—as I was already referring to it—present in some form, even when we did things together?

The feeling of being easily fooled and the shame at having been so stupid burned behind my eyelids. The sheets became damp with sweat. I fantasized about how Eric pushed aside the great stage set that was our mutual childhood in order to demonstrate that behind it there had always been an abyss of solitude.

Those are big words. Big feelings. But they aren't enough to describe what I was feeling.

He came back at dawn.

I must have nodded off, for I was awakened by quick steps against the tiles on the roof. At the next moment Eric stuck his paw in through the still half-open window, heaving himself up over the edge and into the room. It was fascinating to notice how soundlessly he did it. How routinely he did it. It was, as I already suspected, not the first time.

I showered him with indignation. I attacked him with such a cascade of questions that he wouldn't have had time to reply to them, even if he'd wanted to. I wept. I shook him in anger and hugged him with love. After a while I calmed down sufficiently to call him to account in a more lucid manner. Where had he been?

He refused to tell.

Finally he said, "Teddy, it's best for both of us if you don't know."

He said that with tenderness in his voice.

I fell silent. I stared at him. He thought he knew what was best for me.

It was not even insulting.

It was stupid.

I said nothing more, but decided to find out as soon as possible what he was up to. Therefore on the nights that followed I lay awake, waiting for him to climb out of bed, put on his clothes, and climb out through the window. But that didn't happen. It was a refined torture. Knowing that something was going on behind my back, but not knowing what it was. I was worried about him.

I wasn't the only one.

Archdeacon Odenrick was worried, too. Even if he didn't say anything to me. Or to anyone else.

We'd begun our confirmation classes that fall. On Tuesdays we went down to the parish building on Chapel Street after school and learned about Magnus, Magnus's angels, and Magnus's works from one of the deacons in Amberville. On Thursdays we went to Sagrada Bastante, where Archdeacon Odenrick himself waited to instruct us. Exactly what his title was at this time I don't know; he became archdeacon a few years later. He was an excellent confirmation deacon. He dramatized religion so that all of us were drawn into the stories. At the same time he was careful. There was always room for doubt and uncertainty.

I doubted.

And I was uncertain.

I could accept that there was an all-powerful Magnus. Mollisan Town had not arisen out of an empty vacuum. The Deliverymen who transported the newly produced stuffed animals and the Chauffeurs who took care of those who were worn out were not the henchmen of chance. But in the end it wasn't a matter of believing. It was a matter of wanting to believe. That Magnus forgave the penitent and let them into paradise was not something Odenrick tried to prove. Religion was logical in relationship to its own theses.

Except when it was a matter of evil.

Why did the good and all-powerful Magnus allow evil? Why had he created Malitte as his opposite?

One day I raised my hand and asked. Archdeacon Odenrick looked at me inscrutably, posing a counter question. "Teddy, what is evil?"

I was just about to answer the same way as my twin brother had once done. That evil was something that made you feel bad. There were almost twenty of us young animals gathered in one of Sagrada Bastante's many halls. There was a solemn, serious atmosphere at our lessons. Every utterance was a challenge to peer pressure. That "evil makes you feel bad" sounded so childish in this context that I remained silent. I exchanged a glance with my twin brother and saw that he, too, remembered our conversation with Odenrick.

My question remained unanswered. As did Archdeacon Odenrick's follow-up question. But I brooded intensely about the matter during the weeks that followed.

What was evil?

Every night I lay awake, waiting. Eric's heavy, calm breathing mocked me as I lay there on tenterhooks without being able to fall asleep. I was listening for suspicious sounds from his bed. All I heard was a car or two driving along down in the street.

Time passed, and I couldn't sleep.

But it was not only worry about Eric that kept me awake at night that fall. Unfortunately not. After only a few weeks of confirmation classes, something strange happened. As I was on my way into the classroom at Sagrada Bastante, Archdeacon Odenrick asked Eric to remain after the lesson. He did so in a low, discreet voice, but I heard it clearly.

Envy flared up in me as though I'd bitten into a hot pepper.

I had a hard time following along during the lesson. When it was over, Eric remained sitting at his desk while I was forced to go outside. It was one of the most trying moments in my life up to that point.

I lingered in the cathedral a while, but when Eric didn't come I had no choice other than to go home alone. He kept me waiting a whole hour. At first he refused to say what Odenrick had wanted. Then it crept out of him that it was about some kind of special instruction which a few of the cubs would receive.

Eric was one of them.

And the envy almost burned a hole in my stomach. A small, black hole.

During the nights, I brooded about what this special instruction was about. Why was Eric chosen and not me? Then it struck me. As I was lying in my bed without being able to sleep, as I was lying, expecting that my twin brother would again betray our twin-ness by leaving me alone in our childhood room, then it struck me.

I wasn't the only one who had seen what was dwelling in Eric.

For Archdeacon Odenrick there were no lost souls.

For Archdeacon Odenrick there were only wayward souls.

What he called "special instruction" was an attempt to rescue Eric from evil. But it was too late. Despite the fact that Eric was breathing softly and calmly in bed a few meters from my own bed, I knew that it was too late.

Unfortunately I had no plan. I didn't know what I should do if he sneaked out through the window again. When it did finally happen, a few weeks after the first time, I didn't do anything, either. During the entire fall and spring, as long as the confirmation instruction was going on, Eric disappeared through the window at night at regular intervals. I remained lying in bed. Paralyzed.

I realized that there was nothing I could do to rescue my twin brother from Malitte and evil.

That is to say, nothing that Archdeacon Odenrick wasn't already doing.

And doing better.

I wake up in the morning, and my head is full of dream fragments.

It's a split feeling.

I wake up at night from dreams that are pleasant. I forget them in a fraction of a second and fall back asleep. Dreams that are unpleasant I dream in the morning. They linger on. The most effective way to get them to dissipate and disappear is to consciously attempt to remember them.

When I've forgotten the nightmares, I get up to a new day.

With each day new risks ensue. In the evening, when I turn out the bedlamp, I experience a feeling of triumph. It's not something I'm proud of. Neither the feeling nor its origin. During the day which just passed I resisted the temptations and fought down the demons by choosing the difficult decisions ahead of the easy ones. I resisted the whole day.

What was my reward?

Sleep.

To what did I awaken the following day?

A new day of temptations and demons.

It's not difficult to accept my split feelings about this.

It is with a blush of shame that I confess that in moments of weakness I've thought that the day the Chauffeurs come to fetch me from Lakestead House, the battle against evil is finally over. Then I've escaped.

Escaping life through death is like resisting the temptation to scratch yourself on the back by chopping off your paw.

Being good is more difficult than being bad.

My story is a story of suffering.

When I think about evil, I have developed three archetypes for the sake of clarity. They themselves are not evil. These three include all the clichés of evil that I've overheard around me. In newspapers, in books, and during conversations with Archdeacon Odenrick and other thinking individuals. The archetypes are symbols. They have no living stuffed animals as prototypes, nor have I tried to caricature any of them.

First up is the Dictator. He is evil in theory, never in practice. He is intellectual and driven by conceit and self-interest. The Dictator strives for power, sometimes even as a goal in itself. More often, however, power is a means to attain other purposes. It might be a matter of securing the most favorable parking place in the garage at work. Or filling a secret bank account to the bursting point. Large things as well as small. The Dictator archetype dwells in all too many of us. He might be the neighbor who has just been named department head. She might be our mayor who's going to run for yet another term.

I'm not saying that it is like that. It might be like that.

The Dictator might very well have lived his entire life without a single evil intention. It is only at second or third hand that his decisions and actions result in evil.

The Dictator is the general in the army.

The Dictator is the theoretician behind the sect.

The Dictator is the philosopher behind the -ism.

The Dictator is the first tile in the game of dominoes.

The Dictator is the origin, not the intention.

The Dictator never lowers his gaze so low that he needs to see or take a position on the consequences of his self-justifying plans.

The second archetype that I've defined is the Sadist.

The Sadist is a stuffed animal who spiritually and intellectually knows that what he strives for is wrong. Yet he can't resist. The actions of the Sadist have a single purpose. He is out to get satisfaction. He lives in, and for, his feelings.

The Sadist might be the bitter taxi driver who by accentuating his unsuccessful life—for example, by placing a diploma in sailing clearly visible up by the steering wheel—is out to implant guilt in his passengers.

The Sadist is the torturer in the wars of distant times.

The Sadist's intention is not evil. Even if the Sadist has an emotional disturbance, he is intellectually and spiritually exactly like you and me.

The third and final archetype is the one which is most uncommon.

Yet he is the most-often referred to and feared.

I know why. What I call the Psychopath is the person who is seen as the most evil of the three. Nothing frightens us more than the kinds of things we don't understand. No one knows the behavior of the Psychopath. There are theories, but no answers. The Psychopath suffers from a spiritual defect. He can be rational at times, but it's impossible to say when or why. On one occasion he's filled with empathy, the next time emotionally shut off. He is unpredictable.

The Psychopath is a kind grandmother who secretly captures and kills butterflies.

The Psychopath is the office rat who gnaws himself on the legs at night.

The Psychopath is the mass murderer we read about in the newspapers and who pursues us in our nightmares.

The Psychopath isn't evil, either.

The Psychopath is sick.

It took a while before I'd gathered enough courage to follow Eric when he sneaked out through the window. By then we'd finished our elementary school studies, begun our high school education, and turned sixteen.

I surprised even myself.

Like many nights before that night, I heard the rustling of Eric's bedclothes and woke up. The weather was past midnight. Eric stole across the floor. I was lying dead quiet. As usual I was in agony. But inside me there was suddenly a courage that had never been there before.

I don't know what caused it.

I waited until he'd gotten out of the window, until it was silent. Then it was my turn to throw off my blanket and pull on my clothes, which were folded over the desk chair.

Then I crept out after him onto the roof.

He wasn't easy to follow. I ran across the roofs that were Amberville's shield against the rain. The light breeze burnished the sky smooth and black, the moon's glow was reflected in thousands of glistening black roof tiles.

I tried to run as quietly as I could.

Beyond the muddle of Amberville's rooftops, on the other side of Western Avenue, I could see the lights from Tourquai. Some of the façades of the stately skyscrapers were illuminated. Along with the lights down in the street, that light was my salvation.

At regular intervals I caught sight of Eric farther ahead, a blur of motion behind a chimney. As he jumped between roofs, the glow of the streetlights reflected from his belt buckle. Each time he disappeared, he showed up again farther and farther away. I ran as fast as I dared. At last I lost sight of him. By then we had run more than twenty minutes and still the tall buildings in Tourquai seemed just as distant.

I had no idea where I was, other than I was still somewhere in Amberville. Still I went on. The faint breeze sounded like a panpipe. Sometimes an accelerating car engine was heard.

Otherwise it was silent.

Then suddenly a "plunk."

I stopped. I looked in the direction of the sound and discovered Eric down on a red street. He disappeared around a street corner. Remaining on the sidewalk was the empty pop can he'd stumbled against by mistake.

I got down from the roof as quickly as I could. It sounds easy, but it was an adventure, a story of danger, drainpipes, woken-up neighbors who threatened to call the police. Once down on the street, I ran as fast as I could toward the place where Eric had vanished. I, too, rounded the street corner.

I found a granite-gray dead-end alley.

No brother, only this alley.

In front of me: a ten-meter-tall brick wall without windows or doors. The façades on both sides up to the wall were windowless except for a few openings sitting so high up that Eric never could have reached them.

Or?

There was a large container on the street. Perhaps you might be able to climb up on its edge and from there, with an agile leap, reach the lowest window opening to the left.

For me, such gymnastics were impossible. It shouldn't have been possible for Eric, either. But I was no longer sure about Eric.

I remained standing. At a loss. I stood staring at the brick wall—presumably—for a few minutes. The way home would feel even longer with a task that was unfinished.

Then I heard.

"Psst."

I readily admit that I jumped.

"But what the hell, Eric, didn't you just get here?"

I looked around me in confusion.

Nothing. Absolutely nothing.

"Come in, then," said the voice.

With a metallic sound as if from a large metal spring, the short side of the Dumpster opened and I stepped in.

Casino Monokowski.

The container was a container on the outside.

On the inside it was the entrance to Casino Monokowski.

The gorillas in the door nodded to me in recognition. For them, I was my twin brother.

The container itself was nothing worth describing. It looked like a container on the inside as well. With the difference that on the long side there was an opening that led into the building against which the container stood. I went in through the opening and remained standing a few steps inside the place.

My mouth opened wide.

I had never seen anything like it. As large as the interior of Sagrada Bastante. Or like a gutted Grand Divino.
Decorated with gilded draperies along the massive walls
and dark-red wall-to-wall carpets on the floors. Filled with
endless rows of clattering, flashing gambling machines and
quantities of round poker tables, large roulette tables, and
high, half-moon-shaped blackjack tables. Interspersed between tables and machines were long bars whose mirrors
revealed all the tricks the poker players were up to.

A planned-out chaos.

Filled with stuffed animals.

Despite the enormous capacity of the place, it was the
guests who dominated the impression of Casino Monokowski. Mammals and snakes, birds and fish. Felines and
dogs, predators and imaginary animals. The noise level was
deafening. The jingle of one-armed bandits, the clinking of
glasses and bottles, the rustling of bills at the poker tables,
and the murmur of suppressed expectation. The smells
made me dizzy. Cigar and cigarette smoke. Perfume and
sweat. Arrogance and nervousness.

I was inundated with impressions, but I resisted. Slowly I
forced my way over to a bar and ordered a soft drink.

The bartender, who obviously also recognized me as my
twin brother, smiled, amused but amiable.

Somewhere in here was Eric. What should I say if I found
him? Of all the accusations I had formulated, which one
bore being said out loud? Without humiliating myself more
than the one I accused? Perhaps it was better to return
to reality and leave Eric's salvation to Odenrick and the
church?

But he was my twin; our bonds were strong.

I took a swallow of my soft drink and was on the verge
of exploding.

Like a siphon, the alcohol sprayed right out over the bar,

and in my throat there burned a hellish fire. I was sixteen
years old. I had never even tasted red wine at home.

I dried the corrosive liquid from my lips and prepared to
scold the bartender when I realized the obvious.

This was what Eric drank. He was already abusing alcohol. When I ordered a soft drink, the bartender thought it
was a joke.

Still bewildered, someone tapped my shoulder. I turned
around. There stood a chinchilla.

"Table twenty-three," he said. "It's urgent."

I understood nothing. I said nothing in reply.

"Urgent," said the chinchilla with irritation. "Get a
move on."

I shook my head. It was pointless to pretend to understand what he expected of me.

"It's a dog, he's been winning a good while now," said
the chinchilla in order to acquaint me with the situation.
"We're talking big money. I've been looking for you."

Finally my surprise appeared not to be out of place.

"It was Dove who located you," said the chinchilla, nodding up toward the ceiling, as if this dove were Magnus
Himself.

The chinchilla placed a hand on my shoulder and shoved
me away from the bar. I still said nothing. This seemed to
make him nervous.

"Dove is watching," he whispered in my ear at the same
time as he continued to push me ahead of him as if I were
a plow.

"Stop the dog. Quickly."

With that we were at what must have been table twenty-
three, for the hand on my shoulder was suddenly gone. I
turned around. The chinchilla had vanished. In front of
me there was a tall table where three animals were playing
cards. One of them was a dog, and in front of the dog was
a mountain range of chips.

I knew nothing about gambling games, but I wasn't stupid. I realized that the chips were money; I realized that my—or, rightly stated, my twin brother's—task was to play against this dog and defeat him.

I sat down at one of the vacant chairs at the table. The rooster who was dealing out cards immediately pushed a few piles of chips over to me. Then he dealt out the cards; we each got two cards.

The player to the right of me nodded, and the rooster set a third card in front of him. I didn't know what that meant.

"Card?" the rooster said to me.

I nodded.

On the day the green pickup delivers us we are all good. That is my conviction. After that we are exposed to temptations that lead to actions which have consequences which, if we aren't thoughtful, come to be experienced as evil. We all carry within us the conditions for developing into a Dictator, a Sadist, or even a Psychopath. That is why I live as I do at Lakestead House. Carefully.

This sounds bombastic. I'm not ashamed of that. I have devoted my life to goodness. The consequences became infinitely more extensive than I thought, but I regret nothing.

The walls in my room are light blue. I live a great deal of my life in this room. That wasn't the idea, but it's logical.

Evil is found in experiences. Never in intentions.

A classic problem is how evil the evil intention which leads to a good action really is. This line of reasoning can be turned around. It can be asked how good a good intention which has evil consequences really is.

For me this is of no importance. This is the sort of thing Archdeacon Odenrick can figure out. My definition of evil is simple.

Evil is what the victim experiences. Nothing else.

The Dictator, the Sadist, and the Psychopath are not driven by evil intentions. They are out for material gain, emotional gain, or else they're following an instinct without any intention whatsoever.

Their victims are not interested in intentions. Their victims experience pure evil. If the victim knew about the Dictator's plan, the Sadist's bent, or the Psychopath's childhood, the victim wouldn't describe what he withstood as evil. He would talk about fate, about bad luck, or explain it by his "getting in the way" of something.

Pure evil is a result, not an intention.

Pure evil must be "unjust" from the victim's perspective.

Pure evil is an experience.

There was already a six of clubs and a queen of spades in front of me on the table. The rooster gave me the eight of clubs when I asked for one more card. Then that round was over.

My plan had been to figure out the rules during the course of play. That didn't work. On the other hand, it seemed to me as though the dog was getting rid of more chips than me.

The rooster continued dealing out cards. We pushed out our chips. Took our cards. Then it was time for the next round. I had no idea what was going on. But the dog, like the others at the table, became more and more furious.

The fury was directed at me.

"What the hell are you up to?" hissed the dog.

I shrugged my shoulders.

But before there was time for anything more to happen, the chinchilla suddenly showed up by my side. With a discreet nod he got me to leave the table and my chips. He placed the same question as the dog, although in a lower voice.

"What the hell was that?"

We kept each other company away from table twenty-three.

"Are you out of your mind?" he asked. "A few rounds more and they would have had to carry you out."

I didn't answer. We walked slowly in order not to attract attention. Everyone moved slowly inside Casino Monokowski. The heat, perhaps the alcohol, but above all the mass of animals meant that you were forced to take it carefully. We turned to the right into a long corridor bordered by slot machines giving off an ear-splitting din.

"Take this," whispered the chinchilla right next to my ear, slipping me a small package.

He did it so discreetly that the package was in my hand before I noticed that I had gotten it. It was no larger than a matchbox. White wrapping paper and thick, beige tape.

"It's for Otto. He's sitting farthest in, in the Twilight Room."

"Otto?" I said.

"What are you taking this evening?" asked the chinchilla with irritation, and stopped me right before the corridor of slot machines ended. "Otto Orangutan. In the Twilight Room. Shall I lead you there?"

Before I had time to accept his offer, he turned around and left.

There I stood with a small white package in my hand, not knowing what I should do. The clatter was ringing in my eyes, I was still bewildered by my experiences at the gaming table and the taste of alcohol still remained on my lips.

Should I give up and go home?

That was a possibility. Events were running away in an uncontrollable manner, and I was feeling physically ill from the greed and bewilderment that were in the air. True, I hadn't run into Eric, but perhaps that was just as well?

I had uncovered his secret.

It filled me with shame and disgust.

I decided to go home, but it wouldn't be that easy.

That fateful evening at Casino Monokowski was a fore-

boding of the rest of my life. Psychosomatic illnesses, pre-
destination, and religiosity; it's all about faith. Having sufficient imagination in order to be able to twist reality into
faith's more limited framework. If I spend my days searching
for signs, I'm going to find them in the end. Perhaps it's the
same way with that night at the casino. Perhaps I attributed
greater significance to it in retrospect than it had?

Perhaps not.

At first glance, Casino Monokowski looked like a single,
gigantic room. It proved to be more than that. To make
your way from where I stood to the exit was a real hike.
Slowly I walked against the current, with my gaze to the
floor in order to avoid all the "acquaintances" who knew
Eric but not me.

My strategy was simple. I walked along one of the outside walls. That must lead me to the exit.

Golden sheets of cloth were hanging along the walls.
They muffled the sound in the place and gave the miserable
reality a certain degree of class. I assumed that the walls
behind the draperies were unfinished cement. Thus I was
surprised when the golden drapery was suddenly pulled to
the side.

Out through a gap in the drapery a gazelle's head ap-
peared. The gazelle's right horn had come off in the middle.
His eyelashes were so long that for a moment I wondered if
I had been mistaken, if he actually was a she?

"Come!" whispered the gazelle, indicating behind the
drapery with his hooves.

For a moment or two I considered ignoring him and
continuing toward the exit, but it was easier to do as he
wanted.

I stepped in behind the drapery. There was yet another large
room. Here, however, the dimensions were more normal.
Animals were sitting at round tables playing cards, and the
only bar was traditionally located, along the short wall.

The gazelle shoved me to the side so that we ended up in the shadows, at a respectable distance from the card players.

"Sweetheart. You're not Eric," said the gazelle.

The tongue-tiedness I'd shown signs of up till now continued.

"You're not Eric," he repeated.

He didn't sound angry, if anything surprised. His voice was sharp and considerably lighter than I had guessed.

"We're twins," I finally forced out.

"What a surprise, sweetheart."

An ironic gazelle. His laughter sounded like little bells.

He observed me for a long time in silence. I didn't dare move.

"But you're not particularly alike," he said at last. "Other than in appearance."

I nodded. I agreed. After this evening, I knew that the abyss between Eric and me would never close up again.

"I need that package you got," he said.

"You . . ." I stammered, "you're not Otto Orangutan."

"Sharp-eyed as a cobra," mocked the gazelle. "Give it here."

The gazelle attacked me. More or less. Before I had time to react, he had his hooves in my pants pocket, and I pulled back in terror. I must have gotten a bit of the drapery under my foot, because I stumbled and fell backwards. It was not a violent fall, it was more like I sat down.

The gazelle seemed not to care if anyone saw us. In his eyes shone the same desire that I'd seen in each and every animal in here. I admit that it frightened me.

"We can do this in one of two ways," said the gazelle. "Either you just give me the package. Or else I have a little fun with you first. Then I take the package."

I shook my head. The glow in his eyes was so intense that I was forced to look in a different direction.

That was how I discovered my salvation.

Eric came walking toward us.

Before I had time to answer, my twin brother put his paw on the gazelle's back and murmured something I didn't hear. The gazelle smiled, an ingratiating, repulsive smile. Then he backed into the shadows of the drapery and disappeared.

My brother extended his paw to me. I took it, and got up. With that I had used up my last bit of strength.

We stood staring at each other without knowing what we should say. In my soul a cry was being formed, a scream for help, and I understood that it belonged to Eric. It was Eric's scream that was screaming inside me.

I knit my lips together. Not a sound.

Then I turned around and ran as fast as I could, running toward the exit. I continued to run when I came out onto the street, I ran the whole way home, not caring if Mother and Father heard me. I ran up the stairs to my room.

Eric maintains that I'm still running.

CHAPTER 10

Tom-Tom Crow dropped the screwdriver. It fell to the floor with an audible thud.

Eric Bear stopped in his tracks, paralyzed by fear. He could see how the silhouettes of Sam Gazelle and Snake Marek remained standing a few meters farther away in the dark room.

They had broken into Hotel Esplanade less than a minute ago. The weather was past midnight, and the Chauffeurs had neither been seen nor heard for several hours. They ought to be safe. But they were breaking into the house of death. If they were discovered here, neither police nor prosecutor could help them; then they were doomed.

The seconds passed.

The sound from the screwdriver spread through the dark building. Only when the sound had forced its way into every nook and corner without anything happening did Eric dare to set his paw down on the floor.

"We're going in," he whispered to Tom-Tom, who was standing closest to him.

The big crow nodded, and along with the gazelle and the snake they went straight into the hideout of the Chauffeurs.

A few days after the sensational discovery that the Chauffeurs were hanging out a wing-stroke's distance from Yiala's Arch, the four stuffed animals kept Hotel Esplanade under observation. The hotel was an ordinary building with a spackled gray and white finish, but with a peculiar feature. It lacked doors and windows on the street level. Apart from the secret garage entrance, which was a part of the façade itself, there was nowhere to go in.

"But we have to get the hell in," the crow declared wisely. "How else are we going to get hold of the list?"

"It'll work out," replied Eric Bear. "We'll lie low a few days, map out their routines, learn how the opposition looks. Snake is going to think up a plan. Aren't you, Marek?"

Snake grunted. He was unsure whether Eric was flattering or teasing him.

They drew up a schedule. Because the Chauffeurs only worked at night, the four at Yiala's Arch were forced to alter their daily rhythms. Eric returned the cars he'd borrowed, but kept the gray Combi. It was perfect to use for surveillance work, neutral and boring beyond recognition. They parked the car kitty-corner from the camouflaged garage door and took turns spending hours in the driver's seat, making note of every observation.

But nothing happened.

In the twilight, the door to the secret garage was opened and the Chauffeurs drove the red pickup out. Right before dawn, they returned after completion of duty. In between: nothing.

Before the third night, Eric acquired a camera with a massive zoom and a lens that worked in the dark.

"Let's find out who they are, these Chauffeurs," the bear said to his friends. "Tom-Tom says that they're stuffed animals just like us. Perhaps we can find them in one of the windows? If nothing else, we ought to be able to get a picture of them as they drive in and out of the garage."

"Okay," said Sam, shrugging his shoulders. "But why?"

They sat, having breakfast at the kitchen table. A crumb from a piece of toast with orange marmalade was stuck to the corner of Sam's mouth, and his long, red tongue captured it and made it disappear.

"I don't have a real plan," Eric admitted. "But the more we know, the better, right?"

"Maybe," said Snake. "Maybe not. There are occasions when a lack of information can be the thing that—"

"Besides, I'm damned tired of just sitting and staring at that wall," Eric interrupted with irritation. "But anyone who feels he's so occupied with other important matters that he doesn't have time to deal with the camera can just let it be."

"You have a point there, darling," giggled Sam.

Snake sighed. He knew that he was the one who would be forced to process the photographs; only he could do that sort of thing.

The following morning they had the first—and as it turned out only—razor-sharp visual portrayal of ChauffeurTiger. It was a fortunate chance, light reflected toward the hood of a car, lighting up the driver's seat of the pickup at the same moment that Snake happened to snap the picture. He'd set the camera on the dashboard above the steering wheel. But it wasn't until he developed the picture the following evening that he realized what he'd photographed.

The image that slowly appeared in the developer bath

became sharper and sharper. He took the photo paper from the solution and hung it up to dry, but couldn't continue with the rest of the roll. From the drying line ChauffeurTiger was staring right into Snake's narrow eyes and beyond, into his soul. Tiger's face was enormous, his fur gray and battered but his gaze hard and cold. It was a gaze that could kill; these were eyes that had seen everything. During his entire adult life, Snake Marek had struggled with doubt about his own artistic abilities. Faced with ChauffeurTiger's unmerciful gaze, he could hide nothing.

Snake recoiled, shocked and afraid, and wriggled out of the bathroom which he'd turned into a darkroom. During the ensuing night, the friends determined that there were apparently only three Chauffeurs, the tiger and two wolves. They probably went in shifts, and these three would be replaced by three others at some later time.

The wolves were no charmers, either, but despite their sharp, yellow teeth and their scornfully pulled-back upper lips, it was still ChauffeurTiger who gave Sam, Eric, Snake, and Tom-Tom nightmares.

And it was the thought of being caught by ChauffeurTiger that meant that they hesitated another few days before they dared break into Hotel Esplanade.

They came into a kind of all-purpose room which was large, dark, and deserted.

"Snake and Sam, you take the right side, we'll take the left," whispered Eric, making a gesture.

They didn't know what they were looking for. The Death List could be a coffee-stained scrap of paper on a nightstand, but just as likely a document in a leather folder locked up in a safe. They had also discussed the risk that the Chauffeurs took the list with them in the red pickup.

Eric took a few steps toward the door to the left. He heard Tom-Tom directly behind him. The snake and the gazelle were still standing beside him.

"We'll do this as fast as hell," hissed Eric. "Then we'll get out of here."

They worked efficiently for the next few minutes. The bear side by side with the crow. It was easier to search through the premises than Eric had thought. The Chauffeurs had hardly any furniture and very few personal effects. The dust bunnies revealed that they weren't interested in cleaning, but there were nooks where things could be hidden. When, after less than a quarter of an hour, Eric and Tom-Tom went back out to the large room where Snake and Sam were already waiting, they were rather certain that they hadn't missed anything.

"Nothing," whispered Snake.

"Not us, either," answered Tom-Tom.

"Now let's split," said Sam.

The gazelle's entire body was shaking. It had already been shaking when, a half hour ago, they had raised the ladder against the window on the second story. That window had stood ajar since they'd starting keeping an eye on Hotel Esplanade. As the gazelle was climbing up, the ladder had shaken so much that the crow had been forced to use all of his weight to hold the ladder steady.

"We're not going to find any list. There is no list. We're still alive. Let's leave," Sam clarified.

Eric nodded. There was nothing else to do.

They returned to the corner room with the open window. They had pulled the ladder up after them; now they carried out the opposite maneuver in order to make their way back down to the street.

"Fiasco," muttered Snake Marek as they were on their way toward Yiala's Arch a few minutes later.

"We're alive," said Gazelle. "That has to count as a success, old man."

CHAPTER 11

On the morning of Tuesday the thirteenth of May, only five hours after they had returned from their fruitless break-in at Hotel Esplanade, there was a banging on the door to Sam's apartment.

Sam, Snake, and Eric all jumped up from their sleeping spots, as though wakened from the same nightmare. Tom-Tom Crow had forced himself to wake up less than half an hour ago, got dressed, and gone out and shopped for food. Just like for the watch shifts at night, there was a schedule for who would take care of the shopping. Today it had been Tom-Tom's turn.

Again there was a banging.

Eric and Snake looked urgently at Sam, who with an embarrassed mumbling got up out of his bed, pulled on his bathrobe, and shuffled over toward the door.

"Go away!" he shouted. "Get out of here. The store is closed. You'll have to humiliate yourselves somewhere else."

This led to more determined knocks, and with a heavy sigh Sam Gazelle opened the door a crack.

But instead of making a small gap out toward the stairway hall, Sam was pressed back into the apartment with violent force. The gazelle stumbled backwards and fell down on the floor on his side with a bang. Eric and Snake threw themselves out of their beds, but before they had time to go anywhere Nicholas Dove's two gorillas were standing in the room, staring at them. And with a certain elegance, Dove strolled into the tumult, his glance fastened on Eric Bear, a disdainful smile evident at the corner of his mouth.

"This doesn't inspire a great deal of hope," he said, continuing over to the kitchen table, where he pulled out a chair and sat down.

The gorillas remained standing where they were, on either side of the door, the red one to the right. With some effort, Sam struggled to his feet, attempting to regain some element of dignity.

"Nicholas Dove," he said, giggling amiably, "so nice to—"

"Time flies," interrupted Dove, directing himself straight at Eric as if the gazelle didn't even exist. "And I can't say that I'm impressed by your progress."

Dove's concentration was directed completely at Eric Bear. Sam proceeded over to the kitchen counter for the purpose of offering Dove something to drink; Snake Marek stood expectantly by his mattress, the farthest inside the apartment, observing the development of events.

"You know," said Dove, "time is just what I don't have."

"It might seem as though nothing is happening," Eric began in his defense. "But that's not true, we have actually—"

Nicholas Dove held up his wing deprecatingly; he wasn't here to listen to the bear's excuses.

"It's not the case," said Dove, "that I don't keep myself informed."

"Would you like anything? A cup of tea, water, something stronger?" asked Sam.

"I'm assuming that you keep yourself informed," answered Eric. "Anything else wouldn't be you. But this is, nonetheless . . ."

Eric held out his paws. The mood in the room was expectant. Only a few moments ago Snake had tensed every muscle in his narrow, short body, ready to slither in under the mattress or somewhere else where he wouldn't be seen. But with every word that was exchanged between the bear and the dove the snake relaxed. He was not the focus of this visit. As long as neither of the gorillas moved, they mostly resembled stone statues, and Nicholas Dove was, as always, removed in a super animal kind of way. The only thing holding up the nervous energy was Sam, who noisily searched for ice in the freezer. He had decided, on his own authority, to serve Nicholas Dove a glass of water.

"And the worst thing is," said Dove, "I'm not at all certain that you're exerting yourself."

His tone of voice was slightly absent; he didn't look at Eric but rather his gaze swept across the room as though he were searching for something.

"Not exerting myself?" repeated the bear, irritated. "I'm living in a pigsty in Yok, I've turned the day upside down in order to—"

"You don't understand," interrupted Dove. "It's not a question of what you're doing, it's a matter of what you're coming up with."

And with an unexpected intensity, he burrowed his gaze into the bear, who involuntarily stepped back. In Nicholas Dove's normally inscrutable pupils was a desperation that Eric had never seen before, and which he never wanted to see again. It was coal-black and unmerciful.

"I'm forced to make myself clear, I think," said Dove in a low voice.

A scarcely discernible nod, and suddenly things happened.

When both of the gorillas—as if they were guided, if somewhat slow, robots—took the few steps over to Eric Bear and took hold of the bear's arms, the nervous Sam dropped the water glass that he'd finally filled. The sharp crash of breaking glass caused Nicholas Dove to react with surprising speed. Dove whirled around, turning his back to the others. Sam screamed as ice and glass splinters whirled around his hooves, and before the scream had quieted, Nicholas Dove had conjured an automatic weapon from his wing; larger than a pistol but smaller than a carbine. For a brief moment he aimed the weapon at Sam, but then Dove realized what had happened. Without batting an eye he put the weapon back inside his feathers and again directed his attention toward Eric Bear.

Snake Marek had been waiting for this moment of confusion.

In the moment that followed after the water glass struck the floor, Snake was already past the gorillas. He wriggled out through the open door and was on his way down the stairs when the dove pulled out his weapon. Eric looked after Marek. Nothing else was really to be expected of that miserable snake, he thought. Nicholas Dove didn't even condescend to send a gorilla to bring back the reptile; that's how insignificant he was in the dove's eyes.

"It's important to be clear," continued Dove as if this little intermezzo hadn't taken place. "And I'm wondering if you've understood that there is a time factor to take into account here."

"Obviously I have—" began Eric, but he got no further before one of the gorillas punched him in the stomach with a force that completely took the breath out of him.

The surprise also did its part. His legs lost all their strength, and suddenly it was the gorillas who were holding him up.

"You don't have much time," said Dove.

The next blow struck above the bear's eye, gliding across his eyebrow and a little ways up over his forehead. Before Eric had time to feel it the next hit came, against the temple, and then he felt the pain in his belly. He coughed, not seeing the cotton coming out of his mouth, but Sam started screaming from over in the kitchen.

"Shut your mouth, you goose."

It was the first time Dove had addressed anyone else in the room, and he did so in a low but determined voice. Sam became silent immediately.

The gorillas released Eric Bear, who with a heavy thud fell to the floor.

Eric was struggling to retain consciousness, but failed. It was as though Sam's apartment gradually faded away, and instead the beach in Hillevie emerged. With a pleasurable intoxication in his body he was strolling along the edge of the beach, on his way over to the decrepit pier. Eric had experienced many of life's best moments sitting on the worn planks on the pier at the north end of the beach.

He carefully balanced out to the end of the pier, where he sat down with his legs hanging over the edge and his paws a few decimeters above the surface of the water. In the moonlight the sea was lying dark and endless before him, removing all feelings of time and distance.

And he knew that this was the exact same water that had been there a million years before. The cycle of nature functioned like that. Eternity was no more terrifying than the water gurgling under the pier, time was just as inexorably sluggish. The sound of the rippling sea was unexpectedly reminiscent of Nicholas Dove's voice.

"It would be stupid to tear you apart now," Eric heard the water say, "but time is running out. And I thought that if you're having a hard time finding the proper feeling for this assignment, there are a few small things I should be able to use your rabbit for even now. What do you think? Shall we take her to the casino this evening already? Think about it."

If Dove said anything more before he left Sam Gazelle's apartment, Eric never knew it. The bear disappeared back down into his unconsciousness.

CHAPTER 12

Snake Marek returned a few hours after Dove had taken off. He acted as if nothing special had happened. Eric was sitting, bandaged, at the kitchen table; Sam was fixing the dinner that Crow had bought.

"Snake," said Crow, "you know what, I . . ."

But Eric silenced him. He invited Snake to take a seat at the table. All four ate in silence and, over coffee, began discussing how they should go from there. After an hour or two they were in agreement. Snake's theory was simple. If the Chauffeurs didn't operate arbitrarily, there must be some form of communication between them and their employer. Instead of searching for the list, which demonstrably didn't exist, the snake, bear, gazelle, and crow should try to find out how this information reached Hotel Esplanade.

Sam had no difficulty arranging a wiretap. Technology was one of his foremost interests and in the cellar at Yiala's Arch he had an entire workshop. Exactly how the gazelle made use of his tools and equipment in his "work" remained unclear. Without difficulty he located the telephone cables which led to Hotel Esplanade, and in a childishly simple way he jury-rigged them so that calls to and from the hotel were routed to a tape recorder up in Sam's apartment.

It seemed unlikely, however, that anyone gave the Chauffeurs orders over the telephone. The risk of misunderstandings and eavesdropping would be far too great. And because there was no longer any postal delivery in Yok, the stuffed animals felt the possibility that the list was delivered by a courier most likely. This led to a decision to intensify the surveillance of the hotel. If the precision of their approach had been a little slapdash before, Eric now created a schedule without gaps. No one was particularly happy about the increased guard duty, but they all understood that it was needed. During the lonely hours of the night, Sam Gazelle used pills in a way that took a heavy toll on his hiding places and supplies. Eric brooded and agonized, thinking about—longing for—Emma Rabbit. Snake devoted the time to intellectual nonsense and soul-searching; a soul-searching which in the aftermath of the night appeared even more nonsensical than the nonsense itself. Tom-Tom Crow was, however, the one who was most tormented by sitting hour after hour, staring at the hotel's dark brick façade where nothing happened from the time the red pickup left the building a few minutes after sundown until it returned a few minutes before dawn.

Tom-Tom was a simple soul, but he didn't like being alone. He didn't like it at all.

Over the years he had learned to distract the loneliness through a series of empty rituals. He cooked, cleaned, even watched TV according to certain definite patterns. Patterns that demanded discipline. The ambitious handiwork projects were part of that. It was a matter of taming the silence and the loneliness. When evening was over, sleep came as quickly as a sharp right hook.

And he never needed to recall what had happened.

But in the gray Volga, he remembered. There was nothing else to do.

He recalled how cramped it was. How it rubbed against his wings, and how the light filtered down through the cracks in the floor.

He remembered the pain. The terror.

Tom-Tom stared intensely at the façade across the way, at Hotel Esplanade, trying to blot out the unpleasant thoughts by looking even more intensely.

But he was a simple soul.

He needed distractions.

And nothing was happening outside Hotel Esplanade.

He believed that the attacks were for real, all the way up to school age. It was only Papa who could hear the warning sirens, and certainly that was strange, but why should Papa lie? Papa was all Tom-Tom had. Mama had disappeared even before he was delivered. Tom-Tom was Papa's only child.

They were coming from the forests, Papa said. They tortured stuffed animals. They could keep at it for days. When you finally died, said Papa, you could feel content. But Tom-Tom shouldn't be afraid. Papa would never let anything happen to him. That was why they had to practice.

There were a couple of loose floor planks in the kitchen. When Papa heard the sirens, Tom-Tom should run into the kitchen and throw himself down into the hollow place under the floor. But because it was only Papa who heard the sirens, Tom-Tom never knew when it was time. No matter how hard the punishment Papa gave him, Tom-Tom never learned to hear the sirens. The sirens in Papa's head.

It was cramped under the planks in the kitchen. There was hardly room for Tom-Tom. Perhaps that was just as well. The idea of the practice was that he was forced to lie silent as long as possible. If he let out a peep, the enemy would find him. Then the enemy would tear up the planks and torture him. It was for Tom-Tom's own good.

He learned to lie silently for hours.

Tom-Tom Crow stared at Hotel Esplanade, trying to think about Snake, the bear, and the gazelle. He tried to take himself back to reality and the gray Volga and the terrible Chauffeurs on the other side of the street. But after a few minutes, he was down in the cramped space under the floor again.

The pain.

What if the enemy sensed something anyway?

What if the enemy sensed something anyway and started searching for a hiding place somewhere under the floor planks? What if the enemy, for example, poured boiling water over the floor, boiling water that ran down through the cracks? Would Tom-Tom still manage to keep silent? Boiling oil? Melted sugar? Tom-Tom's papa was inventive at the stove. He was doing this for Tom-Tom's own good.

The pain.

When dawn came and the first rays of the sun were climbing up over the horizon, the night of watching was over. Most often, the red pickup drove into the garage an hour or two before sunrise; sometimes the margin was narrower. The Chauffeurs would sleep through the day after completion of nightly duty, and that applied to Eric, Sam, Snake, and Tom-Tom as well. But no one found as great a relief in the hour of dawn as the crow.

During the shift that proved to be the last one outside Hotel Esplanade for the stuffed animals, Sam Gazelle overslept.

It wasn't at all strange; chock-full of interacting and counteracting substances flowing around in his system, the chances of his remaining awake for an entire surveillance shift were generally nonexistent.

Instead of soundlessly opening the car door and nonchalantly strolling back to the beautifully grass-green Yiala's Arch as dawn was breaking, Sam threw open his eyes in surprise and noticed that the day had begun. The Morning

Weather had turned cloudy, nothing more, but this would still demand an explanation. Eric would understand that Sam had fallen asleep, and Sam had no excuse.

He wriggled out of the car at the same time as he tried to gather his thoughts. The ghosts of his nightmares had not yet dissipated, and they made it hard for him to produce miserable white lies.

He shut the car door and took a deep breath. There were a few cigarette butts on the sidewalk right next to him, and only a year ago he would have leaned down and picked them up. Somewhere in the vicinity he heard the sound of an iron grate being rolled up as a shop owner came to work. And Sam was just on his way to begin the stroll homeward when the concealed garage door to Hotel Esplanade unexpectedly opened.

Despite the fact that the sun had gone up and the day had begun.

From out of the garage drove not a red, but a green pickup.

CHAPTER 13

It sounds so frigging unbelievable," said Tom-Tom, who was standing in the kitchen, searching for rusks in one of the cupboards over the counter.

"But I swear," Sam Gazelle whined, wretched and irritated at the same time. "How wrong do you think a person can see?"

"It sounds unbelievable," agreed Eric.

"I'm telling you, it was ChauffeurTiger," Sam repeated for the third time.

The crow found the package of rusks and sat down next to Sam.

"Who had turned into some frigging DeliveryTiger?" said Tom-Tom skeptically, putting a rusk into his mouth.

Sam threw out his hands. That's the way it was. Without a doubt. Without the dramatic hood that the Chauffeurs wore, and dressed instead in the Deliverymen's typical green uniform, a bit reminiscent of the bus drivers' jackets and peaked caps, it had been none other than Chauffeur-Tiger who had sat behind the wheel of a green pickup, with one of the two wolves beside him.

"Hmm," said Snake Marek, for once markedly laconic.

They sat around the kitchen table, Sam on the edge, all staring incredulously at him. The Morning Weather was in the process of letting up and the rain would cease any minute now. It was Tuesday morning, just over two weeks since they'd started their surveillance of Hotel Esplanade, and Eric had almost forgotten how the apartment looked in daylight. The parquet floor shone with an oiled luster, and even the sticky ring marks from beer bottles on the kitchen table looked more pleasant during the day. Sam had emptied out a carton of breakfast cereal, honey-glazed rice puffs, and Tom-Tom sat down by mistake on the chair where the cereal had ended up. The crushed puffs now spread a sweetish smell through the apartment which was not at all unpleasant.

"You may believe what you want to," said Sam bitterly.

"I believe you," said Eric. "But it still sounds unbelievable."

"It's just that . . . oh, what the hell, you have seen things before . . ." said Tom-Tom, swallowing his third biscuit. "The kinds of things you've told us about. Hell's dragons and colors and . . . you know . . . those sort of frigging . . . roller-coaster rides."

Sam put on a wounded expression. The white and black rings that made his eyes seem bigger than they were reinforced his innocence, and the corners of his eyes glistened as though from tears. He put his head to one side and stroked his broken horn.

"I hadn't taken anything for several hours. At least," he whined. "That is really narrow-minded. Believe me, after all the years that I've used a little . . . extra stimulation . . . you learn to see the difference between reality and fantasy. It's only in reality that my little energizers run out."

"No, damn it," Tom-Tom now tried to take back what he'd said, "I didn't mean it like that. It's clear as hell that I believe you. It's just . . . no . . . damn it, then, I believe you."

The crow's words subsided in a silence that might be called reflective. Snake broke the silence.

"It's not implausible," he said, wriggling up onto the kitchen table.

They all looked at him with a certain surprise. Up till then Snake had sat silently, weighing arguments for and against. Finally he'd made his decision, and this despite his contempt for the gazelle, which he no longer concealed.

"Apart from the fact that there only remains a sliver of credibility in our little gazelle, who seems to do whatever it takes to get a little attention from our straight-backed lead bear," Snake began with venomous irony, whereupon protests were heard around the table, "it's not at all implausible. One might say that it's actually just the opposite: rather obvious. Chauffeurs and Deliverymen are only different sides of the same coin. It's so foolishly predictable that it's amazing no one has uncovered them before. In addition, from the perspective of the authorities, it's rational. One contract, one garage, one rent . . ."

". . . and one transfer!" said Eric.

The thought struck him when he had his guard down. He got up from the chair with such force that it fell to the floor.

"The lists," he said, without even noticing Snake's irritation at being yet again interrupted in the midst of a lengthy statement. "I know how they handle the Cub List at the ministry. How the transfer itself takes place. Are you imagining that there really is a Death List, and that it's delivered at the same time?"

Sam nodded enthusiastically.

"Darling, that doesn't sound improbable at all," he said.

"I don't really flipping get it," said Tom-Tom.

He was still hungry, but didn't want to take more biscuits as there were only three left.

"But it's . . ."

"What?" asked Snake.

"It's today."

Eric nodded without anyone understanding what he meant. Since the four of them had shut themselves up in the apartment at Yiala's Arch, none of them had been concerned about what day it was. The nights had come, the days had passed, at a more and more ominous pace.

"It's the sixteenth today," said Eric. "And it's on the sixteenth that the transfer takes place."

He was so agitated he was shaking.

"That's this evening!" he repeated.

"Is he talking about that frigging Cub List now?"

Tom-Tom put the question right out into the room.

"It's about both lists," said Sam. "I think."

"But we don't know that," said Tom-Tom Crow, mostly to make the matter clear to himself. "Eric knows what they do with the Cub List, but if it's the same frigging way with the Death List? We don't know that, do we?"

"It's this evening," Eric repeated to himself.

"Finally we're getting out of here," said Snake.

TWILIGHT, 3

When the sun sank behind the horizon and the last breath of daylight colored the sky dark pink and dull red, when the Evening Storm was at hand and could be sensed in the bushes and the crowns of the trees, sometimes he felt ill at ease, reminded of forces that were beyond his control. Then he fled deep down under the ground, to the catacombs that had been constructed by long-forgotten generations, to which the light of day would never reach. There he might wander around and marvel at these endless passageways and crypts where secret societies had held their meetings, where business deals were struck, and where secrets were buried for all time. Deeper and deeper down under the earth he went along a route that wound through the very bedrock, lit up only by the torch he brought with him. The air became damper and damper, full of earth and stone dust; the chill caused him to shake and feel at home. When he'd walked for over a half hour he reduced his pace. It was getting hard to breathe, and he rationed his oxygen. The system of tunnels was several miles long; neither he nor anyone else knew its full extent; it had been built, extended, and added onto for hundreds of years; there wasn't just one but many architects, and a map would never be drawn. Everyone in the city knew about the tunnels, but there weren't many who knew how to find an entrance. He himself knew of two, but it was maintained that there were ten of them. He'd investigated a few kilometers in each direction from his starting points, but he didn't want to go farther than that. It wasn't necessary, either.

A few meters after the tunnel had become so narrow that he was forced to crouch, it divided in three directions. He took the middle route, a broad but low passage which after ten or so meters came to an end in a small crypt. He extended the torch in front of him and lit up the wall. From out of the ground a cat's head was sticking up.

"Boo," he said.

The cat didn't react. He extended the torch closer to the cat's eyes, and the cat's left eyelid seemed to jerk weakly.

Fascinating, he thought.

He'd buried the cat thirteen days earlier, and there was still life in it. He could of course have buried the cat's head as well, but he was interested to see what would happen. Presumably the loose-tongued cat that had tattled to Dove would never die, but instead live down here in an eternity of eternities. He was not alone in wondering what really happened after the Chauffeurs fetched you.

Soon enough he would see, he thought drily.

He turned around and went back the same way he'd come. He still walked slowly. The chill caused him to move slowly, but it contributed to his thinking swiftly. It didn't worry him that Eric Bear had succeeded in tracking the Chauffeurs to the hotel down in Yok. Without bothering in the least about the matter, he'd known for a long time that the Chauffeurs camped out at the Esplanade. On the other hand, it made him wary that Nicholas Dove had paid a visit to Sam Gazelle's apartment the other day. The harder Dove

pressed, the greater the risk that the bear would be forced
to become truly creative. And Dove was an opponent who
couldn't be defeated without the type of repeated, much-
discussed confrontations that he especially disliked.

He stopped. Had he heard a neighing behind him? Was it
the cat who had managed to pull itself together for a small
sound? He stood dead quiet, listening. Then it was heard
again, the growling from his own belly. He smiled. He was
hungry.

When he came back up out of the catacombs, the sun
had gone down and darkness had overtaken the sky. This
was a relief. He felt starved, and decided to visit one of the
cafés open in the evening which had spread across the city
like weeds the last few years. He didn't like to move about
openly on the streets, he avoided that as often as possible.
Before it hadn't felt like that at all, but now he'd become
furtive. There were occasions, however, like this evening,
when he made exceptions to the rule.

He regretted it the moment he stepped into the café. He
thought everyone was looking at him, and he quickly sank
down into a booth far inside the place. He ordered pancakes, syrup, and coffee, knowing it was unhealthy, but
hunger conquered good sense.

Thank heavens for Snake Marek, he thought. Services
and counterservices. Manipulations and promises. With
Marek on the scene as a mole quite near the bear, he in
any case didn't need to worry that something would happen
that he wouldn't find out about.

They would never get anywhere.

Then the pancakes came to the table and he lost interest
in Eric Bear and the Death List.

HYENA BATAILLE

Worse than pain, worse than treachery and beat-
ings. Worse than the most intense anxiety or the
most dreadful humiliation; worse than all of this is cursed
memory. Days on end can go by, then the clouds draw
in over the city, the sky darkens, and rain dampens the
wrecked cars around the place where I live: large raindrops
that indolently settle onto mangled metal car bodies. Then
the past forces its way through the membrane of time, in the
empty hole in my chest a heart is pulsing anew. And when
I awaken and everything around me is refuse and putrefaction, the collision between then and now is violent. It causes
me to lose my breath. This cursed Garbage Dump was my
destiny long before I came here.

I met Nicole Fox through an editor at the publishing
house—I don't recall his name. I still hadn't published my
first book; my collection of poems, to which I'd given the
title *approach . . . honeysuckle,* would be coming out the
following week and I was already scared to death about its
reception. I don't know if what frightened me most was the

thought of being publicly criticized, or if it would be worse to be passed over in silence. It seemed to me that the looks I encountered everywhere were insidious and scornful and I was on my way to the exit at high speed when I stumbled over Nicole Fox.

She was sitting in an armchair, and her long legs became my deliverance. I fell like a tree, but thank goodness she was the only one who noticed. Together we fled from the place. Nicole became my savior and my deliverance. Life before I met her had been a single long denial, and the poetry collection was the climax of wretchedness. The poems had been written over a period of ten years, and when I locked myself into the cellar of a condemned building in Yok with cigarettes and moonshine alcohol, I didn't give a thought to tomorrow. I'd pissed on my friends, betrayed my family, and done my best to strip myself of all pride and dignity. It was a wreck who stumbled into that cellar in Yok. I drank to fall asleep. I relieved myself on the floor in a corner of the room, but after a few days I didn't shit anymore because I didn't have anything to excrete. It was the pains in my stomach that finally forced me out of that cellar. The poems were finished, I don't know if they'd been finished for weeks or only for a day or two, but with the manuscript under my arm I made my way up to the street. I cringed in the sunlight, I thought that the wind was ripping and tearing my fur, and I thought everyone I encountered was staring at me. I walked hour after hour with my gaze on the colorful asphalt until I suddenly recognized where I was. I was in Angela's neighborhood. Because I didn't have anywhere else to go, and I knew where she hid the key, I let myself into her empty apartment and managed to eat my way through the major part of the contents of her refrigerator before she came home. When she saw me she screamed like the guenon that she was, and she didn't stop screaming before I left. I forgot the manuscript on her kitchen table, but didn't have the energy to go back and fuss about it. The poems weren't worth it. Out of pure sadism Angela turned the manuscript in to Doomsbury Verlag. The result was that an editor from Doomsbury found me at the Century Bar just over a week later. He paid my tab—that was the condition for me being able to leave the place—and with that, half of my advance for the poems was used up. Out on the street I sobered up enough that I could sign the contract. But I was nonetheless pleased; I would make my debut as a poet.

When my first book of poems was reviewed I'd been living at home with Nicole Fox for the past several days. She smelled of meadow flowers, she knew what I would say before I said it, and she had perfect pitch for when I wanted to be close and when I needed space. I was still a miserable animal without anything to risk, without spine or value, but with every day that I spent with Nicole something was growing inside me. It was self-worth.

approach . . . honeysuckle received an effusively warm reception. Without my understanding it—because I was a fool in heart and soul—it was my living together with Nicole Fox that gave me strength, and not the cane-wielding critics at the daily papers. But I believed that my newly awakened power had to do with the book, and, with Nicole's enthusiastic approval, I set out into the city to fill my arms with application forms. My life as a paralyzed hyena was over; I was intoxicated by a sense of my own will. Together with my beautiful fox, I sat the entire day and half the night, filling in small squares and writing my name on dotted lines. I applied for grants and jobs, for the first time in my life.

Everything went so fast. After many tough years of life without content, it seemed as though everything happened overnight. A marvelous everyday life emerged together with Nicole Fox. She was living in a roomy two-room apartment in Tourquai, and her neighborhood was a universe that unexpectedly opened itself to me. There was the bakery that sold bread over counters out toward the sidewalk, which is why there was always the aroma of fresh-baked rolls on the street. There was the café at the corner by the park where the milk foam was always shaped into a heart. Nicole and I lived in this idyllic state. The months passed, and finally we were on our way to being caught by grim reality that sent us insistent reminders of telephone, water, and electrical bills. It was then that I got my grant. One day in August, an anonymous, brown envelope from the Ministry of Culture's Office of Grants was lying on the hallway floor in all modesty. We celebrated that evening with a bottle of champagne, but we had a bad conscience from having been extravagant and skipped breakfast the next morning.

It was a lovely time.

Hindsight's common sense fills us with the knowledge of that which was, and that which is to come. But you have to be loyal to your younger self. What I did then, I could not have done better.

It took time to gather together the sequel to my first collection of poems. I was filled with life: I had begun not just one but two degree programs, one whose purpose was to complement the sorts of things I had gone without, and a second in order to go further in life. The poems I wrote became short and empty, light as air and just as transient. Nicole read them, and, without taking the enjoyment from me, she was definite in her criticism. Between the first collection and the happy verses I was squeezing out of me there was now a chasm. This chasm, said my wise fox, was considerably more interesting than the verses at hand.

We got married. I had no expectations about the ceremony itself. I was neither a believer nor an atheist, I didn't have time to invite either relatives or friends, and yet I felt so proud that I was about to burst. In a little pavilion in Parc

Clemeaux where the Afternoon Weather struck drumrolls against the roof, such that the deacon was forced to raise his voice: there I wed Nicole Fox. It felt like I made her my property, and I was ashamed of that feeling. We had dinner at a nice restaurant on Rue Dalida, and then Nicole fell asleep, worn out, at midnight. I sat up writing without interruption. It became a long suite of poems about hes and shes. The words dripped with self-loathing and shame over my sex, but I had no idea where all these feelings came from. Later, attentive readers would understand that there was something affected about this collection, whereupon I became very upset. But the poems were good. Nicole read them when I was finished the following evening, and she congratulated me for having found the way out that I had unconsciously sought. Here I had a worthy successor to *approach . . . honeysuckle.*

Book number two received respectful treatment as well. By this time I had finished my basic courses and had just begun doctoral studies in comparative literature. The book became the starting point for a debate about genre which I lost interest in after the first article. I applied for a new grant with the Ministry of Culture, and when I got the money, Nicole and I began to think in earnest about having cubs.

We decided to be just as wise and organized in becoming parents as we had been impulsive and passionate in our twosomeness. I immediately began to plan for my next book, and at the same time applied for yet another grant. Along with the miserable compensation I got from the Comparative Literature Department, we could get by on the money. We applied to the Cub List.

The third collection didn't offer the same birth pangs at all as the second had, and my stern, wise fox confirmed what I felt myself. Something new was in the process of being born in my writing career, something grander and more original than I had accomplished before. With every day our application for a cub climbed up the long waiting list, and poem was added to poem without the quality going down. Nicole observed the connection as obvious.

Then my life was crushed. The annihilation was meticulous and definitive. During the years to come I would curse the day I forgot the manuscript on Angela's kitchen table, the evening I stumbled over Nicole Fox's legs; if I hadn't learned what happiness was, it could never have been taken away from me. And it all depended on a single animal. Snake Marek.

I didn't even know he existed. During the entire humiliating and drawn-out process that was my case, I didn't know that Snake Marek existed. I found that out much later, by chance; it's not interesting and doesn't add anything to the story. The important thing is what he did. The decisive thing is the way in which he sat deep inside the dark culvert of the Ministry of Culture, letting bitterness ooze out of every stitch of his insignificant body. With my first two poetry collections I had passed his Argus eyes, but the third time my application forms were on his desk he caught sight of me. And for some reason that spiteful reptile decided to crush me. One day I received a letter saying that my grant money would not be coming. A new decision had been made, it read, and it had been decided to freeze my grant "for the time being."

I didn't take this seriously. I tried to reach one of the assistants at the Office of Grants on the phone, without success. Then I let the matter rest. When I mentioned in passing my worry to Nicole, she became hopping mad.

She initiated a massive apparatus. They couldn't be serious, you didn't do this kind of thing to the few geniuses that the city had produced. Nicole wrote petitions and organized debates (which were not particularly well attended). She wrote letters to the editor and tried to get others to do the same thing (but only one was published). And when at last she threatened a sit-down strike outside the Office of Grants, she finally got a response. An assistant—it proved much later to be Snake Marek himself—wrote an open letter in response. The letter was sent to the arts editors at the newspapers, to the Department of Comparative Literature, and home to me and Nicole. "The quality of Bataille's poetry," it read, "is such that a grant would send the wrong signals." Neither more nor less.

Perhaps I could have brought myself through the ordeal if that letter hadn't been written. I would have been able to lie low for a few months and then dared to come out of the apartment. Looked my colleagues in the eyes again after the summer, perhaps even smiled apologetically at Nicole Fox's exaggerated reaction. But the Ministry of Culture had written its letter, and the wording was diabolical. Everyone could freely interpret what was wrong with my poetry. It proved that I had detractors everywhere, snipers who were only waiting for the right moment.

I didn't retaliate. Despite Nicole's irritation, I didn't retaliate, I pulled the blanket even farther up over my head and stayed in bed. Day and night. The second collection of poems deserved criticism, I knew that better than anyone, I'd known it the whole time without daring to admit it. The pathos that carried the collection was fictional, I'd never been concerned with any battle of the sexes. Whatever Nicole said, I couldn't get away from the feeling of being exposed. I had Nicole bring home alcohol so that I could use the sleeping pills I'd squirreled away over the years. They worked better combined with alcohol, and I slept away a few days in a kind of unpleasant daze. It was too damn selfish; Nicole needed support, but I had a hard time putting up with myself, and the thought of finding the energy to carry her as well was impossible. When the alcohol was gone and I came to my senses again, it was the middle of the night and coal black outside the windows; I jumped out of bed and burned the almost-finished manuscript of the third collection in the sink. Nicole, who'd been sleeping on the couch in the living room, was wakened by the smoke, but by then it was too late. Together we stood and watched how the charred papers writhed in pain.

The animals at Doomsbury Verlag had of course gotten cold feet when I'd been publicly criticized. But because they knew that I had come a long way with the approaching collection, they felt pleasantly secure. When I told them that there no longer was any third book, the news spread lightning-fast across the whole city. I was lying drugged in my bed and had no idea what was about to happen.

I don't know which of all the mendacious versions of my condition reached my colleagues at the university department, but that doesn't matter. They understood that conditions had changed. In our society it's money that rules. Giving me the professorship that I had long considered mine was now out of the question. The venerable professors let one of the mice in the office call and convey the decision. My services were no longer required. How could they do that? Morally it was despicable, and it was a question as to whether it was even legal. One of the professors got in touch with me many years later, clearly tormented by his rotting conscience, and let me read the protocol of the meeting they'd had. The protocol was likely set up as evidence in case I should protest. I was described as a labile lunatic who not only was equally mediocre in my research and my poetic practice, but besides had become an abuser of pills with pyromaniac tendencies. What I needed was hospitalization, not one of the few permanent positions in the department.

I had no more than managed to digest the message from

the university when the real catastrophe occurred. In some weird way the news that I would neither get my grant nor retain my job was all over town in no time, and two days later we got a letter from the Cub List. Without incomes we were being removed from the list for the time being, it read. Impudently we were encouraged, however, to make a new attempt when our personal financial situation had improved. I recall the morning when the letter came; it still lives on in my nightmares. I got up, thinking that everything had been taken from me. I got up, believing that I was already standing at the bottom of the hole of life. But that morning I understood that nothing had been as important to me as Nicole Fox.

Across from me at the kitchen table sat my beloved fox. I had become accustomed to seeing a fire burning in her eyes. It had burned there since the day we met, and the injustices of the last few weeks had caused it to flame up. The letter from the Cub List extinguished that fire for all time.

"My love," I said. "It . . . it's going to work out."

I had nothing else to say. She didn't answer. She remained mute for several days. Our roles were reversed: she went into a kind of coma and I did my best to entice her back to life. For me this was perfect; I could finally put away my own pain and concentrate on someone else. Practical tasks kept me occupied. I bought and prepared food, I did dishes and laundry. And I consoled and consoled. Nicole did as I asked, she got up and got dressed, she ate the food I prepared, and she listened to me talk. But she was in a world of her own where I couldn't get to her, and I didn't know what was going on in her mind.

After a lunch that we ate in our kitchen in Tourquai a week or so after the letter from the Cub List, she got up, went directly into the bedroom, pulled out the suitcase from under the bed, and started packing her clothes. I'd followed her into the bedroom because I felt that something was going on, and when she started packing I asked what she was doing. She didn't answer, simply continued calmly folding her clothes and setting them in small heaps in the suitcase. I asked again. She didn't seem to hear me. I became furious; it must have been the result of the entire drawn-out process I'd gone through. I rushed over to the bed, throwing the suitcase and the neatly folded clothes onto the floor and screaming at her with the full force of my lungs. She looked me straight in the eyes and said with studied clarity, "I'm leaving you now."

And I realized that there was nothing I could do about it.

The rest of the story is uninteresting. I became what I am. I took a swing at someone when I was drunk, I kicked someone else—I don't know who they were, and that has no significance. I again became what I'd been before those weeks in the cellar and my first poetry collection. I fought because I wanted to, because it felt good, and then: because there was always someone who paid me. Much later I wound up in jail; during the first time at the correctional facility I was forced to remain sober and I learned to close myself off. I realized that it was a matter of concentration. I focused, wiping out everything that had happened between the cellar in Yok and the first drunken fistfight. In time I understood that prison was exactly like the city outside. I started fighting again, I got paid just like before, and thanks to the payment I could flee from my memories with the help of drugs. They were needed those days when I didn't have the energy to concentrate. I can forget everything, except this: Snake Marek is the animal who for no reason froze my third grant and crushed my life. This I will never forget.

CHAPTER 14

Eric was fiddling with the key he had in his pants pocket. He was standing, along with the crow, the gazelle, and Snake Marek, in the men's restroom kitty-corner from the Order Room on the ninth floor of the Environmental Ministry's imposing headquarters between Avenue Gabriel and Place de la Libération in the heart of Tourquai. Eric had pushed open the door just enough that he could peek out through the narrow doorway. The half-moon was in place; there couldn't be more than a half hour left of the Evening Weather. The Environmental Ministry was a deserted building except for the guards who were expected to patrol the floors each night. But the guards were apathetic. Eric had heard Edda complain countless times about how the security company was eager to send invoices, but hardly even managed to leave the reception area at night. Despite the fact that two inspection rounds were part of the contract.

The corridor along the meeting rooms was in darkness except for the bluish glow here and there from the plant lights. They were hanging from the ceiling like personal suns for the rubber trees, palms, and ferns, which otherwise would have folded up and died in the windowless dark. The dark-blue wall-to-wall carpeting created a subdued, sober impression.

"Is there usually some particular time that—" Sam whispered impatiently, but was immediately hushed by Eric.

"Someone's coming," hissed the bear.

As though on command, they all stopped breathing for a few long moments. They heard a door being slammed shut with a kind of metallic clang, a lock being turned, and then the sound of footsteps. Against the sound-muffling carpets it was impossible to determine if the steps were heading in their direction or not.

Tom-Tom was the first to start breathing again, like a fish on land gasping for air, and Eric became irritated.

Too many sounds were coming from the crow.

At the same time Eric didn't want to close the door completely. Not knowing what was going on was, he decided, a greater risk than staying completely hidden.

Then all four of them heard it. The crackling sound of a walkie-talkie far away, and a voice that said, "On nine now, read?"

"On nine, yes."

Eric turned around in surprise and encountered Snake's piercing gaze.

"Never leaves reception, huh?" Snake hissed.

Eric hushed him with a hand gesture. "Into the stall," he hissed, gently shoving the crow so that he would understand.

Snake was the quickest to move, but instead of wriggling over toward the toilets he slithered lightning-fast across the floor and glided down into a small wastebasket by the wash basin, where he hid himself under a crumpled paper towel. There were two stalls in the men's restroom, and it was by chance that the crow took the innermost one while Sam and Eric had to share the stall closest to the door.

"You and me in a restroom stall. A fantasy fulfilled," sighed Sam without even trying to speak especially softly, "and then the circumstances are so . . . rotten."

The gazelle giggled, closing the door and sitting down on the lowered toilet seat while Eric positioned himself to peer through the gap in the door.

"Shh," hissed Eric.

"Honestly speaking," said Sam without whispering, "what can happen? Is the guard going to throw us out?"

The gazelle was not afraid of being discovered. Of all the violations of the law he had committed over the years, a break-in at the Environmental Ministry men's room was hardly anything to write home about. Snake had surely come up with an excuse for himself that would make the situation worse for the others, and Tom-Tom was too stupid to even think of lying. In addition, the crow would neither allow himself to be arrested or questioned; in tight situations he lost control and it's the guard you'd be feeling sorry for. The only one who really couldn't be discovered was Eric.

The restroom door opened and the guard came in.

Eric shut his eyes. When he'd played hide-and-seek with Teddy when he was really little, he'd thought he became invisible if he closed his eyes. He waited. Without a single idea of how he might handle the situation. Here I stand, hiding, he thought, inside a stall in a men's restroom along with a drug-intoxicated homosexual prostitute gazelle who is particularly popular with the masochists of the city.

And Eric Bear smiled a weak smile, for the condition of things could hardly get much worse.

The guard's few footsteps across the floor over to the stall were determined. And Eric was imagining the paw on the handle on the other side when there was an unexpected crackling from the walkie-talkie. The sound echoed inside the half-tiled room.

"Yes? Over," answered the guard.

His paw was still on the door handle.

"Food's ready now," said his colleague from down in reception.

"Already? Read."

"I'm not waiting, you can come when you want."

Then the crackling ceased, and for a few, endless seconds the guard hesitated before he made his decision. With rapid steps he left the restroom. The door slammed shut.

Eric didn't open his eyes. He didn't know how long he held his breath, but he felt quite ready to faint. His shoulders sank, he opened the door and stepped out of the stall.

"Damn, I'd almost started hoping for a little action," said Tom-Tom Crow, who was coming out of the neighboring stall.

They felt strangely exhilarated, even Snake, who came winding out of the wastebasket. Eric crossly muttered a reply to the crow that no one heard, and retook his position by the door out to the corridor and the Order Room.

The full moon was old when the courier finally arrived.

Tom-Tom had fallen asleep inside one of the restroom stalls, Sam and Snake were carrying on a low-voiced conversation about nothing in particular over by the wash basin. When the elevator announced its arrival in the south corridor with a mournful ping, Eric was standing at his post by the door, but all three of them heard the sound.

The gazelle and Snake fell silent.

It was certainly not the guard taking the elevator, and it wasn't more than a few moments later that they saw him; it was some kind of feline creature. A well-pressed gray suit and the steel-rimmed eyeglasses concealed his particular features, making him anonymous. He took the direct route to the Order Room, setting his briefcase down on the floor while he dug in his pocket for a key. He unlocked the door, took the briefcase, and went into the room, from which he came out again after scarcely half a minute. He'd vanished before the moment had even become exciting.

Eric remained standing in the doorway and peeked.

"Why are we still standing here?" asked Sam impatiently. "He's definitely gone."

"That was the Cub List," whispered Eric.

And he'd scarcely uttered the word before the elevator announced the next visitor. This one, however, had a quite different appearance.

To begin with, it took a while before he showed himself in the north corridor. And when he finally arrived, it was as though he'd gotten lost. With lingering steps he looked around time after time. He was a threadbare camel with shoes so worn the right heel was missing. His pants looked as though he'd slept in them for several weeks, and the shirt that hung down over his thighs was spotted black by soot or oil. When he proved to have the key to the Order Room on a chain around his neck, they all understood that this was the only possibility: this animal was born with pockets with holes in them.

The camel went into the Order Room and came out again. The whole thing went very quickly, but in contrast to the earlier, correct civil servant with his briefcase, it was impossible to see if the camel had taken a list along.

"Now?" whispered Sam.

"We'll wait until we hear the elevator," Eric whispered back.

He involuntarily put his paw in his pocket and squeezed the key. It was the key that he'd had made when he was young, the key that he'd copied in modeling clay from Mother's key ring. And what if it didn't work? If it was the wrong key, and had been the wrong key for all these years? Or if the ministry had quite simply changed the locks since then? Stranger things had happened.

"Now, then?"

Sam's impatience demanded no explanation. All four of them had calculated what risk they were taking as of now.

If the camel had actually set a Death List . . . a real Death List in the locked Order Room, ChauffeurTiger could arrive at any moment to fetch it. And no one, not even Tom-Tom, had any desire to run into the tiger.

"Now," said Eric.

He opened the door to the restroom and quickly crossed the dark corridor. Without hesitating, without thinking, he put the key in the Order Room lock and turned it.

It worked.

When he stepped into the small room, where, just as his mother had always said, there was only a table and a desk blotter, he immediately saw the two envelopes. The one neat with typewritten letters on the front, the other looking like it had been crumpled up, thrown into a puddle, hung up to dry, and then ended up here. Eric felt Snake's presence right behind him, and intuitively he realized that there was no time to waste. Without appearing any too urgent, he ran over to the table and snatched the battered envelope at the same moment as the snake was making his way up the legs of the table with the intention of doing the same thing. Eric took a few steps to the side and opened the envelope. There was no risk that anyone would notice that the envelope had been opened and closed again; the shabby camel had seen to that.

A piece of paper, and there was a list with names, eighteen of them, typewritten in a column. Eric read.

What was there was impossible.

It was not only Nicholas Dove's name that Eric recognized on the Death List. There was another name that he knew more than well. Terror and shock caused Eric Bear to become dizzy, feel nauseous. He took a deep breath, pulled himself together, and looked up from the paper.

"It's true," Eric Bear said without moving. "There is a Death List."

CHAPTER 15

The bedroom was bathed in the gentle daylight coming in through the drawn, white curtains. On a massive double bed, thick down comforters and a dozen shapeless pillows created a white lunar landscape with high mountains and deep ravines. Resting in this realm of softness was the delicate, unclothed body that was Emma Rabbit. She was lying on her stomach, with her legs scissored around a thick bedspread and her face turned to the right, toward the windows.

The walls of the bedroom were white, the oiled oak boards of the parquet floor had become darker since they moved in, and the bed was the only piece of furniture in the room, besides the round, white rug and the overstuffed armchair where Eric Bear was sitting, observing his sleeping wife. In the bedroom on Uxbridge Street there was an aroma of sleep and well-being, but it had been several years since Eric had noticed that. Today, after having been squeezed in with the males at Yiala's Arch for two weeks, the aroma was more than tangible; it broke over him, filling him with melancholy.

He couldn't see his wife's face from the armchair where he was sitting, but he saw her thin body, and that caused tenderness to bubble up from his heart.

Was Eric Bear sitting there, secretly looking at his sleeping wife?

It couldn't be denied.

Thoughts were moving through his head, slowly but evasively. Memories and associations, scenes and words, all in a single incomprehensible jumble. He let it happen. His yoga teacher had taught him to let thoughts come and go like clouds passing over an early Forenoon Sky. He had never understood what she meant, but finally he did just what she'd said. And slowly but surely he fell through the years down toward his childhood, which is often the case if you simply let your thoughts be in peace. Morning and the bedroom faded away and disappeared, until the scent of a familiar breathing was all that remained.

A sweet-smelling breath, closed-in the way a stuffed animal's breath always is. The warm exhalations that come from the belly, that gather fragments from cotton that has never seen the light of day. From Teddy's mouth came a breath that, to be sure, was lukewarm and stale, with a touch of honey and grass, but which made Eric secure. After the nightmares, he might take the few steps across the room and jump down into Teddy's bed where his breath was waiting on the pillow, and the ghosts and demons that were haunting him disappeared. Or in the classroom, when Teddy turned around and whispered something in his ear, and Eric felt his breath sweeping past a few millimeters away; then it was those two against the world.

Alone was strong.

But two was one stronger.

During Eric Bear's entire upbringing he'd wanted to get closer to his twin brother. It was being close to Teddy that meant something, that gave him power to free himself from

Mother and dare to revolt against Father. And with every year that passed, Teddy became more and more distant.

Perhaps that was why the moments of physical proximity with his twin had survived through all these years. His breath of course, but also how in the evenings they'd used each other's bellies as pillows, and how the feeling of being a part of someone else had been a shield against the reality lying in wait outside the house on Hillville Road. They used to massage each other before they fell asleep in the evening, hard with a solid grip, or loosely with the fingertips. Even the wrestling matches, which Teddy always won as he was the stronger of the two, left behind a feeling of healing nearness despite the bruises and worn fur.

Eric had loved his twin brother. He had needed him. More than he'd loved and needed anyone else in the whole world. It was in the light of Teddy's betrayal that Eric's complicated teenage years should be seen; this betrayal which neither of them could truly say when it occurred. It was not a matter of open conflict. Teddy disappeared by degrees into his own world of peculiar ideas that he refused to account for. It hurt to be shut out. And in his attempts to compensate for the loneliness to which he was inescapably consigned—and which he feared more than anything else—he sought community in circles where community was offered only in exchange for something else.

Eric loved Teddy. Eric did everything Teddy asked for. The only problem was that Teddy asked too seldom. But when it happened . . . when it happened . . . it was such a joy. However peculiar Teddy's requests were, Eric went along. It was as though he stood, freezing, outside a shuttered-up house week after week, and then suddenly someone opened the door and asked him to come up and sit down in front of the warm fire. Coming home. Feeling secure. Not having to wonder and worry.

. . . .

When did Eric discover for the first time that everything wasn't as it should be with Teddy?

This question might be answered in two ways.

The first answer is: never.

The second answer is: at the same moment that they started school and Eric had the chance to compare his twin brother with others who were the same age. But by avoiding judging his brother's singular manner in terms of right or wrong, life went on.

Sometimes it was absurd. In his teenage years it was not uncommon for Teddy to do and say things that appeared patently peculiar. Eric defended his brother by refusing to react to these peculiarities, and together the brothers seemed like certifiable lunatics. Even if Eric didn't know what would happen if it was openly acknowledged that something was wrong, the thought frightened him.

Boxer Bloom was a fundamentalist, a conservative on the border of being a reactionary animal in all questions except political ones, where he gladly appeared to be liberal. Teddy Bear's eccentricities became more extensive the older Teddy got. The boxer became more and more irritated. Rhinoceros Edda's understanding for Teddy was exceeded only by her desire to smooth things over.

"I can't eat this," said Teddy suddenly one evening when all four of them were sitting in the kitchen on Hillville Road, having dinner.

The twins had recently turned fourteen and they were in the eighth grade. Teddy and Eric had spent the last weeks of summer vacation at Hillevie's sailing camp. Since they'd come home from camp and the family had moved into Amberville again, Boxer Bloom had done his best to pretend as though everything were fine. He imagined to himself that Teddy had undergone a magic metamorphosis over the summer, and that everything would finally be . . . normal. Now he was getting desperate. It had nothing to do with food. The reminder that they would be forced to live with Teddy's lack of accountability and compulsive thoughts for yet another year was more than Boxer could bear. When Teddy pushed aside his plate and awkwardly looked down at the table, something burst inside Boxer Bloom. With suppressed rage he muttered, "You can't eat?"

"Papa," said Teddy, who, like Eric, heard how angry his father was, "that's not the idea. I . . . I just can't."

"It's a tomato salsa, potato casserole, and veal cutlet," Boxer informed, "that your mother has devoted hours to preparing. And which you have eaten a hundred times before."

"Well," objected Mother, "perhaps not *that* many times . . ."

"Why doesn't it suit you just now?"

Boxer stared fiercely at the cub.

"If he doesn't want to, he doesn't have to, does he?" said Eric. "He's eaten the salsa and the casserole. Maybe he's full?"

"It's got nothing to do with that," said Teddy.

"Well, now," thundered Bloom. "So what does it have to do with?"

"It can't be right to kill a calf," Teddy almost whispered.

And Boxer struck his paw on the table and got up. He appeared massive where he stood looking down at them. He held one paw pointed right at the cub.

"And what in the hell do you mean?!" shouted Bloom.

But in the moment following, before Teddy had time to reply, despite the fact that the tears were already rolling down his cheeks, Eric unexpectedly flew at his father.

Mother screamed, Father cried out and staggered backwards out toward the living room. Eric was hanging around his belly in something that resembled a convulsive hug.

"No more!" shouted Eric. "No more now."

Eric didn't care about the veal cutlet and his crazy brother. Feelings of impotence had built up for several weeks, just as long as Bloom had tried to imagine that everything would be fine, and finally here was the violent, physical release.

It should be said in Boxer Bloom's defense that he did not forcibly attempt to free himself from his cub. When he regained his balance he simply stood completely still until Eric released his hold. And they remained standing like that, staring at each other, the cub openly aggressive, the father more surprised. Before they recovered enough to say anything to each other, Teddy got up from the table out in the kitchen. The sound caused Eric to turn around, and he saw his twin brother running up the stairs.

"There are limits," said Bloom flatly. "A limit for when it's gone too far and we can't take care of it ourselves any longer."

Eric turned around again and stared into the dog's eyes.

"Your love ought to be boundless," Eric whispered scarcely audibly, "but it never has been."

Whereupon he turned and ran up the stairs after Teddy.

Emma Rabbit turned around in the bed.

Eric Bear gave a start, restored in an instant to the present. He looked at her and how in her sleep she was searching for the blanket because she was cold lying there on her back. She pulled one of the large, white comforters over her, again disappearing out of his field of vision. The tears were running from Eric's eyes without his realizing it. Soundlessly he got up. It was a little more than two weeks since he'd seen her last. But tonight, after he'd put the Death List back in its crumpled envelope, he was compelled to come here instead of to Yiala's Arch. Compelled to see her, to carefully stroke her forehead in her sleep.

He had intended to sneak out of the bedroom and let it be fine like that, but he wasn't able to. Not just now. He stood up, taking a few steps over toward the bed. She turned her head, and her whiskers twitched from the dream she was having. It was strange, he thought, that he dared to love someone like this. Again. To make yourself so defenseless, to risk being wounded so terribly. Again. After everything that had happened with Teddy.

Eric looked at his sleeping wife and smiled. But she wouldn't hurt him. And it was this certainty, this self-assured thought that meant that he'd dared. He loved her because she was worthy of being loved, and he, more clearly than anyone else, could see that.

Carefully he sneaked out of the bedroom, avoiding the plank in the floor right next to the threshold, the one that always creaked. He walked quickly through the living room and out into the hall, succeeded in opening and closing the door without the least sound, and only a few moments later he was en route in his gray Volga Combi.

A Death List existed.

It was not drawn up by the Chauffeurs.

And Nicholas Dove was there on the list.

The list consisted of names and dates, that was all. On certain days no one would be picked up, other days there was more than one. Such was the case the twenty-first of May.

That was the day the Chauffeurs would pick Nicholas Dove up.

That was in four days.

But on the twenty-first of May there had been one more name. Yet another stuffed animal would be taken away from this life in four days.

Teddy Bear.

CHAPTER 16

May I go home now?"

Snake Marek sounded hopeful.

Eric Bear was sitting on a barstool at a minimal bar counter; Snake found himself on the same counter. All the Springergaast boutiques nowadays boasted this kind of bar, situated in the midst of an explosion of colorful boutique furnishings and advertising posters which some advertising-agency genius—perhaps employed at Wolle & Wolle—maintained stimulated sales. The bear and the snake had each ordered a cup of coffee and a blueberry muffin. Around them packages of cookies and chips, bulk candies, soda pop labels, and even fresh fruit competed for attention. There was an aroma of fresh-ground coffee and baked croissants. Eric had chosen to move the meeting to Springergaast on Carrer Admiral Pedro, a few blocks from Yiala's Arch, because he wanted to be alone with Snake. And few customers came to this boutique.

"Lay off," he said.

"I didn't think so," sighed Snake with disappointment.

Yesterday evening all their plans had been upset. When

Eric saw Teddy's name on the Death List it was no longer a question of simply saving Emma.

His first reaction was shock. But intuitively Eric realized that he couldn't show any weak spots with Snake in the room, and therefore he was forced to act as if nothing over and above what was expected was on the list. If Snake hadn't been there, if Eric had given his feelings free rein? Then he would have fallen apart.

"Have you thought about my request?" asked the bear.

"Which one?"

"Saving someone from a soon-to-be dead man's death sentence."

"If you think I'm smart enough to figure out something like that, surely you must realize I'm smart enough to understand what this is all about," Snake answered with irritation.

Eric shrugged his shoulders.

"Presumably," he said.

"Dove has threatened your sweet Rabbit. If the Chauffeurs get Dove, his gorillas fetch the rabbit."

Eric shrugged his shoulders again. This was an acknowledgment.

"And?" he asked. "What do I do?"

"I have no idea," answered Snake, sounding so uninterested that Eric had a hard time not letting himself be provoked, despite the fact that he understood that this had been the reptile's intent.

"You could bribe the gorillas, couldn't you?" suggested the long-tongued Marek.

"Bribe the gorillas?"

"Yes, what the hell do I know?"

"You've worked at Casino Monokowski, you've worked for Nicholas Dove, and you're suggesting that I should bribe the gorillas?"

"Honorably stated and with all due respect, I don't give a damn about either," said Snake.

Eric sat silently. There must be a reason, he thought, for it was apparent that Snake was looking for a reaction. Perhaps, he thought further, it had to do with the Death List? Perhaps Snake, who was sensitive to the weaknesses of animals, understood that something had happened in the Order Room, something that had worsened the bear's situation? And perhaps Snake was out to reveal this through his provocations? Both of them knew that you could never have too much information when power was concerned.

They each took a bite of blueberry muffin and pondered the next move.

"Do you think Tom-Tom can do anything?" asked Eric.

"What would that be?"

"He's a crazy bastard," stated Eric, "deep down inside. Perhaps he'd be able to make them see reason?"

"If you toss in the gazelle too, it's not impossible," said Snake.

They each took another bite; it was a suitably doughy yet flavorful muffin.

The gorillas had reason to fear a berserk crow. But even if Tom-Tom and Sam together might frighten away many gorillas on the way, they could never frighten them all off.

"If I know the dove rightly," said Snake, "he has in addition promised an enormous reward to the one who proves that he took care of your Rabbit. An accountant in some shabby office somewhere in town is just waiting, with an authorization in his desk drawer, for someone to come in with proof. And that means it's not just the crazy gorillas you have to take care of, but the bounty hunters as well."

Eric sighed. That's how it was of course, he'd realized it too.

"And the chance of successfully completing our assignment?" asked Eric.

"You mean removing Dove from the list?"

Eric nodded. Actually he wanted nothing better than to

tell about Teddy, but nothing positive would come out of such a confession. So he nodded again.

"I don't know," said Snake. "We've proved that there is a list. I didn't think we'd succeed in that."

"I knew there was a list," said Eric.

"You didn't know that at all," said Snake.

"But removing someone, pardoning someone . . . ?"

"Among all the legends about the Death List," answered Snake, "there are a few that speak of something like that. And I'm not just thinking of that story about the archdeacon."

While the coffee cooled and Eric ate up both his and Snake's blueberry muffin, Snake told the story of Horse Carl and Admiral Pedro.

Horse Carl was the hero who, more than two hundred years ago, united the four parts of the city after almost a century of civil war, temporary alliances, and betrayed promises. Today all schoolchildren read about Horse Carl, but not many knew, said Snake in a tone of utter contempt, that as a reward for his efforts Horse was awarded the opportunity to pardon one animal each year from the Death List.

"No, wait," protested Eric, "I've never heard anything about that . . ."

"As I said," snapped Snake Marek, irritated by the interruption, "this is about legends, myths. There's nothing that's true or false. But I can understand if the authorities try to keep this type of story from being retold. I have a hard time seeing which department would benefit from the story of Horse Carl . . ."

And then he continued:

Horse Carl soon understood that the possibility of pardoning someone could be used in the power play that had arisen among the leading animals in the four parts of the city. Carl established a new tradition. A small selection of judges, generals, highly placed politicians, and one or two truly significant landowners would get to vote each year for one of the animals on the Death List. The animal who counted up the most votes would be removed, and all those involved could enjoy the feeling of power: power over life and death even greater than what they'd had before the city's unification.

Everything functioned according to Horse Carl's plan up until the year when both David Owl and Admiral Pedro were on the Death List. For many years the admiral had been in command of the rather insignificant fleet in Hillevie, but he was still young, and that his name showed up on the list came as a complete surprise, both to him and to everyone else. Pedro was seized by panic, applied for and was granted discharge from the fleet, and then devoted all his time toward attempting to influence the animals who would be voting to cast their votes for him. When the day for the announcement of the pardon came, it proved, however, that Judge David Owl had nevertheless received more votes than the former admiral Pedro.

Pedro was furious. He demanded to meet Horse Carl. Carl granted the audience and expressed regret at the decision, but explained that he could do nothing about it. The judgment had fallen, the person who would be pardoned was David Owl, that's how it was decided. Why couldn't Carl pardon both of them, asked Pedro.

Horse Carl sighed heavily. It was impossible.

"Why was it impossible?" asked Eric Bear in much too loud a voice.

"It was just impossible," repeated Snake Marek, once again irritated at having been interrupted.

Well.

Former admiral Pedro made the most logical decision of which he was capable, under the circumstances. He went with a military stride directly from the audience with Horse

Carl to David Owl and cut off the judge's head with a saber. Then he took the head into the forest and buried it. In this way, thought Pedro, they should pardon the one who had received the next most votes.

But there former admiral Pedro was mistaken. Instead, the possibility of pardoning animals was taken away from Horse Carl with immediate effect.

"Taken away by who?" asked Eric.

"The story doesn't say," said Snake.

The Death List was classified as secret, no one knew in advance who was on it (and after a hundred years we didn't even know if the list itself existed), and the routine with the Coachmen, later the Chauffeurs, was introduced.

Snake Marek fell silent. After a long while Eric said, "This indicates at least that someone decides, and therefore there must be a possibility of influence."

"Perhaps one might see it that way," nodded Snake.

"Now we'll go home and decide how we proceed from here," said Eric.

Snake nodded, and they slid down from barstool and counter and left Springergaast.

The night of the eighteenth of May became another night of alcohol, cards, and bizarre notions in the kitchen at Yiala's Arch. Just in time for the Evening Storm, the bottles were uncorked. Crow showed signs of dexterity as he shuffled the cards with his longest finger feathers, Snake wriggled up onto the kitchen table and made himself ready for the first deal while Sam stole into the bathroom to make himself a cocktail of pills before it was time to play. Eric lit the tea lights and poured drinks for everyone.

Tom-Tom Crow only pretended to get drunk. When the others weren't looking, he stole away to the kitchen sink, pouring out the vodka and replacing it with water. Then he cawed loudly and drunkenly for the sake of appearances. He couldn't bring himself to drink; the last few days he'd felt strange, sensitive in a way he didn't like; tonight he'd been awakened by tears running down his beak. He knew what was causing it, but he struggled to force the memories back into the deep ravines of forgetting.

Eric Bear, on the other hand, got drunk as a sailor. Drunker than he'd ever been. He'd intended to hold back, intended to guide his intoxicated companions through the night and direct them back up onto navigable paths of association when they slipped down into the ditch.

That's not how it turned out.

When alcohol got the upper hand and Eric could no longer defend himself against his feelings, the bear disappeared first down into deep resignation, where he felt very comfortable because resignation excused him. What could he really do, asked resignation. He was fighting against death, and no mortal was victorious over death. Despite the fact that they'd gotten hold of a Death List, it felt just as unlikely as it had a few weeks ago that they would succeed in rescuing Nicholas Dove back to life. The only thing they had acquired was information about the Chauffeurs and the list that was mortally dangerous. It was of utmost importance that no one said anything, Eric observed anxiously. It was of utmost importance that these idiots for companions in Sam Gazelle's kitchen could keep their mouths shut.

"Airybody," attempted Eric Bear, "gotchto choosed. Now!"

But no one cared to try to interpret his slurring, and it was just as well. The two animals Eric loved most were at risk of dying, and he had only three days to do something about it. He felt inexplicably sorry for himself, and he thought he had the right to immerse himself in self-pity.

But the more he drank, the harder it was to hold on to this almost apathetic sorrow. The vodka heated him up. It was so unfair, he thought. It was as though a higher power was playing a joke on him, as if someone truly wanted to see him suffer and therefore let him discover his brother's name on the list. Dove can go to hell, the bear thought crossly, and the anger chased away the loneliness and caused him to feel strong. Dove can go to hell, he thought again, and fate can go to hell, too.

Eric got up from the table. His chair fell over and the crash caused the others to fall silent and look up. He had absolutely nothing to say. He looked at them, one after the other, and was filled with a powerful love. They were sitting here for his sake; they were loyal. His bear heart was transformed into a cleaning sponge, soggy with alcohol and sentimentality, and tears welled up in the corners of his eyes. His friends. His confidants.

"Eric," asked Tom-Tom, "what the hell are we doing now, actually?"

Eric Bear turned slowly toward Tom-Tom and tried in vain to focus his gaze.

"Yes, then," repeated the crow, "I don't get what the hell we should do."

That swine, thought Eric, perplexed, and all his beautiful feelings evaporated. Does the big crow doubt my ability?

"I think we put Noah Camel up against the wall," said Sam from over by the dish rack.

The gazelle was doing dishes? Eric squinted in order to make Sam out better. Indeed, he was standing there doing dishes. Wasn't that overly zealous?

"Noah Camel?" asked Snake.

"He must have gotten the list from someone," Sam defended himself, assuming that Snake thought badly of the idea.

"Was that camel bastard at the ministry?" asked Tom-Tom.

"You know who he is?" said Snake.

All of these retorts flying back and forth through the

room confused Eric Bear. He understood that something was about to happen, something important, but he didn't know what it was. Noah Camel?

"Noah and I . . . know each other," said Sam, adding hesitantly, "you might say . . ."

"And you're just saying that now?" Snake Marek almost screamed.

His irritation knew no limits.

"But this is good, isn't it?" asked Tom-Tom.

Three days might be enough, thought Eric.

NOAH CAMEL

can't understand it can't understand it can't understand how
someone can want to cause such pain such pain such pain
and tears don't help because I'm freezing 'cause it's cold, it's
always cold cold but I'm not freezing because it's cold, I'm
freezing from fear, I'm freezing down to the marrow and
stuffing and this cold hurts so bad it hurts so bad

saw Sam Gazelle coming, saw him coming from the window
in the hall, saw him coming from the window in the hall and
it made me a little happy even because even if I knew he was
dangerous we were friends he and I we were friends he and I
for we'd met once long ago and I knew he was dangerous for I
knew who he was and what he liked to do but I thought that
was just talk because there's so much talk and there's too much
talk and I opened the door when he rang the bell and asked
him to come into the kitchen and sit down and maybe have
coffee or a beer for you're supposed to be nice to your friends

he took a fork and poked it through my leg, through cloth and
cotton, the metal teeth of the fork right through my leg from

one side to the other so I was stuck to the table and I can't
describe how much it hurt how horribly painful it was but still
I almost didn't feel the pain because I got so scared, so scared
that my whole body started shaking but I didn't scream even if
I should have screamed but I wept silently and looked at Sam
Gazelle who I thought was my friend and I didn't understand
I didn't understand I didn't understand a thing

he questioned me and threatened me and said that if I didn't
talk he would burn me, just like that he said that he would
burn me and I saw in his eyes that he wanted to burn me
whatever the hell I said and by then I was almost happy because I understood why he'd stuck the fork through my leg,
he was after something, he wanted to know what I knew
and that's the kind of thing that happens all the time, it was
understandable and I didn't give a damn who killed who so
I told him, told him everything I knew about where I'd gone
before and where I went after I'd been up to the ministry
and then everything was as it should be, then he'd gotten
what he wanted and then he could go away again, leave
again and I never wanted to see him again

but he didn't go

he did things with me I can't talk about 'cause they're much
too terrible to say with words, things that are so horrible
you can't even mention them and when I think about everything he did I go completely dark inside for I don't want to
tell what he did with me, Sam Gazelle, but he did it over
and over again and he never got enough and I screamed
and I cried and I fainted and dreamed and woke up and he
was still there and said that he'd come up with something
new that he wanted to try and sometimes he laughed and
sometimes he was serious and I don't know if he saw me at
all and the pain was . . . the pain was so enormous that I

almost couldn't feel it despite the fact that it was so great that it caused me to faint

but it wasn't the pain that was the worst it wasn't when he did what he did that was the most terrible but rather it was just before he was going to do it just before in the breath before he said that he wanted to try something new

can't understand it can't understand it can't understand how you can want to cause such pain such pain such pain and tears don't help because I'm freezing because it's cold, it's always cold cold down to the marrow and stuffing and it's burning, the cold, it's burning and it's on fire and it hurts so bad it hurts so bad

and I screamed and screamed that I would tell everything he wanted to know and there was nothing that I wouldn't tell if he only asked me to and I cried and screamed that I'll do everything you want and I'll tell everything you want if you just stop stop stop I'll tell tell tell but he told me to shut up he told me to go to hell he didn't give a damn what I had to tell, he said, and my desperation was greater than . . .

and I screamed and I screamed
and I told and I told
and I fainted and woke up and fainted and woke up
and finally I fainted again

can't understand it can't understand it can't understand how it hurt so bad so bad so bad and tears don't help because I'm freezing because it's cold, life is always cold and life will always remain that way until the fire catches up with me and ignites me and consumes me and eradicates me and only then will I stop freezing, perhaps I'll stop freezing then perhaps

TEDDY BEAR, 3

I move about freely. I am living a free life.

Eleven paintings in narrow, white wooden frames hang in the corridor on my floor. Abstract art. Painted with a lot of water and a knife's edge of pastel paint. I don't like them. I never would have chosen them myself. But in that case, would I have made things too easy for myself?

These paintings, in particular the two hanging before my door, counting from the stairwell, irritate me. Irritation stimulates reflection. Reflection develops me.

With paintings that I appreciated I would have stagnated.

My room is my universe. My bedroom and my bathroom.

I take my meals with the others in the dining hall one floor down.

Every week I go into the city. I take long city walks. I keep myself up-to-date. I know they're performing a comedy by Bergdorff Lizard at the Zern Theater. It's a tragic piece that must be carried by the individual efforts of the actors. Every other week I visit Mother and Father. I call them in advance and tell them I'm coming. I don't want to surprise them at an unsuitable moment. I know that Father thinks my visits can be trying. I wish he himself would choose to see me.

As it is, he chooses not to.

Eric comes out to my place to visit.

Mother and Father never do.

What is more absurd than the life I'm living today is how defensive I get when I have to describe the life I'm living today.

That says something about society.

I shouldn't need to defend myself.

On the other hand, I might agree that it's peculiar that I'm married and responsible for the city's leading advertising agency at the same time as I'm living this life in my own universe.

The mayor appointed our mother as head of the Environmental Ministry the same week that I completed my academic degree.

Mother has worked at the Environmental Ministry her entire life. At the transportation and energy offices, she had been in charge of recycling issues and responsible for the city's road maintenance.

Nonetheless, her appointment came as a shock to those of us who were close to Mother.

There were many of us who were close to her.

I was the closest to her.

Her double identities were so well separated that I had a hard time seeing her in a role as a department head. To me her list of qualifications consisted of slow-cooking and roll-baking. For Mother herself this political success was expected. The animals in the city as well felt that the choice of Rhinoceros Edda was a good one. Mayor Lion knew what she was doing. Her most important mission was to appoint popular department heads. If she made popular decisions, the Mayor's chances of reelection increased.

We celebrated Mother's appointment in the evening. It was a Thursday in the beginning of June. There was me, my brother, and Mother and Father. We sat in the kitchen, and Father had bought a bottle of champagne after work. The news about Mother had been in the newspaper and Father got a discount on the champagne.

I don't recall what we ate.

I smiled dutifully, raised my glass, and toasted.

I was deeply downhearted.

I had applied for an internship at the Environmental Ministry. For several years Mother had been in charge of the Planning Division, which dealt with issues of city planning and resource allotment. Her office was in Lanceheim. I had applied for a job at the Energy Unit in Tourquai. I believed that my future was in advanced energy research.

Now that was impossible.

With Mother as head of the Environmental Ministry my application papers would be questioned. My competency would be closely scrutinized. Even if I were deemed qualified, there would always be a measure of doubt.

I sipped the champagne, feeling confused.

What would I do now?

Time would help me answer that question, but that evening I felt the weight of an unobliging fate. For several years I had set my heart on a career in the Environmental Ministry, a place of employment big enough to hold both me and Mother.

Father gave a little speech.

"In order to gain something you have to give up something else," he said.

His eyes glistened. I had never before seen him cry. Now a tear of pride was rolling down his cheek.

"But what you have given up, I don't know," he continued. "It's not your family, in any case. Not your friends, either. Or your cooking ability. Perhaps it's the other way around, because you've refused to give up, that you have gained?"

He'd intended to say something else, but Mother stood up and silenced him with a hug.

Eric applauded.

I applauded too. This took the edge off my brother's irony. My smile, however, was still strained.

Then I recall a cozy evening in the kitchen. I recall that I set my disappointment aside to be happy with Mother. I recall that Eric and Father for once found something around which to unite. We showered Mother with congratulations and prophesied success for her in things both great and small. Not until I turned off the lamp on my nightstand did I again recall the situation that Mother had unknowingly put me in. I brooded a while, but soon fell asleep.

I was no longer the lost bear I'd been before.

I had become aware of myself.

These words from my late teens still apply. This was the way I saw, and still see, myself:

I am a stuffed animal who cannot commit an evil action. I am an animal who is driven to always, as far as is possible, do right.

With that it was said.

Not so remarkable.

Nonetheless, unusual.

This insight about how things stood grew during my secondary school years, but it was in the final grade that these intuitions blossomed into certainty.

When I understood, it was impossible to understand that I hadn't already understood.

I'd always been the same, but when I was little I was not in command of my actions. Someone else—my parents or teachers or other grown-ups—decided in my place. Besides, I could still not determine what was right and wrong. I was brought up to believe that there was a kind of unwritten rule book in ethics to fall back on in difficult cases, and that you weren't allowed to read that book before you were an adult.

I imagined to myself that I could disregard my intuitive sense of what was right and wrong, and that the anxiety created by the conflicts between my own conviction and the norms of society was just part of being a teenager.

That I would grow into myself.

That it was a matter of maturity.

Poor wretch.

Let me give examples:

I don't walk against red lights.

I don't tell "white lies."

I redid one of my last examinations after I'd accidentally caught a glimpse of the answers my neighbor had filled in and then couldn't figure out what I'd happened to see and which answers were my own. Despite the fact that the likelihood that I was influenced was very, very small. Despite the fact that he'd never done better than me on any test.

I'm not some kind of compulsive truth-sayer who can't keep his thoughts to himself. I don't run over to strange animals and accuse them of living in sin. But I suffer—and I don't hesitate to use the word "suffer"—from an effort to be good and truthful in a way that restricts my life.

When I look back, I realize that it's always been like that.

I talked with Mother and Father and Eric about the matter. They reacted in different ways.

I spoke with Father one morning when he had time and was sitting, enjoying the newspaper with a cooling cup of coffee. That was the way he liked his coffee best. Cold. I did my best to express what I was feeling. Father's sense of justice was almost paralyzing. It was one of the most distinguishing features of his character, and I thought he would understand.

He didn't understand.

He looked at me as if I were crazy. He muttered that life didn't let itself be tamed. That principles were a way of surviving. That terms like "good" and "evil" always had to be put into context. After that he lost interest in his line of reasoning and returned to his newspaper and his cold coffee.

Mother didn't understand, either.

We were on our way to the market hall in Amberville one Sunday the month after I'd finished my degree.

"I had a plan for the future," I explained. "But then it didn't work out. It doesn't matter. My mission is more important than anything else."

"What mission, darling?" asked Mother.

I told her. About being good, and what that entailed. About the illusory simplicity of the promise. How it was a matter of a full-time occupation and that perhaps I would have a hard time managing much more than that.

Mother didn't understand.

I tried to explain three times, three times she changed the subject and instead talked about the red beets that we were on our way to buy.

Eric understood everything. This was no surprise. We were each other's antitheses; if he hadn't understood, it would have been strange.

Eric understood everything, but didn't agree with anything.

Getting Eric interested in goodness was like getting a reptile interested in doing laundry.

After the summer, I applied for a job at an advertising agency.

It was by pure chance. A good friend of Father's had told about a job as an assistant. The pay was better than for an established energy researcher. I sent in my application papers without any expectations. I will never understand why they decided to call me in for an interview. Two days after the interview they called and offered me the job. Father's friend had exaggerated the pay, but only marginally. I arranged to start at the advertising agency Wolle & Wolle the first of October.

Wolle Hare and Wolle Toad had located their office in the Lanceheim district. Of the city's four districts, Lanceheim is the largest. In Lanceheim there are both hectic office districts and broad, illuminated shopping blocks. In Lanceheim there are large, green areas of single-family homes in the north and crowded apartment blocks of high-rises and underground garages in the west. The advertising agency Wolle & Wolle was on plum-violet Place Great Hoch, just over a block from the Star and walking distance from the advertising school where the hare and the toad had once met.

The position I took was as assistant to Wolle Toad, the stingy, bean-counting Wolle in the successful duo.

I didn't think it would mean anything.

I thought my mission in life had to do with goodness. That the job was something I could go to in the morning and go home from in the evening. Nothing more.

It didn't turn out that way. Not at all.

I met Emma Rabbit on the outskirts of my universe.

In a neighboring galaxy.

She was an angel. If I close my eyes, I see her before me clad in white. How she floats up the stairway.

Can it have been at Wolle & Wolle? In that case, Emma must have felt as uncomfortable there as I did.

That was why we sought each other out. We were both in the wrong place at the same time. Forced to be in the wrong place, for different reasons.

Deep down, Emma Rabbit didn't want to work at an advertising agency at all. She despised the advertising industry. It was for art that she lived and about art that she dreamed. It was in her studio apartment in Tourquai that she showed me the minimalist canvases where she, with the finest pony-hair brush and watercolors, created enchanted forests and meadows and fields and mountains.

After that evening my fascination turned to veneration.

In Emma Rabbit's imagination lived primeval forests and wide-branching, richly fragrant deltas.

No one listened like she did.

With her head to one side and those big eyes that followed every thought. From its source to its outlet. I had never been able to talk with anyone that way.

It made me happy.

It made me unhappy. How many years had passed without my having a friend like her?

I brooded.

The job as assistant to Wolle Toad offered independence. I was creating routines on the basis of a responsibility that I myself had defined. This suited me well. My time was required, not my thoughts. This meant that I could devote myself to significant questions.

I was worried.

I was almost alone in putting value on that goodness that ought to be desirable for everyone.

I believe, I explained to Emma as we sat across from each other and her large eyes were locked with mine, that all animals are delivered good. But from the first day outside the factory we are exposed to temptations.

To expose the good to temptations is the challenge and driving force of evil. Evil derives its nourishment by luring the good stuffed animal to commit mistakes.

What worried me was how unequal the battle was. I drew

up a number of maxims in order to make clear the relationship between good and evil.

Evil had a clear advantage.

Like this:

Evil is impossible without goodness. Evil seeks balance, it seeks symmetry. Evil is social, because it only exists in an opposing relationship. Goodness is self-sufficient. It needs no one, nothing. I can be good on my own. But to manifest evil requires a counterpart.

Evil is restless, goodness passive. Evil constantly seeks ways to reach its goal. If one temptation isn't enticing, evil tries another. Goodness seeks nothing, because it knows in advance how it should be good. If evil is dynamic, changeable, and intellectually stimulating, goodness is, to put it bluntly, boring. Goodness doesn't have much to put up in defense in the battle against all the temptations of evil. Evil is incomprehensible and absurd. Goodness lacks a short-term force of attraction.

Against the background of these suppositions, I asked Emma Rabbit, is it possible for an intelligent animal to remain good? Or, in reality, is goodness only possible for fools?

Emma Rabbit shook her tender head and wrinkled her plastic nose.

She didn't have the answer. But in her eyes a possibility glistened.

I showered her with questions.

Are good actions without genuinely good intentions pointless? Are good intentions which result in misery disguised evil? If goodness is a matter of faith, is goodness impossible for the agnostic or atheist? Is there a clear connection between goodness and spiritual harmony? Is there a connection between evil and anxiety? If there isn't such a connection, how will goodness find its adherents?

Emma Rabbit looked into my eyes. She had no answers, but together with her I dared to formulate the questions.

There were no answers, and together with Emma I was secure enough to dare to admit that.

The first time Emma met Mother, we were treated to mushroom risotto with boiled viper's grass and béarnaise sauce in the kitchen in Amberville. With it was served the pickled pumpkin preserve that was Mother's specialty. That same afternoon Mother had baked a rich carrot bread and had time to season the fresh cheese with dill. Mother had exerted herself.

Father thought that the vanilla sauce with lime and confectioner's sugar was a tad bitter when it was served with the rhubarb pie.

Emma thought there was a lot of food.

Eric was, as usual, not at home.

Many times I've tried to recall the conversation we carried on in the kitchen that evening, but I don't recall a single word.

I recall that Emma was tense.

In her eyes it wasn't my mother who, with an apron around her voluminous trunk, stirred the risotto, it was the legendary department head Rhinoceros Edda.

Several months later Emma hinted that she had expected something else. I can only speculate about what she meant. Perhaps candelabras and crystal chandeliers, servants and a political discussion. Politics had never been discussed in the little kitchen on Hillville Road. There we talked about cooking, sports, and everyday things.

Emma was not interested in politics. From that it followed that she was politically unaware. Did Emma say something foolish about politics that evening? Something Mother and Father found inappropriate? Was I ashamed in such a case? I hope that I wasn't ashamed. The shame of being ashamed is heavy to bear.

I loved Emma Rabbit. You shouldn't be ashamed of your beloved.

Love had come stealthily. Love had waited, lain in wait and attacked when I least suspected it.

I'd been defenseless.

The first days I didn't dare say anything. We attended to our roles as usual. She asked how the night had been, I answered that it had been good. She asked if I wanted to have the window open or closed. I answered closed.

But I answered with a joy that I couldn't rein in. Love made me strong and exhilarated. It didn't take very long before I told her how I felt.

I was afraid of how she would react.

In the kitchen with Mother and Father, she was the one who was afraid. Why didn't she let her eyes sparkle and reveal all their warmth and joy? When Mother asked about her ambitions and mentioned that I'd told her about her paintings, why didn't she say anything?

At ten o'clock Emma went home.

It was as if she'd never been there.

Mother and I sat down in the living room. We heard Father upstairs. Often he would sit at the desk in their bedroom and work until far into the night. I needed times to talk alone with Mother. It was a need she'd implanted in me, just as physical as my need for food or sleep. The spiritual closeness I felt toward her was coupled with these conversations.

As usual, we'd each opened a bottle of mineral water and placed them in front of us on the coffee table.

"Teddy, she's marvelous," said Mother as we heard Father's footsteps from upstairs.

Then an insight struck me. When I heard Mother praise Emma Rabbit, common sense forced its way up through my amatory intoxication. For a moment I saw my beloved objectively. As Mother saw her.

I shut my eyes.

But a feeling of uncertainty remained. I understood that there was another way of looking at Emma Rabbit, in a different light than love's rosy shimmer. I understood that the essence of my love was a loss of distance. This sort of absorption in one's self and one's own feelings was one of evil's many temptations. Without distance, I felt myself pleasantly free from responsibility.

This made me afraid.

I consoled myself that this insight about the danger made it harmless. (Later I understood that this thought, too, was an attempt by evil to overthrow my mission in life.)

I tried to restrain myself. In the morning when Emma Rabbit came in I kept my eyes shut.

But it's your deepest emotions that are the most difficult to conceal.

Emma Rabbit was like a drug. I could not refrain from the delight mixed with terror she infused into my heart.

One day we took a long walk on the shore in Hillevie. Emma had come to get me without advance notice.

We have something to celebrate, she said.

She didn't say what it was. The daytime breeze picked up as we came down to the sea. Her ears bumped against her cheeks. She held on to me so as not to fall down. I held on to her. There was a scent of salty damp from the sea and of damp yarn around Emma. In a little more than a quarter of an hour the Afternoon Rain would be over Mollisan Town, while we were walking securely out here in Hillevie, watching the dark clouds passing over our heads.

"Teddy," she said, "I've given notice."

She was beaming with happiness. With happiness.

I was struck with panic. If she hadn't been holding me under the arms I would have fallen flat onto the cold sand.

"Emma Rabbit," I said, "will you marry me?"

I had thought about asking earlier. I had abstained. I'd been wise and strategic. I was through with so-called wisdom now. A seagull was screeching out over the sea.

"Emma Rabbit," I repeated, "will you marry me?"

Later she would tease me about that. It was my need for control that caused me to get to the point, she would say. When I realized that I wouldn't get to see her at work anymore.

She was so lovely on the shore at Hillevie. Happy as a cub at having finally made her decision and chosen art.

I put a damper on the mood with my proposal. I couldn't let be.

"Emma Rabbit," I said for a third time, "will you marry me?"

Her broad smile became even broader. She nodded and whispered, "Yes, thanks." It was enchanting.

In the very next moment I knew that I could never carry out the marriage.

It had to do with Father.

Eric and I grew up with a powerful father figure. Boxer Bloom served not only as our role model; he was a role model for many. The stories about him were legion. The one I personally placed foremost, and which moved me most deeply, dealt with pride, dignity, and respect. It dealt with a stuffed animal's attitude toward his place of employment.

When I started at Wolle & Wolle, it was unavoidable that I compared myself to my father.

Father had been trained as a schoolteacher. Immediately after his education, he started to work at the elementary school in Amberville, where he later remained. He taught chemistry and physics and made himself known for his un-usually just treatment of the pupils. He became the school system's living model, who proved that it was possible to treat everyone alike: cats and chimpanzees, foxes and badgers.

Therefore it was peculiar that Rector Owl called on Father in that particular affair that would transform their lives.

This was at the time when Eric and I were not yet in school, because we were too little. One evening as Father sat correcting papers in his office, there was an unexpected knock at the door. Father stopped what he was doing and looked out through the window. The storm had swept in over the city. Father often worked late, because he could be in peace in the evenings. Now he asked the person who was knocking to come in. To Father's astonishment, Bo Owl was standing outside the door.

"Bloom," said Rector Owl, "do you have a minute?"

Of course Father had a minute for the venerable rector. Owl had already been serving at Amberville when Father had been a pupil at the school. Father pushed his papers aside and prepared to listen. It was the first time Owl had called on him after school hours.

"You do have Nathan in your physics class, don't you?" said Bo Owl.

Nathan was Bo Owl's cub, a beaver who'd been delivered to the rector and his wife late in life. Now Owl's cub was in one of Father's final-year classes, and he had major problems with physics.

Father nodded thoughtfully, and said, "With your help, Bo, I'm certain that Nathan is going to pass his examination."

"Unfortunately that's not good enough, Bloom," sighed the owl. "Nathan wants to continue his studies at the art academy. So he has to have the highest grades in all of his subjects, even in physics. Just passing isn't good enough."

"Then he's really going to have to work at it," declared Father.

That Beaver Nathan would receive the highest grades in physics, Father considered to be more or less impossible.

Nathan had neither aptitude for nor understanding of the subject.

"We're planning to work at it," the rector assured him. "You can be quite certain that I as well as Nathan are going to do everything in our power to succeed."

Father nodded.

"But what I would really appreciate," continued the rector, "were if you, Bloom, also did everything you could."

Father said that he always did his best. According to his opinion, most of the pupils responded well.

Father misunderstood the rector's intentions. The idea of giving Beaver a grade that had nothing to do with his efforts was so preposterous that it didn't occur to Father.

Rector Owl was forced to become explicit to the point of vulgarity. The conversation ended with Owl openly threatening Father. If Beaver Nathan wasn't guaranteed the highest grade in physics, Father would lose his job.

Father left school that evening crushed. When he came home, at first he didn't want to tell Mother what had happened. That an animal he had long admired could behave in this way made him deeply distressed.

He did not consider giving in to the threat.

Toward midnight he told how things stood. Mother's reaction was practical.

"But we'll never be able to afford living here," she said.

Mother understood immediately that Father didn't intend to accommodate Owl. He would thereby lose his job. The monthly payments for the mortgage on the house in Amberville were still high and Mother's career had not yet taken off.

"No, no, there's no danger," said our naïve father. "It's clear that Rector Owl is going to come to his senses."

Father was convinced that the rector would feel regret.

Father was convinced that the rector would call on him the very next day and apologize. The apology would be accepted, Boxer explained to Mother that night; we all react instinctively sometimes.

Naturally Bo Owl didn't make an apology.

On the contrary.

When Owl realized that Boxer Bloom had no intention of doing what he wanted, Owl committed a serious mistake. What drove him to it? No one knows. Perhaps it was as Father believed, an overdeveloped protective instinct that went along with the fact that Owl got Nathan so late in life.

Bo Owl paid some baboons to threaten Father.

The baboons broke the windows at our house, wrote dirty words on our door, and subjected Father's pupils to harassment. This treatment didn't work. Father didn't get scared. Instead Father's empathy with Rector Owl deepened. For obvious reasons, this further provoked the rector.

Finally the apes threatened us.

They threatened Mother and me and Eric.

Then Father had had enough. Rage and terror caused him to make an unwise decision. He challenged the baboons to a duel. I don't know how it went, how he managed to contact them, but so it was. Mother fled the field and took us cubs home to Grandmother.

When the apes came, there were more than twenty of them. I can see them walking abreast in two columns along Hillville Road. I can even imagine the lonely silhouette that stood in the middle of the street outside our house and waited for them. Desperate and furious. Broad and heavy, there he stands, watching them come.

When less than a hundred meters separates them, Father shouts, "Now it's over! This is going to be the last thing you do!"

The apes slow their pace somewhat.

A sense of uncertainty appears in their ranks. There stands a single dog and seems convinced that he can get the better of them. This scene is one of the clearest memories my brother and I carry with us throughout life. Despite the fact that we weren't even there.

The baboons suspect an ambush.

Amberville is not a district that they know, and one of them gets the idea that Bloom has mobilized the entire neighborhood. The rumor spreads in the ranks of the apes. Stuffed animals are sitting in the houses, waiting for Boxer's signal. At any moment they're going to come storming out onto the street and support him. Otherwise he would be crazy to challenge them alone.

When one of the apes in the forward rank stops, they all stop. The uncertainty increases. There is scarcely fifty meters between father and the baboons.

Father lets out a battle cry.

"Now I'm going to get you!"

With these words he starts running toward them.

The apes stand as though petrified. The scene is absurd; they can't believe it. The most cowardly of them turns around and flees. Within a few seconds Father has the moral advantage. He increases his speed and screams at the top of his voice, "Now I'm coming to get you!"

Reality exceeds imagination. One by one the apes turn and follow close on the heels of the first deserter. Father imperceptibly reduces his speed so as not to catch up with the bravest.

The slowest.

He stops when he reaches the spot where the apes began their retreat. He looks far after them, knowing that they are never going to make problems for him again. The apes are going to feel ashamed. They are never going to tell the story as it was. Rector Owl is defeated and cub Nathan will get his rightful grade. Regardless of what that is and what it leads to.

"Now I'm going to get you, said Father."

Eric and I made those words legendary. We told the story over and over again. We repeated it so many times that the reality became a fairy tale. A story of right and wrong. Of integrity and honor. Of decline and corruption.

A few days after Father had defeated the apes, Jason Horse phoned from the Ministry of Culture.

Father was offered Rector Owl's position.

Father accepted.

The epilogue goes: Rector Owl disappeared and was not seen for several years. Later he was said to be at the university library in Lanceheim, where he was working in the archives. His cub, Nathan, is still driving bus number 6.

To summarize, in the autumn of age, a life consisting solely of good deeds is impossible. Apart from the fact that evil constantly tempts us, we are at some point placed in a situation of choice where goodness is not one of the alternatives.

My choice looked like this:

To injure the one I loved in order to remain true to myself. Or to rescue the beloved through false actions.

I could not marry Emma Rabbit.

I proposed to her in April. We set a date for the wedding at the end of August and thereby had time for the preparations. My love for Emma was stronger than ever.

The same applied to the insight that this marriage was insanity.

Both of our mothers were happy to excess about the upcoming wedding. They discussed what songs to sing, which guests to invite, and what flowers to order. Archdeacon Odenrick was spoken with, the band was booked, and dresses were sewn. Mother would prepare the food herself.

Father was more levelheaded and only intermittently took part in the planning. This worked out well, as Emma Rabbit was fatherless. It had always been painful for her to talk about her father, and therefore we let it be. But I understood that she was devoting a lot of thought to him during the wedding preparations.

I held myself at a proper distance from the planning.

I ought to have stopped the whole thing, but I couldn't.

It wasn't a matter of will.

I wanted to love Emma for better or for worse. I wanted to share the rest of my life with her in love and truth.

But that wouldn't be possible.

We were no more than stuffed animals. Against our will we would come to injure one another, quarrel, and perhaps even be unfaithful to each other. Young and inexperienced, we gave our promises because we relied on love. But wherever I looked, in literature and in reality, lifelong pairing was only possible through mutual forgiveness or a similarly mutual lack of interest.

Neither the one nor the other was possible for the one who has chosen goodness.

To enter into this marriage with the knowledge that in five, ten, or twenty years I could betray my own youthful self was impossible.

I ought to have told Emma about my thoughts. But she was just as excited about the impending wedding as her mother. I couldn't break her heart.

Three weeks before the wedding the thought came to me in my sleep. It arrived as easily as a bur in your fur. It was just as hard to get rid of.

Three weeks before the wedding. I didn't know how I would get Mother to understand that I had to back out. I hadn't paid any attention to Emma's comments from the previous evening. She had said that it would be exciting to meet my brother Eric. She asked if he was older or younger.

I heard her ask the question.

I didn't think any more about it.

But the idea came to me in my sleep.

CHAPTER 17

Blood-red Western Avenue continues all the way to Hillevie and the sea. When the developed areas thin out and the forest begins, blue South and yellow North Avenues change to small country roads which after a few miles turn into paths no one has walked on for many decades.

Mint-green Eastern Avenue leads, only a few hundred meters beyond the city limits, to a massive wooden gate. Above the gate hangs a four-meter-long board between two tall poles, and on the board someone has written "Garbage Dump" in tar. The wooden gate stands wide open from the start of the Morning Weather to the end of the Afternoon Weather. If you arrive earlier or later you're forced to pound on the gate, or use your horn, to get someone to open it. But it's far from certain that you'll make yourself heard, and the garbagemen who drive the trucks are careful to keep to the open hours.

The Garbage Dump was a terrifying area. The sun never reached down between the mountains of refuse that lined the streets. Inside the gate there were three roads to choose from. No signs guided the visitor, but there was seldom anyone who came to the Garbage Dump who didn't find their way on their own.

The garbage trucks that transported combustible refuse took the Right-hand Road. If the cargo consisted of worn-out apparatus made of steel or iron, you took the Left-hand Road. In both cases you drove along meandering roads toward a turnaround several kilometers into the garbage region. The garbagemen drove as fast as they could, as the stench became worse and worse the deeper in toward the heart of the Garbage Dump they came, but it was hard to maintain any speed to speak of on the curving roads, and there was always a risk of avalanche from the mountains of garbage.

Once at the turnaround for combustible refuse, the garbageman tipped the bed of the truck so that the garbage fell straight down into a gigantic hollow where tons of soot and ash couldn't conceal the fact that the embers derived nourishment from new trash around the clock. At the corresponding turnaround for steel and iron was the Hole. Magnus's own enormous outhouse, and no garbageman had ever stayed long enough after having tipped his load that he heard the scrap hit the bottom of the Hole.

The Middle Road inside the wooden gate led, via tunnels and unexplainable windings, the whole way up to the top of the dump and a shantytown consisting of a few dozen ramshackle hovels and shacks. Up there, with a view of the dump and the eastern parts of Lanceheim, lived the populace of the dump. Stuffed animals who knew how to run across the mountains of garbage without starting a landslide, those who no longer perceived the stench of decay, who keep the incinerator glowing and the roads drivable, and had forgotten how things looked in Mollisan Town.

In the middle of this settlement disguised as a Garbage Dump lived the Queen of the Garbage Dump, Rat Ruth. Her residence was a veritable temple of refuse, built of pieces of wood, shards of glass, and compacted newspapers. On the roof stood a four-meter-tall plastic Christmas tree that Ruth had found many years ago, and which she'd become attached to. The tree's hundreds of lights blinked red and white and green, day and night.

The garbagemen who thought they had something of value in their load took the Middle Road up to the dump's settlement. On the square in front of the rat's residence was a kind of parking lot, where they parked their cars and awaited the dump's foreman and uncrowned prince, a hyena by the name of Bataille. He was the one they dealt with, a hard negotiator who knew that the alternative to his meager offers were the dump's south or north waste stations. Nonetheless, Bataille was to be preferred before Ruth. The rat most often slept during the day, but on those few occasions when she awakened by mistake and received the terrified garbagemen, there were no negotiations at all. If they wanted to leave the Garbage Dump in one piece, the only thing to do was to turn over the small valuables they'd planned to sell, and then drive away as fast as they could. Hyena Bataille found a certain enjoyment in the actual negotiations; Rat Ruth thought it was more fun to scare the shit out of the garbagemen.

There were two reasons to live at the Garbage Dump. Animals who were driven out of society, on their own account or others', moved here as a final outpost. And stuffed animals which had been produced with a defect were dumped along with other dross and refuse. Those newly produced animals who had never gotten to ride in the Deliverymen's green pickup made up the majority in the dump city. There were discolored birds and gnawers without teeth, stuffed animals without whiskers, arms, legs, or tails, all of whom worked for Rat Ruth. The kind who made their way to the dump after first having lived in the city most often had a hard time getting into the community. It often happened that these animals were forced to live alone somewhere in the wasteland around the burn piles, or else they were compelled at last to return to Mollisan Town.

Ruth was a discarded stuffed animal. She was missing her right paw as well as a left leg when she rolled out of the factory. Instead of being placed with some eagerly expectant couple on the Cub List, she was tossed up onto the bed of a garbage truck and tossed out at the dump.

Two things distinguished Ruth even in her early years. One was that she didn't seem to miss her paw or her leg. She hopped along through life on the stump and on the legs she had, and she didn't run much faster or slower than her friends her age. The other thing that was bewildering was her lack of a need for acknowledgment. Or, put more simply: she seemed not to give a damn about others. The young Rat Ruth turned her back on the world, not because deep down she feared it. She wasn't interested; that was the whole thing.

Rather soon the grown-ups at the dump joked that Ruth's leg and paw were the lesser amputations. Her lack of social needs was worse. She went her own way, and when she did go with others, she did so by coincidence. She wasn't asocial, but everything she did, she did on her own terms and on her own account, and in that way, in time, she won respect.

It wasn't Rat Ruth who asked to be crowned Queen of the Garbage Dump after the King of the Garbage Dump died. The title, like the ceremony, was something the animals at the dump thought up themselves, nothing that had been authorized by any department. A leader was needed from which a hierarchical system could proceed. In a place like the Garbage Dump it was important to know your place in order to fill out your life. And having a king or queen was ostentatious in a way that livened things up.

"Me?" a confounded Ruth had asked when they came to

see her after the Chauffeurs had picked the king up early
one winter morning. "Well, why not?"

And thereby it was decided.

Rat Ruth was only twenty-six years old when she was
named monarch of the dump, and the role made her visible
to the garbagemen in the outside world as well. This forced
her to take an active role in the life of the dump, which she
did with the same nonexistent commitment that marked all
of her endeavors. In the residence that the defective stuffed
animals insisted on having built for her, the largest hall was
set up for audiences. The animals understood that they had
chosen a queen who would not eagerly seek out her subjects, and therefore set up a throne. With patches of jeans
over the holes in the pink, flowered cloth of a discarded
armchair, complemented with a footrest which in its previous life had been a vacuum cleaner, Ruth sat night after
night dozing, drinking lukewarm beer, and letting herself
be talked to by her foremen. They told about their duties,
which was the everyday life of the Garbage Dump. She had
reduced the number of foremen to three—during the old
king's time there had been eight. One of them kept watch
over the road to the incinerator, another took care of the
Hole and the road there. And a third, the one who was closest to her, Hyena Bataille, was responsible for the wooden
gate and for the winding, treacherous road up to the queen's
residence and the dump city.

This was a prosperous kingdom Rat Ruth had inherited.
The Environmental Ministry had calculated roughly how
high the rent should be for the animals in the dump to be
able to manage, and even manage nicely. The ministry had
great respect for the work that was carried out at the Garbage Dump, and were aware of how quickly the situation in
the city would degenerate if the dump didn't function. What
they didn't know was that the trade in used goods was a
secondary occupation.

The bigwigs in the city's underworld had become accustomed to the fact that the King of the Garbage Dump was paid well for causing animals to disappear. Nonetheless they wished him back when the Queen of the Garbage Dump stated the new conditions. She understood that she could set any price she wanted; the Garbage Dump was one of the few places where the Chauffeurs lost the game. An animal that was torn apart could always be sewn together at the hospital. Even a torn-off head could be filled and replaced. But the animal that failed to pay its gambling debts, that didn't respect the gangster kings or their gorillas, only needed to be reminded of the Garbage Dump and its incinerator and the Hole to meekly step back in line.

Rat Ruth was not a numbskull.

Hyena Bataille had appeared as if out of nowhere. One morning he was sitting on top of an old Volga wreck that stood along the road toward the Hole. His paws were hanging nonchalantly out over the edge of the roof and his stained, black, narrow-brimmed hat was shoved back on his head. He was smoking a cigarette, squinting toward the sun that was coming up, and didn't seem to be bothered by the collection of animals that in a few short moments gathered around him.

He was so haggard and his fur so matted that no one who saw him that morning was especially concerned. Perhaps you could sense that he was an aggressive type—he had presumably made his way to the Garbage Dump of his own free will—but it didn't appear as though he was in a condition to win a fight. The animals didn't bother to call a foreman over; they thought they would have a little fun on their own.

"Who are you?" asked a brave rooster.

He was sky blue with a cloud-white comb, aspired to a

foreman's job in due time and therefore had a particular purpose in appearing cocky.

At first the hyena didn't seem to have heard the question. He sat unmoving, smoking his cigarette and letting the tender rays of the sun stroke his whiskers.

"Who's asking?" he said at last.

His voice was deep and harsh. Friendly, but commanding respect. When he turned his face toward the rooster it was the first time the animals saw the hyena's eyes. They glistened like black mirrors, refusing entry to onlookers.

"It's me who's asking," answered the rooster, without letting himself be concerned by the challenge that the hyena had assumed, and reciprocated, without hesitation, "and when I ask I'm used to getting an answer."

"That sounds about right," mumbled the hyena in his dark voice, as though he was mostly talking to himself, "I've heard that you all have a special way of treating strangers here."

"And you came here anyway?" said the rooster ironically.

The hyena took a final drag from the cigarette and put it out by crushing the ember against the roof of the car where he was sitting. He furrowed his eyebrows, and his sudden displeasure made the animals standing in a semicircle around the car feel ill at ease.

"Lay off now," he said, "and leave me in peace. I'm sure we'll find some way to relate to each other in due course."

"'Relate to each other'?" the rooster imitated in a voice full of scorn. "Did you hear? He wants to 'relate,' in 'due course.' Listen, the only course you need to do is . . . is . . ."

But the rooster couldn't think of any cogent irony because he was uncertain what the word meant.

"Leave me in peace," said the hyena again.

This time it wasn't a request, it was a direct order. And for a fraction of a second—a second that could have saved the rooster's life—the rooster actually considered doing as the stranger asked. But then the blue rooster realized that it was too late, that fate had already brought him here and that fate always knew what it was doing. He was forced to follow it to the end. He took a step forward and kicked at the car door. The sound that arose, an imposing boom, surprised him. It was the acoustics of the car's empty compartment that caused the rooster to overcome his terror when he heard for himself what powerful legs he had.

"Beat it," he said to the hyena. "There are already enough mouths to fill here."

The rest happened in just a minute. Nonetheless, that minute would be talked about for several years.

The hyena jumped down from the roof of the car and in the same movement took out a bottle which he must have had concealed inside his worn-out jacket. The glass bottle reflected in the sun, and the rooster as well as the observers intuitively perceived the bottle as a weapon, something the hyena would strike with. But it was the hyena's other paw that shot forth like a projectile and encircled the rooster's neck in a merciless grip. In a moment the hyena screwed off the cap of the bottle with his teeth, and when the rooster opened his beak to gasp for breath—the grip on his neck hardly allowed him to get any air—the hyena forced the bottle down his throat instead. The animals stood bewildered at the sides of the fighters, watching how the contents of the bottle ran down into the rooster.

How many of them understood what was really going on? Some. Perhaps a few. But not many.

It took a while before the bottle was empty. To judge by the rooster's heaving, flapping, and more and more frantic body, the liquid that was running down his throat was foul-tasting. But despite the fact that the rooster kicked in every direction and desperately tried to wriggle out of the hyena's grasp, he had no chance. The scene even looked ridiculous, because the rooster's exertions didn't seem to concern the much stronger hyena whatsoever.

It took perhaps half a minute before the bottle was empty. An endless time. When there were only a few gulps left, which the rooster apparently couldn't get down, the hyena threw the bottle onto the ground and from the inside of his jacket conjured forth a lighter.

It was then that the animals understood.

And in the following moment, when they saw the yellow-red flame of the lighter, someone started to scream. A scream that immediately became polyphonic. During the seconds that followed, as the hyena mercilessly brought the lighter toward the rooster's beak, almost all of them screamed. Some fled headlong from the place.

The hyena had filled the rooster to the brim with alcohol. When the flame of the lighter came in contact with the alcohol, the rooster's beak flared up and in the following moment a kind of inner explosion was heard, but by then all of them had turned their gaze from the just-ignited animal, and only the stench of burning insides told of the rooster's agony.

When the Queen of the Garbage Dump heard talk of what had happened later that afternoon, she immediately had Hyena Bataille called to her and asked if he might consider becoming one of the Cleaners.

Bataille accepted immediately, and it wasn't long before he was one of the Garbage Dump's foremen.

CHAPTER 18

That's enough now."

Snake Marek slithered up a drainpipe and over to the lid of one of several trash barrels that stood outside the entryway to Yiala's Arch. In this way he was almost level with Eric Bear, and they stared angrily at each other. Twilight had fallen a few hours earlier, Tom-Tom and Sam had gone in the car in advance, and there was no longer any time to lose. They had tomorrow and the day after tomorrow, then the Chauffeurs would pick up Dove and Teddy. The last thing Eric Bear had a desire to do was to stand jawing in this narrow, green alley that stank of urine.

He said so, too.

"We don't have time to shoot the shit now. I'll listen to your objections on the way there."

"We're not going there. And absolutely not at this time of day."

"Like I said, we'll talk about this in the car."

"The reason that you wanted me to be part of this was?" asked Snake, his gaze not wavering a bit. "Do you remember why you thought it was important that I should take part?"

Eric considered his reply. There were a number of sarcastic remarks that appeared enticing, but he wouldn't gain anything by arguing. The original reason was that he assumed he needed Snake's brain, his analytic ability. But the memory of Snake's talents appeared to be embellished. What had Snake Marek actually contributed, apart from this constant complaining?

"Do you recall?" nagged Snake. "You forced me along because I understand things that you don't get. This is one of those things."

Eric threw out his paws. He didn't know what he should say; he lacked arguments.

"We have no choice," he said.

"We can choose to let things be," said Snake. "And we ought to choose to let things be."

It was of course possible to let Snake stay at home, but at the same time Eric sensed that this was exactly what the sly reptile was after. And he wasn't going to get off that easy. No one liked making their way to the Garbage Dump in the middle of the night; not Eric, either. But if they were going, all four of them were going. It was an irrational decision, but for Eric this was not negotiable.

"Now we're going," said Eric firmly. "I've heard what you're saying, and now I hope you'll hear what I'm saying."

"This is idiocy," said Snake.

"There are no alternatives."

"And if the camel was lying?"

"Neither you nor I believe that," said Eric.

Sam Gazelle had been exhilarated when he came home late in the afternoon. Snake was down at Springergaast buying cigarettes, Tom-Tom and Eric sat reading the evening papers and had just put on a pot of coffee.

"Now you'll hear," said Sam, clapping his hooves with delight.

He was bubbling with giggles, little bells sounding through the room. Eric set aside the newspaper and inquisitively observed the exhilarated gazelle, who sat down at the kitchen table.

"Noah remembered me," said Sam proudly. "I knew he would remember me."

"Noah remembered you," repeated Tom-Tom, who was infected by Sam's exhilaration and giggled obligingly at his own amusement, "but Magnus knows if that was good or bad."

"Sweetheart, I'll say this: he opened the door," declared Sam.

"The question is, will he open it next time?" asked Tom-Tom.

Sam giggled knowingly.

"But he'll no doubt remember you again?"

"He will," promised Sam. "Absolutely for sure he will."

"I don't want to know," said Eric.

"For once, darling," answered Sam, "I think you're right."

"I want to know," objected Tom-Tom with a sneer.

"Reconsider," said Sam.

They laughed as if they'd heard a funny story. Eric became impatient.

"And?" he said, getting up and going over to the coffee-maker to pour a cup of strong, black coffee for himself.

"Darling," said Sam, trying to collect himself, "forgive me. It was like this. The camel told me where he got the list."

"Just like that?" panted Tom-Tom, giggling like a little she.

"Just like that," Sam confirmed, giving the crow a roguish smile that caused Tom-Tom once again to break into a loud laugh.

"And?" shouted Eric in order to drown out the crow.

"Excuse me," Sam asked again, pulling himself together. "Noah got it from the Garbage Dump. The camel goes out to the Garbage Dump and picks up the envelope with the lists."

"Ruth?" said Eric.

Sam shrugged his shoulders. "Darling, have you heard of anything coming from the Garbage Dump that doesn't come from Ruth?"

"Ruth," repeated Eric to himself. "Obviously."

Eric Bear had met Rat Ruth on a few occasions in his life.

Together with Tom-Tom Crow, Eric had been assigned to escort a terrified ermine from Casino Monokowski out to the Garbage Dump early one morning just over twenty years earlier. He had no idea what was behind the break between the ermine and the casino. At that time, Eric was popping almost as many pills as Sam Gazelle, and even connections that were explained to him often remained unclear.

Tom-Tom carried the quivering ermine out to the car where Eric was waiting. They sat in the backseat. Eric drove as fast as he could up toward the Star, then continued out on Eastern Avenue and without touching the brakes was at the dump's wooden gate just under twenty minutes later. There he tooted the horn three times, according to instructions. The black Volga limousine from Casino Monokowski was an often-seen vehicle at the dump—just like black limousines from other establishments—and the gates were opened at once. At the fork in the road immediately after the entrance stood a duck in black sunglasses (despite the fact that the sun had not yet come up) who waved him forward. Eric drove along the Middle Road, a ravine through refuse and scrap, eerily narrow and deep. Onward, onward he followed the road until he was suddenly forced to put on the brakes because a rat was standing in front of him.

The ermine and the crow in the backseat were thrown forward, but Tom-Tom pulled himself up quickly and burst out, terror-stricken, "It's Ruth."

Eric knew who Ruth was, even if he'd never seen the young Queen of the Garbage Dump. Dove always talked about her with equal amounts of respect and irritation.

"What the hell is she doing here, in the middle of the road?" whispered Tom-Tom with a hoarse anxiety that infected Eric. "You just about ran her over."

The last statement was an anxious declaration which in the car's mute compartment sounded like an accusation.

"Throw him out," said Eric.

"What?"

"Throw him out!" repeated Eric.

And Tom-Tom understood, opened the back door, and heaved out the ermine. Whereupon Eric shifted gears and started to back up. He backed up as fast as he could for more than a kilometer before the ravine opened into a passage wide enough to turn in, and then they drove in silence toward the wooden gate that they both feared would be closed when they got there. But it was open, and on the way back along Eastern Avenue the sun came up on the horizon and they laughed at their adventure and for several months talked about that morning when Eric almost ran Rat Ruth down.

The second time Eric Bear met the Queen of the Garbage Dump was more than fifteen years later, at a large, polished conference table inside Sagrada Bastante.

Eric counted the telephone call that had preceded this meeting as one of the high points of his life, proof that he had not only succeeded in a general, superficial, and material sense, but that he'd truly forced himself into the innermost core of contemporary history.

He and Emma had been having a late dinner in the kitchen on Uxbridge Street when the telephone rang. Emma shrugged her shoulders inquiringly and shook her head. Eric got up from the table and took the phone in the serving corridor.

"Eric," an authoritative voice was heard, "I beg your pardon for calling so late, but . . . oh, forgive me. This is Archdeacon Odenrick."

"I recognized your voice, Archdeacon," said Eric. "It's been a long time."

"It really has been," said Odenrick, "but I have nevertheless had the benefit of following your career at a distance."

"You can't believe everything you read," replied Eric with feigned humility.

"Don't say that to your mother," said Odenrick jokingly. "She's insanely proud of you."

"No danger. She reads and hears what she wants to read and hear. Selectivity is one of her greatest talents."

"I think you're underestimating her," answered Penguin Odenrick, not without a certain degree of merriment.

"I'm sure I'm not," said Eric. "What's the occasion for this late call?"

Odenrick was a straightforward penguin, an animal who set high value on his time, and he appreciated Eric's direct question.

"I'm calling about A Helping Hand," explained the archdeacon. "We have a vacant place on the board of directors—old Goldman became ill, actually last summer, but she wasn't picked up until a few weeks ago. Very tragic nonetheless, of course, and when we were talking around the table about successors your name came up."

"It did?" said Eric.

"You can believe that I felt very proud," said Odenrick. "Having known you since you were a little cub."

"Do you mean that . . ."

"We would be very happy to have you on the board, Eric."

When Eric Bear returned to the kitchen to his waiting Emma Rabbit it was as though his paws didn't touch the floor; he was flying a few centimeters above the parquet floor. Emma had only heard portions of the conversation, so Eric told her. Of all the city's aid associations, there was none so influential or respected as A Helping Hand. For more than a hundred years the city's archdeacon was chairman of the board. Only the upper crust of society sat on the board, the most irreproachable animals that could be found.

"And now, me," said Eric Bear.

Emma Rabbit was most often moderately interested in Eric's achievements; she defined herself in different arenas than her spouse. But a place on the board of A Helping Hand impressed even her.

The first board meeting followed a few months after the archdeacon's telephone call, and it was with genuine reverence that Eric made his way along the long, dark corridors within Sagrada Bastante en route to the boardroom with its enormous oak table and the stern, tall, and hard chairs.

The first thing he saw when he came in was Rat Ruth.

None of the other animals held any surprises, it was more or less those he had expected. Mayor Sara Lion sat to the left side of the archdeacon. But Ruth? During the years that followed—the board met approximately every fourth month—Eric realized that Ruth was just as obviously anchored in society's upper crust as the archdeacon or the mayor. She seldom took part in the discussions; she walked by herself during the breaks and always departed before the lunches, or the less-frequent dinners. But nonetheless. She was asked for advice with proper respect in all matters, and no one ever wrinkled their nose when Ruth or her operation were brought up.

Eric assumed that everyone on the many-headed board knew how Ruth supported the city's gangster kings. Yet they let her sit in and revel in all the social patina that the board work entailed. Eric wasn't naïve, nor was he a moralist, but in the circles around A Helping Hand both of those types were represented. When Eric, in time and very carefully, tried to raise the question about Ruth with individual board members, he got nowhere.

Eric realized that the board members, with their years of experience from the backside of life, had all been forced to become thick-skinned pragmatists. They appreciated the significance of garbage being gathered and knew that if Ruth didn't carry out this bad-smelling work someone else would be forced to do it. But could that be the entire reason that they accepted her at the table? Eric was doubtful.

And now, from a completely different direction, he was presented with a possible explanation.

Noah Camel ran errands for Rat Ruth.

Rat Ruth was not only the queen of organic and industrial waste, she was also life's own waste composter. Rat Ruth was the one who drew up the Death List. The reason for the esteemed board members' respect was purely and simply that they were scared to death.

And they had every reason to be.

The snake and the bear stood silently across from each other in the narrow alley. It was already so late that it was getting cold, there was a smell of hairspray from one of the open windows, and on the lid of the trash barrel where Snake was standing someone had stuck a wad of chewed-up, pink bubble gum.

The animals scrutinized each other.

Snake understood that love for Emma Rabbit was Eric Bear's weak point. True, Snake had never experienced love, but he was an artist: he had written mystery novels based on crimes of passion, written poem cycles with a starting point in lust, and made hundreds of nude studies in charcoal. Taking love with such seriousness as Eric Bear did, however, was simply ludicrous.

"Perhaps it's time," said Snake Marek, "to put things in their proper perspective? This whole business with Dove is . . . there were certainly good reasons to call together the old gang and remind us all where we've ended up in life, but now it concerns our security. Emma Rabbit, with all due respect, but a bear of your position can quite certainly find . . . alternatives . . . and I think for my part that—"

"That's enough," said Eric, holding up a paw, whereupon Snake actually fell silent. "That's enough. We have to go now. Someday, perhaps, we'll sit down and talk this out, you and I. But not today. We don't have time. After you."

And Eric waited patiently while Snake Marek extremely unwillingly wriggled down from the trash barrel and headed off toward the car, where the gazelle and the crow had been sitting a long time.

TWILIGHT, 4

They were sitting in the conference room and couldn't see when the sun sank down below the horizon. True, there was a row of windows looking out on the street, but he had drawn both the blinds and the heavy curtains so that you could see neither in nor out. He liked that the room was dark and gloomy, he liked this austerity: oak-paneled walls and black armless leather chairs around the large conference table, creating a solemn, quiet atmosphere. Under the table there was a sizable beige rug with the beautiful emblem. It protected the varnished parquet floor from the scraping feet of the chairs. Nowadays he had moved almost all his meetings to this room, whether they were large gatherings or, as this evening, it was a matter of speaking in confidence with an old friend. It felt too intimate to invite outsiders into his own office. It hadn't always been like that, but now it was. His cramped, cluttered office was his secret command bridge, to which he didn't dare risk taking someone who by mistake might catch sight of . . . of anything whatsoever that wasn't intended for eyes other than his own.

He was standing with his back turned toward the conference table where Rat Ruth sat at the far end. He poured mineral water into two glasses. The sideboard contained two roomy refrigerators. The crystal glasses in the lower cupboard were always freshly washed. It's in the details that laziness is most easily revealed and where arrogance resides; he saw to it that all the glasses, plates, and silverware in the sideboard were cleaned every day. It wasn't for him, but out of consideration for his guests.

As far as Rat Ruth was concerned, the gesture was wasted. Even from where she was sitting, five meters away, he smelled the stench from her clothes. At least he hoped it was her clothes. Her rough fur was covered with a layer of filth—he couldn't call it anything else—and her nose sat crooked in a way which truly irritated him. Why couldn't she just turn it a few millimeters, so that it was over and done with? Considering how maimed she'd been when she was manufactured, a nose that sat a few millimeters crooked was of course not something that worried Ruth.

"What do you want?" asked Ruth in an aggressive tone that didn't surprise him.

He calmly filled both glasses, turned, and carried them over to the rat. He sat down as far from her as he reasonably could without appearing obviously impolite, and gave her an indulgent smile.

"We're going to talk seriously," he answered at last. "Sometimes you just have to do that."

The rat shrugged her shoulders.

"You're comfortable, aren't you?" he asked.

She shrugged her shoulders again, but at the same time shook her head as if to declare that she didn't understand what he was talking about.

"I know that you're comfortable," he continued, mostly to himself, "since you're still around."

The rat observed the glass of mineral water on the table in front of her. Her small, peering eyes were unfathomable. He could not possibly determine what was in her thoughts at this moment.

"And I'm happy to have you there," he said. "It feels secure. Reliable. Self-interest is a predictable motivator. And I don't have time to wonder."

"Hmm," answered Ruth.

He observed her morosely. She would not let herself be scared.

"I'm happy to have you there," he repeated, "because you're reliable."

He felt frustrated by her indifference. He had a sudden desire to put her in her place, get her to react, show her who decided. But at the same time he realized that this desire was idiotic, an expression of a type of weakness that he was above. He got up from the table because he was forced to get rid of a little energy and strolled back and forth along the outside wall. The rat didn't turn around, despite the fact that he was moving behind her back. He didn't know if that was foolhardiness or confidence.

"You've met Eric Bear before, true?" he asked rhetorically.

"Nah," she said.

"You certainly have," he hissed with irritation, stopping a short distance away from her so as to be able to fasten his eyes on her. "He's the bear that's a member of A Helping Hand."

"I don't recall any bear," she admitted.

"But, what the . . ." he went on, "are you weak in the head or what? He's been a member for several years. He sits three chairs to the right of you."

She shrugged her shoulders.

"Sometimes I wonder why you are part of that group at all . . ."

"Me too," replied Ruth quickly.

"You're a member because I want it that way!" he screamed.

"That's it, yes," said Ruth.

Was she toying with him? He suddenly became uncertain. He took a few deep breaths and calmed himself. Sat down again on the chair by her side.

"Eric Bear is coming to see you," he said in a normal tone of voice. "Tomorrow or the day after tomorrow or the day after that. I don't know exactly. But he's coming, and rather soon at that."

"So?"

"And I don't know what kind of plan he thinks he has, what he intends to threaten you with . . ."

"He's thinking about threatening me?"

For the first time during their conversation there was emotion in her voice. She sounded surprised.

"That I don't know," he cut her off. "I don't know what he's going to do, but I know what he's going to ask. He wants to know about the Death List."

The rat looked straight into his eyes. In her pupils there was only blackness.

"So?" she said.

"And whatever he has to say, whatever he maintains or threatens, whatever he pretends or demands, I know how you're going to treat him."

"So?"

"Yes, if he gets as far as the whole way up to you," he said, "and not even that is for sure, you'll listen to him and then send him on his way. Amiably and courteously. You and I know that there isn't any Death List."

The rat sat silently.

"The Death List doesn't exist," he said again.

He stood a while observing her. Then he grew tired. She would do what he said, she always did.

"You can go now," he said.

There was only a moment's hesitation, then she got up from the chair, leaving him alone in the conference room.

CHAPTER 19

Eric Bear drove in silence along the mint-green avenue.

Snake Marek sat in the passenger seat, keeping demonstrably silent. This particular night the others for once would have appreciated his prattle, but Snake's pride was wounded, and he was punishing them with his silence. He sat stiff as a stick, staring down at the dirty rubber mat, where clay had dried and cracked. In his mind he tried to construct an iambic verse with a starting point in the patterns on the mat.

He got nowhere with that.

Tom-Tom was sitting behind Eric. It felt secure to sit in the car and see the city go by outside, thought the crow; considerably more secure than sitting in any of the buildings, watching the cars pass.

Sam was listening to his heartbeats. Since yesterday morning his heart had been beating double: thump, thump, thu-thump. He'd taken a whole fistful of the pink tablets he believed were good for his heart, but apart from the fact that he felt tired, nothing happened. Sam had never talked with Rat Ruth, but he had seen her several times. She gave him the creeps, she was one gigantic bad omen. Driving to the Garbage Dump in the middle of the night, when the rat was awake, was a very bad idea.

Thu-thump, thu-thump, said his heart.

Eric's plan was so simple that it scarcely even deserved to be called a plan.

Eric intended to turn off Eastern Avenue a few cross streets before the Garbage Dump and take the road through the outskirts of Lanceheim up to the city limits. The wooden gate, the main entrance to the dump, was guarded at night. On the other hand, Ruth and her crew didn't fear thieves who came on foot; no one could climb over the mountains of trash at night. True, the entire area was equipped with a fence, but that was because the animals in Lanceheim had demanded a clear boundary between themselves and the dump. In many places the fence had been torn down and never put back up again.

So, park on one of the cross streets north of the wooden gate. Find a hole in the fence and make their way in. Make an evasive movement toward the northeast and then make their way south, down to the Middle Road. After that, follow the road up to the Garbage Town and Rat Ruth's residence. Eric had no illusions that they would be able to make it the whole way to the residence without being discovered. But if they only managed to get far enough they would surely be granted an audience with the Rat Queen. And, eye to eye with the rat, Eric Bear—this naïve advertising bear—was certain that he would be successful in making her see reason. Get her to realize that she had to remove both Teddy and Dove from her list.

How this would come about he hadn't yet figured out.

And he himself knew how it sounded. Like pure nonsense. Therefore he hadn't shared his plan with either Sam, Tom-Tom, or Snake.

. . . .

The neighborhoods in northeast Lanceheim consisted predominantly of single-family houses with small, poorly
tended gardens. On the expansive hills that farther east
changed to sparse pine forest were patched-up single-story
houses with flaking paint. There were often wrecked cars in
the yards, there were rusty bicycles and mysterious, sealed
black garbage bags. These were houses you lived in while
you were looking for something else.

In the glow of the streetlights Eric Bear drove slowly
through the night. He was searching for a suitable parking place and didn't want to attract unnecessary attention.
Finally he found a place in front of a pair of apartment
buildings unexpectedly ensconced in the middle of a low-
lying precipice, and he positioned himself next to a red
Volga GTI.

"From here we'll go on foot," he reported.

Eric turned off the engine before anyone had time to
comment on this surprising information.

"On foot?" Snake finally spit out, but Eric had already
gotten out of the car.

"On foot?" repeated Snake, now turned toward the backseat. "He must be joking!"

"He's not joking," Sam answered laconically.

"A little fresh air will be nice, damn it," said Tom-Tom
encouragingly.

The crow got out, too, joining Eric at the parking spot.

"You know that this is idiocy," Snake said to Sam.

They sat alone in the car.

"Sure, old man. In contrast to your normal, healthy life,"
Sam answered.

"Strolling into a Garbage Dump in the middle of the night
might be a way to cause our normal, healthy lives to come to
an end," Snake retorted. "If it's life you've grown tired of."

"All ways are good except the bad ones," Sam asserted, he, too, getting out and onto the parking place.

Eric, Sam, and Tom-Tom started walking east. They heard the car door open and shut again, and soon all four of them were on their way toward the Garbage Dump. Just as silently as they'd recently been sitting in the car.

Hyena Bataille saw them from a distance.

The animals at the dump had built a handful of lookout points. These were not regular towers. On the contrary, from a distance it was almost impossible to determine that there was anything special about these collections of scrap which here and there rose a few meters above the rest of the peculiar landscape of refuse.

Like many nights before, Bataille had been deeply embroiled in conversation with the hot-tempered Louise, a beige-brown terrier with deformed eyes who, based on some sort of principle, never agreed. For many months they had discussed the relationship between inherited instincts and inherited desires, but their quarrels were not particularly committed. They sat in a couple of deck chairs that were patched together with black tarp. Far away were the abandoned streets of Lanceheim, and for Bataille and Louise the four stuffed animals who made their way into the Garbage Dump were as obvious as an armada on the open sea. If not equally terror-inspiring. Bataille didn't even stop talking.

"Do you think they're on their way here?" asked the terrier, when the hyena paused at one point.

"Who?" asked Bataille.

Louise nodded toward Lanceheim.

"Anyone you recognize?"

Louise shook her head. "Not at this distance."

"No," said Bataille. "But that doesn't really matter, does it?"

Louise giggled.

. . . .

"Is this the plan?" asked Snake.

Because no one answered, he continued in a tone of voice that was just as unnatural as it was indignant. "Are we just going straight into the Garbage Dump, look up the rat, and convince her to change the list? Is that the plan?"

Tom-Tom snorted.

"Damn, how ridiculous you are now, Marek," said the crow. "It's clear as hell that Eric has a plan."

"Do tell, Eric," Snake asked scornfully, "about this plan. Let's hear it."

Eric Bear was walking a few meters ahead of the others and finally discovered a hole in the fence, farther north than he'd thought, but here it was. He nodded.

"We go in here," he said, pointing.

Sam took a few quick steps up to the bear and whispered, "You're sure about this?"

But Eric didn't answer, pretending not to hear; he was already on his way into the Garbage Dump. He climbed carefully up a mountain of trash where you had to keep your wits about you so as not to step on something that would give way and slide down. The lights from Lanceheim didn't extend more than a few meters into the area, after which the moon would have to guide them where they slowly and with great care climbed alongside one another up the trash mountain. Each time someone stepped on an object that fell down, all four of them stopped until the sound died out. Only after having assured themselves of renewed silence did they continue to climb. They'd all heard what happened to animals who made their way uninvited into the Garbage Dump.

Higher and higher they climbed, and when after more than half an hour they stood atop the mountain and looked out over the threatening contours of the Garbage Dump, which seemed to stretch into infinity in the moonlight, they were thoroughly out of breath.

Without uttering a word, Eric pointed out the direction, and they started walking south. He realized that they were forced to climb down onto the Left-hand Road and up onto the trash mountain again before they could make their way onto the Middle Road and begin the march toward the Garbage Town. Judging by the climbing they had just carried out, it would take them at least a few hours. But the night was long and there were no other alternatives. The despair which had been growing all day in his heart now burst out in full bloom, and the steps over the treacherous terrain felt heavy.

"We're going right into a trap," whispered Snake to Sam, who was walking beside him. "And you know it."

Sam didn't answer.

"What are they doing?" asked Louise.

She was standing on a stool next to Hyena Bataille and thus could whisper the words right into the hyena's ear. The hyena shrugged his shoulders and shook his head. He was holding a telescope to his eyes, and slowly lowered it.

"They're on their way south," he said. "Toward the Left-hand Road."

"Should we take them there?" asked Louise.

"You can bet your sweet ass on that," said Bataille.

"Who are they?" asked Louise.

"Three strangers and an animal that I hate more than any other animal on this earth," answered Bataille.

This surprising answer caused Louise Terrier to feel ill at ease. A Bataille in a bad mood was a danger to everyone.

When the four stuffed animals came up to the precipice that led down to the Left-hand Road, they had been in the

Garbage Dump for almost an hour. They had proceeded in silence, and their misgivings grew in step with their fatigue. The dump was silent and deserted, a fact that partially calmed them, but sometimes the stillness seemed unnaturally mute. At one point Sam thought he'd seen something moving far away, but he kept that observation to himself, afraid that Snake would use it against Eric.

But not even Snake was saying anything anymore.

"We'll go down here," whispered Eric, pointing toward the road.

The others nodded. It felt good that the bear seemed to know where they should go, seemed to know what he was doing. Carefully they started climbing down toward the Left-hand Road. It went easier now, not just because they'd become more used to balancing on the treacherous trash, but also because it was downhill.

When they'd made it all the way down, they discovered that the cliff that rose on the other side was much too steep to climb; it was a vertical wall that stood before them.

"We'll try walking a bit," whispered Eric to Tom-Tom, who stood closest, and the bear nodded eastward, in toward the dump.

The four started walking, happy to have solid ground under them again. The moonlight that had guided their way up on the mountain couldn't reach into the narrow valley path that was the Left-hand Road, and they walked in a blackness that forced them to walk even more slowly. After a few hundred meters the precipice on the north side grew higher and higher, and they were now surrounded by steep, sheer walls of trash on both sides. Here and there objects were sticking out which they tried to avoid.

Then a voice was heard.

Thin and faraway but quite distinct. The four stuffed animals stopped in their tracks. Then the noise broke loose.

The sound which unexpectedly broke the silence in an

explosion caused the ground below them to shake. Tom-Tom fell down on his knees with his wings covering his head. Sam ran to the edge of the road, pressing his back against the trash wall while, not moving, he gazed in the direction of the explosion. The snake wriggled as fast as he could in the other direction, away from the boom that still continued. Eric stood completely still, trying to understand what was happening.

And despite the fact that he saw it with his own eyes he had a hard time understanding. A torrential stream of trash was sliding down the trash mountain's south face. Metal and wood, plastic and plaster, twisted objects and forms that he couldn't make out, all running in a single thick-flowing porridge down the mountain and quickly filling in the road behind them. And when the bear understood what was about to happen, he turned around. In front of them a similar avalanche of odds and ends and muck was flooding down onto the road. It was a trap. It had happened so quickly that not even Snake had time to wriggle out.

Then it became silent.

Eric could hear the sound of his own breathing, like a rushing rapids in a deserted landscape, but otherwise nothing. Snake was ten or so meters farther ahead, Tom-Tom stood right next to him, and Sam a few meters to the right.

"Now?" a clear voice was heard to say somewhere in the night.

Instinctively the four companions turned around. It was completely silent. Then the sound of a large number of paws and claws was heard, running on the south side of the ravine. Eric twirled around and stared up toward the southwest.

"We wish no one harm!" shouted the bear.

He tried to see some of those he'd just heard, but the mountain walls were too steep and too high.

"Hello!" he shouted.

Now there seemed to be stuffed animals moving everywhere up there. Snake as well as Sam had made their way in toward Eric and Tom-Tom in the middle of the road, and all of them were standing tightly together, staring up toward the night sky, where stars were shining.

"Hello!" Eric shouted again. "We have come to speak with your queen!"

The words produced no response. The stuffed animals running around on the sides of the ravine didn't take any notice, they were still moving around, taking up positions. For what?

"Hello!" Eric shouted a third time. "I am Eric Bear. I have come to speak with Rat Ruth."

Slowly silence descended over the ravine. Sam Gazelle stood quite close to Eric, and he whispered in the bear's ear. "It's over now, isn't it? Are we going to die?"

Eric didn't reply. He didn't have the answer.

CHAPTER 20

They lifted Eric out of the ravine.

Down from the sky came a chair in slow motion. It was an absurd experience, because they could neither see the arm of the crane nor the wires, only a large armchair slowly gliding down out of the gray-black night sky. They caught sight of it at roughly the same time. Soundlessly it landed a few meters from them.

"The bear will sit down," said a gruff voice that echoed down to the bottom of the ravine.

Eric looked from one friend to the other, and they nodded. They had confidence in him. Even Snake looked hopeful.

"You'll manage this," said Tom-Tom, giving Eric a pat on the shoulder. "Damn it."

Sam nodded in agreement, and Eric took the few steps over to the armchair and sat down. Immediately the chair began to be hoisted up, and with a tense hold on the arm of the chair Eric Bear vanished into the night.

His friends down on Left-hand Road could hear the tumult that broke out above them when the armchair finally became visible to those who were waiting. The snake, the crow, and the gazelle stood completely still, listening to the sounds from the Garbage Dump's animals as they departed with Eric. Then it became silent again.

Unpleasantly silent.

Sam looked at Snake, who slowly let the green tip of his tail sway back and forth.

"I'm not saying anything," he said. "I'm not saying anything."

Sam took a hoof-full of light-blue pills out of his pants pocket, generously offering some to his friends. The snake and the crow declined, the one with contempt and the other courteously and amiably, whereupon the gazelle—not without a certain amount of difficulty—swallowed the pills himself.

They carried Eric on the armchair to the Garbage Town. His plan was to try to commit the route to memory so as to be able to make his way back on his own, and this demanded concentration. They carried him through tunnels and over a bridge. Back and forth, it felt like, across these mountains of refuse in a dark world which stank of putrefaction and where none of the contours were comprehensible to him.

Four stuffed animals carried the armchair on their shoulders. Eric perceived their strong odors and guessed that they were horses of various types, perhaps dromedaries or donkeys. Around them a dozen shadowy figures were moving in the night, and after a few minutes Eric identified Hyena Bataille as the group's commander. He had heard about Bataille. Up to now the bear had succeeded in maintaining a certain composure, but now the feeling of displeasure became much too strong. He abandoned his ambition of memorizing the many right and left turns, and instead closed his eyes. Images of Teddy and Emma filled him. But despite the fact that he exerted himself to refrain, again and again his thoughts slipped over to Bataille. Could everything he'd heard be true?

After perhaps a quarter of an hour, the surrounding sounds became louder and louder. Eric opened his eyes and understood that he was on the outskirts of the Garbage Town he'd heard talk of but never seen. In the moonlight—there surely remained a half hour before the full moon would become half again—hovels formed of refuse were outlined. Walls and roofs leaned at odd angles, or else the constructions were on their way to sinking down into the dump's clay blanket of refuse. But the more compact the settlement became, Eric observed, the higher the walls rose.

When he saw Rat Ruth's residence he realized that he had reached the center point of the Garbage Town. The queen's residence consisted of a mass of free-standing, multi-angled hovels connected to each other by a network of winter garden–like passageways. Shards of glass of various colors had been pieced together in the passageways, and in the moonlight the mosaic sparkled to great effect.

The animals who led Eric to the residence handed him over to two bats. They led him along the multicolored glass corridors. The impression was kaleidoscopic; up was down and down was up, and several times the bear involuntarily stumbled where he was walking. It stank of muck and anxiety. The hyena had thankfully stayed outside, and from the howling crowd of animals that met Eric in the open area in front of the residence—and which reminded him of the angry mobs he'd read about in history books many years ago—not a sound was heard.

They passed through buildings that seemed to be empty and suspended in oblivion. In the glass corridors Eric was blinded by light; in the pitch-black hovels between them he couldn't even see where he was setting his paws. The floor was uneven and sometimes crunched when he stepped on something. Here and there he believed he heard stuffed animals whispering as he passed by, animals concealed by the solid darkness but who had become accustomed to it and therefore could see him without him seeing them.

It was only when they came into the queen's hall that Eric could make out the contours around him. He was led in through an opening in the farther wall. Directly across, on the other side of the room, was Ruth's throne. He sensed how a mass of movements occurred at the same moment as he came in, and he glimpsed tails and hind legs hurrying out through the door openings on the room's opposite side.

Ruth was slumped on her throne, apparently bored, and hardly looked up as they approached. Eric, who had become accustomed to seeing her at the meetings of A Helping Hand, was shocked at how she suddenly seemed to fit in. From being a suspect rat who through her mere presence transformed the individuals around the conference table to normalcy, here she was in her right element. She radiated a power that Eric had never even suspected, and—this impression he had the moment he stepped into the hall, and it was reinforced during their conversation—she possessed a kind of passive goodness that took him completely by surprise. She was nonetheless the Queen of the Garbage Dump.

"Ruth," he said, "I'm sorry to have to . . ."

He didn't know how he should continue.

The rat was surprised by the direct address, and she sharpened her gaze. When she recognized him she seemed to be surprised, and she signaled to the bats to take a step to the side so that the bear wasn't standing pressed in between them.

"Eric Bear?"

He nodded. "I'm sorry to have to look you up like this in the middle of the night," he said, "but I have a matter which I must speak with you about. And it cannot wait."

Above all else this seemed to amuse the rat. She sat up in her throne, signaled to Eric to come closer, and leaned forward a little, as one did to listen to a little cub. When Eric took a few steps forward, the bats followed along. The bear did his best to pretend not to notice this.

"It concerns a . . ." and he looked around again, into the darkness along the walls of the hall, "it concerns a list."

The rat looked uninterested.

"A list?" she repeated.

"A list," Eric confirmed.

But when he didn't see even the hint of understanding in her gaze, he made himself clear in a whisper: "The Death List."

The rat's eyes narrowed. She leaned back, as if the cub she'd taken him for had shown himself to be more naïve than she'd thought.

"Leave us alone," she commanded.

Both of the bats turned around and disappeared before Eric even had time to react. Judging by all the commotion along the dark walls, there had been several animals in there. When the silence resumed, Ruth looked at him commandingly at the same time as she raised one eyebrow.

"And so?" she said, and in her small, dull, pearl eyes he saw nothing either confirming or denying.

There he stood, alone and defenseless, in the Garbage Town queen's innermost hall. The rat reposed heavily in her overwhelming power where she sat, but still, Eric felt no fear. He remained tense, however, uncertain whether she was trying to lull him into a false sense of security.

"I know," said Eric, "that you draw up the Death List."

"How is that?"

The words fell with an indifference that caused Eric to tremble.

"It has come to my knowledge," he repeated, "that it is you who are behind the Death List."

Ruth continued staring at him, and then burst out in loud, surprising laughter. It sounded like a quick succession of snorts and contained no joy whatsoever, but it was still a laugh.

"That's the stupidest thing I've heard," snorted the queen. "Would Magnus allow me to decree over life and death?"

"It's not the idea that you're putting on airs," said Eric in a voice which he hoped sounded convincing. "I know what I know."

"Nonsense," snorted the rat.

"Noah Camel," said Eric.

The rat stiffened. "Who?"

"Your courier has been gossiping. And you don't need to concern yourself about punishing him, he's already gotten his punishment."

"I've never heard talk of any camel," said the rat, but there was a hesitation in her voice that hadn't been there before.

"This is my story," said Eric Bear.

Then he told everything that had happened. He told about Emma, and about the passion he'd experienced during their years of being in love, a passion which made him tremble with excitement and shake with jealousy. Love, said Eric Bear to Rat Ruth, had caused his heart to become heavier than an anchor from sorrow and dejection, and at the same time it had caused him to feel as exhilarated as a helium balloon. He told how passion deepened and turned into unselfish love, and then: the self-sacrificing, lavish love that made him courageous, invincible, and beautiful. Finally he told about love as the deep commonality that withstood trials and temptations by quite simply making him blind. How could he be lured by someone else, when he didn't see anyone else, filled to the brim as he was by his soul's one and only, Emma Rabbit.

Then Eric told about his twin brother Teddy, and about the life that Teddy was living which just as easily might have been Eric's. And vice versa. And how the closeness and tenderness that ached in him became harder and harder to endure with every year since their teens. The same pain, Eric admitted to Rat Ruth, was in Teddy, the same closeness, although with other indications, and it had always been like that. They were each other's fate, they could not be separated and therefore it must be so, that if Magnus took one of them, he must also take the other. If only one of them remained, an asymmetry would arise which wasn't possible, like east without west.

At the start Rat Ruth shook her head at Eric Bear's swarm of words, and she yawned to show how bored she was. More than once she raised her paw to silence him, but he didn't let himself be silenced. And slowly but surely he won her interest. Word by word, sentence by sentence, and minute by minute he pulled her into his emotional life and stuck her solidly between love and desperation. He could see that what he was saying actually meant something to her, that deep within the rat's soul was a little rat who recognized itself.

And when he fell silent after having for the first time dared to formulate all the pain he'd closed up inside himself since last Tuesday up at the Environmental Ministry, the rat sat silently for a long time on her throne, staring at him.

Then she made her decision.

She waved him up to the throne, and showed with a gesture that he could take a place on one of the stair steps right next to her right back leg. It was only then that Eric noticed that Rat lacked a right claw, and it demanded a real exertion of will not to stare at the clawless leg.

The bear sat where he'd been shown, and Ruth spoke to him in a kind of hissing sound that could not possibly be heard by anyone else.

"It's not me," said Rat Ruth. "I have it here, it's true, and I send it on. With the camel or with someone else, and that's true as well. But I'm not the one who makes the list."

A confession.

Eric was amazed.

The confession came directly, without awkwardness or pride. It was too simple, thought the bear. Why did she confess? So thoughtlessly? How could she be sure that Noah Camel really had squealed; perhaps she'd already spoken with Noah in the evening and knew that the game was up? Had the Queen of the Garbage Dump been seriously moved by Eric Bear's sentimental stories?

"I don't know who does it, and even if I did know," said Ruth, "I wouldn't tell. And, believe me, there is nothing you or your friends can do to force me."

She had to lie. The list must be hers. She was, after all, the Queen Over the Decay of Everything. Eric Bear refused to accept what he was hearing.

"Thereby," said Ruth, "I believe that your business is—"

"It's not over," he interrupted.

"What?"

"After the Chauffeurs come. It's not over, it's just the beginning of something new."

Rat shrugged her shoulders.

"I'm not getting involved in that," she said.

"And everything you can do for me now," he said, "will be counted in your favor then. In the next life."

"You're out of your mind," hissed Ruth, but there was an amused look in her eyes. If nothing else he had lured her into extending the conversation.

"It's not about wisdom," he said.

"You're a lunatic," she answered matter-of-factly. "Just by the fact that you believe it's possible to remove two names from the list."

His pulse beat faster. Was he about to talk her into a new, and greater, admission?

"I've heard the stories too," he said. "Many of them. It's possible to remove one name . . ."

"Possible? I wouldn't call removing a name from the Death List possible," hissed Rat Ruth, still with a degree of exhilarated scorn in her voice.

". . . but two names are impossible," concluded Eric.

"Let me put it like this," said Ruth, "and I'm not the one who thought of it, I'm only repeating something someone said to me a long time ago. 'One removal is for the divine, more is for the unborn.' I don't know what that means, but it sounds as though you're up against the impossible."

It was Eric's turn to shrug his shoulders.

"Madness," repeated Ruth.

After that she raised her voice and shouted, "Guards!"

The bear got up with a jerk. He was standing only a few decimeters from the rat and realized that he was exactly the same height as she. But before he had time to consider his options, the bats were again at his side.

"Take him to his friends," ordered Ruth. "And throw them out of here, all four of them. Their business is going to remain unfinished. Eric Bear, to find a treasure, the treasure has to be buried."

And with that the bats took a rough hold of his shoulders and led him away.

At the same moment as he stepped back out into the cool night the stench struck him. Eric Bear had nearly forgotten about it inside with the rat. Certainly it smelled of mold and slime inside the residence as well, but it was nothing compared to the stench here at the top of the Garbage Dump. Instinct caused him to start breathing through his mouth, and thereby he released an involuntary sigh. The bats' grip on his shoulders was achingly tight, and despite the fact that he obeyed their slightest suggestion of where and how fast he should walk, they held him just as hard the whole time. He shuddered at the thought of the long march back to the ravine where Sam, Tom-Tom, and Snake were waiting.

Then these words came as though out of nowhere: "Release him."

The bats stopped in their tracks.

The deep voice that had spoken these words was accustomed to being obeyed. In the next second, Eric realized that they had already released him. From the frying pan right into the fire. Eric, too, had recognized the harsh voice.

Hyena Bataille.

"You can go," said Bataille, now at an angle behind them, and the bats were gone without Eric seeing how it happened.

He stood dead still. Should he run? No one was holding him back, and the darkness might conceal him. If Bataille caught up with him? Strength, setting, and speed were in the hyena's favor; all Eric could hope for was luck.

That would scarcely be enough.

"We have something to talk about," said Bataille. "But not here."

The bear remained motionless. He had no idea what the hyena meant, but he sensed that the words were intended to distract or possibly fool him.

Then Bataille was standing there, less than a meter away.

"Follow me," he said.

He turned around and started walking.

It was now or never.

With a leap the bear would catch up with the hyena, onto him, over him. Possibly Eric could get his paws around his neck, around his throat . . .

Bataille turned around. "Are you coming?"

And when Eric saw the hyena's face and it became clear to him that this truly was the legendary Hyena Bataille, not some little mole in the schoolyard, he also realized how ludicrous the thought had been. Flee? Overpower Bataille?

Eric nodded and followed.

Bataille led the bear away from the Garbage Town, back toward the ravine where his friends were prisoners. After a little more than five minutes they passed a windmill-like propeller that was fastened to a low tower. The hyena pointed.

"This way."

Under the propeller was a hovel in which there was a three-legged table and two gray corduroy armchairs. Bataille made a gesture toward the bear, and Eric sat down.

"I don't know what I should say," sighed Bataille, "but Ruth can be difficult."

Eric nodded.

He would agree with whatever Bataille said, and he would reply courteously to whatever question was asked. Keeping yourself alive was more important than anything else. Without him, who would rescue Emma and Teddy?

"I've known her for . . . I don't know how many years," said Bataille in his dark, harsh voice. "And yet . . . I don't know."

Eric nodded again, then shook his head. He hoped that these were movements that were in agreement with Bataille's state of mind and insinuations.

"If I kill all four of you," said Bataille, "then . . . I don't know. Perhaps she won't give a damn? But, then . . . you two sit on some board together?"

"A Helping Hand," confirmed Eric.

The hyena nodded. Thought about it.

"I'm taking no risks. She gave me the task of bringing you to your friends and releasing all of you. But I can't let the snake go now that he's finally come. I want Marek."

Eric stared. "Marek?"

"But that's not what she ordered me to do. So I need your

permission, Bear. I don't intend to get in trouble with the rat."

Hyena nodded. "Give me your blessing, say that you allowed me to take Marek. That will be enough for her, it's you she's interested in. Then you'll get something from me."

"But . . . I . . ."

"For I know who writes the Death List," said Hyena Bataille.

TEDDY BEAR, 4

I always had time to have coffee at Nick's on brick-red Uxbridge Street. If I didn't do anything else when I went into the city, at least I did that. Nick steamed the milk scalding hot and baked his apple muffins with cardamom. He worked the register himself in front of shelves filled with bread loaves and baguettes. We'd gotten to know each other over the years. We said hello.

I sat in the first booth, by the window facing the street. It was always unoccupied. Other regulars preferred sitting in the booths farther in. The place was long and narrow and all the booths looked alike. A round table, fastened to the floor, with a white laminated surface. A red leather couch that encircled the table in a U shape. Tall backrests that created a sense of isolation. The regular customers came to Nick's for isolation.

The lighting isn't worth mentioning.

With the spoon I poked a hole through the milk foam, watching warm vapors from the coffee rise up toward the ceiling. Like a thought.

Across from Nick's is the building where my twin brother, Eric, and my wife, Emma Rabbit, live.

Number 32 Uxbridge Street. They live on the fourth floor. The windows that face the street are from the living room and dining room. From my booth in the café I might see them walking across the parquet floor.

The day I'm going to tell about, I couldn't see them through the windows.

The day I'm going to tell about was twenty-two days ago.

The day I'm going to tell about, a powerful red gorilla came out of the entryway to number 32 Uxbridge Street. This occurred as I took a bite of my muffin, which included a large piece of apple. The gorilla held open the door, and out onto the street stepped a well-dressed dove. After the dove followed yet another gorilla. I was certain that this peculiar company did not live in the building, because I knew who lived there. The gorillas and the dove pointed across the street, directly at me where I was sitting on the seat by the window. They couldn't see me. You couldn't see in through the windows to Nick's Café. This was due to the reflectivity of the glass.

It was the café itself the dove was pointing at, and all three of them crossed the street with rapid steps.

Before the situation became clear to me, the little troika was standing inside Nick's, a few meters from my booth, ordering coffee and croissants.

I pulled myself all the way in against the wall and concealed my face behind a dessert menu that was always on the table. Hidden behind types of ice cream, various toppings and flavorings, I heard, to my terror, that the dove and the gorillas were taking a place in the booth next to mine.

"That ought to have scared the shit out of the bear bastard," said a harsh voice that must have belonged to one of the gorillas.

"Firewood out of the table," laughed a similar voice that must have been the other gorilla's.

"Shut up!" hissed a high-pitched voice that with certainty belonged to the dove. "Eat your croissants and keep your mouths shut."

I could not marry Emma Rabbit.

I loved her. I'd proposed to her. The date for the wedding was set. My parents and her mother were happy. Each in their own way.

Nonetheless, I couldn't.

It was unavoidable that Father's story had something to do with it.

I think best after dinner.

When I've had a cup of coffee after eating. For dessert I eat dried figs straight from the bag, up in my room. Across from me hangs an enormous painting depicting the sea. Emma painted it a few months after we'd met, but I had it framed a few weeks ago. The painting must be three by five meters. Apart from a lighthouse far to the left, the canvas is filled by the sea and foaming waves. Hundreds of dark-blue nuances have been painted with a brush, giving the impression of never having been lifted from the canvas. The artist seems never to have hesitated. The technique suggests an aggressive impatience. It must have been inside her. Somewhere.

You see what you're looking for.

You see the sort of things that are within yourself.

I must have known that there was something about Father. Intuitively I already knew that there was something about Father when I was very small. I knew it during my school years. This knowledge was no more than a twitch in my eyelid. No more than the ripples on the surface of the bathwater. I carried the secret around in the same way you constantly carry around the decisive moments in life.

You know about them both before and after they have taken place.

I knew about my father's secrets. I knew that life is not for all time. I knew that in the end you always stand alone. I knew that my free will was my greatest enemy. How did I know?

I can't explain that.

Our father, Boxer Bloom, the wisest and most just animal in our city.

When the secret was on its way to reach conscious awareness, like the sand that inexorably runs out of the hourglass, I turned the glass upside down again. Then I did the same thing again and again and again. But with the years I didn't have the strength to resist.

Was it maturity? Perhaps simply fatigue? It wasn't courage.

I had learned to see through the underlying structures of society. On the other hand, the breeze in my fur in the twilight can go right by me. I don't perceive the aroma of boxwood or the sun's warmth against my nose.

Shame hides when we're not searching for it.

Shame's best hiding place is right in front of our eyes.

Father always worked late. This wasn't strange. It was better to correct the pupils' papers at the office than to drag everything home. There were conferences to prepare for and carry out. A series of social activities demanded his presence.

It happened that I saw him sitting in the car on the school's parking lot, conversing with one of the other teachers. Perhaps it was a female teacher? That wasn't strange. A rector was no better than his teachers. A rector's priorities must be respected.

On one occasion they got out of the car just as I was walking across the parking lot. I didn't ask him why they'd been sitting in the car.

I never asked him.

It was my fault, and I am living with that.

There are philosophers who maintain that evil is passivity. In our secularized, transparent, and democratic city, passivity is the only kind of evil that remains. All others have been rooted out. Taken into custody. All other kinds of evil can be controlled and limited.

So it's said.

Rhetoric. Empty rhetoric. Nothing is new under the sun.

The unwillingness to help a stranger has to do with laziness. It has to do with cowardice. The result of laziness and cowardice is passivity, but we can read about the reasons behind it in theology.

Laziness and cowardice.

I was not blind to my shortcomings. Nonetheless, I wasn't able to confront Father. You speak of codependency with regard to substance abuse. Those who are close to the substance abuser make themselves a part of the behavior by not confronting it. That isn't passivity, it's guilt.

Father's cowardice became my cowardice.

I hope that his guilt was as hard to bear as mine.

I have excuses. There are always excuses. I was forced to transform my amazing father, the unsurpassable Rector Bloom, into a cowardly wretch who didn't dare admit that he was unfaithful. That was asking a lot. While I was growing up I had filled the image of my father with everything I respected in life. When I realized the truth, it was not just Father who fell from his pedestal.

It was my life that came crashing down.

Eric already knew. He didn't care. He kept silent.

I did, too. Every morning my father met my mother in the kitchen with a big smile, a warm embrace, and a cup of coffee. It was my fault that her life became false and distorted in one stroke. My fault. Not because of what I did. Because of what I refrained from doing. My passivity.

My cowardice.

Never again.

I will never again be a part of such a tragedy.

I don't intend to react. I act.

I couldn't get married to Emma Rabbit.

There were a number of reasons.

This was just one of them.

I had become, and intended to devote my life to remaining, a good bear.

I didn't hear what they were talking about. After the dove's reprimand the gorillas lowered their voices. The murmuring from the next booth was impossible to make out.

I never eavesdrop.

Usually there's nothing to hear.

It was different at Nick's that day. If I'd had the opportunity, I would have committed their conversation to memory. But I drank my coffee, wiped the foam from my whiskers, and gave up on hearing what they were saying. Outside the window a car or two drove past. The Morning Weather was getting old and I considered leaving the place. Usually I went to Nick's in the afternoons. Fate and an unexpected change in my routine out at Lakestead House had caused me to go into the city right after breakfast.

When she came walking up the street from Balderton Street I didn't recognize her at first.

It was so unexpected.

She never left the studio before noon. She lived for her art and knew that the victories were in the obstacles. If the work felt empty and sluggish she understood not to give up and go away. It was a matter of suffering through it and persevering. On the other side of difficulties was the creativity that made her forgetful of time and space. Then she could work until far into the evenings. Sometimes into the night.

She never left the studio before noon, and yet Emma

Rabbit was strolling nonchalantly on Balderton Street this morning. Astounded, I watched her direct her steps right toward Nick's.

Wearing a long, thin coat with a fur collar. She had on high brown-leather boots with suns embroidered on the calf. She carried her head high, as she'd always done. Even though she seemed to be on her way to Nick's I was sure I was imagining things. She would go home. It did happen that I imagined things. Now I was imagining that she was looking right into my eyes through the window toward the street that I knew was impossible to see through.

Instead of turning the corner on Uxbridge Street, she continued straight across the crosswalk at the intersection. For that reason she disappeared from my line of sight for a few moments. The following second the door to Nick's opened, and there she stood.

Emma Rabbit.

Less than five meters away.

She could not be allowed to see me. Under no circumstances must she see me sitting here.

I improvised.

My half-eaten muffin was on the plate next to the coffee cup. With a quick movement I bumped against it. It bounced toward the seat and fell down onto the floor under the table. I produced a gesture of irritation—however, not the slightest sound—and followed the muffin down under the table. From there I saw how Emma wiggled the toe of her right boot in expectation that Nick would serve her. My muffin and I remained under the table as Emma ordered a cup of tea, paid Nick, and took her small tray and carried it past my booth.

She didn't go far.

I heard her before I'd even managed to climb up and set myself on the couch again.

"So there you are!"

She was talking to the dove and the gorillas in the neighboring booth.

I went to see Eric. I went to see him in enemy territory. We of course had no place to meet.

The external circumstances of my life had been transformed. Right before I started at Wolle & Wolle I moved away from home. I moved out to the coast and Lakestead House. The move must have occurred before I started at the advertising agency, because when I met Emma Rabbit I was living out here.

Eric and I never saw each other at home with Mother and Father on Hillville Road. He maintained that he had regular contact with Mother. He despised Father like the plague. I saw our parents once or twice a week. We never talked about Eric. Father and I were not in agreement about everything, but we agreed on the fact that Eric hadn't been able to hold his own against evil.

He had fallen.

Father didn't forgive him.

I forgave him.

I went to see Eric at Casino Monokowski, despite the fact that I'd promised myself never to set my paw there again. I was desperate. I couldn't get married to Emma Rabbit, despite the fact that I loved her.

Just like the first time, I was admitted by a doorman who mistook me for my brother. The Afternoon Weather was no more than approaching, but inside Casino Monokowski it might just as well have been midnight. I found Eric in a distant corner, at a small table that was hidden behind one of the many bar counters.

He was not surprised to see me.

"What time of day is it?" he asked.

"It's the middle of the day," I answered.

"Doesn't feel like it," he said. "I've got to have something to wake up."

He called to the duck behind the bar and ordered black coffee and some type of alcohol. I presume. I shook my head, I didn't want anything.

"Tell me how the Angels are doing," Eric asked.

In last year's finals the Yok Gigantes had defeated our Amberville Angels in the seventh and decisive final match. We hadn't been that close to a victory in fourteen years. It was fourteen years ago that we'd last taken home the great goblet. Until now the season had alternated between heaven and hell.

"I've missed it all," said Eric.

"It's not impossible that it'll happen this year," I said. "It's not impossible at all. Harry's form is holding up. He's made more goals than he did in the whole season last year. He's on his way . . ."

"But defensively?" asked Eric, putting his finger on the sore spot. "Are we going to manage the defense?"

While I expanded on how I perceived this year's team lineup, animals were circling around us. We were, and always had been, an attraction. Identical twins were unusual. The most curious were the employees of the casino. Eric's workmates. Waiters and waitresses, croupiers and bartenders, guards and stewards. Eric didn't pay any attention to them.

When I had exhausted the subject of the Amberville Angels as thoroughly as I could, silence fell between us. It was never uncomfortable.

"Is there something in particular?" he asked.

I nodded; there was.

"And if it had been something simple, you would have already spit it out," said Eric.

I nodded again. We were twins, we understood each other.

Eric called for more alcohol, I ordered a cup of coffee to have something to do. The attraction value of looking at twins receded. The table where we were sitting was isolated, and there was nothing to keep us from having a frank conversation.

I didn't know where I should begin.

"There's no difference between small crimes and great crimes," I said. "It is said that you can overlook some but not others. But whose arbitrariness should apply?"

Eric shook his head, shrugged his shoulders, and sipped his drink. I let my coffee cool in the cup.

"I refuse to compromise," I said. "And, besides, that's impossible. Walking against a red light and making a killer of a law-abiding driver can't be less serious than stealing an orange at a Springergaast."

Eric shrugged his shoulders.

"Is it so impossible to understand? It seems to be impossible to understand. They say I have to be reasonable. Even Mother thinks this is getting crazy. She says that I have to see the context. Making judgments is an art in itself, she says. I don't need to make judgments. It's a matter of courage. To have the strength to keep from compromising."

"And you think I have problems," said Eric.

"I've never said that," I answered.

"No," Eric quickly agreed. "No, Teddy, that's right. You've never accused me of anything."

And he smiled at me and took my paw over the table.

Then I wept. I couldn't help it.

"Eric," I said, "I'm not here to ask you for a favor."

His gaze was sharp despite the alcohol.

"I've come to propose a businesslike agreement to you. Between brothers. Without papers and signatures. But no less binding for that."

"An agreement?" asked Eric.

I nodded. Now I knew what I should say. It didn't make the words easier to get out of me.

"I get something, and you get something in exchange," I said.

"What do I get?" he wanted to know.

There was expectation in the air.

"Money," I answered at last.

"You intend to pay me?" asked Eric.

"Yes I do," I confirmed. "You'll get paid."

"I get paid at Casino Monokowski, too," he said.

"You're going to get more from me," I said. "Lots more."

"I don't know if I want to hear the rest . . ."

"I have problems. With my life, Eric. It's hard being good."

This sounded pathetic. I couldn't continue. But Eric understood me. He had always understood me. He nodded. I swallowed, collected myself, and continued.

"Being good and at the same time living an everyday life . . . it's . . . I'm forced into situations that . . . where all the alternatives are equally impossible. And I cannot . . . Eric, I'm serious, I . . ."

Then I whispered.

"Either I die, Eric. Die now. Quickly. Before I fall for the temptations. Before I'm seduced by the sort of things that others regard as bagatelles. Little things. That's how evil tries to lure me. With the little things. Or else . . . we find a way out."

He remained sitting silently. I dried my tears. I cleared my throat and did my best to focus. What I had to say demanded a certain degree of dignity.

"Eric, the agreement I am proposing . . . I want you to take my place. When life forces me to make a decision . . . when life forces me to do things . . . that are not compatible with goodness."

He met my gaze, and I looked down at the table.

Now it was said.

The silence that followed became a long one.

"Okay," he said at last. "Okay, we'll do it. Shall we go?"

And with that I left Casino Monokowski for the second, and final, time.

I couldn't stay under the table.

As long I could see her brown boots with the suns on the calf I didn't dare risk anything, but when they disappeared out of sight I assumed that she'd sat down with the dove and the gorillas. With a certain difficulty I wriggled myself back up onto the red seat. I didn't want to risk Nick coming over to my booth and asking what I was doing. It would have been difficult to explain.

A single thought echoed in my head. I ought not to have been this close to Emma Rabbit. Not at Nick's Café, right across the street from number 32 Uxbridge Street, that sober, brick-red street.

She had just arrived. I had to go.

I had to get out of there.

I evaluated my chances. Could I make my way from my booth and over to the door without Emma seeing me? It was likely that she was sitting on the outside of the booth behind mine. If she were seated facing in, the possibilities of succeeding were reasonable. But if she were seated facing the exit . . .

And if I remained sitting?

They were carrying on a conversation which I still could not hear, but Emma's soft, clear voice went right into my heart. It was painful.

So near.

After a few minutes I'd had enough. I had to do something. It was impossible to remain sitting. I moved carefully along the table. I held on to the menu in order to conceal my face if that should be required.

It was required.

Suddenly the tone from the neighboring booth changed. Departure. Farewells. I ducked down behind the dessert menu. A few seconds later Emma Rabbit was standing right next to me. She stood with her back turned toward me. The dove placed himself alongside her. I peeked over the edge of my dessert menu. The dove and Emma were embracing each other. They were hugging. Thank goodness the dove closed his eyes as he hugged her, otherwise he would have seen me. I ducked down behind the menu again.

"Bye-bye, Papa," said Emma Rabbit.

"Bye-bye, honey," said the dove.

"And, Papa," said Emma, "if you forget my birthday again this year I'll never forgive you."

The dove laughed a high-pitched laugh, and I heard how Emma turned and left the place.

I don't know what I did then.

I remained sitting behind my menu until long after the dove and his gorillas had left the café.

I had just seen the fatherless Emma Rabbit's father.

It was a lie. She was a lie. Thoughts raced through my head, like balloons bursting.

My Emma. Who was she really?

CHAPTER 21

They say that a stuffed animal can get used to anything, but each time he returned, Eric Bear found Yiala's Arch just as repugnant. It had as much to do with the narrow alley, reeking of urine, as with Sam Gazelle's claustrophobic apartment. Despite all that was at stake, Eric was forced to overcome the most intense revulsion each time he returned to Yok after having carried out an errand somewhere else in the city. When he passed Eastern Avenue and continued south, it was as though he were crossing a border. His identity was wiped out in a single stroke. In the rest of the city there was a surrounding world which reflected him as the sum of his actions. There animals understood how to interpret his ironic humility. In Yok he was nobody.

It was terrible.

And with heavy steps he turned into the grass-green alley and with bowed head went over to the entry to number 15. Eric Bear was so filled up with his dejection that he didn't sense trouble. All his concentration was directed inward. Perhaps otherwise he would have noticed that someone had knocked over the large cactus—the one that bloomed with small red flowers—that stood in a cement planter right inside the entryway.

Slowly Eric walked up the stairs. The memory of Snake Marek's helpless cries caused him to stop on the first stairway landing.

Eric, Sam, and Tom-Tom had sneaked away across the Garbage Dump. Hyena Bataille had promised not to let himself down into the ravine before the three were out of sight and earshot. He had broken his promise. The memory of Snake's desperate cries echoed in Eric's head.

He sighed heavily and continued up the stairs. He was so occupied with his own pain that he didn't perceive the smell of a cigar, or think about the fact that the door to Sam's apartment was ajar.

After the night at the Garbage Dump Eric Bear had devoted Friday morning to a stop by his office. He didn't recall when he'd last slept, but fatigue had become a constant condition which no longer worried him. At Wolle & Wolle people came and went more or less as they pleased. You were often working on projects, and right before the appointed deadline it was not unusual that you practically lived at the office. And the other way around: after the assignment was delivered, you gladly took a few days' well-earned vacation. Over the years, a work environment had been created where no one bothered keeping track of anyone else's working hours, and therefore no one made a big deal of the fact that Eric hadn't set his foot at Place Great Hoch in almost three weeks.

A massive pile of documents and folders that he was expected to sign and authorize were waiting on his desk; there were so many papers, he didn't even try to understand what he was signing. When after a little more than half an hour he was finished with the authorizations, his calendar awaited. In the neglected calendar that he and his secretary helped each other to update, the past weeks' rescheduling and cancellations had created a chaos which the coming weeks' rescheduling and cancellations would worsen. There was nothing, it appeared, that couldn't be delayed or that someone else couldn't take care of. Nevertheless, sooner or later most things seemed to return to his desk. In comparison to what he was up against, all these meetings were as paltry as the problems they aimed to solve. Yet he knew it was important to maintain the idea that life would go on as usual. Nothing was more valuable than hope; nothing else could give him the same strength.

One of Nicholas Dove's two gorillas took hold of Eric Bear at the same moment as the bear stepped over the threshold to Sam's apartment. The gorilla placed his massive hand on just that place that the bats some ten hours earlier had so carelessly mistreated, and Eric moaned with pain.

"Finally," said Nicholas Dove, getting up from the chair and putting down his cigar right on the kitchen table's laminated top, where it continued to glow.

The cigar would leave a large, black mark on the tabletop before the dove's visit was over.

"We were just talking about you, and wondered if you were intending to come back or not," said Dove.

Eric didn't hear him. In the corner of his eye he caught a glimpse of Sam Gazelle, thrown onto one of the mattresses on the floor by the terrace door. In the kitchen, with his back against the kitchen sink, sat Tom-Tom Crow on one of the wobbly kitchen chairs. He was tied with black insulation tape that had been wound around his wings and legs. They had even taped his beak. On the floor around the chair were piles of black feathers.

They had plucked him. The crow's belly shone white.

And on the diaphanous white cloth there were three or four burn marks that Eric immediately understood came from Dove's cigar.

Tom-Tom's gaze turned toward Eric. The humiliated entreaty, the pain and terror that shone in the crow's otherwise friendly, peering eyes caused the bear to completely lose his head. With a growl he tore himself loose from the red gorilla that had been holding him and rushed across the room. At that moment he had the power to take on anyone whatsoever. He threw himself against the gorilla alongside Tom-Tom. The gorilla stumbled backwards a few steps, but his large ape body was caught by the sink, which kept him from falling. Then everything happened very quickly.

Eric managed to hit and roar and bellow a few more seconds. Then a massive gorilla hand took a firm grip on his neck and lifted him up into the air. Eric had forgotten the red ape on the other side of the room. Eric Bear was thrown through the air, over the kitchen table, striking against the hard metal of the refrigerator. He pulled himself up, dazed but not yet defeated. The gorilla who had thrown him was on him again before he regained his balance. He lifted him up again by the neck, then slammed him against the kitchen table. The table fell apart with a crash. One of the splinters was forced into the back side of the bear's thigh and came out the front side.

The pain waited a few seconds before it reached his awareness.

Somewhere in the tumult Dove's clear voice was heard, but Eric couldn't make out any words. With a certain effort he got up, the adrenaline muting the pain in his thigh for the time being, and picked up a long, rough splinter of wood that he found on the floor. He staggered forward toward the nearest gorilla. The idea was to mercilessly drive the splinter right through the ape's eye, but Eric was neither quick nor strong enough. The ape easily warded off the attack, and with the back of his hand struck Eric across the face so that the bear fell backwards down onto the floor and finally came to rest.

When Eric Bear awoke, he saw Nicholas Dove's worried face looking down at him.

"Have you . . ." said Dove, but the bear heard no more before he disappeared back down into unconsciousness.

In the following moment—which wasn't the following moment at all but rather a few minutes later—the dove's head was replaced by a gorilla face that was grinning happily.

"He's alive now," said the ape.

After that the bear was out.

CHAPTER 22

But that's ridiculous," said Emma. "You must go to the doctor."

Eric Bear had made an attempt to go over to the kitchen island to get the red wine he'd uncorked shortly before, but he didn't manage more than a few steps. The pain in his thigh prevented him from moving freely, and in shame he had to limp back to the chair and sit down.

"It's not so bad," he assured her again.

He'd maintained that it was a strained muscle he got when he tried to run a race with Teddy on the beach.

"Idiocy," Emma had snorted. "Fifty-year-old bears shouldn't run at all."

Eric had been away from home for almost three weeks; he told Emma that there were only a few days left. A truth with an ominous import: it was still Friday when he granted himself this short leave in order to have dinner with Emma Rabbit.

On Sunday the Chauffeurs would pick up Teddy Bear and Nicholas Dove if Eric didn't succeed in preventing it.

"I've never understood who you think you impress with

your suffering," said Emma, letting all the city's males be summarized in this "you."

Eric threw out his hands.

"There's nothing to do. I'll take some painkillers and rest, then it'll get better."

Eric had taken Tom-Tom with him to Dr. Thompson when Dove had finally gone away and the bear and crow had recovered consciousness. The doctor had sewed a few stitches in the bear's thigh, and then Eric exited the doctor's office leaving the crow, who needed more extensive bandaging, behind. But instead of returning to Yok, Eric drove home.

Emma Rabbit carried the plates of *vitello tonnato* over to the table. Then she put out the salad, wine, and bread and lit the candles in the large candelabra they'd bought at an auction a year or two ago, one of A Helping Hand's many events. She dimmed the ceiling light and sat down.

"I want you to come home," she said with a tender smile, "because I'll soon get tired of waiting."

And then she lifted her wineglass in a toast. Feelings of melancholy caused Eric Bear to shiver, leaving behind a clump of anxiety in his throat. It grew so quickly that it closed up his esophagus before he'd even managed to bring the wineglass to his mouth. He wanted what she wanted. He, too, wanted to come home, more than anything else: home to her embrace, where time stood still and all there was, was the scent of her fur and the beating of her heart against his chest.

She fixed her eyes on him. Pretended to look stern. And he wanted so much to laugh at her little play-acting but instead felt how the tears were burning inside his eyelids and he knew that he couldn't cry, couldn't expose himself: he loved her and would never be able to lose her.

It was that simple.

. . . .

"I don't know exactly who is writing the list," said Bataille, "but I know how she gets the information."

The large propeller was slowly set in motion as the light breeze picked up, but the horizon was still hidden by night. Eric sat rigid as a stick in his corduroy armchair, trying to control his facial features, the nervous twitches of his whiskers, and the indulgent smile that he knew made him weak. Across from him sat the fear-inducing hyena. True, it appeared unlikely that this whispering conversation they were carrying on would end with him getting up and torturing the bear to death. But nothing was impossible.

Eric Bear's senses were on tenterhooks. At the Garbage Dump he saw not only the outlines of a discarded frying pan, a wheel-less baby buggy, and the prow of an old rowboat sticking up out of the gray-black mass of rubbish; in addition he could make out the odor of decaying coffee grounds from the stinking entirety, heard two horses neighing in the distance, and perceived the structure in the armchair's fabric, as if it were braille.

It was clear that Bataille had overheard the conversation Eric had recently had with Rat Ruth. Perhaps the hyena had been sitting in the darkness along one of the walls and listened; it didn't need to be any stranger than that.

"It wasn't the idea that I should know," hissed Bataille. "She doesn't know that I know."

The hyena was proud of his cunning and that he'd figured out how the one thing was connected to the other. The used clothes that the well-situated residents of the city donated to the church were gathered together and driven out to the dump once a month. Sometimes the deliveries were so extensive that a burly funeral director came with a whole truckload of clothes. Other months all you got was a package of coats that had been wrapped in brown wrapping paper and placed on a wheelbarrow that was pushed by a creaky old doorman or some former cantor with rheumatism.

The clothes came to good use, the hyena assured him, fingering the short, worn leather jacket he himself was wearing. All the animals at the Garbage Dump had clothes that came from the church's donations; there weren't any others. And sometimes, when the shipments were especially large, Rat sold back some of them to the stores in the city that dealt in used goods.

"It took a while before I noticed it," said Hyena. "But whether it was a delivery truck or a wheelbarrow, it was always the queen herself who took in the delivery."

The breeze that had caused the large propeller to whirl like a mighty windmill presaged the arrival of dawn. If Hyena's story had been disturbed earlier by creaking from the blades of the propeller, for a while now the sound had been a constant whine. Eric pushed the armchair closer to the table and leaned forward as well, whereupon he came so close that he could perceive the hyena's musty breath. There was a burnt smell from the predator's mouth. The dark of the night would remain dense for a while yet, but the starlight caused the hyena's eyes to flash as he twisted around and stared out toward the dump. It was an ice-cold radiance.

"I already knew that we were involved with the Death List," said Bataille. "When I came here I didn't believe in the list, but . . . but even when I knew . . . I didn't know more than that."

From the very start Bataille had become one of the Cleaners at the dump. The Cleaners were divided into three teams of five animals each. Once a week, sometimes more often but never less often than that, Ruth gave them written orders. These were crumpled scraps of paper which she solemnly handed over inside the great hall, where, in her terri-

ble handwriting, she had scribbled down a few addresses—
she'd learned to write as an adult—and the assignment was
always the same. Empty the apartment. Throw away what
should be thrown away, bring back the valuables. Clean out
everything. And leave the place as though no one had been
there.

The first months, Bataille thought this was a matter of
tips that Ruth had gotten from part of the criminal network
she worked for. A kind of repayment for services rendered.
They supplied her with information about when families
went on vacation, stayed with relatives, wound up in the
hospital, so that she could empty their abandoned houses.
What the hyena didn't understand was why they were
forced to clean up after themselves so carefully. Perhaps, he
thought, this was a manifestation of some sort of vanity?
Ruth was not always easy to understand.

Bataille came onto the trail of the truth in the form of
an old female cat whom they met in a stairwell one morning when Hyena and the Cleaners had been on their way
up to the sixth floor in a newly built apartment house in
Lanceheim.

"Are you going to Kohl's?" the cat had asked, and Bataille had nodded since "Kohl" was one of the names that
was on the week's crumpled scrap of paper. "Poor devil,
may his soul find peace now."

And the cat had shaken her head and continued down
the stairs.

Only the hyena had heard the cat's comments, and he kept
it to himself. Bataille knew that his reputation was growing,
that the animals feared what was a fortunate combination
of imagination and a lack of empathy. He also knew that
the moment he lost the queen's favor his hours were numbered. As soon as it was possible, the hyena gathered information which perhaps might prove valuable the day Ruth
no longer shielded him.

During the following months he tried to get evidence for his hypothesis. When it was possible—and it wasn't always—he strayed from the ongoing cleanup work in search of neighbors who could confirm that the apartment or the house they were going through belonged to an animal who had been carried away by the Chauffeurs the day before. Sometimes it was impossible to find anyone to ask, and the hyena had to return to the Cleaners with unfinished business. But he was not in a hurry, and often enough he got the answer he wanted. Finally he was certain.

The Cleaners were, without knowing it, the Chauffeurs' rear guard.

Eric Bear loved to listen when Emma Rabbit told stories.

After dinner they went in and sat in the oversized lounge suite of thick, beige cotton that dominated their living room on Uxbridge Street. The armchairs were so massive that it was impossible to sit normally in them. Involuntarily you ended up in a kind of half-lying position, with your legs under you on the chair or pointing straight out over the armrest, and it was in the latter manner that Eric Bear made himself comfortable and listened.

Emma was sitting on the couch. She had brought her wine with her, and she held her glass on her lap while she told about the past week. She spoke without gestures, without dramatizing her tone of voice, but her urgency was not to be missed. She had been working on a new project for the past few months, she told. It was a suite of memory tableaux from her early childhood; to be more exact, seven scenes which she repeated in various perspectives and techniques, sometimes all seven on the same canvas but more often one or two at a time. In the previous week she had worked exclusively in oils.

Eric listened and nodded. Never, he thought, was she anywhere other than here. Not even when she devoted herself to her childhood, which she often did in her art. It had to do with her energy, thought Eric, the quiet, burning force that caused Emma Rabbit to follow through with all the projects she embarked on. Some with a certain success, others best forgotten.

"Now I'm coming over to you," he said in the middle of a sentence, and she continued to talk as he—carefully, so that he wouldn't bump her wineglass—rolled out of the armchair and crept over to her on the couch. He sat right next to her so that he could feel her warmth. With his head against her shoulder he continued to listen with closed eyes.

"Despite all my theories, I never believed, not once, that it was Ruth who made the Death List," said Bataille.

He suddenly fell silent.

Eric had heard it, too. A kind of clicking somewhere in the darkness out in the dump, and they both turned around, trying in vain to see something. A long way off the lights from the hovels of the Garbage Town could be glimpsed like a will-o'-the-wisp in the blackness, but otherwise the dump was concealed by the night. To be on the safe side, the hyena lowered his voice to a hoarse whisper as he continued.

He hadn't connected the clothing deliveries with the Cleaners. There was no reason to make such a connection. But that Ruth took in the clothes on her own had aroused his curiosity, and he decided to find out why she didn't let anyone else do the job.

This proved to be more difficult than he'd thought. Rat Ruth met the courier, wrote a receipt for the delivery, and took the packing slips back to her room while the clothes were being unloaded. There was no possibility of ferreting out anything at all. On a single occasion Bataille managed to catch a glimpse of Rat sitting in her room, bowed over

a massive binder where she apparently stored the papers
having to do with the clothes. But why she, who otherwise
preferred to sleep through the days, always remained awake
for this delivery, remained a mystery. It certainly had nothing to do with Rat's interest in clothes.

Bataille understood that the answers to his questions
were in the binders that Ruth stored in her bedroom. Bataille didn't relate to Eric Bear exactly how he'd managed
to worm his way into the queen's bedroom, but after a long
period of purposeful efforts he'd finally gotten a friendly
invitation.

The hyena leaned across the three-legged table and in a
whisper described the scene with great care. How the queen
rat had lain down on her back on the bed after they'd shared
a bottle of calvados and was soon snoring audibly while Bataille snooped around in the room, which was filled to the
brim with the rat's valuables. That is to say, things that the
rat considered valuable, which could be a diamond neck-
lace or a half-eaten package of alphabet cookies. Bataille
sneaked around, lifting up piles of clothes, rummaging
through piles of papers and books that had to do with the
administration of the Garbage Dump. He searched through
clothes closets, which apparently functioned as some type
of pantry. The binders were nowhere.

At regular intervals the rat sighed or moaned from the
bed. Each time, the hyena was forced to break off his search
and make certain she'd fallen asleep again before he could
continue. He didn't want to think about what would happen
if she realized that he'd fooled her.

Finally he found her hiding place. Under a pair of loose
floorboards by the window closest to the bed. But he'd only
managed to start leafing through the binder when the rat
awoke with a jerk. Bataille threw aside the binder and poked
the loose floorboards back with his foot. All he'd seen were

pages filled with handwritten columns of names, dates, and the type of garments that had been donated.

It took almost half a year before he got a chance to inspect the binder a second time.

"But, you understand," said Bataille and the icy cold in his eye glistened yet again in the light from the stars, "I am made of time."

Eric nodded as though he understood what the hyena meant.

The next time it had gone better. Bataille had immediately gone to the hiding place by the window and so had significantly more time. What he'd thought was a single binder proved to be an entire little library. Lists of names, clothes, and dates. Page after page. The hyena didn't know what he was looking for, he mostly sat and leafed through it at random in order to discover a pattern. He believed that he was looking for some kind of code when his glance fell on the name Kohl. Kohl had donated a shirt and a pair of pants. The date that stood next to the clothes was a little more than a year old. Bataille thought about it and realized that Kohl must have donated clothes right before the Cleaners had been up in Kohl's apartment.

He started searching for more familiar names. And there they were. One by one he ran across them. The animals in whose homes he and the Cleaners had been those past months, the animals who had been picked up by the Chauffeurs the day before.

It was asserted that all of them had donated clothing on their dying day.

When Emma Rabbit finally fell silent, he hadn't heard a word of what she'd said the last ten minutes, despite the fact that she spoke without interruption.

"You haven't heard a word of what I've said the last ten minutes," she complained to him.

"Sure I have," lied Eric Bear. "Test me."

They were still sitting next to each other on the couch, he with his head against her shoulder. He put a paw on her leg and experienced how her warmth went right into his body.

"I'm not asking any test questions. Never have," she lied.

"You don't dare," he declared triumphantly and slowly lowered his head down onto her lap. "That's the whole thing."

"I don't want to embarrass you," she answered, stroking him across the ears.

"It's true," he said. "Not being able to conceal my superiority would truly have embarrassed me."

"What you just said you didn't even understand yourself," she laughed.

"I've never maintained that I was smarter than you."

"But that's what you think, isn't it?"

She looked down at him, and her entire face smiled. She was teasing. Seen from this perspective, upside down and from below, her eyes were even larger. There was his whole future.

"Never," he answered.

"Liar."

"And not that, either. You and I have one of the few equal relationships that I know of."

"Bullshit," she smiled.

"I think I'm smarter than you, you know it's the other way around. And I would have exposed you long ago, but I prove how much smarter I am by not saying anything," said Eric. "It can't get any more equal than that."

"You're a deeply deranged bear . . ."

"Which, naturally, is further evidence of my smartness," he smiled.

And he lifted his paws and pulled her down onto the couch in a heartfelt embrace.

When Bataille gave Eric the last piece of the puzzle, a feeling of euphoria passed through Eric. An insight so revolutionary that it caused him to feel dizzy.

They got up from the wobbly table at the same time, the bear and the hyena, and walked with silent, determined steps back west toward the ravine where the snake, the crow, and the gazelle still were.

Eric tried to take in what the Hyena had actually said: the donated, used clothing was really a way of sending a list of names—the Death List, to put it bluntly—to Rat Ruth. From the packing slip she wrote out two lists. One she sent by courier to the Environmental Ministry and the Chauffeurs. The other she gave to the Cleaners.

All stuffed animals have asked themselves questions of life and death, at some point, when young or old. Why must the factories manufacture new animals? Why must those who were already living in the city be carried away by the Chauffeurs? Why did they all live in open or concealed terror of what would happen in the next life? And who had established a system so cruel?

This day had been the longest in the bear's life. He had seen the day dawn from the stinking mountaintops of the Garbage Dump, spent the morning in his old reality at Wolle & Wolle, and then been half torn apart by Dove's gorillas in the afternoon. After that, this evening together with Emma. Home on Uxbridge Street where time stood still and where security dwelled.

But it would never be like before.

Now Eric Bear understood.

Everything functioned as it did for a reason.

In the same way that Rat Ruth always took in the shipments

of used clothing that came to the Garbage Dump, Hyena Bataille had found out that the same conditions applied in a corresponding way on the other side. It was always the same person who drew up the packing slips and saw to it that the clothes were packed the right way.

Archdeacon Odenrick.

The archdeacon sat in his beautiful cathedral, untouchable and above suspicion, writing down names and dates for the animals that the Chauffeurs would pick up the following month.

So simple.

Eric should have figured it out earlier.

TWILIGHT, 5

He seldom lost his concentration during a sermon. When he climbed up to the pulpit it was as though the everyday world turned pale, the words he'd chosen to proceed from seemed more significant than anything else, and his powerful voice carried unwaveringly throughout Sagrada Bastante, out to the very last row. He filled the cathedral with his presence. He didn't leave even a possibility for doubt. In that moment his voice, even every single word, was all that meant anything. His preaching had come to be widely talked about; the pews were, as usual, filled to capacity. A feeling of calm rested over the congregation. To be able to turn yourself, and your faith, over to someone as resolute as he, was a flight from everyday demands that was not only innocent but even purifying.

Therefore a discreet sigh passed through the church when on this late afternoon he suddenly hesitated between two words. He left a pause which must have been unintentional, a pause which suggested that he didn't really know which word should follow the one he had just spoken. When in the following second he again took up the sermon, uncertainty spread along the rows of pews. Had they all imagined this hesitation? The memory of the collective sigh was soon clearer than the archdeacon's momentary mental pause, and he still brought an unctuous sermon to a successful close.

But he had hesitated.

He had lost his concentration.

Accursed Eric Bear.

Afterward he walked slowly back to the office from the sacristy. He made use of the seldom-exploited corridors that ran in all directions through the massive building. There were grand colonnades and halls in a long row which connected all the more important parts of the cathedral with one another. Why the architects had once upon a time insisted on constructing these ant tunnels alongside the main corridors remained a mystery to him.

Perhaps, he thought, it was for occasions such as this: when the world weighed like a yoke across his shoulders, and the mere thought of encountering a colleague and smiling amiably was the worst kind of torture.

He was certain that Rat Ruth had followed his instructions. Nonetheless, something had happened at the Garbage Dump which he didn't know how to analyze. No one seemed to know where Snake Marek had gone. Without Marek he no longer had control over events, he didn't know what the bear was planning or how he was reasoning. This was not at all satisfactory. Not at all.

What was the worst thing that could happen? he asked himself.

That the stubborn bear finds me, he answered himself in the following moment.

The worst thing that could happen was that the bear, in some unfathomable way, worked out that the trail led straight into Sagrada Bastante. True, he didn't understand how that would be possible; he had refined the system he'd inherited from his predecessors and no one had ever revealed it before.

But someone has to be the first, he thought.

And what am I worrying for? he asked himself. If the bear comes here, then I can take care of him.

If the bear comes here, thought Archdeacon Odenrick, he'll never walk out again. There's room for yet another animal alongside the cat down in the catacombs.

CHAPTER 23

It was the last evening at Yiala's Arch.

Tomorrow the Chauffeurs would pick up Teddy Bear and Nicholas Dove.

Tomorrow it would be over, if Eric didn't succeed in the impossible.

Sam Gazelle stood at the stove, frying sausage. He poked at the sausages with a certain distaste and with a Teflon-coated spatula, causing them to roll back and forth in the pan without getting burned. The kitchen fan emitted a dull buzz and at regular intervals the fatty sausage casings burst with little pops. Tom-Tom Crow had just set the kitchen table, and all that remained was folding the napkins. Now it was Saturday evening and all; he thought about folding them like peacocks. It was a self-assigned task which the crow, mumbling, swore over; there was a big difference between folding linen—like he'd done at Grand Divino—and folding paper napkins.

Eric Bear was standing by the balcony door, looking out over the gloomy inner courtyard. Snake Marek's absence filled the apartment. Where the bear's gaze fell, he was reminded of how the little green reptile had crawled in just that place.

Tom-Tom and Sam hadn't said anything. Had not accused him with a word, not with a glance.

After Tom-Tom had been hoisted out of the ravine and lightly embraced Eric and Sam, he'd gone back to the edge to be watching when the dangling armchair would be lowered for Marek. But the crane stood still. And without saying anything, Eric Bear started walking in the opposite direction, back toward Lanceheim. A few seconds of confusion ensued. Sam and Tom-Tom looked at each other, and between them a grim mutual understanding arose. They followed the bear. A few minutes later all three of them could hear Snake's cries, but the sound was so distant that it was possible to dismiss it as the wind blowing across the treacherous expanses of the dump. The bear, the crow, and the gazelle continued toward the city in a silence that remained unbroken, for the most part, the entire day.

"You can eat now," declared Sam, taking the frying pan with the evenly browned, although split open, sausages from the stove. "If anyone wants it."

They hadn't eaten the entire day, because no one had felt hungry. But finally Sam got tired of Tom-Tom's growling belly and found a few long-forgotten sausages in the freezer. The gazelle seldom ate dinner. If his vanity didn't forbid it, his pills caused him to lose his appetite.

Eric didn't feel especially hungry for the fat sausages either, but didn't want to risk an out-of-balance crow and therefore pretended to be hungry. They sat down at the table, unfolded the peacock napkins that had just been finished, and served up the sausages. The crow ate three, Eric and Sam shared the one that was left.

"It's Penguin Odenrick," said Eric at the same time as

Tom-Tom was spraying ketchup over his sausages as if he intended to drown them. "Only Odenrick can remove Nicholas Dove from the list."

Sam stared at the bear. The crow stuffed a substantial piece of sausage into his beak, trying to look interested at the same time.

"How long have you known?" asked the gazelle.

"Since yesterday morning," said Eric.

Sam nodded. That fit together with the ravine, with the rat and the snake.

"And now?"

"I have to confront him," said Eric. "I have to get him to admit what I already know, and then force him to remove the dove from the list."

"You don't have a lot of time."

The gazelle looked out through the window.

"The sun is just going down. Tomorrow morning it will be too late."

"This evening will do," said Eric with certainty.

"What the hell are you thinking?" asked the crow while he carefully chewed what he had in his beak. "What the hell do we do?"

The bear didn't respond to this. He stared ahead of him, as if the question had put him into a trance of some kind. Tom-Tom continued chewing and Sam looked down at his plate, where his half of the sausage sat, sad and untouched. By the time Eric finally had an answer, the crow had already forgotten what he'd asked.

"I want you to go to Owl Dorothy," said the bear.

"Who?" asked Tom-Tom.

"Is she alive?" asked Sam.

"She's alive. She's been working for the archdeacon her entire life. I believe she was his governess when he was little. Then she became his secretary. Took care of his appointment calendar, his correspondence, all the daily chores that popped up."

"And what the hell is a governess?" asked Tom-Tom, who wasn't familiar with the concept.

"Dorothy lives in Amberville," said Eric. "I'll write down the address. On Fried Street. She's lived there as long as I remember, she was living there when I was small. If you mention my name she'll ask you to come in. She enjoys serving cakes."

Eric smiled. The memory of the massive cake plate with its cakes sometimes too old for words put him in a better mood for a moment. Tom-Tom, whose hunger was stimulated by the sausages, waited with interest for the bear to say something more about the cakes, but that didn't happen.

"Then," Eric continued, "we'll meet up at Sagrada Bastante. When the clouds disperse and you see the half-moon. You should take the back way; I'll write down the address, too. And 'when you see the half-moon' means just that, not a minute before or later."

"Finally there's a plan?" said Sam.

It was a kind of statement, but his voice carried such clear hope that it even surprised Sam.

Eric got up.

"We have no time to go into details. But there are a few things before we go. . . . I'll tell you what I want you to do at Dorothy's. . . ."

CHAPTER 24

There are occasions when the most direct route is made up of more detours than you could have believed in advance. The evening when Eric Bear strolled up toward Sagrada Bastante in the Evening Storm was such an occasion. Massive cloud formations moved rapidly across the sky, but all you could see were the edges of the clouds, cautiously colored by the sun's lingering rays. Sam and Tom-Tom had taken the gray Volga so as to have time to drive to Amberville and back to the cathedral before the half-moon. Eric was thus faced with the decision to take the bus or walk. He chose to walk. Despite the urgency, he feared the moment when he would get there. Instead of walking up to Eastern Avenue and taking the direct route over to the Star, Eric walked westward through Yok's rainbow-colored muddle of streets and in this way gave himself time to think.

Without an end to a stuffed animal's life, he thought, the church would not exist.

Of course it was no more difficult than that.

All the rituals and writings, ceremonies and regulations that made up the world of the church and the world order, gained power from this simple fact: that life, as we knew it, came to an end. And that the life after this one, which for understandable reasons we would only come to know somewhat later, only existed in the form of faith and mild hope.

Long, long ago, thought Eric Bear, before the church—the church as he and his contemporaries knew it—got a hold in Mollisan Town, had animals been exchanged at all then? Had there even been a stuffed animal factory that kept the system going, or was the factory itself something the church was behind?

The thought was dizzying.

Eric stopped himself, remained standing a few moments keeping that thought alive. Then he saw the next connection in front of him, as though in letters of fire above the sidewalk. For even if the church's entire existence rested on the idea of everything's perishability, this idea also suited the power of the state extremely well. How else could all these millions of stuffed animals, thirsting for growth but at the same time pleasure-seeking, be kept in check?

The bear stumbled over a leek that was on the sidewalk, but managed to avoid tumbling and went on, in thought as well. In order to institute laws and rules and see to it that they were followed, it was of great help that our lives had a clear beginning and end. It was a matter of understanding stuffed animals' inner motivations, and with a limited amount of time we were in a hurry to reach our goals. Who would long to have cubs at the age of thirty if life continued until you were more than two hundred years old? Who would get an education before the age of twenty-five, who would fight to be able to succeed the next generation in professional life before the age of forty?

Eric Bear turned right, onto a champagne-colored avenue lined with furniture stores closed for the evening. He had no distinct recollection of ever having set foot here before.

It looked more like a street up in Tourquai. Deserted and silent, with no beggars or drunks and not a wrecked car as far as the eye could see.

This made him nervous; he didn't have time to get lost.

The cycle of life, thought Eric at the same time as he increased his pace somewhat, led to us continually repeating ourselves; we became predictable, such that the authorities could more easily manage us. We were all delivered with the same instincts for the most part. Generations before and after us are going to react in the same way we do; that's a given. Therefore the mayor could simply decide how education was allotted, fortunes distributed, and natural resources exploited. For despite all the advances in technology and medicine, despite the fact that the material conditions of life had been transformed so dramatically during the last two hundred years, a stuffed animal continued to be ruled by its love, its hate, its empathy and its jealousy, its greed and its laziness, completely uninfluenced by progressing civilization. Our instincts caused us to act as our forefathers did—thanks not least to the fact that in secrecy we all feared the day when the Chauffeurs would knock on our door—and thereby the powers that be could control us much more easily.

The bear continued down the champagne-colored avenue.

We were forced to live as intensely as we dared, he thought further, because our days were numbered. But at the same time we lived cautiously, because the life after this in some way seemed to be related to everything we did today.

At least that was what religion and the church maintained. And the state didn't deny it.

Eric Bear randomly turned left and the aroma of melted cheese struck him like an open door.

A compromised, predictable, and spiritual existence of frustrated restraint for the good of the afterlife, this was how we consumed our lives.

On the basis of the Death List.

In his imagination Eric saw Penguin Odenrick sitting in the mysterious dimness of his office. How he was hunched over the desk, writing in one of his large notebooks with leather covers. The flames of the candles in the massive candelabra on his desk danced in the draft from the leaky stone walls. In his eagerness a fourteen-year-old Eric Bear had run along the entire colonnade, pulled open the door to the innermost regions of the cathedral where no unauthorized person was allowed, and continued in a more and more breathless run through the dark corridors where only wall-mounted torches lit up the stone-clad floors. Farthest in and farthest off in the massive cathedral building Eric arrived at the archdeacon's office, and without knocking he opened the door.

Archdeacon Odenrick had as usual been sitting bowed over his writing. Surprised and angry at the interruption he looked up. When he caught sight of Eric Bear, his stern look softened.

"We're finished now," said Eric proudly.

"And what did it end up being?" asked the archdeacon.

"Thirteen overcoats, five pairs of pants, three pairs of boots, and a large blanket," answered Eric.

"That's wonderful!" said the archdeacon, nodding in approval.

"We went into that deserted lot that's over by—"

Odenrick interrupted.

"Ah, ah, ah," said the penguin, "no details. I don't want to know."

"But . . ."

"No. This is a part of the agreement. Keep the secrets to yourselves, the big ones as well as the small ones. That's the hardest part. The equipment is easy, keeping secrets is hard."

Eric nodded. When Penguin Odenrick spoke it was as

though every word was carefully weighed. It had taken several days before Eric understood that what the archdeacon called "the equipment" was the used clothing.

Getting to listen to the archdeacon's sermons was generally considered to be a privilege. It was hardly every Sunday that he himself gave the sermon in the cathedral, but when he did the church was always fully occupied. The same careful emphasis, the same seriousness and reflection that he made use of in the pulpit of the church, he used both with his confirmands and now, in his comparatively small office, one-to-one with Eric. The effect was lasting. Eric Bear would never be able to free himself from the feeling of being a chosen one created by these meetings with the archdeacon. Neither would he ever be able to lose the deep respect he felt for Odenrick, a feeling which originated in the bear's need for affirmation. To be seen by this giant, if only for a few moments, was a triumph.

"No," said the young bear, "I know."

"And I'm counting on the fact that you've instructed the others."

"I have," said Eric, nodding feverishly. "No one's going to say anything. Even if we have to yank our tongues out to keep from doing so."

"I hope that won't become necessary," answered Odenrick without smiling, and Eric remained uncertain whether he was joking or not.

The bear remained standing a while in the dark room, unwilling to leave, until the archdeacon asked whether there was anything else. Then Eric was forced to admit that that wasn't the case, and he slinked away. Slowly he returned to the packing rooms through the muffled corridors of the cathedral, and the feeling of pride caused him to smile to himself. When he once again saw his little band of workers—a crocodile and two cats who were both named Smythe—he exaggerated the archdeacon's praise as much as he dared without risking credibility.

"He's going to yank out our tongues if we ever breathe a word of this," Eric Bear concluded.

The crocodile and the cats nodded. They were all fourteen years old, and they all felt equally, marvelously special.

Eric Bear suddenly found himself in a dead-end alley. He had turned off from the champagne-colored alley onto a violet-green street that was now cordoned off by a three-meter-tall iron grating with no openings. The buildings that lined the sidewalk were the same run-down apartment buildings that he had been seeing the last ten minutes. They appeared to be deserted, but in their moldy insides lives were passing that in one way were closely related to his: one day they would all cease.

Eric stopped a few meters in front of the grating and looked around. It wouldn't be impossible to force it open, but he still didn't know where he was. Perhaps it would be quicker to turn around and make his way toward the avenue along some other street?

Eric suddenly discovered that the storm was in decline. He was seized with panic. He didn't have time to carry on like this. When he realized that it must have been his sub-conscious playing a trick on him and that he hadn't gotten lost from negligence or carelessness, he started to sweat. Tomorrow morning was much too late. And here he was wandering around the streets in Yok.

He turned around and started to trot. Uncertain whether he was on his way west the last fifteen minutes, he ran all the faster without knowing in what direction. There was no one to ask either; the streets in Yok were empty. He turned to the right toward what he guessed was north, but he was unsure. He'd never been an outdoor enthusiast; he recognized the Milky Way but no more than that. And with a pulse that continued to race faster, he ran on through anonymous blocks of run-down buildings where hardly more than a third of the streetlights were functioning, and it felt as though he were running a race with time itself.

Why Penguin Odenrick had chosen him in particular remained a mystery through the years. The natural choice ought to have been Teddy. And at first Eric believed that the archdeacon had actually made a mistake. Up to that day Odenrick had joked many times about what a hard time he had telling one twin from the other when he was at their house for dinner with his parents on Hillville Road.

But it was Eric he'd summoned during the first weeks of confirmation instruction, and it was Eric he'd intended. Odenrick had from the start already made it clear that Eric was not allowed to tell about his new assignment, not even to his twin brother. And Eric didn't question this, because the special position the archdeacon had all of a sudden granted him caused the bear's young heart to swell with satisfaction and pride, just as the archdeacon had intended.

Those first weeks, however, the secretiveness remained incomprehensible. Once a week, Eric, along with the crocodile and the two cats, had the task of gathering in used clothing that kind citizens had donated to poor animals through the church. Eric and one of the cats folded the clothes while the crocodile and the other cat wrapped them in brown wrapping paper. Outside the churches in Amberville, Lanceheim, and Yok were collection stations to which Eric and his new friends took the bus. It took several hours to make their way around the whole city, but the youngsters were so filled up with the gravity of the moment that the time passed quickly. The remaining confirmands believed that the four received special instruction from the arch-deacon when they were actually collecting clothes. There was a packing room in Sagrada Bastante where they could hang out. The cubs were ordered to tell the story about special instruction, even if someone from the church asked where they were going. The first four weeks, there were clothes at one of the collection stations at least; the fifth week it became apparent why the archdeacon demanded such secrecy.

Empty-handed, they returned to Sagrada Bastante, but instead of going to the packing room Eric Bear went to see the archdeacon in his office. The cats and the crocodile waited outside.

"We have to send out at least one small package every month," said the archdeacon. "That's the least we can do for the unfortunate in society."

"But there are no clothes," Eric explained again. "There's nothing."

"But we don't need much. We actually only need something, whatever. Perhaps you can find that something somewhere else?"

"Somewhere else?" repeated Eric without understanding.

"Wherever," the archdeacon clarified.

Eric remained uncomprehending, and a few additional questions were required, and answers equally evasive and encouraging, before the bear understood that the archdeacon was actually suggesting that they should steal clothes. Still, when Eric left the room he was afraid he'd misunderstood the matter.

"What should we do?" asked the cats at the same time as Eric closed the archdeacon's door behind him.

"We're going to see to it that we make a package of clothes," replied Eric. "Because nothing is as important as that a package of clothes is sent away from here once a month. That's exactly what he said. And sometimes, he said, you have to do something a little less good in order that something else, something more good, is able to happen."

"Huh?"

The crocodile hadn't understood a word, and he dared to show it.

"Should we steal the clothes?" asked one of the cats who, on the other hand, could follow that kind of circumlocution.

"Yep," answered Eric. "Neither more nor less."

With his heart in his throat, Eric Bear ran straight out onto Carrer de la Marquesa, the ash-gray street, and finally he knew where he was. The wind was still blowing briskly; it wasn't too late. He continued running up toward the intersection to dark-blue Avinguda de Pedralbes, from where it was no more than a few minutes up to Eastern Avenue. If he could keep up the pace, he would be at the Star and the cathedral before the storm died out.

The few animals who were outside in the lukewarm Evening Storm in Yok's run-down blocks were careful not to turn around or stare at Eric as he ran past. A running animal meant bad news.

On Eastern Avenue, Eric Bear reduced his pace, although his stride remained long. When he saw the cathedral's hedgehog-like silhouette against the cloud-draped sky, he was still so focused on arriving in time that he forgot to feel nervous.

Yesterday morning, when Hyena Bataille had told him about the clothes that were delivered to the Garbage Dump, Eric Bear understood for the first time that he had neither been the first nor the last confirmand chosen to lead a small league of clothing stealers. And it was then as well that he'd understood that it was the archdeacon himself, and no other, who was behind the Death List. It was that simple.

That was why it could go on, year after year, with ever-new groups of children taken in hand by Penguin Odenrick.

The wind was milder as Eric went up the stairs to the cathedral's massive portal and opened the rather modest door that led into the church. He passed through the great halls, across the inner courtyard, and along the colonnade. He continued through the dark corridors with torches along the walls, and only when he came up to the door that led into the archdeacon's office did he stop. For a moment he was once again fourteen years old. He knew that he had one full hour, no more.

Then he pulled himself together, quickly knocked, and pushed open the door without waiting for an answer.

TEDDY BEAR, 5

Emma Rabbit was the most beautiful bride I'd ever seen. But Archdeacon Odenrick saw her first.

Odenrick stepped into the narthex where Emma and her mother were waiting. He had explained the procedure to us in advance. He wanted to say a few words to the bride and bridegroom before the ceremony itself. Emma and I had chosen the shorter variation.

To me, religion remained a two-edged weapon.

It was a matter of daring to believe in the unbelievable, which in all other contexts was described as stupidity. I'd devoted my life to pure goodness, and I sensed a double standard in the kind of goodness advocated by the church. It focused on good actions, while the soul and the self were allowed doubt and uncertainty. The church in Mollisan Town was a proselytizing church. If for no other reason, the church's religion was simplified and systematized. Its greatest advantage was that it lessened our fear of death.

Emma and I met Archdeacon Odenrick in one of the meeting rooms at Lakestead House. It was just the three of us.

"And you, Emma?" said Odenrick. "Do you also think

that the primary contribution of religion is to lessen the fear of death?"

"I'm not afraid to die," said Emma.

Archdeacon Odenrick smiled victoriously in my direction.

"I'm not a believer, either," Emma added.

The archdeacon's smile disappeared.

We were sitting one flight up. Outside the windows it was already dark. The lighthouse out on the promontory swept its light over us at regular intervals. There was a smell of coffee from the kitchen.

"But you're in agreement about marrying in the church?" the archdeacon asked with some skepticism in his voice.

"If you're going to get married, then you should," said Emma.

"Many times Magnus's sense of morality coincides with mine," I said. "In the remaining cases I'm prepared to forgive."

"To forgive is divine," replied the archdeacon.

All three of us nodded.

It was going to be a beautiful wedding.

"Emma Rabbit," said Archdeacon Odenrick as he stood outside in the small narthex only minutes before the ceremony, "you are a very, very beautiful bride."

"Thank you, Archdeacon," said Emma.

When the choir began singing I shed tears.

We had come in contact with the Red Bird Singers through Father. Despite the fact that they seldom performed at private events, they had agreed. When the eight, pale-red birds stood on the platform and the distinctive harmony caused the church's hollow timbers to quiver with hope and melancholy, I knew that it had been worth the trouble.

However much Father had paid, it was worth it.

Before the second verse the door to the narthex was

opened and Emma Rabbit and her mother appeared. Emma was a revelation. The guests sitting in the pews were listening to the exquisitely beautiful singing and for the time being didn't see the bride. The church was almost full. A few hundred stuffed animals. Most of them were friends of Mother and Father. There were seventy-eight animals invited to the dinner afterward.

The Red Bird Singers concluded the introductory hymn and the singers sat down. The procession with Odenrick, Emma, and Emma's mother began its short but symbolic course along the middle aisle of the church. Mother and Father sat in the first row. They didn't turn around. Mother was already crying and didn't want to show it. Father sat next to her, straight-backed.

A murmur went through the church. A collective inhalation that spread in time with Emma's measured progress.

I've already written it.

I'll write it again.

She was so beautiful.

The bridegroom stood at the altar, waiting. He looked terrified.

The guests didn't see his sweaty paws or his shaking knees. However, he couldn't conceal anything from my critical gaze.

The bear was fingering a small etui that he had in his trouser pocket. It was an inappropriate gesture that expressed nervousness and uncertainty. When he assured himself that he hadn't forgotten the rings, he took out his paw. He nodded toward the congregation, toward Emma and toward Mother, but he didn't appear relieved.

In the bear's eye was the expectation and happiness shared by everyone in the church. But for the bear at the altar, that feeling was diluted with anxiety. It wasn't obvious, a sharp gaze was required to notice it.

I saw it.

It was my twin who was standing up at the altar. He couldn't conceal anything from me.

He had taken my place.

We had an agreement.

I myself was concealed inside the sacristy, peeking out through a crack in the door. Neither Emma Rabbit, Archdeacon Odenrick, Mother, Father, nor anyone else in the church was aware of what was about to happen.

Emma Rabbit was getting married to the wrong twin.

I didn't promise anything that I couldn't keep. Eric promised without caring about it.

I sat hidden behind my door and saw my brother get married to the she I loved with all my deplorable heart.

The tears I shed were not from melancholy or sorrow.

I was weeping for joy.

One morning in December, Wolle Hare threw open the door to my office and shouted, "Now you can't hide yourself anymore!"

Then he laughed his snorting sales-laugh that he'd been practicing for many years. It wasn't particularly contagious. On the other hand, it induced thoughtlessness and made it feel less dramatic to make a decision. Let's make the deal, the customer who heard Wolle Hare's laugh would think. Let's make the deal, life isn't so terribly serious.

I wasn't affected by his laugh. For me, life was serious.

"Hide myself?" I repeated.

"We need you," shouted Wolle Hare, "you and no one else."

"You have for a long time," I answered quietly.

I had worked at the advertising agency for almost eighteen months and knew my position. I didn't need to be flattered by either Wolle or Wolle.

After the first six months I realized how things stood. Everyone in the agency wanted to be in the spotlight. The animals competed in proving themselves smart, smarter than each other. Those who weren't part of the competition that day sat on an invisible jury and judged the others. It was a matter of being creative or successful. Certain ones strove to be both. Everything could be measured in money.

No points were awarded for administrative tasks. No points to the one who saw to it that the rent was paid on time, that the pension allocations were taken care of, or to the one who had the welcome mats changed when they got dirty. No points to the one who took care that the green plants stayed green.

When I started working at Wolle & Wolle we had stretched our suppliers' patience, and credit limits, to the breaking point. The authorities awaited an opportunity to sic the sheriff on the gentlemen Wolle and Wolle.

I became the firm's rescuer in distress.

It didn't happen overnight. Slowly I won the confidence of our external suppliers. I convinced them. The hedgehog who came with new doormats relied on the fact that from then on he would be paid within twenty days. An eagle at the tax office knew that I was always available to take his questions. The animals who worked at the agency became used to the office-supply storeroom being inventoried and replenished.

After a year of assiduous labor, my exertions produced results. Thanks to my exactitude and my absolute conception of right and wrong, Wolle & Wolle had become a model of business practices in the industry.

Naturally there was no one in the agency who saw what I'd accomplished. For these self-centered designers with colorful clothes and flexible consciences I remained a gray mouse without apparent purpose.

Good.

In contrast to them I had no need of winning their ironic competition. I knew my value.

It was greater than theirs.

Considerably greater.

"Come," said Wolle Hare, "then I'll tell you."

I showed no enthusiasm. In one leap, Wolle was over at my desk, taking me by the arm. He pulled me up out of the chair. Brutally he shoved me out of the office. I felt secure inside my office. My binders and document files controlled my professional life, set its limits and gave it meaning. Out in the office landscape that was the advertising agency itself, a different order prevailed.

A lack of order.

My status made me invisible, but this morning as I was shoved across the floor by Wolle Hare, I received numerous glances. Some wondered who I was. Others wondered enviously why Wolle Hare was devoting attention to me in particular.

I shared that wonder.

Wolle Hare and Wolle Toad had furnished a joint office in a corner room that extended into a conference room overlooking Place Great Hoch. Toad was waiting for us at his desk when we came in. A small group of designers who were called in for especially significant pitches was sitting at the conference table. I knew them all by name.

"Here he is!" the hare cried out triumphantly and pointed at me. "Didn't I say that he would help out?"

The exhilaration in Wolle Hare's voice was not met by any reaction. The group at the conference table looked skeptical.

"Who is that?" someone asked.

"No idea," answered someone else.

"Are you volunteering, Teddy?" asked Wolle Toad.

I didn't know what this was about. I shrugged my shoulders.

"They want to use you in an ad," said the toad, making a gesture over toward the creative group at the table, and toward the hare. "It's about banking services."

"Me?"

No one in the room could take my question as being coquettish.

The toad nodded.

"It's about building trustworthiness," he said in order to explain why the choice had fallen on me.

I was completely unprepared. Before I had time to collect myself, Wolle Hare placed an arm around my neck and led me away from the toad's desk.

"This is a chance for you, Teddy," he explained in a low voice. "You can't be an administrative assistant at an advertising agency your whole life."

"I'm very comfortable with . . ."

We had stopped halfway between the creative group at the conference table and the toad at the desk.

"I don't mean that you have a career as a model ahead of you," Wolle Hare clarified. "But if you volunteer for this type of thing, it's not inconceivable that we'll have you in mind the next time a management job comes up."

"Is it the head of accounting's job that you . . . ?"

Our accounting head was an old blue jay who was going to retire at the end of the year. So far I hadn't heard about a successor.

"There's no reason to be that specific," the hare interrupted me. "And this is of course not a punishment we're talking about, appearing in a commercial for the Savings Banks' Bank."

We were standing in front of a large whiteboard. I looked over at the designers, but they didn't seem to care about us anymore.

"The Savings Banks' Bank?" I repeated. "But we use Banque Mollisan. I don't know anyone at the Savings Banks' Bank."

"We'll make an attempt, then," Wolle said smoothly without having heard my objection.

"I don't even know if I . . ."

"So the job is yours, shall we say that?" said Wolle. "Head of accounting, you said? That's not so bad, is it? Shall we say so?"

"I don't know if I . . ."

"Good," he called out, patting me on the back in confirmation.

The designers looked in our direction. I thought I glimpsed a smile or two. Perhaps it was only because Wolle sounded happy.

"Teddy's on board," shouted Wolle Hare.

The hare went over to the others to discuss the consequences of the good news. I remained standing by the whiteboard. No one seemed to notice me. The designers and the hare talked, the toad sat at his desk and wrote. Should I leave? Before I had time to make up my mind, a cat detached himself from the group of designers. I knew who he was. He'd gotten a prize for a campaign for light beer.

"Cool," he said, shaking my paw. "Not a difficult thing. Just you, in your normal clothes."

The cat inspected me up and down and nodded in approval.

"We drive in the studio. Backdrop. It's raining," he said. "You're just standing there, like. Straight up and down. But you smile."

"Smiling in the rain?" I asked.

"A bank for us who are tired of being run over," the cat said. "That's what it's about. That's the message."

"Am I the one who's been run over?" I asked.

The cat shrugged his shoulders.

"You're the one who's tired of being run over."

"But I'm the one who's been run over?"

"Bear," said the cat, smiling amiably, "it's possible that you're a steamroller. But in the picture you'll represent the one who's tired of being run over and chooses Savings Banks' Bank instead."

"Banque Mollisan is better," I said.

"I have no opinions whatsoever about that," the cat said and went over to the others.

Assuming a role and expressing an idea in a certain question has nothing to do with evil or good. I wasn't naïve. A photo model who depicted a bad character was not a bad animal. Investigating your dark sides was necessary if the object was to live a good life.

I don't intend to go into that.

The point is: placing yourself in front of a camera in order to swear that the Savings Banks' Bank was the city's best bank had nothing to do with evil or good.

On the other hand, the consequences were impossible to accept.

Suppose someone who saw the advertisement actually believed the message. And changed to the Savings Banks' Bank.

Making an ad, said Wolle Hare and Wolle Toad, was a job. We did our job. Those who saw the ad had to take responsibility for their own lives. To influence was neither to betray nor mislead. There were no hidden intentions. Recommending one bank before another was not a crime.

The argumentation was impeccable.

But I knew that the Savings Banks' Bank wasn't the best. I knew that anyone who changed banks due to the ad would not get better banking services. It was not about the photography. It was about taking responsibility for the chain of consequences that every action unleashes.

Eric helped out in my place.

We had an agreement.

Eric had no misgivings regarding advertising photography.

He was the evil one. I was the good. It was a few months before the wedding with Emma Rabbit. Or a few months after. It was the start of something or a natural continuation. Eric and I got the job as head of accounting. Possibly we became head of marketing, or some other kind of manager. I have a hard time committing titles to memory.

Together we made a successful career at Wolle & Wolle.

The advertising world suited my twin brother perfectly. He surprised the trend-sensitive designers with his self-promoting attitude and his unexpected leaps of thought. He had nothing to lose. I don't know exactly what he said or did. For obvious reasons we were never at the agency at the same time. But I'm sure that it wasn't a matter of anything remarkable.

I was, without a doubt, the one between us who had the intellectual capacity.

Eric turned his shortcomings into advantages.

He never expressed a definite opinion about anything.

Things went fast. I was at the office one day a week. Two or three days a week. The rest of the time Eric was there. He is an extroverted animal. Seeks contact. I'm not like that at all. He found out things I'd never heard discussed. He ended up in the management group. I did, too. It became our platform.

We became good friends with Wolle Hare.

It was incomprehensible.

The hare was an animal who was certifiably hard to get close to. Nevertheless, Eric picked open his defenses as though Wolle were a cheap bicycle lock. After a few months, Eric was his closest ally.

These are not profundities we're talking about.

The hare was convinced that the agency would go under if it didn't expand. Eric knew nothing about business. Nevertheless he expressed his opinions. I could hear when they were talking on the phone. My ignorant twin was using words like "synergies" and "fusions." One day he would enthusiastically promote the idea of opening a casino. The next day it might just as well be a real estate holding company.

It was pure madness.

I witnessed a careening carriage en route to the precipice. Personally I dutifully sorted the papers that came my way. I watered the flowers. I refilled the coffee in the coffee machine.

I waited for our bluff to be exposed.

Eric's behavior became less and less acceptable. When Wolle Hare called us into the office one day after less than a year as head of accounting, I thought it was all over.

It was Eric who was at the office that day.

He wasn't even surprised at being named assistant managing director. It was a natural development of his collaboration with Wolle Hare, said Eric.

A natural development.

I won't fatigue the reader by describing the astonishment that subsequently struck me, time and time again through the years. My time at the advertising agency lessened. Eric's increased correspondingly.

His successes increased as well. I stopped seeing them as ours together. I followed his career from a distance. A distance that Lakestead House provided me. Eric was not reticent about what he was occupied with. On the contrary. He told me everything. As if he were atoning for guilt.

The job dealt with communication and manipulation. He was cunning where any type of marketing was concerned. The explanation was simple. He wasn't afraid to lie. To assert that one dish soap was more economical than the others. One car safer than the others. One type of insurance more comprehensive than another.

Even if that wasn't the case.

He treated the personnel the same way. He promoted or slandered them on the basis of his own shortsighted purposes. He didn't reflect on whether his judgments were objective or not. When I pointed this out, he didn't understand what I was talking about.

Eric achieved one success after another. At the beginning it was about Wolle & Wolle. Later this continued up and through all of the city's power elites. Sooner or later, I was certain, someone would expose him.

I didn't look forward to that day for myself; *Schadenfreude* is for the envious. On the other hand, I did look forward to that day for the sake of justice. It was a matter of balance. Eric's life had capsized long ago, and the waves that struck against the pier below Lakestead House during the Evening Storm always struck again.

But the years passed, and nothing happened.

I became less and less interested in Eric's professional life. I lost track of how many boards he sat on and how many commissions he was elected to.

Sometimes I felt ashamed that he used my name.

Sometimes I wished that he would leave me in peace with his stories.

I was unspeakably naïve.

This is not soul-searching. This is about pride. Naïveté is something I cultivate; to me, naïveté represents a pure conscience, good intentions, and the genuine trust in the outside world which is the basis for having the strength to carry on the struggle against cynicism.

I was unspeakably naïve. I believed I could take over when Eric had sworn the marital vows that I myself wasn't able to swear.

The wedding reception became a taste of what was to come.

I sat in a café across from the reception venue and

watched how the stuffed animals Emma and I had invited passed by on the sidewalk. I watched them through the illuminated windows, how they toasted the bride and groom. I could hear music carrying faintly out onto the street. Music I myself had chosen. Along with my mother I'd planned the napkin folding and what sort of flat-bread would be served with the appetizers. I knew what was going on without being there.

I presumed that the bride and groom were very happy.

I was happy.

I didn't understand what was about to happen.

When I slipped up the stairwell on Uxbridge Street the next morning, ready to change places with Eric, a surprise was waiting.

As we'd decided, I stood and waited out on the stairway. The rain had just ceased and the Forenoon Weather had begun. I wasn't thinking anything in particular. My senses were wide open. It didn't bother me that Eric had woken up with my Emma that same morning. Eric and I were each other's opposites. We were one and the same. I stood in the stairwell and waited. My heart was wide open and my mind was pure.

I would replace Eric and reinstate order.

The door opened, and there stood my twin brother.

"You are a very fortunate bear," he said and smiled.

"I know," I said.

"And if you need my help again, you only have to call," he said.

"Thanks," I replied.

"See you," he said.

I nodded.

I slipped into the apartment and left Eric on the stairway.

The apartment was larger than I'd thought. Lots of rooms and corridors. Closets and corners. Finally I found Emma

Rabbit in the bathroom where she was brushing her fur. She was humming one of the songs the orchestra had played last evening.

"As if November were too late," she said as I stepped in.

"No," I answered, then changed my mind. "Yes?"

I didn't know what she was talking about.

"But Alexi is going to see what a green bicycle can mean," she said.

"Sure," I answered.

I didn't know who she was talking about.

"Despite the fact that you realize that it's going to hurt?" she asked.

I nodded.

I didn't know why it should hurt.

"Darling," I said, "excuse me a moment."

I ran out of the bathroom. I ran out into the hall. I ran out into the stairway and down onto the street where I ran as fast as I could in the direction I assumed Eric had gone.

I caught up with him before Wright's Lane.

"It didn't work," I panted. "You have to go back. We have to plan better."

But it wasn't a matter of planning.

Every day that Eric spent in my stead with my wife, they created common memories. Every memory created references, solidarity, and a communion into which I had no entry.

For another eleven months I continued to arrange meetings with Eric on the stairwell outside the apartment. Full of hope, I went in to Emma Rabbit and tried to take over the life that was going on without me. In the best cases I managed for two hours. In the worst cases, for less than a minute.

My will remained unbroken. My love for Emma conquered my good sense. During these months I constantly laid out new strategies. I left no idea untested. However absurd it might appear.

It became clear to me that I was forced to copy my brother's life down to the smallest detail so as to be able to take his place.

I subjected my twin to intensive interviews that I prepared for several days. I carried out regular interrogations where I demanded complete openness. I observed Emma during all hours of the day. I sat at Nick's Café and stared at their doorway, ready to get up and follow her at any moment. I tried to live and breathe their life without them noticing it. Walk along the streets where they walked, visit the department stores or restaurants that they visited. The idea was simple. If I got the same stimuli as Eric, my reactions ought to be rather like his.

During this year of painful desperation I continued working at Wolle & Wolle. Work was my salvation, a place of clear demands and monotonous routines in a chaotic life of pain and degradation. I commuted back and forth from Lakestead House. I was en route to the office or to Emma and Eric's apartment. Then I was on my way back again. Lakestead was strict where time was concerned. I was always in a hurry. I was always short on time.

I had a hard time keeping certain days under control. I stood outside Wolle & Wolle, wondering if Eric was there. I stood outside Uxbridge Street, wondering if Eric was there. I stood outside Lakestead House, wondering why I was there. I stood outside Hillville Road, wondering if Father was there. I stood alongside myself, wondering if Eric was there.

The pain of failure receded. I knew what to expect from my encounters with Emma. My hopes overcame my clear-sightedness. My hopes invited self-deception. I was balancing on the brink of the dishonorable.

Finally a day arrived when reality overcame fantasy.

It's so simple to write.

Finally reality conquered fantasy.

But these fantasies had been my lifeblood. The castles in the air I'd erected every time I ran after Eric in desperation and induced him to turn around. When reality caught up with me, it took the dreams out of my life, and what was left was almost nothing.

I retreated. I left it to Eric to uphold my life. I don't think anyone noticed.

I retreated.

There are occasions—for some, several times during a normal day, and for others a few times during a lifetime—when you feel impatient with your situation in life.

A kind of existential vacuum.

A thought loop that arises when the majority of physical and emotional needs are met. You feel boredom, despite the fact that you ought to be happy. You lack connection, a sense of belonging, and ask yourself if life really is no more than this.

I never experience such a vacuum.

I wake up in the morning when it's time to get up, approximately when the Morning Rain starts to fall. I'm not a morning person, but I force myself to get up and do my morning toilet. After that I carry out a simple exercise program, then I go down to breakfast. After having carefully read the newspaper, I go back up to my room. Take care of my things. I have time for a walk in the garden before lunch.

In the afternoons I sometimes still go into the city. Especially on Tuesdays and Thursdays. I go to Nick's, have a coffee, and look over at the doorway to 32 Uxbridge Street.

If Emma Rabbit comes, I follow her. Not always, but it does happen.

Eric comes to see me at Lakestead House. More often than he needs to. I don't want to forbid him. He does it for his own sake.

I can't tell him that Emma Rabbit has lied to us. That she's not fatherless at all, but rather that she has a father who's a dove.

There are situations where what is good isn't obvious.

Not to tell is to withhold. To withhold is to betray. To tell is to tear down something that has been built up for a long time. If Eric knew that his Emma had long been keeping a secret from him, it would crush him.

Why has she chosen to keep her father secret? I don't know. Is the reason perhaps reasonable? Perhaps there's a simple explanation? In order to set yourself in judgment over another animal, you have to close your eyes to the whole truth.

I never close my eyes.

I know that my life isn't Eric's. That his life isn't mine. We have become two individuals for certain reasons. There are reasons in the background. The truth, which for me is a part of goodness, means nothing to him. Emma Rabbit means everything to him. She has become who she is through a long series of events which, thanks to their definite sequence, have defined her character. She has her reasons to conceal her father. I don't know them, I can't set myself in judgment over them.

I keep silent.

Not a word passes my lips.

This is how I might think, in the afternoons as I walk along the coast.

This is how I was thinking today, as I was walking along the coast.

I spoke every third or fourth idea out loud to myself. When the black clouds drew in over the mainland in the afternoon, I got raindrops on my tongue. Then, as usual, the gates of heaven opened. I hurried back home. For those who wish, rusks and tea are served in the afternoon. I myself waited until dinner, which I ate early.

In the evenings, I reflected.

At night, I slept.

CHAPTER 25

Eric, what a surprise!" said Archdeacon Odenrick, but there was no joy in his voice.

Eric was standing one step inside the threshold to the archdeacon's office, not knowing what he should do. Outside the small, aperture-like windows he glimpsed reality in the form of buildings and streetlights, but he had a strong, unpleasant feeling that he would never return out there again. He closed the door behind him and tried to gather his courage.

"Come in, come in," the archdeacon invited with a smile that was broad and warm.

Eric tried to smile back, but was unsure whether he succeeded. Slowly he walked over to the ample visitor's armchair that stood in front of the archdeacon's massive desk, and which he'd never dared sit in when he was little. Now he sat down, but he sat on the edge of the armchair, straight-backed, and with his paws in his lap. He still hadn't said anything.

"Eric, that you come to visit this late . . ." said Odenrick.

"Yes," the bear finally forced out.

"You were passing this way, or . . . ?"

"Yes, exactly."

"But no one visits a deacon so late in the evening without some purpose, do they?" said Odenrick.

Eric nodded in shame, found out.

"There's no problem, no hurry. How are your parents? I see them all too seldom nowadays."

Mother and Father. That was a topic of conversation to dwell on. It was solid ground. Eric told what he knew about his mother and her hardships at the ministry, and for a few minutes they helped each other choose the best desserts she'd served over the years. For once Penguin Odenrick, who was also close to Eric's father, asked whether Eric had reconciled yet with Boxer Bloom. Eric shook his head. No, they still hadn't spoken since . . . for a long time.

"That grieves your father, you should know," Odenrick said seriously. "Even if you don't believe it, for I know you don't. If you knew how much pain you cause him, I'm certain you would call and put things right. You're not a bad bear, Eric."

The thought of Boxer Bloom irritated Eric as always, and even now, in the archdeacon's office, where so much was at stake and so much had to be said, he had a hard time letting Odenrick's words pass by without comment.

"As if he couldn't call," muttered Eric Bear.

"The two of you are equally stubborn," smiled Odenrick mildly. "It's terrible. It's inherited, and that makes it doubly painful for your father. It's his own stubbornness he encounters in you."

"That is not at all . . ." said Eric with a scornful tone of voice, and immediately regretted it. Of the church's theoretical foundations, he'd always considered the idea of genetic inheritance to be one of the most hard-to-swallow bits.

"We've talked about this before, haven't we?" said the archdeacon, recognizing the bear's hesitation.

Eric nodded.

"And if I don't misremember, I placed the rhetorical question whether you truly believe that the Deliverymen bring the cubs out by chance. Do you believe that it was fate alone that made it that just you and Teddy ended up with Bloom and his rhinoceros? Or was it somebody's intention? Sounds more likely, don't you think?"

Eric wanted to nod but didn't dare. He knew that was how the archdeacon always handled the question of original sin.

"But aren't we all born good?" protested Eric somewhat lamely, leaping over several trains of thought to get to the point.

"We are all born with the possibility of doing good," said the archdeacon diplomatically.

"But, Archdeacon, do you really think that stuffed animals come directly from the factory that are evil? Evil, because the animals that will become their parents, or their ancestors, had done wrong at some time in their lives?"

Eric couldn't hold back his acid irony, and involuntarily he leaned forward a little.

"The sin which has been committed through the ages we all carry with us, collectively. Then it is the church's task to forgive. That's just how our roles have been assigned to us," said the archdeacon, adding, "You take this all too literally, all too personally."

"Is it the church's task to forgive?" Eric repeated. "How often should that happen? How soon after my evil action does forgiveness apply? And after I've been forgiven, has a deacon then transformed me from evil to good?"

Eric spoke quickly, stumbling over the syllables; he had to make his way past this side track in order to get to his actual business.

"Whether you regret the evil you've done," the archdeacon replied without raising his voice, "is more important than anything else."

"Anxiety is the answer," clarified Eric.

"Remorse," corrected the archdeacon.

Eric got up from the large chair. His frustration over the conversation and the dogmatic penguin was so great that he could not possibly sit still.

The archdeacon misunderstood the gesture.

"Is that why you're here?" asked Odenrick, thereby giving Eric an opportunity to refrain from asking what the archdeacon knew he was thinking about asking. "For something you've done? To ask for forgiveness? That's far from—"

"No," interrupted Eric, making a gesture with his arm as if the archdeacon were some kind of porter. "I'm not here to beg pardon."

The archdeacon leaned over the desk, carefully observing his visitor. The humble tone that had previously concealed the bear's actual state of mind fell to the floor like the drapery from a sprawling work of art, and here stood his true self.

"I'm here to appeal for help," said Eric Bear without the hint of an appeal.

"I'll naturally do everything in my power to—" began the archdeacon, but once again he was interrupted.

"That remains to be seen," said Bear. "This is about the Death List."

Whatever expectations Eric had had, they came to naught. The penguin behind the desk didn't bat an eyelid. No surprise or rage, no fear or even lack of understanding. Penguin Odenrick looked just as pious as ever.

"The Death List?"

"I know how it fits together," said Eric. "I know that it's your list."

"My list?"

"That it's you who writes it, you who chooses the animals who will die."

"You know that?"

"And I need help," repeated the bear.

"Sit down," said the archdeacon.

It was an order, the tone of voice was sharp, and no more than what was required to transform the self-assured bear into a former confirmand.

Eric sat down and tried to encounter the archdeacon's gaze. It could no longer be described as mild.

"You should think carefully about what you're planning to accuse me of," said Odenrick, "because when the words are spoken it's going to be difficult to take them back. I've learned to forgive, but I have a hard time forgetting."

"I'm not afraid of you," replied Eric.

And in the same moment as he said that, he knew that it was true. He was not afraid. Here sat an idiotic penguin with the power to let his beloved wife and his biological twin live. And the power to force them to die. What did Eric have to be afraid of, what more was there to lose?

"I'm not afraid," repeated Eric, "because I know who you are, and your power consists of your secrets."

"You think you know what power is," said the archdeacon, "but you know nothing."

The penguin got up from his chair, and Eric was happy that the large desk stood between them.

"The worlds where you move, where the struggle for material advantages is carried on with more or less criminal methods," said Archdeacon Odenrick with all of his breath support, "and here I include your fancy corporate directors; that's only the lobby. You're so occupied with comparing yourselves with each other that you don't see it. That someone has granted you the arena in which you fight, and that as long as you restrict yourselves to it you're left in peace. But if you start searching for doors that lead out of there, then comes the punishment. Hard and merciless. And that, my upright friend, is power. Which you'll continue to experience, but never taste."

The penguin remained standing behind the desk. He looked down at the bear, and his breathing was excited. Just then he was a demonic figure, but Eric Bear still felt no fear.

"Power," repeated the bear, nodding to himself as if he'd understood something. "Of course. That is a motivating force."

The penguin didn't let himself be provoked. "It's a matter of managing it. I've striven for it, I'll gladly admit that. And the reason is that I want to make use of it. Otherwise it would be meaningless. And I'm good at making use of it. Because I understand that I am a temporary servant."

"I know what you can do," said Eric, nodding.

"You know nothing," answered Odenrick slowly and with such contempt that it surprised Eric.

"You're wrong there. I know a great deal. And I won't hesitate to make use of it."

"I certainly believe that," replied Odenrick, sitting down in his chair again. "You're good at that. That's the way you got yourself a wife."

That was a punch below the belt, and it was just as intentional as it was painful. Eric had intended to follow through his train of thought, but completely lost the thread. The past returned to the present with violent force, and Eric was unprepared. Despite the fact that the archdeacon's provocation was completely obvious, he couldn't refrain from reacting to it.

"That's bullshit," he said in a loud voice, "and you know it."

"Oh," the archdeacon smiled, "there seem to be several of us here who know a few things, and who should be able to make use of that."

"Teddy knows," said Eric. "He's always known."

"And your lovely wife?" asked Odenrick amiably. "What, exactly, does she know about how the whole thing happened those days before you got married?"

"She certainly recalls that the esteemed Archdeacon Odenrick conducted the ceremony," said Eric. "I'm sure of that. And she recalls how the archdeacon spoke with us the day before. She can probably recall the entire conversation, she has a good memory."

This didn't make the archdeacon's smile any less condescending.

"But does she know that it was your idea? Does she understand that Teddy—"

"Teddy was the one I was thinking about the whole time, and you know it!" screamed Eric.

"Do I know?" sneered Odenrick. "Do I know?"

"And I know that the clothes you send to the Garbage Dump are actually the Death List!" continued Eric in the same overexcited tone of voice.

He was still sitting on the very edge of the armchair. But the reason was not respect or humility. The bear was like a pumped-up muscle only waiting the chance to be used. By revealing that he knew how the Death List was sent to the dump, he had gotten the archdeacon to fall silent. Without himself being aware of it, Eric's upper body slowly started to rock back and forth.

"I want you to remove two names from the list," Eric said with suppressed rage. "That's my purpose, that's why I came this evening. I want you to remove two of the names."

"You're crazy," said the archdeacon with his gaze aimed down at the desk. "You're completely crazy. What you're asking for is impossible."

CHAPTER 26

"Everything looks flipping alike," swore Tom-Tom Crow.

He shook his head, trying to see what was on the street sign. Amberville's endless blocks of mute townhouses made him ill at ease, and he drove slowly.

"This violet one here is Seamore Mews," Sam Gazelle read on the sign. "It's the next one, the turquoise."

In his lap he had a torn-out page from the telephone directory where, to be on the safe side, he'd circled Owl Dorothy's address. Number 24 Fried Street.

The car smelled of cheese doodles. When Sam forced the crow to stop at a Springergaast on Balderton Street to try to find a map in a telephone directory after far too many random right and left turns, Tom-Tom had taken the opportunity to buy a few bags of snacks. Now the acid odor had taken over the car, the crow was orange around the beak, and Sam was feeling carsick.

"There," said Sam, pointing at the next sign that sat at the exact same height on an identical façade. "The turquoise one, like I said. Fried Street."

Tom-Tom turned off.

"Now, let's see . . . number 56. Go on a little, then we're there."

Tom-Tom drove slowly, passing building after identical brick building before he turned gently and noiselessly in and parked. The dark-red rows of buildings extended both north and south through a gently rolling landscape. Two stories high, black roofs, white windowsills, just as well cared for as everything else in Amberville.

Tom-Tom stepped out onto the sidewalk, Sam went around the car, and together they hurried up the ten steps to number 24 Fried Street. Sam rang the doorbell. They waited a minute or two, hearing footsteps en route down the stairs to the hall, and then the outside door was opened by Owl Dorothy.

The storm had just abated, but the sky was still covered with clouds.

Dorothy was a threadbare owl, a very old bird who pensively let her peering eyes wander from the gazelle to the crow and back again. They had awakened her, it was obvious; she had her ears in a kind of nightcap and had wrapped a dressing gown around her thin body. She concealed a yawn behind her wing.

"Good evening, beautiful queen," said Sam in an attempt at lightheartedness, "my name is Sam. I beg your pardon that we're disturbing you at this time of the evening, but Eric Bear asked us to come out and say hello."

"Eric Bear?" Dorothy repeated.

The gazelle and the crow nodded.

For a moment Dorothy seemed to be considering how likely this statement was. Then she made her decision and took a step to one side, such that the strangers outside her door were transformed into guests. Sam stepped in, and Tom-Tom followed behind. The old owl guided them with vigorous steps to the kitchen, where she invited them to sit down at a small, round kitchen table while she herself put the teakettle on the stove.

"It's been a long time since I've seen Eric," she said. "Is he well?"

"He's lovelier than ever," answered Sam.

"Superfine," affirmed Tom-Tom.

"Anything else would have surprised me," nodded Dorothy. "Do you take milk or sugar in your tea?"

"Just milk, thanks," Sam replied.

"I'm okay," said Tom-Tom. "Tea is not . . ."

"Would you like something else instead?"

"No, no, I'm fine."

Tom-Tom felt troubled by the fact that the old lady, whom they would quite soon be forced to shout at and frighten, was treating them so politely. If he hadn't accepted anything to drink, it would be easier to threaten her a little later, he reasoned.

Dorothy served Sam a cup of tea and placed a glass of water in front of Tom-Tom. Then she sat down across from them at the kitchen table.

"I don't know how I should say it," began Sam Gazelle.

"Just say it," suggested Dorothy. "Things are the way they are."

"Yes, but this is special," said Sam. "And it sounds strange if you just say it."

"Say it," repeated Dorothy. "I'm old, I've heard most things."

"Yes, but not this. This is the kind of thing you don't talk about willingly. And it feels a little strange to just say it."

"Say it," said Dorothy for the third time. "It's not going to get easier in a few minutes."

"Say it," agreed Tom-Tom irritatedly. "Otherwise I'll say it."

Sam held up a hoof. He would say it. Rather than let the stupid crow start talking.

"Sweet little auntie, we need the archdeacon's manuscripts for the Death Lists," he said.

So it was said. Owl Dorothy reacted neither with surprise nor with consternation. She appeared completely uncomprehending.

"Excuse me," she said. "Now I think that I don't understand."

"The Death Lists," repeated Sam. "We know how it's arranged. Everything the archdeacon writes out by hand, you type up on a typewriter."

"That's right," said Dorothy, not without pride. "It has to do with the archdeacon's handwriting. You understand, despite all the education and wisdom that the penguin possesses, it's almost impossible to interpret his handwriting. It took me many years before I could clearly distinguish his 'j' from his 'g.' Not to mention the little pole that sets an 'h' apart from an 'n.' But in time you learn, and—"

"I'm sorry," interrupted the gazelle, "this is certainly a lovely art. But we're in kind of a hurry. The manuscript to the Death Lists?"

"The Death Lists?" repeated Dorothy. "That sounds gruesome. Do you mean this is something that Archdeacon Odenrick would be involved with? In what connection, then, if I may ask?"

"Auntie, you know what we're talking about," said Sam.

"I do beg your pardon," said Dorothy, "but I cannot say that I—"

"Come on, then, dammit," roared Tom-Tom. "We're in a hurry. Now you bring out those damn lists, ma'am. Otherwise I'll see to it that you . . . bring out those damn lists."

"My," said Dorothy, looking horrified.

"Exactly," said Sam, without enthusiasm.

It was clear that the old owl was afraid. She stared in fright at Sam and nodded frantically, her short beak bobbing up and down like a float in the waves.

"Well?" said Sam.

But Owl Dorothy seemed to have gone into some kind of

gridlock of fear and confusion, and beyond continuing to nod she didn't react at all.

Sam looked at Tom-Tom, who shrugged his wings to show that he didn't know what should be done.

"Do you have an office here, auntie?" asked Sam. "Show us where you usually hang out, where you work on the archdeacon's things."

The changed tone of voice worked, partly. Dorothy managed to take herself out of her temporary paralysis. She shook her head in confusion, mumbled a few words about her not knowing what they were talking about, then got up from the kitchen table and guided them into her small office, which was next to the kitchen. A pedantic orderliness prevailed there. Neat piles of correspondence, paperwork, and archived material were on the desk and on the shelves next to it.

"Exactly," Tom-Tom burst out triumphantly when he saw all the handwritten papers with just that unreadable writing the owl had just described.

Sam sat down in the desk chair, Dorothy stood alongside and nervously tried to explain what the various piles contained at the same time as she watched with mounting terror how Sam rummaged through the papers without regard for order.

"Worthless," he said after a while. "This is just worthless. Where are the lists of names?"

"But," said Dorothy, "I don't know what you're talking about. What lists of names? The only lists of names I have are the lists of confirmands and . . . wait, the guests who are invited to the home of the minister tomorrow evening. Is it the invitation list you want?"

"Could it be some damn code?" said Tom-Tom.

"Have to see what you have," said Sam. "But you're not fooling us."

"I don't want to fool anyone," said Dorothy, leaning

down to take out tomorrow's invitation list from the hanging folder in one of the desk drawers.

The crow and the gazelle ran down the stairs, two steps at a time, over to the car. Dorothy stood in the doorway, watching them.

The bum was sitting on the sidewalk, leaning against the gray Volga. There weren't many street people in Amberville, and it was quite unbelievable that one of them would get in Sam and Tom-Tom's way this evening.

And yet it happened.

It was a llama. In the glow of the streetlights the car cast a shadow over his upper body, and they saw only the legs lying outstretched across the sidewalk. When they came closer they saw that the llama was long and hairy and dirty and seemed to be sleeping half upright against the Volga's front tire.

Without a word Tom-Tom increased his speed and ran ahead of Sam. In a few seconds he was at the car, where he took hold of the llama's shoulders and lifted him up. Perhaps the llama awoke, perhaps he never had time to come to his senses before Tom-Tom, with all the force of which he was capable, threw him down on the sidewalk headfirst.

It had been enough so that the llama would not awaken again that night.

When his soft skull struck against the stone of the sidewalk hardly a sound was heard, but when the crow took hold of the llama's legs and swung the animal right into the side of the Volga, the distinct but hardly dramatic sound of a seam bursting could clearly be heard.

The llama remained lying next to the car, and Tom-Tom positioned himself with one leg on either side of the unconscious body. Sam screamed.

"Crow! We have to leave!"

But Sam's words only sounded like a weak sigh in the ears of the crow, like a breeze in a tree. With his foot Tom-Tom shoved the lifeless body so that the llama rolled around onto its back, exposing the tear under its right arm.

Tom-Tom fell down on his knees and pressed his wing feathers into the opening. He dug in as far as he was able and tore the stuffing out of the llama with a frenzy that caused Sam to turn his head and look in a different direction. This pulling and tearing of the llama's insides went on until almost all the cotton was lying in piles alongside the animal on the sidewalk.

Then Tom-Tom's strength ran out, and slowly he rose and got into the car. Sam hopped in on the passenger side, and they drove away in silence.

The sky was far from starry, but here and there they could still see the moonlight between breaks in the cloud cover.

They were in a hurry.

EMMA RABBIT

Magnus, I'm tired of waiting. I know this is a waiting room and I know that this is where you wait, but that doesn't matter, I'm still tired of waiting. Besides, there's a pitiful assortment of animals in here; it was like that the time before in Dr. Sharm's waiting room and it's like that here, too. On the couch by the aquarium, in the armchairs by the ugly coffee table, old hags all over the place who refuse to accept that time passes, that they're no longer young, that their fur has seen better days. I'm not much better myself, I'm not saying that. But it's still somewhat different, I haven't even turned forty, and apart from my knees I don't look so bad. You might take me for thirty. Perhaps even twenty-five, some evening when I'm made up. The old lady who's staring at the guppy can't possibly be under sixty-five, and what does she think? That she looks like she did in her fifties? It's tragic. When I turn fifty I hope I've aged with dignity. I'll keep my head high, dress like a lady, and try not to cling to my youth as though I wasn't finished with it. As if youth wasn't already lived and completely, thoroughly explored. I'm not a stuffed animal who looks back. What has been, has been, and will never come back. I can't understand those who go over and over all their old injustices, bitter about things that have happened, things that you can't do anything about anyway.

Waiting.

No, it wasn't my turn. It was the stuck-up lion who was just inside the door. Wonder what she's doing here? Perhaps she's acquainted with the doctor? She could use a new tip for her tail, but I doubt if she's noticed that. If you close your eyes to shit, you don't see it. One of Papa's words of wisdom. He throws thousands of such proverbs around, that he's thought up himself and that sound like true wisdom but aren't wise at all. I learned them all, and Mama went crazy every time I repeated them out loud. They were never a happy combination, Mama and Papa. She is too ordinary for him. Still, it's easier for me to understand that he put up with her than that it was the other way around. Why has she let it go on, year after year? I would never have been able to stand it. I would have put my foot down. But it's clear, deep down inside she must be afraid. Who isn't? He isn't much to look at, but appearances are deceptive. Perhaps he's threatened her? Said that if she leaves him he's going to . . . well, something unpleasant. Sometimes I've heard him when he doesn't know it. When he's at the office and I'm just on my way in but have stopped outside the door because I hear that he isn't alone inside. The first time when I was really little. I've always known. Long before Mama knew that I knew. Papa is good at making threats. It is, so to speak, a part of his job.

Waiting.

Now?

No. Not now, either. Every time that nurse comes out to call someone in, everyone sitting in the waiting room thinks it's their turn. But we have to wait. I hate waiting. I've already thought that too many times today. I hate waiting. The wallpaper in the waiting room is green, with thin, white stripes. The ceiling is rather low. There are two small windows facing the street. The closed door into the doctor's receiving room remains closed. It resists our gaze. When the door out to the stairway opens and a new patient comes in, we all stare angrily at her. We want to have the doctor's undivided attention for ourselves. We don't want to share. At least I don't want to. I've always had an eye for doctors.

Once I worked as a nurse. That was long ago, and I kept at it less than a year. But I've never had any other job that lasted as long, at least not a real job. Besides, that year was the longest of my life. It was Papa's idea, I'm not pretending anything else. He came up with the suggestion one day when he got angry because he thought I'd been shopping too much. He always thinks I shop too much. I have several girlfriends who are a lot worse than me, but he doesn't care about that. You might say that the thing about becoming a nurse wasn't a suggestion at first, it was more like a threat. Yet another threat. But something caused him to keep it in mind, and later in the evening, when he'd calmed down, he picked up the thread again. It could be useful for me, he maintained, to have a regular job. And in health care besides. I don't know if he used the phrase "character building," but I assume that's how he was thinking. My life had been too easy, and it was time for a little resistance. This was one of the few things Mama and Papa agreed on, that my life had been too easy. Much easier than either of theirs. I had a hard time understanding how that could be my fault, but now I would be punished. Mama was ecstatic. Papa arranged a position for me the very next day, and we drove off to meet the director of the hospital. Perhaps I don't need to say that I was against the whole thing. I was dating a chaffinch who thought a nurse's uniform might be pretty, but that was the only amusing thing about the proposal. I believed, in my stupidity, that Papa would think better of it when he realized what all this would entail. I thought it was still mostly a threat, and if I promised to stop shopping I could get out of it. The director of the hospital, a doctor whose name I forgot the moment we left, went over the work duties. As I understood it, it was at least as much about being some sort of maid as it was about taking care of patients, and in the car on the way home I tried to get Papa to change his mind. That this was, as it were, beneath our dignity. But he thought exactly the opposite, and he truly enjoyed the thought of all the scrubbing and cleaning and laundering and dusting and carrying and toiling it involved. Then I started to smell a rat. Then I started to get that this was really going to happen. That I would start working. I protested wildly the whole week. Stopped talking, stopped eating, and screamed what idiots they were, but nothing helped. I think this was the only time Mama and Papa were actually on the same side. Then . . .

Waiting.

Now, perhaps?

Yes, now it's finally my turn.

It was still a waiting room. Inside the door, where I believed Dr. Sharm would be found, there was a smaller room, still with the same green wallpaper, but now with a single couch suite.

In here two nurses sit behind a low reception counter, and there are only two of us animals who are waiting. It's me and the lion, who is still pretending not to see me. It must be lovely to live so completely in your own little bubble. To be like her, filled up with herself to such a degree that she doesn't need to concern herself about anyone else. I really wonder what she's doing here. Perhaps it's a real disease? But Dr. Sharm doesn't see the sick, only us: the vain. The lion knows that I'm looking at her, she must feel it, but she twists her head a little to the right and looks out through the window. That profile . . . I know her! I recognize her from somewhere, but I can't think of where it is. It will come to me. All good things come to those who wait, but it comes faster if you do something about it, as Papa always says. The two nurses in reception are shuffling papers. One is an ostrich, the other might be a hyena or a dog or possibly some kind of bear. I'm not good at types of animals, I never have been.

There are some newspapers on the coffee table. I pick one up and leaf through it. This is waiting. I hate waiting. A large painting is hanging on the wall behind the nurse in reception. Expressionism, or whatever it might be. Brushstrokes in an explosion of color. I've never liked art. I don't know how I came up with the studio. A little white lie that led to another and then, presto, I was an artist with a studio. It was just perfect. I avoided making up pretend friends, I avoided coming up with false explanations about real friends who might have revealed me afterward. I'm not the housewife type, never have been, and when the studio was really there I realized that it was exactly what I needed. I was free. I could come and go as I wished. I avoided a lot of demands, always had a valid excuse if Papa wanted to see me or if I wanted to see someone. Life with Eric Bear was, and is, perhaps not the world's most exciting, and the fabrication of being an artist gave, and gives, me every possibility.

The first time Eric was going to come by and look there were a few hours of panic. First I was forced to acquire an apartment. Papa had several, all around the city, I don't want to know why or what he used them for. But he let me have one of them, it was good enough to serve as an artists' studio. Then I rushed around up in Lanceheim an entire morning, buying paintings in every single antiques store I could find. They thought I was crazy. I asked the antiques dealers to give me only the paintings themselves, the canvases that is, because I didn't want the frame. A few refused, but most of them did as I asked, because I never tried to haggle over the price. Into a taxi and back to the newly acquired artist's studio, it was down by Swarwick Park. There I set the canvases carefully around an easel I'd also found in an antiques store, and it looked rather nice. I breathed out and sat down on the couch that Papa had surely purchased, for it was leather and enormous and black just as he liked, and then I saw. Eric would ring the doorbell in exactly one half hour, and there were neither paints nor brushes in my so-called studio. I set off again into the city, and by pure chance discovered a store with artist's materials as we went past light-blue Up Street. Into the store, make a real raid, and then back to the apartment again. I completed the image of a hardworking artist who was occupied with her new masterpiece by "spilling" a little paint on my slacks. At the very next moment Eric rang the doorbell. Fortunately, it was an old pair of slacks.

I've never had anything against Eric Bear. It's not about that. He's a nice bear with social ambitions, and I provide him with extra credibility by pretending to be an artist. He is less superficial, thanks to me. He acquires a little depth and heft. I'll gladly offer him that. He doesn't bother me, he cooks on the evenings he eats at home, and when he cleans he puffs the cushions on the couch, something I hereby confess that I've never done.

"Isabelle Lion," says the dog or the hyena in the reception in a loud voice.

Isabelle Lion. As she gets up and without a glance goes over to the door to the left of reception, I remember where I recognize her from. Her husband borrowed money from Papa a few years ago. There were some complications, I don't remember exactly what they were, but it was in the process of ending badly. I've seen her and her he at Papa's office, not just once but two times. Lion opens the door and goes in to Dr. Bee Sharm and ignores me completely. In other words, she recognizes me, too.

I've never had anything against Eric Bear. He doesn't scold me for shopping too much, even if I shop too much, and he doesn't sniff at me to uncover the aftershave of other hes. He doesn't bother me, and I can squander my life exactly as I wish. Because that's what Mama says. You're squandering your life, she says, because I can't account for anything I've actually done during the day. But the days pass nevertheless. I go out in town, shop a little, meet girlfriends, and have lunch. Sometimes there's a little flirtation to play with, sometimes not. Sometimes Mama and Papa want me to be involved in something, sometimes not. But Eric doesn't demand much, other than that I am referred to as his wife. That much I can do.

Now.

Finally it's my turn.

Dr. Bee Sharm is, exactly as his name suggests, a very small stuffed animal, the smallest I've seen. He sits behind a large desk in his white coat, smiling broadly as I come in. Apart from the customary cot along the long side of the room, there isn't much in here that's reminiscent of a hospital. No anatomy charts or horrid stainless-steel tools that always scare me to death. I sit on the stool he is pointing at, and when he asks what I'm looking for, I tell him.

"It's my knees, doctor," I say.

"Uh-huh," says the doctor amiably, jumping down from his chair.

He disappears behind his desk, but comes strolling around the corner and he hardly even comes up to my knees. I can't help it, I lean over so as to be able to see what the little fellow is doing down there. He's supposed to be the best in the city. I wouldn't be here otherwise.

"In my humble opinion," says Dr. Sharm, "you have very beautiful knees, Mrs. Rabbit. And I doubt that it's time to fill them in or shine them up."

"But, but . . ." I start to stammer, because I'm amazed at

an animal who doesn't seem to want my money when I'm fully prepared to give it away, or at least pay handsomely for a simple service.

"There are artificial fibers," Dr. Sharm interrupts me, "that are very true to life, and with which I can absolutely fill in the shallow parts of your knees. But I'm not sure that will be really successful because there's really nothing like original hair-covering."

"Not successful?" I repeat, and I know I sound irritated, but I can't help it. If this little doctor is supposed to be the best in the city, and he doesn't know if the results will be good, who's supposed to know? Not successful? What kind of foolishness is that?

"Oh, ma'am," says Dr. Sharm, "however much we might wish it, and despite all its advances, medical development still has most of its work ahead of it. We think we're becoming wise, we research our way along a winding road, but even so we can't know completely for sure."

I'm dumbfounded. At the same time I shouldn't be surprised. My own experience of health care is exactly the same. At Lakestead House a gaggle of doctors in white coats ran around with furrowed brows looking sadly at you, so that you gained confidence in them and became a little afraid at the same time. The majority at Lakestead House had lived there their entire lives, and would continue living there until the red pickup came and got them. They were almost all there for psychiatric difficulties. The doctors were a threat to health. You never knew when they might come steaming in with a shot or an idea for a small intervention that might be of help. At first I was scared to death. I had such respect for them. But by the final months I knew that the doctors were loonier than the patients. And believe me, the patients were loony. Completely loony. I took care of three of them, an eagle who thought he could fly, a rose-colored badger who thought he was a general, and Teddy Bear, who carried on about how he was fighting against evil. I met Eric Bear when he was up to visit Teddy at Lakestead, so I got to know Teddy first. Compared to all the other crackpots, it was easy to like him. True, he belonged in the home, but if you just kept to the right topics of conversation he wasn't strange at all. Not as strange as the others, in any case. And with that I'm including the personnel. I met Teddy at least three times a day. I gave him breakfast, I took him out on a walk in the afternoon, and I saw to it that he took his tablets before he went to bed. It was primarily during the walks that we talked. About everything imaginable, high and low. He told me a great deal about his family, of course—it was Teddy who got me interested in Eric. He sounded exciting. Dangerous. I liked dangerous males.

"Twenty-five thousand," says Dr. Bee Sharm. "But, as stated, I can't guarantee that it will be especially successful. If I were you, I would wait a few years until the fur around the knee is a little less . . . lively."

But you're not me, you little bee, I thought. Instead I said out loud, "Okay, but I've heard so many good things about you, Dr. Sharm, that nevertheless I'll take the risk. Can I schedule a time for the procedure itself?"

The doctor nodded and referred me back out to reception.

Every weekend I was off and went home to Papa and Mama in Amberville. Coming into the city from Hillevie and Lakestead was such liberation that the trip back on Monday morning was sheer torture. I whined about wanting to quit. Every weekend I whined, but Papa was rock solid. Now he'd finally gotten me a job, he said, and now I had to show that I could endure. But once, out of all the times that I nagged him and tried to describe how indescribably miserable things were for me as a nurse, I happened to mention Teddy Bear's name. And even who Teddy Bear's mother was. That changed everything. From brushing me and my nagging aside as though I were a little fruit fly, Papa suddenly became extremely interested. At first I didn't realize why, but later I understood. Rhinoceros Edda. A contact that led straight into Mollisan Town's political network would open enormous opportunities for Papa. Now I would never get to quit. I cursed myself and wondered how I could have been so dense. Perhaps some of the idiots out at Lakestead were contagious? Papa drove me to the bus the following Monday himself, and he made it completely clear that I should take especially good care of Teddy.

What happened then wasn't my fault. I don't really know how it came about. I'm not interested in politics, I'm not interested in clever plans and long, convoluted chains of thought. Sometimes I think that's what gets my parents to remain a couple. Each of them, in their own way, seems immensely fascinated by keeping track of such things. Figuring out that if She does this, He is going to do that, which leads to She doing that while Her Cousin does this. That kind of endless speculation in people's futures. I don't give a damn about what everyone's up to; personally they can do what they want, and where it concerns the Bear twins it simply turned out as it did. I couldn't help that both of them fell in love with me.

It was less surprising that Teddy Bear should maintain that he loved me. That was part of his disease profile, the doctors said. I didn't really know what to do when Teddy confessed his love, so I asked the doctors for advice. They smiled with embarrassment and gave each other conspiratorial glances and asked me to excuse them but I shouldn't take Teddy's tokens of love seriously. It was not me, Emma Rabbit, he loved, but more what he imagined that I stood for. He had designated me as some sort of object of goodness and tenderness, security and consolation; that was what the doctors said. The only thing to do, they advised me, was, as usual, to agree with the patient. This applied to everyone who was admitted to Lakestead House. Don't end up in any conflicts, agree with or ignore their peculiarities. So I kept on working as usual. Made Teddy's bed and cleaned his room in the morning. Saw to it that he took his tablets and ate his food. Listened to all of his thoughts and agreed with most of them. But not in some sad, passive way; on the contrary, I gladly took part in the conversation. Teddy had a sense of humor and was actually rather wise. But when he descended into strange arguments about evil and goodness, I tried to divert him. Often I succeeded. What I had the most difficulty overlooking was when he mixed up his own life with his twin brother's. Then I really had to concentrate so as not to say something stupid. Eric Bear came to visit Teddy at some point every week, and often Eric talked about his job. I couldn't help that I happened to hear their conversations, it wasn't as though they were whispering or tried to be secretive. And when Eric left, Teddy might repeat Eric's words later the same day as though they were his own. He quite simply borrowed Eric's life. I knew exactly why that in particular made me so ill at ease. It was the clearest sign of how sick Teddy really was, and of course that made all my conversations with him become less interesting.

Out in reception I set up a new time with the dog, who I am now rather sure is some sort of panda. This is not a return visit, but rather a time for the procedure itself. The panda and I agree on a date at the beginning of September. I don't see a trace of the haughty lion. But I follow her example, and when I pass by those waiting in the outer waiting room I stick my nose up in the air. I don't see the animals in the lounge suite or by the aquarium but rather stare straight toward the outside door. In a few seconds I'm out on the stairway and on my way down toward the street. I can't maintain that it feels good to be mixed up with the old, worn-out wrecks sitting in Dr. Bee Sharm's reception. It feels liberating to get out of there.

But I must complete this train of thought. It wasn't particularly strange that Teddy Bear fell in love, nor was it something to take seriously. That Eric Bear also fell in love with me was more odd. Personally I've never been in love. Neither when I was little and went to school nor since. I don't know why. There was a time when I was sorry that it was like that; I felt isolated and different in a bad way. But finally you have to accept yourself for who you are. For good and bad, as Teddy would have said. Since I'm not the romantic type, I haven't incited especially many romantic feelings in the animals in my vicinity, either. Now and then, of course. I'm not ugly. But Eric's courtship surprised me. We didn't know each other, he'd only seen me when I was taking care of Teddy out at Lakestead, and I suspected that above all it was Teddy's description of me that aroused Eric's interest. We greeted each other, exchanged a few words when we met in the corridors up on the nursing unit, but no more than that. Nevertheless he asked if I wanted to go out with him, and when I didn't answer immediately he flattered me so crudely that I was astonished. We were in the assembly hall one flight up, where the patients sometimes drank coffee in the afternoon. Only he and I were there. He was brazen and insistent, but at the same time rather cute, and he smelled nice. We went out a few times. It was no more than that, a way to pass the time in my monotonous, work-filled life that Papa refused to let me out of. However much I complained and swore, he sent me back to Lakestead every Monday.

At last I figured it out. I don't intend to maintain that it was my own ingenious plan, but when Eric Bear proposed to me after only a few months—which, to say the least, came as a surprise—I realized that this might actually be my salvation. If I said yes to the proposal, I would have to leave my job as a nurse. Papa would be jubilant, his only cub would marry into the ministry, and with that I had achieved more in my life than he had ever hoped for. Of course I couldn't foresee all the secretiveness that would ensue. Papa was sure that Eric would call off the engagement if he found out who my papa was; I was sure of the opposite. But it turned out as Papa wished, as usual. I said that my papa was dead.

I still don't know how it happened that Teddy proposed to me two days after Eric. True, they were twins, so perhaps it was a coincidence. Or else Teddy heard what had happened and didn't want to be worse than his brother. If there is anything I regret . . . or perhaps don't regret, but if there is something I'm not terribly content with, it's the entire charade with Teddy. It felt completely wrong to pretend. But all the doctors told me to do it, and Eric told me to do it, and, of course: Papa threatened all sorts of things if I didn't see to it to wind up in the church with one of Rhinoceros's cubs. The deacon wanted it, too. We fooled Teddy. Penguin Odenrick play-acted. He had a serious talk with Teddy and me for several hours, as though he was really going to marry us. And later the same day the whole procedure was repeated, but then with Eric and me. It was weird. Especially because the twins were more or less identical in appearance. Odenrick mostly seemed to think it was funny. Eric, I believe, did it for Teddy's sake. I did it mostly for my own, and a little for Papa's sake. I got married to Eric, I avoided working at Lakestead House, and Eric never found out that he'd married the cub of a gangster king.

I never believed that our marriage would last as long as

it has. I saw it mostly as a way of getting out of being a nurse. Can it be that it hasn't fallen apart because I've never really cared about it? Sometimes when I'm talking with my friends, I think that might be so. All the others seem so filled up with their love. They take betrayal so hard—both their own and their spouse's. Personally I could care less about either.

My life works well. And with a freshening up of my knees, there's nothing to complain about.

CHAPTER 27

Through the window opening in Archdeacon Odenrick's office, Eric Bear could see that the clouds in the sky were about to break up, and he knew he had to hurry. Soon Sam and Tom-Tom would arrive.

Archdeacon Odenrick stood leaning against the door, but he had no intention of leaving. For the past few minutes he'd been wandering restlessly back and forth on the small floor area between the door and the desk, to the right of the armchair where Eric was sitting. The penguin had let so much pent-up frustration run out into his legs that he was getting out of breath as a result. Now he was leaning against the door to gather strength. He was breathing with an open mouth; the odor of old mustard and parsley spread around the room. Eric Bear's provocations had gone on for almost twenty minutes, and if it weren't for Eric's close relationship to the archdeacon, and the archdeacon's close relationship to Eric and his family, the attacks would perhaps have been possible to shake off. But slowly the bear found ways through the pious defenses.

"This is meaningless," hissed the penguin. "You're still not listening."

"It was you who taught me to let be," Eric smiled. "But I'm making myself important, right? Isn't the reason that you, Archdeacon, don't need to listen to criticism is that you and Magnus are so terribly close to each other? I'm not. I ought to be humble. Between the archdeacon and Magnus there is . . . yes, there's hardly any difference at all."

Eric remained seated on the edge of the armchair before the desk; it no longer felt quite so uncomfortable. The conversation had been rancorous, but nevertheless it moved forward with an implacable logic. The archdeacon was driven by a lust for power that he would be ashamed of when it was exposed. But like all stuffed animals, he basically wanted to be loved, and if that wasn't possible, then he at least demanded to be understood. That was his weak point.

The penguin fixed his eyes on the bear.

"What do you want? Really?"

"Remove one name from the list," the bear answered simply. "To start with."

He had revised his request; he had to start somewhere.

"I stole clothes that I packed as a young confirmand," Eric repeated. "Rat Ruth checks off the names on the clothing lists. But you don't need to be a master detective to understand how it fits together."

The archdeacon was breathing heavily, and finally he let a hissing whisper grow into a shout. "Yes, of course it's me!"

Now it had been said, once and for all.

"Of course you're right, Bear. I'm the one who makes the list."

And Archdeacon Odenrick laughed. This was the first time Eric had heard the archdeacon laugh. The sound was jerky and dry; it came from the penguin's throat.

"This has nothing to do with me, you stupid bear," hissed

Odenrick. "You sit there and look like it was something I thought up. Stupidities. This is a task that goes along with the office. The archdeacon of Mollisan Town has always made the lists. That is our function, we are Magnus's implement. Justly measuring out the lives of animals can't be turned over to anyone else."

These were words that had waited to be spoken. The syllables followed one another, dominoes set up long ago that finally fell into place. Odenrick sat down, relieved and at the same time agitated. Eric remained silent. He knew that he'd broken a logjam. He sneaked a peek out through the opening behind the archdeacon. The clouds had still not broken up. But there couldn't be many minutes remaining now.

Archdeacon Odenrick's forehead creased, and smoothed out, like the waves on the sea; under them thoughts were wandering back and forth. When he finally decided to speak, he did it with a calm and measured voice which was gradually filled with greater and greater passion. He spoke as much to himself as to Eric Bear.

Odenrick told how the tradition of the lists had been inherited through the centuries. From having once been a secondary occupation for the archdeacon, over time the Death Lists had come to be the very heart of the office. And what Eric had heard was true, that every year one chosen animal was pardoned. It was the archdeacon's responsibility and duty to do so, a reminder of the Great Mercy.

Penguin Odenrick opened wide the door to his innermost self. And the satisfaction the archdeacon experienced as he now parted with these deep, chafing truths caused him to go deeper and deeper into the details around how the Death List functioned and how the power of the church finally came to rest on this list. How its function governed and maintained the norms of society, completely in line with what Eric Bear himself had been thinking an hour or so earlier, en route to the cathedral.

Without the promise of a life to come, the church would lose its stature, said Odenrick in a loud, theatrical voice. Without the promise of a life to come, the laws that formed the basis of society would become incomprehensible.

"Because the stuffed animals that you and I encounter every day are basically simple fools who are helplessly guided by their pathetic attempts to escape from time and death."

Only in one point, Eric realized as he sat silently and tried to keep from being disgusted by the condescension with which the archdeacon referred to his world, was what Odenrick said a surprise, and a disappointment.

"There is an additional list."

Odenrick nodded with feigned reflection and pointed toward his head with the tip of his wing.

"There is an additional list, which is even more significant than the one we've been talking about up to now. It's the list of those who should be removed, the day their names end up on the Death List."

His tone of voice remained droning, as if he were speaking to a large audience.

"But if you don't want them to die, why do you write them up?" Eric asked with sincere astonishment.

It was the first thing he'd said in almost ten minutes.

"Because otherwise I couldn't remove them," the archdeacon laughed scornfully. "Otherwise Magnus would not be able to remind us of His mercy."

And his laughter sounded as though it hurt. This time he laughed so long that finally there didn't seem to be any connection between the sound and what he'd said, and Eric felt sincerely sorry on the archdeacon's account. A lunatic was sitting on the other side of the desk. The bear looked out again through the window opening. Sam and Tom-Tom ought to be here quite soon.

"And you," Odenrick snorted between the convulsions that he tried to get past without succeeding, "you are never, ever getting at the list in my head."

And the thought of the opposite was apparently so ridiculous to the archdeacon that his desperate cheerfulness received fresh nourishment. He coughed forth another laugh, and the archdeacon was compelled to scream in order to make himself heard: "Because you're completely insignificant!"

Eric nodded to himself. Imagining that the archdeacon would insert some minor lies into the middle of this ejaculation of truth was completely unlikely. This was not the evening for circumlocutions. The archdeacon's power included no more than a single reprieve per year. Eric would not be able to remove both of them, so he was forced to do the impossible.

He was forced to choose between Teddy and Emma.

"What you've told me makes me anything other than insignificant," the bear replied quietly. "You've made me powerful. That's worth more than even you can pay."

"You know nothing!" screamed Odenrick. "Everything you've heard are only fever dreams. You are only one of thousands of animals who've tried to reveal the origin of the Death List, one of tens of thousands of animals through the centuries who've tried to become immortal by removing their own or someone else's name. You know nothing, for in the same moment that you leave here, this conversation has never taken place. If you ask me, you've never even been here."

Eric looked out through the window and seemed to perceive the sound of the engine of a gray Volga. Perhaps he was imagining things?

"I think neither you nor I can fathom what would

happen if this gets out," Eric continued with a calm that stood in such contrast to the archdeacon's theatrical gestures and outbursts that it seemed almost inappropriate. "If everything you've said about the list's far-reaching significance holds up, what would happen if the animals in the city knew that it was you who arbitrarily wrote down their names on a piece of paper?"

"You cannot challenge me," screamed the archdeacon, sounding sincerely surprised. "You cannot challenge me. Haven't you understood a thing? Next week I'll sit down here and write the next list. Perhaps your name will be on it. You cannot challenge me."

The archdeacon's laughter changed into a dry cough.

"Of course I understand," said Eric Bear implacably. "I already said that when I arrived. I understand more than you want to know. That's my payment. Your list, the one you have in your head, of animals to pardon, you may postpone it one year. This year you have to remove the name I ask you to remove. Otherwise the animals in the city are going to find out what's been going on."

"But this is . . ."

"Ah," said Eric, nodding toward one of the window openings, "here come Sam and Tom-Tom. I don't know if you know them, they're just as insignificant as I am."

At the same time as Sam Gazelle parked the gray Volga on one of the cathedral's cross streets, the final clouds broke up and the half-moon was hanging up there, crystal clear, in the black sky. Through the window the penguin and the bear both saw Sam get out of the car, holding up a piece of paper.

"Do you see?" asked Eric. "Those are your handwritten Death Lists. Sam and Tom-Tom have visited Dorothy, you know. And Dorothy, she has a sense of orderliness, she saves everything. Even your original manuscripts, before she redoes them into catalogues of used clothing."

. . . .

The gazelle shut the car door after him but continued waving the paper the way he'd been told to. Along with Tom-Tom Crow he walked slowly toward the cathedral and the unobtrusive door that Eric had promised was there, even if it couldn't be seen from a distance.

"What should we do when he sees that this is a frigging invitation list you're waving around?" asked Tom-Tom.

"No idea," answered Sam.

"I should have killed the owl instead," the crow said regretfully.

"Sweetheart, that wouldn't have helped, either," said Sam. "Presumably this is still just a deadend."

"You swine," hissed Penguin Odenrick.

The archdeacon was standing with his back toward Eric, staring out through the window opening onto the street. He stood stiff as a block of salt. Even from faraway he could see that it was the church's paper with his own characteristic handwriting the gazelle was holding in his hooves.

"You don't understand what you're risking," the penguin hissed warningly at the bear without turning around. "These are structures that have been built up through the centuries. This is a world order that knows no alternative."

"We're risking nothing," replied Eric, unimpressed by the big words. "You give me the list, I remove one name, you tell the rat, and then you'll get your manuscripts back the day after tomorrow."

"That's much too short notice," whispered the archdeacon without taking his eyes from the gazelle and the crow, who slowly continued their walk toward the church. "I can't do it."

"You'll manage," Eric promised.

"How could I rely on you?" asked Odenrick, finally turning around.

Something in the archdeacon's eyes had gone out.

"How could you not?" asked the bear.

They remained standing like that for a few brief moments, before the penguin sat down heavily at the desk and in the same movement bent over to pull out one of the drawers. He took out a copy of the packing slip that had come with the latest weekly delivery of clothes to the Garbage Dump, set the paper on the table, turned in the bear's direction, and pushed it over.

"I'm tired," he confessed. "I don't have the energy to think."

Eric remained silent. He took one of the pens that was in the penholder on the desk and searched along the row of names.

One whose life he rescued at the cost of the other. It was the most difficult moment in his life.

"I never want to hear this mentioned again," said the archdeacon while Eric found the name he was looking for, and drew a broad stroke through it.

"Never again," repeated the archdeacon.

The bear pushed the packing slip back to Odenrick, set aside the pen, and got up from the armchair. Without another word he turned around and left the archdeacon's office.

Sam and Tom-Tom stood chatting in the street as Eric came out. He greeted them with a nod which perhaps was a kind of thanks, but he said nothing. With rapid steps he went over to the parked car. The gazelle and the crow were forced to jog to catch up.

"How did it go?" asked Tom-Tom.

But Eric Bear didn't answer; he sat in the backseat of the car and shut the door.

"Presumably not so good, huh?" said Tom-Tom to the gazelle before they opened the front doors and joined Eric.

The gazelle shrugged his shoulders. Tom-Tom started the car.

"Eric, dear, we didn't get hold of any manuscript," said Sam. "She maintained that she had no idea about Death Lists and gave us an invitation list instead."

"Where are we going?" asked Tom-Tom.

"Now we're going home," said Eric Bear.

EPILOGUE

To Be Read As Needed

Eric Bear sat on a ruined pier at the north end of the long beach in Hillevie, dangling his legs over the water. It was the morning of the twenty-second of May; yesterday he'd slept the entire day, got up at six in the evening, eaten a couple of sandwiches, and then gone back to sleep for the night. He'd slept quietly, a dreamless sleep, hard and heavy; it was his body's way of healing a portion of the tension that had been a strain inside as well as outside in the recent weeks. His body ached with stiffness when he woke up early in the morning.

As he opened his eyes he knew that he had to drive out to the sea. He took a cup of coffee with Tom-Tom at the kitchen table; there was nothing to eat, not in the fridge or in the pantry. The crow had been up since early that morning. During the previous day he'd swallowed his pride and phoned Grand Divino. The department store management, in any case the head of the house and home department, had agreed to meet with him, and he would be going up to speak with him in a few hours.

"Blame me," whispered Eric.

"I've already done that. What the hell do you think?" whispered Tom-Tom and smiled.

Sam was sleeping; the crow and the bear were talking with lowered voices.

At nine o'clock, Eric pulled on his clothes and left the apartment. The gray Volga Kombi was still parked within walking distance of Yiala's Arch. Eric bought a croissant and a second cup of coffee to go from Springergaast and ate while he drove. On the end of the pier, with the sea before him, there was hope of finding some kind of calm, for a few hours anyway.

And what would have happened if Teddy hadn't phoned the day before yesterday? The thought was unthinkable; if Eric lingered on it more than a few seconds his world would fall apart.

When Eric was telling Tom-Tom and Sam about his plan regarding Dorothy and the manuscript, the telephone rang unexpectedly. The sound was alien, Eric could scarcely recall a single telephone conversation during the more than three weeks he'd been staying at Yiala's Arch. Even Sam had looked bewildered. They nodded to the gazelle to go and answer it, which he of course did. With an even more surprised expression on his face he listened a moment, nodded, and then extended the receiver to Eric.

"It's for you."

Eric took the few steps over to Sam, grasped the phone receiver, and just by the breathing on the other end of the line could hear that it was his twin brother.

What Teddy related was impossible to believe.

In the world of imaginary beings and illusions where Teddy lived, at first what he was saying couldn't be taken seriously. Emma Rabbit had no father. It was a dream, a fantasy, there was some motive behind it that Eric couldn't see, but it was impossible to grasp.

They talked for a few minutes. Eric tried to work out how Teddy even knew that there was a Dove who went around the city with a pair of gorillas. Madness. Eric became more and more restless, Tom-Tom and Sam stood, stamping their feet alongside to get going.

Then Teddy mentioned the brown boots. Emma's new brown boots with embroidered suns on the calf. Teddy could describe them in detail.

Then Eric finally realized that it was true.

"You have to help me," said Teddy.

Eric turned around and smiled. Teddy was balancing on the rotted planks out toward the end of the pier. It looked to be a dangerous project. The personnel up at Lakestead would never forgive him if he let Teddy fall in. He got up, took a few careful steps in toward land, and helped his brother across an especially difficult passage where only two planks were still intact. Together they then sat down alongside each other on the narrow end and looked out toward the horizon.

It would be another lovely day in Hillevie.

"This is the same water as a million years ago," said Eric, nodding toward the sea that was so still it resembled ice. "Exactly the same."

Teddy nodded. After a while Eric added, "It feels good."

Then Teddy placed a consoling paw around his brother's shoulders, and they remained sitting that way.